To my godmother, Lois

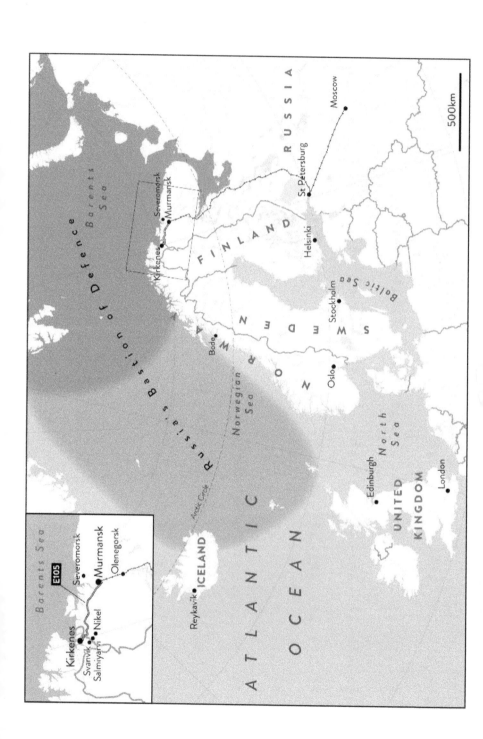

ONE

Colonel Ruslan Yumatov recognized the unlit flatbed truck parked at the side of the road. He flashed his headlamps, turned them off, and slowed his Land Cruiser to pull up behind the vehicle. The terrain was flat, dark, and cold with gales that shook the ground, not a night for any human to be out. Yumatov kept the engine running, touched his companion on the shoulder, and said in English, 'Sorry, Gerry, we have to help this guy.'

'We're on the clock, Colonel. What's happening?'

Gerald Cooper looked at Yumatov with a mix of confusion and irritation. They had driven three hours from the drab, filthy city of Murmansk to meet a Norwegian businessman who would take him across the border into Norway. The rendezvous was in ten minutes, and half an hour from now Cooper was to deliver a tiny flash drive containing classified Russian information destined for the Pentagon. His job would be done, and he'd be well paid.

Yumatov zipped up his jacket, rolled a woolen hat over his ears, and tightened a scarf around his neck. 'Let's find out.'

He opened his door. Cooper did the same. A stream of iced air streaked through the vehicle. The two men were very different. Yumatov loved and understood his country. Cooper was an adventurer from Britain, resentful of his country, craving to fill life's emptiness after the army. He was here for the money.

Yumatov's boots sank into inches of freshly fallen snow. Condensation from his breath created a cloud that vanished in the gale. He pulled his scarf around his face. A man got down from the truck, walked around to the other side of his vehicle, and out of sight. 'Come,' Yumatov said to Cooper. 'It looks like he's hit an animal, a bear or a reindeer.'

He snapped on a flashlight, swept its beam along the side of the silver-gray truck stained with dirty ice. The beam picked out a set of antlers speckled with snow, curving up majestically like a candelabra.

Cooper held Yumatov's arm to keep him back. 'Our mission, Colonel, is to get to the border. Now.'

Yumatov kept walking. 'In my culture, you do not drive past a person in trouble in a place like this.' His flashlight showed the full body of a beautiful buck reindeer, six feet long from head to tail, with a dark-tan hide. He played the light over the carcass. The legs were strong, but slender and agile for the unpredictable lay of its home landscape. When standing, the animal would have been at least four feet high. Instead, it lay on a large, thick green groundsheet which Cooper had also seen.

'Don't seem like a bloody accident.'

'You're right.' Yumatov nodded, his expression stern. 'Give me a moment.'

He walked around the carcass to the driver, who stood by the reindeer's rear legs, appearing unfazed by the cold. He wore no gloves, a black wind-screening jacket, and a flat black cap that didn't cover his ears. He was a solid officer from one of Russia's elite special-forces units.

'On course?' Yumatov asked.

'Yes, sir.'

Yumatov walked back to Cooper. 'You're right, Gerry. It is not exactly as it seems.' He beckoned Cooper to join him as he crouched at the reindeer's head. He pulled back the ear to reveal an insignia, carved on the inside, shaped like a rugby football. 'This is a herder's individual marking. From the way it's shaped, we know he's from across the border, probably jumped the fence piled with a snowdrift. There's been an agreement between the countries for many years to return reindeer that have got through from Norway. The Norwegians pay, not much, but for a trucker like him, it's worth it.' Yumatov pointed to the vehicle. 'See, no damage on the truck. He could have found the reindeer, killed him, then waited for people like us to roll up.'

'For Christ's sake!' Cooper stood up, bristling with frustration. 'He's not in trouble and this is nothing to do with us. We need to—'

'This isn't the London rush hour. It's the Arctic. We're going to lift this beast onto his truck. The driver will deliver him to the border guards who will give him his money and we will have helped oil the wheels of corruption that keep my poor country afloat. Within the hour, you will be enjoying fine whisky at the bar of the Thon Hotel in Kirkenes.'

Cooper first glared at Yumatov, then switched to a shrug of acceptance. 'What can I do to make it quicker?'

'Help us lift him.'

The snowfall was heavy, the wind too harsh for it to settle. Some tracks would be covered, others randomly revealed. The driver switched on the headlamps, lighting up the reindeer as if on a stage. Cooper shielded his eyes so he could see Yumatov. 'Why are you doing this?'

'No man can lift an animal alone in this weather.' Yumatov smiled. 'You try it.'

'No, I mean why are you working with me, because you know what I'm carrying.'

'I know more about what you've got in your pocket than you do.'

'Don't that make you a traitor?'

Cooper's flash drive contained naval technology on submarine warfare. He'd been hired by an American intelligence agency to bring it out of Russia.

Yumatov stepped closer so the wind wouldn't drown his voice. 'No, Gerry, I'm not a traitor. Russia is deciding whether it looks east toward Asia or west toward Europe and America, and I am more afraid of China than I am of Europe. I want my children to grow up as Europeans, and to do that we have to show that Russia is Europe's friend. What you are carrying is a gesture, a symbol of friendship, a handful of naval secrets, none worth dying for, compiled by a senior vice-admiral who, like me, is a patriot. It is technical information that most of your guys know anyway, to show we are willing to share our future with Europe, not fight over it.'

'Good, sensible words, wasted on the likes of a foot soldier like me, so are you talking now or when your President Lagutov quits?'

'It's a process. I'm hoping Sergey Grizlov wins the job.'

'The new Foreign Minister?'

'Very pro-European.'

The driver killed the headlamps and made a phone call. Cooper checked his watch, annoyance spreading back across his face.

Yumatov said, 'He'll be calling the border guys, telling them he's on his way. We need to work with him. He and they are as thick as thieves. You and our contact need to have a smooth ride through.'

Cooper clapped his hands together. 'Fuck, it's cold.'

'A couple of minutes. I'm sure you didn't know that during the Cold War spies used reindeer to take microfilm across the border.'

'You're bloody kiddin'.' Cooper examined the carcass. 'What'd they do, strap it to an antler?'

Yumatov knelt with the flashlight and ran his hand over the coarse brown hair of the haunch. 'They'd cut open a flap of hide, slip it underneath, and sew it up again. Then send the reindeer back across the fence.'

'Reindeer aren't that obedient, so I know you're 'aving me on.'

'And if I'm not, you buy me a pint and fish and chips in a London pub.'

'I'll buy your whole family fish and chips.'

Yumatov showed Cooper his phone wallpaper. 'That's my wife, Anna. On her left is Max. He's seven and says he wants to be a soldier like his dad, and that's Natasha. She's five and dreams of dancing ballet at the Bolshoi.'

'You from Moscow, then?'

'St Petersburg, the city Peter the Great built to make sure Russians knew they were part of Europe.'

Cooper had his phone out, a wallpaper of a blond boy holding a football. 'Meet Ricky, turns eleven next week and I'll be back for his birthday.'

'That's a good-looking young man you have there. His mother?'

'With someone else.' Cooper snapped off the phone. 'She married me, a soldier, and didn't like when I went off to war.' He zipped the phone back into his pocket.

The driver got out of the cab and shut the door. Yumatov turned off his flashlight. 'Finally, we're good to go. Come. Next to me. You do the legs. I'll take the middle. He'll handle the head and antlers because he knows how.'

Cooper squatted down, feeling for a good grip of the ankles and hooves through his gloves. He looked up. The driver had his back to them, staring out into the empty night as gusts dusted snow along barren land that stretched to a dirty white horizon. Yumatov took a step toward him.

Cooper stood up. 'Now what?'

Before Cooper could react, Yumatov plunged a double-bladed steel knife into his neck and cut through arteries and muscles from side to side. He lowered Cooper to the ground sheet as he bled out and died. Yumatov took the flash drive from Cooper's jacket and zipped it securely inside his own pocket.

TWO

Rake Ozenna woke in an apartment, not a hotel room, nor a home, something temporary without personal touches, stylish with timber frames on the ceiling and snow covering half a window that winds had blown in overnight. A doorbell broke his sleep, an alien sound in a bed never slept in before, with indents and crumples in the sheets showing that someone had lain beside him. No one answered the door. The bell rang a second time.

Rake stepped into his pants that lay heaped on the warm tile floor, plucked his vest from there, and his white down jacket hooked over a bedroom chair. He chambered a round in his revolver and slid it down behind his belt, before remembering he was in Norway, but he kept it because he wouldn't have felt right handling an unknown doorbell unarmed.

A short corridor led from the bedroom to the kitchen, part of an open-plan, Scandinavian-style living area with floor-to-ceiling windows and a view over a snow-laden landscape. An icy road ran past, heading straight and long and flanked by trees. On the other side was a frozen lake, a streetlamp, and a road-salting truck parked for the night. Rake looked through the front-door spyglass to see the distorted face of his friend Mikki Wekstatt. He opened the door. Mikki's face creased. 'Oh, Jesus, Rake. What the hell you doing here?'

Rake knew. Mikki knew. Rake said, 'You looking for Nilla?'

'Who else? This is her place.'

Rake didn't know much about Nilla except anyone able to leave a bed without him knowing meant he had either been too far gone or had skills he needed to learn. He remembered she was taller than he, something Rake, who was only five ten, had a habit of noting in women. She spoke fluent English and had a strong body with long black hair that ran halfway down her back.

'We've been asked to pick up a dead reindeer,' Mikki said.

'A reindeer?'

'Yeah. Like Santa Claus and his sleigh. They live up here. Think "caribou".'

Rake corralled his scattered thoughts into a pattern that made sense. Two days ago, he'd been wrapping up an operation in the Uruzghan Mountains in central Afghanistan. This morning, he was in an Arctic town on the border with Russia because Mikki had asked him to help with a baby-sitting job, someone due to cross from Russia.

Mikki and Rake had been raised on the Alaskan island of Little Diomede on Russia's eastern border, a remote place and small community of less than a hundred. They were orphans, whose parents had died or vanished. Their adoptive parents were now in their sixties, and Mikki was ten years older than Rake. They hadn't been close until Rake had joined the National Guard on Mikki's urging. They had been deployed together in Afghanistan, Mikki made it to sergeant. Rake broke through to officer.

Mikki left the military to join the Alaska State Troopers, and was now a detective, technically on secondment to the Norwegian Police Service. There was a lot of common ground with Alaska, people going crazy with nights that never ended, foreign enemy, the border. Rake only learned he was going to Norway when his commanding officer signed off his deployment and told him Mikki was already there. Rake got in in the late afternoon. On the way from the airport, Mikki told him they were a security backstop to a classified US government operation. They were expecting someone across the border in the next few days. Mikki wanted Rake with him, just in case.

Kirkenes was small, a handful of streets, ugly concrete buildings, and a fjord where the police station was. They had dinner with local cops at the Thon Hotel. Along the evening, people slid away, Mikki, too. When Rake was left with Nilla, the dynamics changed. He became alert. It took a day or so to switch mindsets from being in a dangerous place to a safe one. He could have left but didn't. Nilla surprised him by drawing from her bag a locked case with his pistol and ammunition inside. Rake had taken a military flight from Kabul to Germany, but civilian to Oslo and then Kirkenes, so had to check in the weapon, which was taken straight to the police station for registration. Nilla had collected it for him. 'Don't tell me,' she said, pushing it across the bar table. 'You feel naked without it.'

That had to be a signal, but Rake let the work talk go on. He asked her about snow tracking, and she knew things that interested him, the way the sun melted snow, how to read tracks on the steppe, and the talk moved on to how they got into their work, not married, no kids to put to bed, forgotten what a weekend was, Rake's island home thousands of miles away, Nilla raised on a farm thirty miles south, family still there, the kind of fore-play conversations that rang warning bells or opened doors, depending.

Sometimes, at this stage, Rake would use his ex-fiancée's name as his safety cordon, deploy Carrie like the ring he didn't have because she had closed down on him. But Rake found himself in a screw-Carrie mood, at a bar with a beautiful, intelligent woman. He asked Nilla to his room. She took his hand, led them to her car, then her apartment.

Rake leant his hand on the door jamb, eyeing his friend, fellow orphan, step-brother, whatever the hell Mikki was. 'You wanna come in?'

'It's not your house to ask me into.' Mikki stayed where he was. 'There are a million stunning women in this country, and you had to shit on my doorstep.'

'Where's this reindeer?'

'Knocked down across the border. It must have got through the fence. Probably across the lake. Its markings say it belongs to a Norwegian herder. The Norwegians and the Russians have an arrangement to return reindeer. The Russians have just called for us to go across to collect it.'

Rake's expression stayed flat. 'You're hammering on this door because you need to collect a dead animal.'

'Told you life here was different.' Mikki grinned.

'What about this crossing we're meant to be watching?'

'I've heard nothing. They know where we are if they need us.'

Rake dropped his hand from the door jamb. 'Give me a ride to the station.'

'You sure Nilla's not here? How in hell's name could you lose her?'

'Maybe she's gone looking already.'

Nilla appeared behind him, clipping up her hair and putting on a police hat. 'Hi, Mikki. What's going on? You want coffee? Come in for God's sake and close the door before this wind freezes the freezer.' Nilla kissed Rake briefly on the lips and ran her hand affectionately down his arm. He had known her less than twenty-four hours. Spousal. Normal day around the house. Rake found himself not minding.

Mikki stamped his boots free of snow and stepped in. 'The boss called. There's a reindeer down on the Murmansk road, about ten miles across the border. He wants us to go get it.'

'Is it tagged?'

'A herder in Elvenes.'

Nilla made a call, speaking in Norwegian, namechecking Rake twice. When she finished, she said: 'We'll get coffee at the station and be there in less than an hour.' She tilted her head toward Rake. 'You can come with us. Not your weapon.'

THREE

L ight snow lay like dust along the road to the Russian border. Nilla was at the wheel of a white and yellow police van towing a trailer with a snowmobile and enough space to take the animal carcass. She had the wiper on slow, sweeping away crystallizing flakes every few seconds. Mikki sat with her in the front. Rake was in the back.

'See, there,' enthused Nilla, waving her hand to the right. 'Across the water, those hills, that is Russia.' Rake looked through ice-speckled trees where snow was settling on a fjord of ice. Nilla swapped driving hands to point to the other side. 'And that hotel. They have cabins with glass ceilings so you can fuck and watch the sky turn green with the Northern Lights.'

She drove, switching hands back and forth, talking like a tour guide, capturing Rake's gaze through the rear-view mirror.

'So, when are you guys off exploring Europe?' she asked.

'Day after tomorrow,' said Mikki. 'Oslo, then Paris. Never been to Paris.'

'So tomorrow, come down to my farm. Do you dog sled, Rake?'

'Sometimes.'

'Sometimes. Bullshit,' said Mikki. 'Rake's done the Alaska Iditarod, a thousand miles – Anchorage to Nome.'

'Great.' Nilla slapped her hand on the wheel. 'So, come to the farm, talk to our students. Meet my brother, Stefan. Meet the dogs.'

Mikki glanced at Rake as if to say, *Let's do it.*

'We're close to the border now,' said Nilla. 'We cross under an agreement between the Norwegian Border Commission and Russia's Federal Security Service. We call it the FSB. They handle internal security. Same as your FBI. I know the guys there. Norway and Russia get along well. We have not fought a war for more than a thousand years. Here in Finnmark, this is the only conquered territory anywhere in the world from which

Stalin voluntarily withdrew. Big territory. Finnmark is bigger than Denmark—' She noticed Mikki's blank response. Who the hell knew the size of Denmark? Or maybe he had heard it all before. She caught Rake's eye in the mirror. 'New Jersey. More than twice the size of New Jersey. Get the proportions. Hitler burned Finnmark. Stalin gave it back to us. What do you reckon about that, Major Rake Ozenna?'

It was a flirtatious challenge. 'I like places where people don't fight wars.'

'He's holding back,' said Mikki. 'Rake's an expert. He's been lecturing about war. I suggested he became a detective. Instead he sends himself to college.'

'I thought you'd been in Afghanistan,' queried Nilla. 'That's not college.'

'Before that. Tell her what college you went to?'

'Mikki's exaggerating like he often does,' said Rake. 'I did three months at a military academy.'

'Which is fucking West Point, isn't it,' smiled Mikki. 'My little brother at West Point.'

'What course?' asked Nilla.

'Mid-career on leadership and social behavior.'

'You took it and taught it, didn't you?' said Mikki. 'They loved you because of how you handle the Taliban. They parade you, then send you off to another war.'

'What a man of mystery!' Nilla turned sharply in her seat as if she were assessing Rake for the first time, even more favorably.

'Like Mikki says, post-deployment, a lot of guys get back, wanting to work out why the world is so fucked up. At West Point, they teach it.'

'So, tell us, Nilla,' said Mikki. 'How come you and Russia love each other so much when NATO has got an exercise about to start where they practice blowing Russia up? Rake, what is it called?'

'Dynamic Freedom,' said Rake. 'Next week. They do it most years, aimed at testing Russia's defenses.'

Nilla laughed. 'The biggest threat we have is Russian women coming across to marry drunk, no-good Norwegians. They live in Nikel, a few miles from here.' She pressed down her window, breathed in hard, did the same with Rake's window. Snow smacked harsh into his face.

'Taste the pollution in the air.' Nilla opened her mouth to expose her tongue. 'Nikel's a filthy place. Chimneys and smoke. Smelters. Factories. There's a visa-free arrangement for thirty kilometers on both sides. The Nikel women come across, marry, wait seven years to get Norwegian citizenship, then kick their husbands out. Between Nikel and Kirkenes is one of the world's biggest income gaps. If I were a Nikel woman, I would do exactly the same. If your stupid President lifted sanctions on Russia, we could do great business, from here to Murmansk to China. Instead people stay drunk and poor.'

A large blue sign appeared ahead of them. White lettering in English, Norwegian, and Russian read: 'Schengen Border. Restricted Area. Border Crossing Only.' Schengen was a vast area in Europe of twenty-six countries. Once inside, travelers could move freely without customs or passport checks, which was why securing the border with Russia was so important. Nilla pulled into a rest stop. Through two stone gate posts, Rake saw light-brown, modern low-rise buildings.

'This is Storskog, the only crossing point on a hundred and twenty miles of border,' said Nilla. 'Away from here, there are posts every four meters. The Russian ones are red and green. Ours are yellow with gray on the top. On the Russian side, they have a fence right along, but inside Russian territory, some of it just a few meters, some of it several hundred meters. They have sensors, CCTV, alarms. Bears break the wire, but the reindeer we're collecting most likely jumped over because of snow piled up against it, then got hit by a truck.'

Nilla adjusted the satellite navigation screen. 'We are here. A couple of miles back is Elvenes, where the herder lives. The carcass is on this road, E105, about ten miles down. The closest Norwegian settlement is Svanvik, here where I come from. My family has a farm there. Huskies. Tourist sledding.' She turned to Rake, her expression tighter. 'We used to have family across the border. Stalin moved them all to Siberia.'

'He did the same out east,' said Rake. 'We had family across the water. Stalin moved them miles away and set up a military base there.' Rake's home of Little Diomede lay at the opposite end of Russia with no border markings, no immigration posts, no flags, no signs of any kind. No crossings allowed. In Europe they had called it the Iron Curtain. In Alaska, they still called it the Ice Curtain.

A gray saloon car, engine and headlights on, was stopped at the border. Men in uniform inspected. A truck pulled up behind it. 'Switch off your data roaming,' said Nilla. 'Or you'll get billed high by the Russian networks.' Her eyes found Rake's in the mirror. 'You don't have the exact right papers, but it'll be fine. I know the FSB guys. Stay quiet, behave, and we'll have a good time.'

She pulled out, gauging her acceleration against the weight of the trailer. A Norwegian border officer waved them on. Flakes drifted from a drab, leaden sky. By now the sun should be rising. Rake couldn't see it. The light was like dusk. Fresh snow brought a quiet whiteness to the gray. They crossed into Russia. A black Land Cruiser pulled off the edge into the road. Its headlights flashed. Nilla flashed back. Rear orange hazard-warning lights blinked in recognition. The cruiser speeded up, steadying the wheel with both hands. The trailer juddered as it hit a pothole in the Russian road.

FOUR

The reindeer carcass had been dragged to the side of the road and cordoned off. Red tape was strung between six silver metal poles stuck into the ground like tent pegs. Nilla positioned the trailer against the tape, its end a couple of feet from the antlers. The Russian FSB Land Cruiser stopped behind her. On the other side of the cordon, two local cops got out of their car. Nilla cut her engine. The Russians left theirs running. Doors slammed. Boots crunched on snow.

There were two FSB men. Nilla gave a wave. One older in a civilian dark-blue greatcoat, a thickset man with a big smile whom Nilla greeted with a handshake. A younger one wore a dark-green military uniform with a hood, black lace-up boots, and a pistol holstered around his waist. Nilla embraced him with a kiss on both cheeks. She spoke in Russian, introducing Mikki and Rake as colleagues, no other explanation.

The carcass lay battered and twisted, frozen hard, pools of blood where its limbs had been crushed. A coating of snow covered the brown and gray hide. Icicles hung from the elegantly sprawling antlers.

The sun began to puncture through the dreary gray sky. Here and there, toward the horizon, Rake identified low sloping hills. Clumps of trees peppered the white expanse. Such a landscape with sunlight flashing back and forth could play tricks on the eyes. Rake took time. All snow was different, its powder, the way it fell, sometimes silent, sometimes in a gale. In Alaska, in Afghanistan, up here in the Arctic, none of it the same.

Mikki examined the reindeer. Nilla went over documents with the Russians. Rake gave them a wide arc and walked to where he judged the reindeer would have been knocked down. He crouched to inspect the lay of fresh snow, thin enough, if the light were right, to spot marks underneath. He waited until a swift glare of sun gave him what he needed. There were regular tire tracks on old ice, brushed near invisible by the new fall. He looked for new ones, skewed tracks, brake marks, something sudden and harsh that came from hitting an animal that size, something that would have been a few hours old.

Nothing.

Caribou or reindeer were always on the move. They traveled in herds, could be a few dozen, could be several thousand, but not just one, unless sick. Even then, there was a sense of family and caring. Others would stay with it. So why could he find no fresh hoof marks? He saw what might have been the marks of an Arctic fox, a five-paw print, and possibly a bear with a glove-like tread with five toes. They were old, edges faded with weather. There was a handful of reindeer markings, a herd from some time ago. The clearest showed four hoof marks. The rear ones fell slightly outside the front ones, which would be a doe. The carcass was of a stag. Tracks could be a week, a month, even a year old, depending how they had been pressed into the earth and ice.

Rake spotted distinct vehicle markings, tire tracks of a truck and a lighter vehicle like an SUV. The tracks were clear and heavily indented, meaning they would have been stationary. There were well-defined boot marks of human beings, imprints of soles sharp, edges clear, hours old. They were scattered. Some were covered completely, some visible to the eye. But they were away from where the reindeer was meant to have been found dead.

Rake stood up, brushing snow off his legs. Nilla and the Russians talked expressively, a lot of laughter. Nilla examined the buck's ear where the Norwegian herder would have engraved his family's identity marking.

'You done one of these before?' Rake asked Mikki.

'No, but I heard them talking about reindeer retrieval and I know what you're thinking.'

'I'm thinking that the buck was trucked here and dumped.'

'I'm thinking that, too.'

'No reindeer hoof marks. Boots. Tire tracks. Why would they do that?'

'The Norwegians pay the Russians for handing back reindeer.'

'How much?'

'I asked Nilla once and she avoided answering. Has to be worth it. They find a Norwegian reindeer, kill it, and make out it's been hit by a vehicle. Norway pays. Money gets shared around.'

'This is your first?'

'First I know about.' Mikki was about to say more when they saw two sets of headlamps driving north toward them. Nilla noticed them, too. Her mood changed, her face flaring. She beckoned Rake and Mikki. 'We need to lift him onto the truck and get out of here,' she said.

Not a chance, thought Rake. They were coming too fast. The buck's weight would be at least 200 pounds before allowing for ice. It was no easy lift. They needed to be slow and careful so as not to damage the velvet coating of the antlers. If this were a money scam, big and expansive antlers like these would be worth a few hundred dollars.

Rake had underestimated Nilla. She took charge, bringing everyone round, shouting for the local cops to help. She jumped onto the trailer and laid down a tarpaulin. She instructed the younger FSB officer to help her with the head and the antlers. Rake and Mikki were allocated the right leg and haunch.

'Ready?' Nilla commanded in Russian. 'One, two, three, and lift.'

The FSB officer next to Rake lifted hard. A sheet of ice slid off the reindeer's hide and shattered on the ground. The legs were rigid. As Rake tried to maneuver them, he saw a frozen strand of something that looked out of place, not fur, thread of some kind. They raised the carcass high, smoothly took it in, and laid it on the tarpaulin. When the antlers were clear of the trailer's edge, Nilla shouted: 'Now, slowly, bring him in.'

The approaching vehicles were close, spraying up snow under the wheels. One was a white SUV with a flashing blue light on the roof. The other a military green armored vehicle that Rake identified as a GAZ Tigr, a smaller version of the American Humvee. They stopped in a way that blocked the road in both directions, the SUV to the south, the armored Tigr to the north, a slab of dark color against the white landscape. Nilla sent a message on her phone. She stayed on the trailer. The older FSB officer made a call. Three men in dark-blue military cold-weather clothes got out of the SUV. The younger FSB officer glanced nonchalantly at Nilla, as if to say *What the hell?* and went to meet them.

'Which agency are they?' asked Rake.

'Glavnoye Razvedyvatel'noye Upravleniye,' muttered Nilla in Russian before switching to English and meeting Rake's Gaze. 'GRU. Russian military intelligence. The FSB has problems with them, more now with the NATO exercises. It's like the CIA, FBI, and the Pentagon having a public fight with guns in America.'

Copy that, thought Rake familiar with inter-agency fights over budgets, turf, and power. 'But you've had nothing like this?' he asked.

'With an armored car? No,' said Nilla. 'We need to hold back and let them sort it out between themselves.'

'Or we just go?' said Mikki.

'No.' Nilla jumped down from the trailer. 'But we get in the vehicle, just in case.'

The older FSB officer saw Nilla move toward the driver's door and patted his hand in the air for her to wait. They stood by the hood. The younger FSB officer ended his conversation and beckoned Nilla over, out of Rake and Mikki's earshot.

'Does she know anything thing about the border crossing that doesn't seem to have happened?' asked Rake.

'She doesn't. Just me and Norwegian intelligence.'

'This has got to be connected.'

Nilla tapped her hand impatiently against her thigh as she listened to the FSB officer. When he finished, she abruptly turned to go back. He put his hand on her elbow to stop her. She brushed it off and jogged over to her driver's side door.

'Get in,' she snapped.

Rake heard an order screamed out, then a familiar metal-on-metal clicking. He turned toward the Tigr to see its heavy weapon being readied for use.

FIVE

A taut quietness fell. The sun gave a dull silver sheen to the clouds. The Tigr's 7.62mm all-purpose machine gun ramped up the tension. It might even be a 12.7mm. From where he stood, Rake couldn't tell. Not that it made much difference. A heavy machine gun on an armored vehicle commanded the scene.

The older FSB officer spoke angrily to two of the GRU men. The third had his pistol out, holding it awkwardly, not sure what to do with it. The FSB officers kept their weapons holstered. Mikki's revolver was concealed. Rake had none. Nilla was openly carrying, her expression cold, her eyes steady. 'This isn't about them,' she said. 'It's about you two. The GRU say NATO's Dynamic Freedom exercise is a preparation for the invasion of Russia. You are foreigners who have been sent as spies.'

'How do they know we are foreigners?' said Rake.

'That's what I asked. They want to take you to Murmansk for questioning. The FSB guys are trying to fix it. We're within the thirty-kilometer agreement zone where the FSB has prevailing jurisdiction.'

'Not if the other side bring in armored vehicles,' muttered Mikki.

Rake and Mikki were not just any foreigners. They were Americans. Mikki was legitimate, working under the protection of the Norwegian police, Rake a gatecrasher. There was no way they were going anywhere near Murmansk.

The Tigr armored vehicle stood across the road about fifty yards to the north. They could skirt around. The ground on either side was solid. The Russians stayed out of their vehicles, talking in a cluster, breath clouds and cigarette smoke collecting in front of their faces. Their concentration was on each other. Between them and the trailer lay the now empty cordoned area, its metal poles skewed, tape trailing on the snow, smeared with reindeer blood. Nilla's vehicle was backed up facing north. The E-105 was a good winter road, ice-packed and smooth.

The question was the Tigr and how to stop it. Once that was done, with Nilla at the wheel, they could put in some distance. If the Tigr opened fire, it would chew them up. But why risk killing a Norwegian and start that war between Russia and Norway that hadn't taken place for a thousand years?

Mikki said, 'We've weapons in the back.'

'No,' answered Nilla firmly. Saying nothing, Rake walked away from the vehicle toward the Tigr. He kept his hands loose at his side to show he wasn't carrying. He trod heavily in the snow, his steps measured. Nilla was about to follow. Mikki touched her shoulder and said something in her ear. She held back. The Russians hadn't noticed. They kept arguing. Rake wanted to see the Tigr's weapon, how ammunition was fed, who was behind the trigger.

Twenty yards out, the Russian gunner shouted: 'Stop!' Rake held his arms out further, stretched like a bird's wings. He kept walking.

'Stop, or I'll open fire.'

Rake was close enough to be heard. 'What the hell you guys doing?' he said in Russian. He jerked his hand back behind him. 'She's Norwegian, for Christ's sake.'

'I'm following orders.' He was a conscript, no more than twenty. He wore goggles, so Rake couldn't see his eyes. His finger was unsteady, tapping the trigger guard, ridden with uncertainty. No hatch opened from below. No senior officer showed his face to back him up.

'Are you with those losers,' challenged Rake, 'or are you army?'

'Halt,' he repeated. 'Right there.'

Rake stopped and raised his hands fully above his head. 'If you're army, don't answer to these idiots. We'll shoot our way out, if need be. You kill any of us, you'll be the fall guy. You'll die in the next few minutes or be sent east for the rest of your time.'

The gunner's finger darted in and out of the trigger guard. He put his left hand to his earpiece, checking orders. Rake expected the GRU men to be running toward him. They were looking skywards. Rake heard the clatter of helicopter blades. He couldn't see the aircraft, but it was coming in from the east, wrapped behind clouds. Nilla got into the driver's seat, Mikki the other side. She started the engine. The gunner took his hand off his weapon and slipped off his goggles. Rake gave him a thumbs up. The young face filled with relief. Mikki reached over and opened the back door. Rake walked back to the vehicle. His best guess was that the helicopter belonged to another agency, called in to see off the GRU. An armed helicopter would prevail over any other weapons.

Rake closed his door. Nilla was on the phone, speaking in Norwegian. The GRU men headed for their SUV, the FSB to their Land Cruiser. They pulled out, drove past, and Nilla followed, skirting round the Tigr. The gunner gave a hesitant wave. Rake brought down his window to look for the helicopter, flying low, and the noise was growing, a thousand feet and descending. It loomed above them, blue-gray and stubby, a Russian navy Ka-27, designed for fire-fighting, anti-submarine work, ferrying troops, available at short notice. The downdraft sent vibrations though the vehicle and snow and ice skidding across the ground. The noise obliterated all other sound.

Nilla kept driving. The helicopter stayed where it was, hovering at about twelve feet, tearing the poles out of the ground, getting close to the GRU vehicle, keeping up the pressure until they drove off. It ascended and headed north-east toward Murmansk or, probably, Severomorsk, the big naval base twenty miles to the north.

Flying time would be at least an hour, and they had been at the scene less than that, which pointed to the helicopter deployment being linked not to Nilla and the FSB, but to the GRU, who were based out of Murmansk. Had the Russian navy been brought in to counter whatever the GRU was planning? Before any military exercise, especially one as intricate as Dynamic Freedom, there would be a web of communications between Russia and NATO to ensure nothing erupted by mistake. A plan to take two Americans into military custody smelt of a rogue operation. Rake looked out the back window. Two local cops were pulling up the cordon poles. The helicopter was a speck, identified only from a flashing fuselage light.

'I'm sorry you had to go through that,' said Nilla.

'Only hope we have a reindeer worth dying for,' Rake said dryly.

Mikki laughed. Nilla met his eyes in the mirror. 'How long you been here, Rake, and how much trouble you caused?'

'I heard it was Mikki they wanted,' said Rake. 'They planned to marry him off to one of those Nikel beauties.'

Nilla slowed as they approached the border post. The Russian Land Cruiser pulled off the road to the parking bay. There was no goodbye. No wave. No friendly hazard-warning lights. At the Norwegian post, a customs official waved Nilla to stop. She lowered her window. He peered into the back at Rake. 'Sir, you have a visitor waiting in the rest bay by the shop. Says it's urgent.'

As Nilla drove on, Rake said: 'Pull up.'

'Your visitor?' She looked at Rake with uncertainty.

'Just do it,' he instructed sharply. 'Something we need to check.'

Nilla brought the trailer to a rumbling halt. Rake climbed onto it, felt around the right haunch of the reindeer carcass until he found the thread he had spotted. Nilla jumped up beside him. Mikki leant against the side of the vehicle keeping watch both ways. A brown nylon thread made up a series of stitches that formed a square about two inches each side. Rake got out his pocket-knife, cut the thread, and pulled it out of the hide. Nilla had a forensics bag ready. He dropped the thread in. Frozen blood lined the edges of the square like glue. The hide had been cut on three sides. Rake eased in his knife blade to prize it open. He raised it gently and wasn't sure what he was looking at, something curved and oblong, smeared in blood.

Nilla put on a pair of blue surgical gloves. With her forefinger and thumb, she lifted it out and held it up in the low midday light. A clot of blood fell off, and a mask of horror spread across her face. From the hide of a reindeer, they had extracted a severed human ear.

SIX

Rake in the back seat held two transparent bags of evidence on his lap as they drove through the stone posts to the rest stop just beyond the blue border sign. A Norwegian police car was parked there together with a black jeep showing US military plates, which must be the visitor waiting for Rake. The wind had dropped, and soft light cast a yellow hue on the snow and trees. Two men in civilian clothes walked toward them from the police car.

'NIS,' said Nilla. 'Our foreign intelligence service.' She reached for the two bags. Warm and melted, blood streaked the sides of the plastic. 'You deal with your guys. I'll deal with mine.'

They watched Nilla hand over the bags, gesticulating, telling the story, body language rigid, stepping back, turning to point to the carcass on her trailer, hand on hips, taking off her hat, banging it against her leg, putting it on again, talking, listening, never taking her gaze off the two intelligence agents in front of her.

'I'm thinking that our man tried to come over last night and didn't make it,' said Mikki. 'Instead, he loses his ear, which gets sewn into a reindeer hide. Does that even begin to make sense?'

Rake showed him phone pictures of the thread and severed ear. 'See the cut inside the ear.' He pointed to a rough but defined circular shape. 'That isn't laceration, that's a carving.'

Mikki grimaced. 'Sick, the work of a psycho?'

'Yes, but a well-organized one.' Rake opened his door.

Nilla saw them and broke away from her conversation. 'We're stood down,' she said angrily. 'They're taking the buck and the evidence down to Tromsø.'

'What's in Tromsø?' asked Mikki.

'Bigger offices.' Nilla kicked a clump of snow. Loose hair fell onto her face. She took time pushing it back under her hat. This had been her gig. It ran into trouble and had been taken from her. Rake showed her the phone picture of the curving arch of the cut, a jagged black line set against dark red blood and the pale yellow of the flesh of the human ear. Rake thumbed to another shot, close up, with a right-angled edge coming out of the curve. 'They need to see this.'

The two Norwegian intelligence agents came over. 'Major Ozenna, I am Einar Olsen,' said one. 'What do you have for us?'

Rake held out the phone. 'It's elaborate. Organized. It's a message of some kind. A statement.'

Olsen studied the screen. 'We have these criminal problems with the Russians all the time.' He shifted his gaze across the road to a wooden shack that sold souvenirs. 'But I think you have bigger fish to fry.'

A US Marine sergeant in full Arctic fatigues emerged from the shack and sprinted over, looking at the trailer with the rigid, frozen reindeer with curiosity. 'Major Ozenna, sir, I've flown in from Camp Setermoen and have orders from Camp Denali for you, sir, and Detective Wekstatt is to accompany you.'

The sergeant took an envelope from his tunic and handed it to Rake. Camp Denali was the headquarters of the Alaska National Guard, to which Rake was officially attached. Setermoen was the Norwegian military base, five hundred miles to the west, where US troops were stationed. Rake slit open the envelope and read the printed email inside. He didn't like what he saw. 'Thank you, Sergeant,' he said. 'Finish your shopping, I need a few minutes to finish up here.'

'Sir, they said immediately, and we have a plane—'

'We could have been days over there, Sergeant. Let's agree on a few minutes.'

Rake handed Mikki the email.

'What the fuck!' Mikki read out the beginning. '"Following your lecture at the War College on military–civilian cooperation in Afghanistan, you are needed for a panel at the Center for Political and Global Studies in Washington, DC entitled *Military and Civilian Liaison inside Hostile Peace-Keeping Operations.* Your contribution—"' He mimicked the voice of a mythical desk officer who had never seen combat, then broke away from it. 'You gotta be kidding. Who are these people?'

'Marching orders. They want us the hell out of here.'

'But a fucking panel?'

'My guess is that whatever this operation is or was, it's gone bad. The US now wants the Norwegians to own it, meaning you and I have to get out of here.'

Mikki handed back the letter. 'That's why you made officer and I didn't.'

'Norway doesn't want its long, complicated friendship with Russia confused by two American soldiers accused of being spies.' Rake put the envelope in his pocket and gave Mikki a self-conscious grin. 'Besides, not all bad news. Carrie's just moved to Washington, got a job at a big hospital there.'

'Oh, shit!' Mikki face broke into a half smile and half frown. Mikki knew more about Rake's tempestuous relationship with Dr Carrie Walker than he would wish on anyone. 'Will you contact her?'

'Don't know.'

Carrie had sent a message about the new job. Rake congratulated her but got no reply, which was how it had often been, him chasing, her not responding.

'Carrie's not who you are,' said Mikki. 'She'll want you changing, and it won't work.'

Nilla came back and Rake asked: 'Are you taking shit for what happened over there?'

'They're telling bare-faced fucking lies that we have criminal problems like this with the Russians all the time. It's bullshit and I'm off the case.'

Rake pointed to the US Marine sergeant and showed her his orders. Nilla read it and put on a brief smile. 'Started good, turned into a shitty day.' She took both Rake's hands, leant forward and kissed him on the mouth, deep enough and long enough for Rake to sense a stirring that this was a woman he wanted more of. Mikki was smiling. Nilla's colleagues didn't seem to mind. This was Scandinavia, local permissive culture. He had read about it in magazines.

'Let us know what happens to our buck,' he said when she eased back. 'How come he had his antlers and—'

Nilla played her finger sensually around the edges of his lips 'Hush,' she whispered. 'He's not our buck anymore.' She gave him a light kiss and jogged back to her colleagues. The sergeant held the car door open. They climbed in. Mikki directed him to the hotel to pick up their stuff. Rake messaged Carrie: *Heading to DC. Coffee?*

SEVEN

Washington, DC

Rake's message stayed unseen on Carrie Walker's phone because she was striding alongside a gurney into the Level 1 Trauma Center at Washington General Hospital. Paramedics relayed the condition of a cycle accident patient, suspected internal bleeding, trachea injury and falling blood pressure, a dangerous 80 over 50.

Blood soaked into the gurney's left side. Air bubbled up around the patient's neck. Carrie had seen young men cut up. Her experience lay mostly with bullets, shrapnel, and stones propelled by bombs, or with a human body seemingly unharmed but knocked about so badly that the nerves and fluids would never settle back. She reminded herself this was a routine peacetime road accident.

The patient was white, male, and twenty-seven years old, a bicycle messenger who smashed into the wall of the Dupont Circle underpass after being winged by a truck. A spoke from his mangled wheel was now embedded in his throat.

Trauma surgery was about self-confidence and risk, about making quick decisions with only scraps of information, a truth that didn't change whether in a desert with nothing or in one of the world's best-equipped hospitals. Not acting fast enough, even by a few seconds, spelt the difference between life and death.

'E.R. Now,' snapped Carrie.

'Trauma Room Two!' shouted a nurse.

Carrie had no idea where Trauma Room Two was. This was her second day at the hospital, a lifestyle decision to move from New York, away from family who kept telling her to do this and that, mainly find a man, stay in one place, just like that when Carrie wasn't that sort of person. She needed something big, complicated, and edgy among people who traveled and understood blood, sand, urgent sex, and power outages. She balked when a friend suggested Washington, DC, an opening at Washington General Hospital in Foggy Bottom, State Department territory. She didn't like her government, didn't understand why it kept picking fights with other countries. Her friend begged her to be open to the idea. 'The heart of the empire that starts the wars where you fix hurt people.' She thought about it, realized she wanted the job more than anything, and kissed goodbye to the filthy sidewalk of Flatbush, Brooklyn, when the job came through.

Today she was rostered to shadow a trauma unit and, in the afternoon, to take a course on building familiarization about restrooms, fire exits, and cafeterias. The hospital shone with endowment, quality white paint, wide airy corridors, signposts to departments, but none to Trauma Room Two. Her patient was taken down a corridor into the ground-floor area where urgent life-threatening conditions were identified and, if possible, fixed.

Carrie had noted three, maybe four, that might kill her patient within minutes or leave him with permanent brain injury. His airway needed to be secured. The spoke needed to be removed from his throat. There could be injury to the carotid artery, the main blood channel between the heart and the brain. If that were the case, the patient risked bleeding out before they could get him to an operating room.

Carrie flipped open the medical bag she always had with her and brought out doses of propofol and fentanyl to use as anesthetic. She slipped them into her pocket. Medication in the pocket violated the rules of most hospitals but was usually overlooked because every surgeon knew it saved lives. Often in the places she had worked Carrie had been the only doctor. Keeping strong drugs in her pockets had become second nature. She looked back across the gurney, and saw she was standing face to face with a young medic in a freshly laundered white coat.

'You the anesthesiologist?'

He shook his head. 'Peter Reynolds. I'll be shadowing you.'

He thought she was someone else. Carrie looked around for a hospital trauma surgeon and saw none, only two nurses and three paramedics waiting for her lead. There was no time for scrubbing and gowning up. Right now, infection was the least of the dangers. She sanitized her hands, pulled on surgical gloves and mask.

'Airway,' she said softly. She swabbed the neck and injected a dose of her local anesthetic.

'Scalpel.' A nurse was beside her with a stainless-steel tray. Avoiding the bicycle spoke, Carrie identified the thyroid cartilage, then the cricoid cartilage about an inch down. She made a short horizontal incision. She took a tracheostomy tube to give the patient an alternative breathing pathway and slid it in, just under an inch. She attached a resuscitation bag over his mouth, put her hand around the air balloon, and squeezed two short, sharp bursts of air, paused for five seconds, and squeezed again. The chest rose, faltered, picked up, rose again. Carrie gave it two more breaths. The patient's breathing stabilized. She looked at the monitors. Blood pressure dropping, heart rate increasing. Carrie had to deal with probable arterial bleeding which could create a build-up of fluid around the heart. Untreated, even if her patient lived, he would wake up brain dead.

They needed a fully-equipped and controlled operating room.

'OR now,' she said.

'Room Four,' said a nurse.

The porters moved the gurney. Reynolds eyed Carrie quizzically. She second-guessed his thoughts. He was shadowing her. She had a duty to explain. 'There's a risk he may bleed out on the way to the OR. But his injuries are too complicated. If we stay here, he dies.'

Reynolds might not have agreed but it was Carrie's call and she liked the way he accepted it. He walked on the other side of the gurney to her. OR Four was a short distance down the corridor. Nurses, medics, technicians were waiting. Reynolds pushed open an adjoining door to the preparation room where she stripped off her coat jacket to scrub up.

'Jenkins is in Two. Sanchez is on his way,' said Reynolds.

'Your prognosis?' she asked.

'A carotid tear that is partially but not completely closed by the presence of the rod.' He gowned up.

'Agreed.'

The door opened from the operating room. A thin, late-middle-aged doctor was about to speak to Reynolds, then, seeing Carrie, asked: 'Who the hell are you?'

'Carrie Walker. From King's County, Brooklyn.'

The doctor pulled down his mask. 'Greg Thatcher, anesthesiologist.' He glanced at Reynolds. 'No Dr Perkins?'

'Fifteen minutes, max.'

'Fifteen minutes, our patient will be dead,' said Carrie.

'Perkins messaged that we need a CT angiogram for the neck and chest,' said Thatcher. 'He wants to know the damage before intervening.'

'He could bleed out,' said Carrie. 'We control the bleeding first.'

'Perkins insists,' said Thatcher.

'Perkins is wrong. I am here. He is not.' She finished fixing her gown.

Quiet fell among the three of them. Carrie had some idea how seniority would work. It must be Thatcher, but he wasn't a surgeon. Reynolds was inexperienced. He could do basic emergency room but not this. Or her, but she was an unknown. These were intelligent people. They needed a few seconds to make up their minds. Part of the reason she wanted this job was to break her loathing of red tape and big institutions, to learn how they worked, see if she could fit. Right now, she knew that as soon as her patient was wheeled away for a CT angiogram or anyone picked up a phone to get instructions, treatment would be dangerously delayed. CT angiogram would achieve legal protection for the hospital. Everyone in the operating theater would be covered for insurance. The young messenger could die.

From the expressions on Reynold's and Thatcher's faces, she realized the same thought might be running through their minds. 'You done this before?' Thatcher asked.

'Iraq, Afghanistan, Brooklyn.'

Thatcher nodded. Reynolds checked Carrie's gown. They pulled their masks over their faces and went in.å

EIGHT

B lue pastel light dimly lit the edges of the theater. Two circular lamps illuminated Carrie's patient, who was now under general anesthetic, a safety strap across his thighs, ankles, and chest and his wrists secured to the operating table's side boards. His right eyelid was gashed, hanging like cloth. Skin peeled from his forehead was stapled down to stop excessive bleeding. His blond hair was ripped along the right side of the skull. That was just what she could see. Invisible and silent, blood could be leaking into his abdomen or chest in a way to end his life at any moment.

Carrie sanitized the entry point of the bicycle spoke and made the incision exactly where the spoke had entered the neck. She cut a five centimeter line, pulled back the skin, and secured it with a clamp to stem bleeding. She used forceps to draw back muscle and tissue and saw immediately the damage caused by the path of the spoke. Most dangerous was a partial tear to the carotid's outer wall. The artery had two branches. The external one carried blood to the face and scalp. The internal one fed the front part of the brain. She needed to make safe the wound before withdrawing the spoke.

'Vascular Prolene suture,' she said. A nurse was ready with it. One millimeter wrong, a few seconds too slow, and the patient would die. Breathing steady, hand firm, Carrie passed a tapered needle through the outer layer of the carotid artery. She made a pass either side of where the spoke protruded, creating a figure of eight, leaving the ends loose to be tightened once the spoke was out. She created a second layer of stitches to reinforce the first.

'Now,' she said to Reynolds, who slowly drew out the spoke. Normally carotids would spray powerfully. With Carrie's cordon of protection, blood pumped out, but not with unexpected force. She sealed the loose ends of the stitches, knotting both sets several times to keep blood inside the artery. She stepped back, took a breath, then moved in again to look behind the windpipe to ensure there was no injury to the laryngeal nerve that could affect the voice and to the esophagus, the muscular tube that runs from the throat to the stomach.

'Prognosis?' she asked Reynolds, moving aside so he could see.

'Clear,' he said.

'Agreed. Let's wrap it.'

'Blood pressure seventy-six over forty-two,' said a nurse.

'We have a cardiac output problem,' said Carrie. Blood pressure is controlled from the heart, not the throat. The electro-cardiogram showed critically weak low-voltage pulses around the heart.

'Tension pneumothorax,' she said, looking at Reynolds.

'And pericardial tamponade,' he said.

'First, tension pneumothorax.'

'Agreed.'

The low blood pressure was caused by a build-up of fluid and blood in the narrow cavity between the heart muscle and the pericardium, its outer covering. There was every chance that air was trapped around one of the lungs. Trauma surgery rule was ABC, Airway, Breathing, Circulation. The tracheotomy had dealt with the airways. In the next few minutes, Carrie had to carry out two more procedures, lungs and heart. The lung procedure should take less than ninety seconds.

Carrie made an incision just above the rib. She separated the muscles and tissue, inserted a tube, and there was a hiss of escaping trapped air. A nurse sealed it in. Carrie moved on to deal with the heart and blood pressure. The door opened, and a surgeon, scrubbed and gowned, with Andrew Perkins on his name badge, walked in from the changing room.

'Tracheotomy? Cycle accident? Is that right?' Perkins was beside Carrie. Behind his mask, he looked mid-forties, dark hair. Confident. Or arrogant. Or both. He spoke as if this were his operating room.

'About to do a pericardial window,' said Carrie.

Perkins' eyes scanned for her name badge which she didn't have. 'Do I know you? Are you cardiac?'

'General trauma, sir. We have to—'

Perkins cut her off to speak to Thatcher. 'Greg, what's going on here?'

Thatcher was unfazed. 'Ride with it, Andy. We're on the clock.'

'We can't just ride with anything, and you know it,' countered Perkins.

A nurse walking toward Carrie with a steel tray of surgical implements stopped mid-step. The operating room quietened. Perkins read instruments, examined charts, looked back at Carrie. 'You're a shadow. Not authorized for this.'

'I'm qualified.' Carrie recognized Perkins as a stickler for protocol, a general-trauma surgeon, but uncomfortable with high-risk-taking. 'Unless you want to do it?' she challenged.

Perkins ignored the question. 'The patient has multiple injuries. If the pericardial window is a success, but another procedure fails, we will all be held responsible, together with the hospital because you are not authorized.'

'Meaning the patient dies.'

'I can't permit you.'

Carrie was unfamiliar with a situation of having too many doctors. She was used to working with a shortage, just her, no nurse, a tent, no refrigeration, no sanitation, guns pointed at her. She said to Perkins, 'You stay and shut up, or you leave now.' She caught Reynold's eye and gave him a gritty look, making clear he had to decide whether he was with her or against her.

Perkins hesitated, his confidence fading. If he stayed, he would have to take charge and risked being implicated. He turned and left. Thatcher adjusted the anesthetic. Reynolds ushered forward the nurse with the steel tray. Carrie cut where the breastbone met the abdominal muscles. She worked through until she could make an incision in the membrane that enveloped the heart to bring out the blood that was crushing it. Moments later, she was finished. The heartbeat strengthened. Blood pressure increased.

'Good work,' said Reynolds quietly. Thatcher tilted his head in acknowledgment. Carrie opened the door of the changing room. Perkins was sitting on a bench, leaning forward scrolling down his phone. 'All yours, Dr Perkins,' she said. 'Once he's stabilized, you can do the CT angiogram and he has a broken—'

'I'll make my own assessment,' said Perkins, washing his hands. 'And you'll be hearing about this.'

Carrie had her hand on the door. 'Yeah, and if you try to screw with one of my patients again, you'll be hearing about it, too.'

Perkins pushed past her into the operating theater. Alone in the changing room, Carrie let her adrenalin subside. That was the dumbest of the dumb thing to say. How in hell's name could she know what power Perkins yielded? She had given him her in-the-field treatment; don't mess with me, not with this patient, not now. Which worked well in difficult places because of Carrie's height and her powerful face. She had sharp blue eyes with defined contours that ran through her high forehead and cheek bones. Her jaw was narrow and prominent, often giving a false impression that she knew exactly what she wanted and what she was doing. With medicine, yes. Most other things, she didn't score that well.

She checked her phone, ran through messages, and saw the one-liner from Rake. *Heading to D.C. Coffee?* Typically, he didn't say when or why he was coming and, right now, she didn't have the mental bandwidth for Rake Ozenna. He had taken enough of her space over the years. She needed to keep her mind on the patient, the hospital, and her stupid threat to Andrew Perkins.

She took off her disposable surgery cap and loosened her light blonde hair, letting it fall long just above her shoulders. Since splitting from Rake, Carrie hadn't worked out how she wanted her hair. She had tried it short, bobbed it, streaked it, grown it down her back, and had it styled just below the ears with a low curving arch exposing the back of her neck. When she and Rake first met, he had been a carnal, unfiltered lover, alive with instinct and lust. Carrie couldn't get enough. Then, she taught him nuance, guided him to kiss her slowly where nerve ends all over different parts of her body gave her thrums of pleasure. Rake learned quickly. 'Like hunting,' he had told her, 'slow love needs the patience of the wilds.'

She changed into her blue denim jacket and wrote a note for Reynolds to give her a call, let her know the patient's condition. Carrying her woolen coat, she headed out into the busyness of the hospital corridor, arriving late at the lecture hall for her familiarization course. She wore an apologetic expression which turned the trainer's face from reprimanding to amicable acceptance. She slid quietly onto a bench at the back of the hall.

Outside the hospital entrance on New Hampshire, in the early evening winter darkness, Carrie buttoned the collar of her coat

NINE

Carrie turned to see Peter Reynolds wearing a slight smile, half assured, half tentative. She stalled her reply: 'Is he still stable? Out of danger?'

'So far so good and don't worry about Perkins. You have the support of the OR team.' Out of his surgery gown, Reynolds wore a beige trench coat and jeans and exuded confidence.

'Thanks. I'm glad you were there.'

'So—' Reynolds kept up the smile. 'You got time for that drink?'

'Sure, if you know a place.' Carrie was unfamiliar with Washington etiquette, but she had no problem of medical professionals relaxing together after surgery.

'The Hive rooftop. I think you'll love it. It's only—'

Before he finished, a cyclist in a high-visibility yellow jacket pulled up next to her, skidding to a halt, the tire briefly losing grip on the packed snow. 'Dr Carrie Walker?'

Carrie nodded. The cyclist reached into a large bag strapped around his shoulders, drawing out not a package, but a phone, its screen on. He pressed the keypad and held it out to her. He stayed astride the saddle, one foot on the pedal and the other on the sidewalk. He leaned toward Carrie, a few feet away. She needed to take a step to get the phone. She didn't move. The cyclist put it on open speaker.

The caller's voice was gravelly, heavily accented. 'Carrie. Carrie. That you?' There was static on the line.

Carrie listened, tried to work out who it was. The cyclist kept his hand stretched out, palm flat, phone screen lit. His gaze stayed on Carrie. His face wasn't threatening. It was an open street. He was just a messenger. Carrie took the phone. The cyclist straightened up. She turned off the speaker and put it to her ear. 'This is Carrie.'

'I am your uncle. Your mother's brother. Uncle Artyom.'

Her Uncle Art lived in Russia. Last time she heard from him

was ten years ago, no, fifteen at least. 'Hi, Uncle Art. What's up?' Her tone was upbeat and calm as if they spoke all the time. It didn't reflect that a bicycle messenger had tracked her down and waited until she finished work.

'I have something, Carrie.' His reply was in Russian, which Carrie spoke as a kid at home, an urgent edge to his voice. 'Tell them, please.'

'Tell who?' Carrie switched to Russian. 'Tell who what?'

'I saw you on television. Two years ago. That island.'

Carrie had been famous for a few days after she and Rake became caught up in a Russian attempt against Rake's Alaskan home island of Little Diomede right on the border. They had been engaged to be married, and Rake had been brave enough to take Carrie to meet his island community. Neither had yet worked out why those few days had impacted so badly on their relationship. Carrie wasn't convinced of the identity of the speaker. 'Tell me something about myself or my mom that no one else would know,' she said.

'You gave your first medical injection in India when you were a kid because there was no one else to do it. Your mother showed you how and you administered morphine to a gunshot victim.'

She had told Rake. No one else. Only her mom, dad, and sister knew that.

'Are you OK, Uncle Art?'

'I'm fine. Thank you, Carrie.'

Then why not call Mom at home?

'Tell them I have it,' he said. 'Ask: How do I get it to them?'

'I don't understand.'

'Call me, Carrie. Please. Only this phone.' The line turned to static, then quiet.

Reynolds yelled: 'Hey. You. Come back.' Carrie looked up to see the messenger gone, pedaling north into the traffic around Washington Circle.

'What the hell was all that, Dr Walker?'

'I don't know.' Carrie checked the phone's incoming calls, only one, dialing code, 7 for Russia, 8152 for the city and region; not Moscow or St Petersburg; Carrie didn't know further than that. A full seven-digit number.

'What language was that you were speaking?'

Carrie put the phone in her pocket and pulled out her gloves. 'Let's rain check that drink? Next time. On me. Owe you one. The Hive. Great suggestion. I hear it's really good. They have roof heaters.' She spoke in a rapid flow, too fast for Reynolds to object. Confused, he stepped aside for her to walk off, which she did briskly, aware of the ice.

Carrie headed in the direction of her apartment, less than a mile from the hospital, an eighth-floor studio on Virginia Avenue, opposite the famous Watergate building. But she didn't go there. She circled round the neighborhood, letting the cold stimulate her thoughts.

Only Artyom Semenov, her uncle, would have known her morphine story. Carrie was a child of the torn-down Berlin Wall. Her parents had met on a Soviet naval base in Estonia on the Baltic Sea, her father an Estonian doctor, her mother a Russian nurse. Her Uncle Art worked there as a naval engineer. They were all Soviet citizens, even Carrie briefly. When the Soviet Union collapsed, tensions flared between Russians and Estonians. Her parents got out with jobs in a hospital in Calcutta, India. One afternoon, her mother took Carrie along when a train had been blown off the track by insurgents. Patients needed morphine. Carrie learned to administer it. Uncle Art knew the story.

So, Uncle Art had hired a bicycle messenger with a throwaway phone and his cell number punched in. He had asked her to tell 'them' he had 'it' and how did he get 'it' to them. To Carrie, there were three elements. First, someone in the US was expecting her uncle to deliver something. Second, the agreed method of delivery had collapsed. Third, he told her to relay his message. But to whom? Not her mother or he would have said. He knew she was in Washington, DC, and where she worked. But if he meant Carrie was to get involved with the US government, she had no idea where to start. She wouldn't trust any of them with a broom to sweep the streets.

As she came close to her apartment block yet again, the person who came to mind was not American but British, Stephanie Lucas, a friend from way back, an independent woman like her, self-contained, unsettled, more clever, better with people because Stephanie had ended up elected to the British parliament and then ambassador to Washington and was now doing a second tour as ambassador in Moscow.

Carrie fobbed the outside glass door of her apartment block, stepped into the heated foyer, smiled at the concierge, and took the elevator to her apartment. A family photo sat on the window-sill, her parents and sister, Angela, married with two children living a block away from home, an ENT doctor in a local hospital, a stalwart of the community. The apartment's decoration was made up of Carrie's travel booty, shrapnel from Iraq, Kalashnikov prayer rug from Afghanistan, pastel wooden mask from the Congo, and, for some reason that would need months of therapy, she kept by her bed a small face with a headdress of seal fur. Rake had given it to her when they first met. It was carved from driftwood by one of his many cousins, a kid called Ronan.

Carrie put her medical bag on the big dining table, placed the phone from her uncle next to it, and used her own phone to call Stephanie Lucas. She was put onto voicemail. 'Steph. It's Carrie Walker. Call soonest, please.' She repeated the message by text. Stephanie would get back to her. She was that type.

Carrie checked her medical bag. Even now, she made sure it was stocked as if she were in a Syrian desert. She called the hospital to see how her patient was doing and got patched through to the senior night administrator.

'Dr Walker, I have a note here that you have broken every protocol in the book.'

Carrie drew a breath. 'Yeah. I'm dealing with that tomorrow. But, right now, I need to know the condition of my patient.'

'Dr Perkins has accused you of irresponsibly exposing the hospital.'

'Is my patient still in intensive care?'

'You are now officially under supervision, meaning you cannot lead in theater until this has been sorted. That's the message and don't shoot me. I'm only the night manager. But, having worked at this hospital for more than twenty years, I am curious as to what the hell you thought you were doing.'

'Saving a life.'

'And if you had got it wrong?'

'That's trauma surgery. It's what I'm paid to do while you're paid to tell me the condition of my patient.'

'He remains stable and in intensive care. The consensus is that you are lucky, and my advice for what it's worth is that Perkins is not a man to cross. Send him a note of apology.'

Carrie pushed away the urge to say that if Perkins wanted a career-busting fight, she was up for it, when her phone rang with an unidentified number, which Carrie would not normally answer, except for the odds-on chance it was Stephanie Lucas.

'Thanks. I'll do that tomorrow.' She cut the call and answered the other.

'Carrie, it's Steph.'

'That was quick. Thanks. How's things? Are you able to talk?'

'I am and the line at my end is secure.' Stephanie's voice was measured, professional. Carrie reached for a pen and notepad. She told the story, ending with the request 'tell them I have it.'

'With this government tearing itself apart, Steph, I had no idea who to call and you know—'

'Have you still got the phone?' interrupted Stephanie.

'Yes.'

'Tell no one, particularly your family. Give me half an hour. I'll track down Harry.'

Stephanie spoke as if Carrie knew her ex-husband, Harry Lucas, former Chair of the House Intelligence Committee, Iraq and Afghan veteran, and marriage-wrecker who ran a private defense contracting company. Carrie had never met him. On a few bar-hopping nights when Stephanie couldn't work out what was going on in Harry's head, Carrie had been her sounding board.

She put the burner phone on charge, stepped into her tiny, one-person kitchen and opened the well-stocked refrigerator. She enjoyed cooking when there were people to cook for, at least once a week for herself, something new, something healthy, Mediterranean usually, oily fish, peppers, plenty of salad. She had too much on her mind to cook tonight. She would go to the little hotel down the road, which did the best crab cakes in North America, so they claimed. She would eat and think alone.

Stephanie's call came through. 'Harry's expecting you. Take the phone. Tell him exactly as you told me.'

TEN

Harry Lucas lived in an old-style apartment block between Dupont Circle and Rhode Island Avenue with no concierge, the front door up half a flight of stairs on the left, a surveillance camera outside, three locks on the door and more that Carrie couldn't see. She rang the bell and the door opened straight away, not by Lucas but a woman in her twenties, elegant, and expensively dressed.

'Harry Lucas,' began Carrie. 'He should be expecting me.

'Who the hell are you?' Irritation creased across her eyes. 'He hasn't said a woman's coming.'

'Dr Carrie Walker.' Carrie allowed a fast, vanishing smile that she had perfected on ward rounds.

Harry Lucas appeared in jeans and a dark-blue polo shirt, looking unflustered by the exchange. He gently removed the woman's hand from the door jamb, turned her towards him, and kissed her on the forehead. 'Sorry, Jane, got work to do.'

She pushed herself away from him. 'You should have told me.'

'Give us a moment, please.' Lucas closed the door. Carrie waited. A draft blew from outside, an edge of ice in the warm air. A couple of minutes later, Lucas opened the door to let Carrie in. Jane must have gone out another way. She smelt coffee and heard low, bluesy music. The apartment lacked personal elements, like hers, things from all over the world and photos of Lucas' time as a Congressman, the ego wall, handshakes with famous people. Nothing about his ex-wife. Stephanie. No new girlfriend; nothing of Jane.

He took Carrie's coat. She gave him the phone. Lucas unlocked a door with another thicker door behind it that opened with fingerprint, facial recognition, and a six-digit pass code. 'Fiber optic goes straight into the street, which is why I took this floor. Anyone who gets in here would be professional, meaning I could track them. Chances are they wouldn't want to take me on, unless it was government and then you're screwed whatever you do.'

He spoke conversationally, as if they had an old-friend familiarity, which in a way they had through Stephanie, although this was the first time they had met. He pressed the button on a coffee machine, which hissed and whirred. 'Help yourself if you want some.' Lucas placed the phone on a desk surrounded by screens and indicated a stool at a work bench for Carrie. 'I'm going to strip down this phone, then if we can, you're going to call your Uncle Art. We'll run voice recognition, location, all that stuff, and work out where we go from here.'

Lucas took the phone apart, putting each tiny bit on a cloth laid flat on the bench. He used an eye glass, like a watchmaker, to examine the insides and ran a cable from the phone to a computer from where figures and maps flashed onto one of his screens. While doing that, he kept up his chatter. 'Steph once said you were getting married. Did that ever happen?'

Carrie was taken aback. 'Off topic, don't you think?'

'Or we can talk about this freeze-your-ass-off weather? Or I could bore you by telling exactly what I'm doing, which is finding out if it was your uncle who called, why, whether he's been compromised, and what the hell's going on.'

The phone was now in kit form. Lucas examined each part with the eye glass. Photographed them, sent the images off somewhere. 'I ran into Rake Ozenna at Bagram, on his way to the mountains. We'd never met, but what you guys did in the Diomedes is now being taught at military academies. I crossed the canteen to shake his hand and pay my respects. His first words were to ask how you were.'

'How was he?' Two post-traumatic-stress therapists over six months had failed to dent Carrie's confusion over Rake.

'Thoughtful like anyone back from a mission.'

Carrie's changed feelings for Rake hadn't made logical sense. All he had done was show himself to be an adept soldier, and some hormone had kicked in asking if she wanted her kids to have a killer as a father, didn't matter that Rake's killing was necessary. Hormones didn't do logic, so she had tried to shut down her feelings for him.

Lucas looked up from his magnifying glass. 'When did you last talk to him?'

'The Diomede.' Carrie found herself blushing.

'Call him sometime. Soldiers like that.'

She had tried a few relationships since the split; one during a Colombian earthquake deployment; fast and gone. Another, a Brooklyn architect who she thought could become a relationship. She took him back to her apartment. He treated her work as something she would grow out of. He didn't last the night.

'Almost done,' said Lucas. The screen image closed like a crab claw, opened again, made another somersault, then settled. 'Here we go. This is what we've got on your Uncle Artyom Semenov.'

Carrie slid her stool closer. Lucas scrolled up and down, made notes, checked a serial number, split the screen into three columns. Maps swept around Russia; satellite shots zoomed down to a city, a street, a license plate, a face. He pulled up mugshots of her uncle similar to those her mother kept, even a shot of Carrie with her name in Russian from a conference in Moscow. Another from the Diomedes.

'The man who called was indeed your uncle. He bought four phones in cash and registered them to a shell company based in Murmansk. He kept two, couriered the other two to Washington, and hired someone to hand one to you with a number keyed in for the matching phone.'

'There's another one?'

'Yes, suggesting another courier commissioned with its delivery to you.'

'An individual or a company?'

'We'll know when we get the CCTV outside the hospital.'

'Why me? Why not my mother? My sister?'

'My guess is from your Diomede fame, Semenov concluded you knew the right people to tell, which he got half right because you ended up here. What puzzles me is why he doesn't know the right people.'

'Couldn't he have sent whatever it is electronically?'

'Depends how much data and whether he is being watched. The Russians have the Spetssvyaz, the Special Communications and Information Service, their equivalent to our National Security Agency. He might be able to encrypt the material, but he cannot hide the file size. Anything outside his usual pattern or of substantial size would be safer to deliver by flash drive.'

'Which he could not have done on the phone he sent me?'

'Exactly. That he didn't suggests he could have gigabytes of data important to us given who your uncle is.' Lucas brought up a picture of Artyom Semenov in naval uniform. 'See, the two black horizontal bands on the gold of the sleeve and the two stars on the shoulder. Your uncle is a vice-admiral. Did your mother ever mention that?'

Her mother rarely brought her brother's name into an already fractious home because her father constantly ranted against Russia. On the rare occasions she spoke of him, it was of her little brother Arty who smoked too much and didn't look after himself.

'Semenov worked at the Hara Soviet naval base near Tallinn, Estonia.' Harry flipped through to a technical diagram with Cyrillic Russian script. 'His specialism was on propulsion plant of the Kilo-class diesel-electric submarine, the workhorse of the Soviet navy. His task was to make it quieter. In the early 1990s when your mom and dad left—'

He cut himself off, checking another screen. 'You lived in India before settling here? Is that right?'

Carrie nodded.

'That was when Semenov left Estonia to continue working on the Kilo-class submarine.'

'But why betray his country?' asked Carrie.

'My question, too, if his life's work has been to build the world's finest underwater weapons.'

'And if he wanted to, why not just come over for a family visit?'

'His security clearance might get in the way.'

'He came over . . .' Carrie paused, calculating, 'around twenty years ago.'

'Before Putin started making Russia great again. But you're right. There are international conferences in Moscow; Vienna; anywhere. Why the urgency?' Lucas reassembled the phone and gave it to Carrie. 'You need to call him back.'

Lucas spoke as if it were an instruction. Carrie should have expected it, a natural next stage. But the sharpness of Lucas' tone took her aback. He explained: 'Submarine technology is the biggest deal in military secrets because a submarine is capable of smashing anything anywhere in the world. The technology is about hiding it, disguising it, keeping it quiet, which is your uncle's specialty. That's why this is important.'

'What do you want me to say to him?' she asked.

'Tell him that you have passed on his message and they need to know more. If I signal, ask if he wants to visit. If yes, say you'll get back to him within the next day and end the call. We'll conclude from his tone if he feels safe, how nervous he is, how confident. If I signal he's in trouble, say you'll get back to him within the hour and ask if there's any other number you can reach him or a place he'll be. Keep it bland. Do not use key words like America, Brooklyn, safe, dangerous because they may be keyed in for tracking.'

Lucas ran the phone through his system. Carrie would speak into the mouthpiece. Her audio came through a headset. Lucas turned on ambient outside noise so it would sound as if she were standing on a sidewalk. He pressed the call button. Carrie adjusted the headset, hearing long, single ring tones and the click of an answer.

'Carrie?'

'Uncle Art, I've passed on your message.'

'Thank you. I am most grateful.' Semenov's tone was assured, his cadence unwavering.

Lucas nodded.

'Do you want to visit?' asked Carrie.

'I would. Yes. Very much. Shall we make it a surprise for your mother?'

Lucas nodded again. 'Yes. That would be great. I'll get back to you within the next day.'

'Thank you, Carrie. It'll be very good to see you again.' Semenov cut the call. The Russia map appeared on the screen, with circles expanding and contracting around each other as software found his location. 'My God!' said Lucas. 'He's in Severomorsk, a closed city, just north of Murmansk and the center of Russian naval operations for the North Atlantic.' Lucas lapsed into a short silence, arranging his notepad and pen. 'I need to take this to government.'

'Which bit of government? It spends most of the time in a shit fight with itself.'

'That's my labyrinth. Are you at the hospital over the next couple of days?'

'Tomorrow, yes. Then I'm off.'

'Can you switch?'

'Probably.' Carrie thought of the cyclist in intensive care, paperwork she needed to catch up on, the complaint she needed to prepare for.

Lucas gave her the phone. 'You need to be able to answer this twenty-four/seven.' He unhooked her coat from the stand and held it for her to put on.

ELEVEN

Harry Lucas shut down the system and headed out. Fifteen minutes later, he was four miles north-west of Dupont Circle. The neighborhood breathed political authority. On this property, though, there was no ostentation. Halfway up the short path a lamp snapped on and the rotund figure of CIA Director Frank Ciszewski stepped onto the porch. He wore a tuxedo with a bow tie hanging loose.

'You caught me at a damn fund-raiser,' he said as Harry approached. 'But if a man gets a call from Harry Lucas, he knows two things. First, it'll be important. Second, it'll be quick.'

'Thanks for seeing me, Frank.' A clump of snow fell from a tree onto Lucas' shoulder. He brushed it off. 'You're still in the same place. I must have had twenty different homes since you moved here.'

Ciszewski and Harry had worked on security issues when Harry was in Congress. Harry's private-sector work had led to their paths crossing since. Harry lost his career and his marriage and rebuilt. Ciszewski stayed steady as a rock with both.

'Three lines of advice I give young folk.' Ciszewski stepped back, letting Harry in. 'Unless it's unavoidable, do not change your house, your car, or your marriage because all that shit takes so much damn time to sort out.' He led them to a neat open-plan kitchen looking over a deck and a fenced, snow-covered lawn. He pulled out two chairs at a large light-wood table. 'Coffee or anything?'

'I'm good.' Harry stayed on his feet. 'We may have a Russian defector.' He unfolded a photograph of Artyom Semenov in his naval uniform and told the story of Carrie and the phone.

'What's he offering?' asked Ciszewski.

'With his background, it has to be stealth submarine technology. But there's a lot not right.'

'When isn't there?'

'That he's suddenly decided to hand over his life's work to the enemy.'

'You never know what's going on deep inside a man's mind.' Ciszewski tapped his forefinger on the tabletop.

'Has Semenov ever crossed your desk?' Harry asked.

'Not that I recall.'

'His expertise is cloaking, acoustic cladding, the Kilo-class. If he was willing to offer us Russia's latest technology, then should the CIA Director know about it?'

'Nowadays, who in the hell knows? The White House runs its own parallel government. DIA doesn't share everything. Nor does State. You know the score, Harry.'

Ciszewski's reputation was as an oasis of clarity in Washington sandstorms. He had been appointed during Christopher Swain's presidency, stayed on through the brief, ill-fated administration of Bob Holland. The new President, Peter Merrow, had given no signs that he wanted Ciszewski out. 'Merrow's view is that there's too much flawed intelligence swilling around, and there's already a shitstorm brewing about this Dynamic Freedom exercise.'

'What kind of shitstorm?'

'Merrow wants it wound right down. He sees China as the real threat and aims to bring Russia on our side against it. Defense, State, Treasury are pushing against that.'

'CIA?'

'We argue that Russia remains a clear and present danger, that the exercise is routine and takes place every year. They are NATO exercises, which spelt out is the North Atlantic Treaty Organization, which requires European and North American defense forces to train together in the North Atlantic just as we do with Japan and our other allies in the Pacific.'

'Merrow doesn't buy it?'

'He wants a Nixon-in-China moment with Russia and sees Dynamic Freedom as a hindrance to that.' Ciszewski picked up the photograph of Artyom Semenov and studied it again. 'Bringing in a defector and stealing technology doesn't fit his narrative that we need Russia as an ally against China. We might have thought Holland was bad. He didn't hold a candle to Merrow.'

The abrasive Bob Holland had lasted just ninety-four days in office, resigning before being impeached. His crime was to open negotiations without authorization on national security issues with both Russia and China when president-elect. Little-known

Vice-President Merrow moved into the Oval Office, declaring he had no plans to run for re-election, which gave him free rein to run a tight, secretive White House.

'My instructions from the President are to switch resources from Russia and Europe to China and Asia,' said Ciszewski. 'He told me that the Russians were our friends in the Second World War and they'll be our friends again in the next one.' Ciszewski fixed Harry with a gaze of steel. 'So, no, Harry, I can't take it anywhere. Not this month at least. But you can, Harry.'

Ciszewski's stripped his loose black tie through his collar and dropped it on the table. 'Mary likes the windows shut tight in winter. I like the fresh air. One of those unresolved issues.' His forehead shone with sweat.

'You can't be suggesting we go private?'

'Don't lose Semenov. Keep me looped in. I'll have your back. When you know what he has, we talk again. If and when the President needs to know, I'll take it to him.'

If the Semenov operation went wrong, Harry's fingerprints would be everywhere. Both he and Ciszewski knew no one would have his back. Both knew Harry would do it. Ciszewski opened the door. Snow was whipped up. An icy wind hit Harry's face. He stepped out the door, tightening his scarf.

'Carrie Walker, the niece whom Semenov called,' said Ciszewski. 'Is she half Russian or all Russian?'

'Mother Russian, Father Estonian. Both US citizens.'

'I remember now, we ran that check during the Diomedes crisis.'

Not bothering with a coat, Ciszewski walked Harry down the path to the road. 'They've got sensors all over the place. Either I call my security guys and tell them you're coming out or I walk you down and they watch. They've given me four guys, two cars twenty-four/seven on the street to keep the CIA Director safe. I can't take a piss without it going on my record.'

Harry noted cameras rigged high on the lampposts.

He pressed the key to unlock his car. Orange light from his lamps streaked through freshly fallen snow. Ciszewski held the door as he climbed in. 'Moscow's playing cat and mouse games with us. Dynamic Freedom weaves into that.'

TWELVE

Harry left Jane sleeping in his bed to call his ex-wife about Artyom Semenov. The British Ambassador to Moscow listened without interruption. 'If the Brits want skin in this game, Steph, this is your chance. You bring him in.'

The British were good on Russia. Harry could send in trusted freelancers who knew Moscow. But they wouldn't have the resources of British agents.

Stephanie took time to formulate her thoughts. She was on her second ambassadorial tour in Russia, tasked with either fixing Britain's fractious relationship or exposing enough weaknesses to break the regime. Harry and Stephanie had become used to working together as if they had never shared a bed and never split up because they should never have gotten together. Marriage and divorce had made them both better people, according to the one time they had shared a marriage counselor. Whatever the hell being a better person meant.

'The risk is too high,' Stephanie finally said. 'We don't have resources to bring in a man of Semenov's caliber. I would have to go through London, both King Charles Street and Vauxhall Cross, which contravenes what Frank Ciszewski asked you to do. I also have to ask myself why our American cousins would want to hand someone like Semenov to us on a gold platter. I can't answer. Can you?'

'Frank doesn't buy Merrow's argument that we can't risk trouble with Russia because we need help against China. But he can't do anything right now because of Dynamic Freedom. He asked me to handle it until we know what he's got.'

'Coming to the British Ambassador in Moscow isn't—'

'I know, Steph. But it's too big for private.'

'Is Frank aware?'

'He might guess.'

'Then why doesn't he come directly? Why throw it back to you?'

'He doesn't want a paper trail.'

'Frank can't fart without a memo. Why break a habit of a lifetime and go memo-free with Harry Lucas?'

'Suppose you don't bring Semenov in as such,' suggested Harry. 'Suppose he walks into the embassy. Once inside, you debrief. He's yours. You own him and his secrets, and your call on how it's shared.'

'I still love you, Harry.' Stephanie gave a short laugh. 'The big picture guy, unperturbed by the thousand nails that shred footfalls along your fantastical glittering pastures.'

It took a second for Harry to work out Stephanie's tangled imagery, which he concluded was positive. 'Is it a go?'

'It's a discussion. First scenario, Semenov's a whistle-blower. Not a defector. The Russians don't know. He's experienced, trusts Carrie, his sister's daughter, wants to do the business, then go back and get on with his life.'

'The second?'

'He's a defector. He comes to the embassy. We're obliged to get him out of Russia. He can't stay here like another bloody Assange and we have to assume the Russians know.'

'He's made it to vice-admiral. He'll know how to duck and weave.'

'Russian navy vice-admirals don't just walk unannounced into embassies of NATO countries.'

Harry didn't disagree with her, but he wanted to maintain momentum. Stephanie was the only daughter of a South London used-car dealer who had been raised forging vehicle documents and went on to use her looks and brains to make her first million in the chaos of post–Berlin Wall Russia. 'Let's speculate the second scenario,' he said. 'Semenov does want to defect. He is a high-value asset. Everyone wants a slice. You have him. Then what?'

'We get him out. Airports and ports would be out of the question.'

'Land border.'

'First choice would be through Storskog in Norway.'

'Not Finland?'

'Finland is not in NATO. Norway has better protection. The thirty-kilometer visa-free agreement means the Norwegians could put people inside Russia once Semenov is close enough. I deliver him to the Russian side of the border. You get him through. That way he stays within Moscow station, keeps it away from London, and Britain gets her slice.'

'Is that a deal, Steph?'

'I'll get back to you.'

Harry ended the call. He went to the bedroom. Jane was awake, bed covers up to her chin, hands behind her head, staring up at the high ice-white ceiling. She was eighteen years younger, Harry's first generational gap affair and he hadn't been good at it. He had been attracted to Jane as an outsider, an ornithologist, specializing in tropical birds. She was refreshing, new and brimming with enthusiasm and youth. But with all that was going on, it had been a mistake to ask her back tonight.

She flicked her gaze towards him, then angrily back to the ceiling. 'You're still in love with her, aren't you?' she said.

Harry stood at the end of the bed, like a visitor. 'I'm working. Can I get you—'

'I understand. It takes time for feelings to pass. I get that. I'm not stupid. But if we love each other we can work it through.' She propped her head on her hand, looked at him and looked away again. 'What are you doing this time of the morning? Locking yourself away, talking to her all the time. A lot of men can never let go. I can understand if you let me.'

Harry lifted her denim jeans and blue top that hung over a chair and laid them on the bed. He picked up her underwear from varnished teak floorboards, 'Sorry it hasn't worked out, Jane. I really am.' He was about to say *I should have known I couldn't give you what you wanted*, but it sounded like a bad line from a movie.

'You've never had feelings for me, have you? Just say it, Harry. Be brave. Be a man for once and say it.'

'I never had feelings for you.' Harry wasn't sure what feelings entailed. Complete trust. Unequivocal love. Total control. Ownership.

She threw off the covers, flipped her hair so it fell half down her back and half over her breasts. 'So, you fuck off to your work and I'll go get on with my life.' She stood up, her unclothed body bathed in soft ceiling light as if to show Harry what he would be missing. His phone vibrated with a call from Stephanie. He left and took the call. 'Guarantee that Semenov isn't tailed,' she said. 'Ensure Moscow doesn't know we have him and yes, Harry, we have a deal.'

'Done,' he replied, knowing that in the world of intelligence nothing could be guaranteed.

THIRTEEN

Washington, DC

Rake walked into the hotel bar in the Holiday Inn Hotel on Rhode Island Avenue and Mikki said, 'There's a general looking for you. Says he'll be back.'

The bar was functional, plain, and near-empty, which suited Rake fine. The less glitz the more he liked a place. There was a wiry Hispanic guy washing glasses, a hulk of a black guy with a vacuum cleaner working the dining room next door, and Mikki with a beer, on one of the dark faded pink stools that lined the bar.

'Was it about Norway?' Rake took a stool next to Mikki, who said to the barman, 'He'll have a Bud.'

'I asked him that and he looked at me blankly, but he must have known we came from Norway, knew who we were and where we were.'

Rake laid his phone on the bar showing the clearest picture he had of the marking cut into the severed ear. 'Been trying to work out what it is. Any idea?'

'It's something, Rake, but God knows what.' Mikki examined the small round patch in the outer ear, dirtied with blood, but a distinct line following the contours, could be a full circle, could be just a short curve. He ran his finger around his own ear. 'Damn thing's got ridges and dips.'

Rake enlarged the picture. 'There's a line at right angles to the curve.'

Mikki narrowed his eyes and peered. 'Looks like a frigging ice pick. Could be a million things. Not our job anymore.'

A Pentagon car had brought them to the hotel, a few minutes' walk from the Center for Political and Global Studies where Rake was speaking. A full-dress uniform had been sent to his room. Somewhere deep inside the Pentagon were people deciding how Rake Ozenna should look, what he should say, and who he was. Media advisors had told him to get rid of his buzz cut because it gave him a bullish, hostile look. He now had neatly trimmed black hair. They told him a soldier needed to have a good family story. Rake argued that his family skills were rusty, if they had ever existed at all. He hadn't really known his mother and father, had no siblings, just orphaned kids he had grown up with. Rake had made best efforts with relationships, even been engaged to be married, but shit got in the way and no sensible woman with ideas about children and a settled home would give Rake Ozenna a glance. The army was undeterred. Families had fragmented like broken vases on redeployments from Iraq and Afghanistan. They used Rake's lack of family as a story of its own. How to pick yourself up, dust yourself down, and keep walking.

The Pentagon had sent through talking points for his panel, familiar jargon, insurgent marginalization, counter-ideology, population-centric, as if the more syllables in a word the more credible it would be. Rake showered, changed, checked that Carrie had not replied to his message, decided against sending another, called to check in with his adoptive father, Henry Ahkvaluk, on Little Diomede, and headed to join Mikki at the bar.

Rake closed his phone. Mikki was right. He was intrigued by Norway, but he needed to shut it out of his mind. He curled his fingers around his cool glass of Bud. 'Did you get the general's name?'

'General Jim Whyte, US Marines.'

'Is it me or both of us he's looking for?'

'Said I would need to leave because you and he would be having a private discussion. Hope that don't mean we might not be hitting those bars in Miami.'

'We might not, anyway.'

Mikki gave Rake a thin, curious smile. 'Don't tell me: Carrie called. You're getting married and I'm your best man.'

'Even better,' said Rake. 'I spoke to Henry, told him we were back from Europe. Turns out he's gotten Ronan into an exhibition at the Museum of Contemporary Art in Chicago, asked if we could be there for him.'

Ronan was another of Henry's adopted sons, around twenty years old, no one knew his exact age. Ronan didn't want the army. He had a skill in carving walrus tusk. Rake had been paying for his college. A couple of other youngsters from the Diomede and settlements around were getting drawn into the trade because of Ronan. Rake and Henry had started a company to sell the carvings. Mikki wanted no part of it.

'Jesus, Rake.' Mikki rolled his eyes. 'You know how I hate this shit. Have us carve an animal, call us Native Americans, plaster us with a sheen of goodness, and everything will be wonderful.'

'This is different.' Rake took a long, measured drink of his beer. It hit the back of his throat perfectly. 'Ronan's got a thirty-seven-inch tusk. One of the biggest. Nine and half inches in diameter. It's intact, beautiful, and curved like a hammock. The boy's a genius. He's carved it like one of those Indian erotic pieces with everyone fucking everyone, walrus, seal, bear, humans, Russians, Americans all entwined.'

'You have a photo?'

'Nope. Needs to be kept secret until it's unveiled. But here's the selling point. He's built a glass showcase framed from walrus penis bone.'

Mikki chuckled.

'The people in Chicago had never heard of a penis bone,' Rake continued. 'They don't know a lot of mammals have them. That's the draw. The penis bone brings in the crowds because they think sex. The walrus tusk is the art. Ronan's created a masterpiece. The top exhibit in this Chicago show on Arctic Native Art.'

'Arctic, not American Native—'

'Correct.'

'The Diomedes ain't even in the Arctic.'

'Walrus is. It's an Arctic tusk.'

'Arctic is good. They keep calling us Native Americans, but we're not. We're Eskimos from the Diomedes and we must never let ourselves forget it.'

Rake was familiar with Mikki's dogmatism about identity. They had all had unusual childhoods. Henry and his wife Joan had been their only anchors. Things like real family, language, heritage had been tossed about and never settled. Downtime moments like this, Mikki would have a few beers and chase impossible answers. Rake found women a better fix. Warm human flesh, a little talk, no chemical unleashing monsters in the mind. Today Nilla. Yesterday Carrie, although over the past few years, Carrie kept butting into other women's space.

'Yes. You're right. Never forget it.' Rake softly agreed and was about to talk about Chicago bars when he saw General Jim Whyte striding toward them. Whyte had a long, thin face with cold, marble-gray eyes. He wore a jungle camouflage uniform, tunic sleeves neatly rolled above the elbow, a matching cap held loosely in his right hand and brown leather bag hooked over his shoulder. He ignored Mikki and said, 'Major Raymond Ozenna?'

Rake nodded.

Whyte showed his room tag to the barman. 'Charge whatever these gentlemen have had to my room.' His gaze shifted through to the empty dining room. 'We'll move to one of those tables.'

Mikki stayed. Rake followed Whyte past a water cooler and through an arch to a dull empty dining area with tables laid for a breakfast. They took a corner table by a stainless-steel buffet counter which had nothing on it.

'I'm the reason you're in DC, Major.' Whyte pulled out a chair and sat down. 'We're both speaking on the panel tomorrow about military–civilian operations. You speak for seven minutes and make no direct reference to any operations. Do not mention Norway. In the Q & A, if you don't know the answer, say you cannot speak for security reasons. Is that clear?'

They could have had this conversation in the morning. Whyte was moving in as if he owned Rake, which he didn't. Whyte was a US Marine and although many of the public did not realize, the Marines were under US Navy command. Rake's orders came from the Brigadier of the Alaska National Guard, whose commander-in-chief was the Governor of Alaska, unless the President put it under Federal control, which he hadn't. In Afghanistan, Rake had been seconded to a unit of the 1st Special Forces Command, an army operation. Paperwork would be underway to have him transferred back to the National Guard or anywhere else. Maybe to Whyte. But as of now Rake hadn't received any orders.

'Before your latest deployment, you were assigned to examine vulnerabilities on remote US military bases,' said Whyte. 'Is that correct?'

It was, but Rake wasn't going to say. In Afghanistan, he had tested outlying positions and found gaps that insurgents could use to breach defenses. After that, he was assigned doing similar work on home soil.

'Much of my work is classified, sir,' he said. 'I make a point of not speaking about any of it, so I don't mix stuff up.'

Whyte drew a tablet from his case. 'Says here you inspected defenses at the Tin City Long Range Radar, the Eareckson Air Station on the Aleutian Islands, Eielson Air Force Base near Fairbanks, the Acoustic Measurement Facility at Ketchikan, and a couple of others. At Ketchikan, you identified a vulnerability that intruders did later try to exploit. If it were not for your work, they may have succeeded.'

Whyte had the tablet on the table. Rake read the list. He hadn't heard of the breach at Ketchikan, a place in southern Alaska that recorded the unique signature sounds that every submarine emits through noise from engines, propellers, ventilation, and the rest.

Whyte slid across a letter that carried the Alaska National Guard logo, authorizing Major Rake Ozenna to 'liaise' with General James Whyte on matters of national importance. Rake didn't recognize the signature.

'I will need to speak to Camp Denali,' Rake said, referencing the Alaska National Guard headquarters.

Whyte tapped the letter. 'Your orders are here, Major.'

'The authorization needs to come from the Brigadier-General. This isn't his signature.'

Whyte's face was like rock. He didn't look at Rake. His eyes bore into a black-and-white framed photograph of old Washington on the wall behind him. His hands were clasped, resting on the table. The US military, like rival agencies, was a bed of sharpened knives. Each arm competed for budgets and glory. Each career officer planned for a stamp on history. Each had a different definition of national interest and patriotism.

So, what was Whyte in all this and how did he know about Rake's classified work in testing vulnerability at small bases? His first had been on an outpost in Ghazni, in southern Afghanistan, remote, less than fifty men. The landscape comprised arid scrub, dried earth, and clusters of bushes. From the way the sun fell and clouds hung at that time of day, Rake identified sloping ground that could be a threat. He sensed it more than knew it. He tested himself by setting up a sniping position, which, when the sun was dropping, became invisible from the base watch posts.

Back in the US, he was sent to inspect Tin City across the water from Little Diomede and then the others that Whyte had listed. Next, he was being asked to lecture. They came up with a category for his skills, Environmental Situational Awareness.

'Watch how the birds fly,' he would tell his audience. 'See if they move differently. Note how wildlife moves, where it goes for safety, how it seeks out danger; where the wind comes from and what a gust exposes and hides; how the rain falls and where it floods and drains; how the snow lies and where it blocks and melts. Nature is unusual, changing all the time. When you look for a hidden enemy, you automatically look for something unusual. Change your mindset. Everything around you is unusual. Look for the usual. The more normal something looks, the more dangerous it could be.'

The media people loved the usual–unusual line. They told him it was counter-intuitive and high concept.

'So, you're telling me you need to confirm these orders?' said Whyte.

'That is correct, sir.'

'You gave the right answer, Major.' Whyte's rigid face creased into the edge of a smile. A flicker of humanity came into his eyes. He shut down the tablet and pulled back the letter. 'I run counter-insurgency operations in Asia. We're looking at Papua New Guinea, East Timor, and in the South Pacific, Fiji and Vanuatu, small, isolated, vulnerable. A handful of troops. Some ours. Some local. I want you to work your magic and help keep them safe.

'I'm a cold-weather soldier, sir,' said Rake.

'A cold-weather soldier who has done remarkable work in hot climates.'

'Who is the enemy?'

'China has a long record of sponsoring insurgencies. We expect the Chinese to stir up rebellions, whatever it takes to weaken us, and that's where you come in, Major. If they don't get successes against our forces, we can hold our ground. If they do and body bags come back with an American flag draped around, we'll end up handing Asia to the communists.'

The cry to bring troops home had skewed Vietnam, Afghanistan,

Iraq, given Syria to Russia and Iran. 'I'm a soldier, sir,' said Rake. 'If I'm needed for this work, of course, I will do it.'

Whyte's chair scraped back. 'We leave at 13:00 tomorrow, after our panel. You'll have the general's letter by then.' Whyte slid his tablet into his case and hitched it onto his shoulder. He left Rake in the desolate dining space.

FOURTEEN

On the first ring, neither asleep nor registering the real world, Carrie imagined her phone was buzzing with her mother at the other end of the line. It was two twenty in the morning. She glanced through the window toward the Watergate building, where a blizzard raged. Her mind had been swirling with the injured cyclist. She couldn't erase the image of the thin steel rod protruding like a bent flagpole from his neck, mixing up against her argument with Perkins in the hospital. Less an argument. More her sharp, answer-back words. Stupid. Losing it like that. Why pick a fight, risking her job the first day? Well done, Carrie! Not as smart as you think. Your first real attempt at making a career for yourself and you— Jesus, woman!

The buzzing came not from her phone, but the internal apartment block intercom. 'Yes?' She kept that single syllable, soft, measured, a middle-of-the-night voice of normality.

'Dr Walker. A Mr Harry Lucas in the lobby for you.'

'OK. Right!' Relief drained through her voice. 'I'll be down.'

'He says better if he came up.'

Carrie's studio was fine for visitors when the bed was turned back into a sofa, the white cover brushed down, the colored cushions arranged nicely, clothes neat in the closet, table polished and uncluttered, no bra hanging on the back of a dining-room chair, no red T-shirt on the maroon and orange patterned carpet from Herat; no denim jacket, one sleeve pulled out as it caught on her wrist when she took it off; no trail of a single woman, living alone, undressing by dropping garments as she walked around fixing herself coffee, cruising playlists. 'Tell him to come up in ten,' she said.

Lucas could have called, and she would have said 'no'; she would come to his place again. Five minutes away. He must need to be here. Turning up was a smart move.

Carrie dressed quickly, running a brush through her hair,

smoothing down a fresh blue shirt, buckling her jeans, while picking up clothes and tidying the dining-room table like a secretary. She topped up water in the coffee machine, refilled it with freshly ground beans, and turned it on. The door buzzer went.

Looking like a mix between a lawyer and a television-repair guy, Lucas wore a dark woolen overcoat, no hat, and carried two large briefcases. With overnight stubble and determination streaking through bloodshot eyes, he bore shades of a guy who had just walked out of a bar, except he hadn't because there was no trace of alcohol on his breath. He walked past Carrie, put his cases on the floor by the table, squatted down, flipped combination locks, and opened them. Not alcohol, but an alcoholic's obsession.

'Mind telling me—' she began.

'In a moment.' Lucas opened computers, trailed wires, plugged in phones, set up on the dining table. Carrie poured them a coffee, put his on a mat on the table, large cup, black, no milk, no sugar. He sipped it while setting up a work-station which resembled a compact version of what he had in his apartment, two keyboards, two screens, boxes, colored lights as strange to Carrie as operating-room equipment would be to anyone outside of medicine. He pulled chairs up for them both. He brought the schematics of a building onto one screen and a coastal city map on the other. On both, there was a slow flashing blue dot.

'This building is an apartment block for high-ranking military officers in the closed city of Severomorsk on the Kola peninsula on Russia's Arctic coast,' he explained. 'It's the base of the Northern Fleet, on the Barents Sea. See here is the huge statue, the Monument of the Heroes, and over here are Russian warships and a couple of submarines. This is where your uncle's phone is. He could be there now.' He paused, looking across to her. 'It's mid-morning, 10:48. I need you to call him, Carrie. Do not mention your previous conversation. He will know it's you so don't identify yourself. You are calling on behalf of the British Ambassador—'

'Why British? He's expecting the Americans.'

'For us now, with the Brits, it's easier. Less red tape and Steph's involved because you called her, so she gets a slice of the action. Say you are calling on the chance that he might be in Moscow on Thursday and, if so, might he be free to go to the Ambassador's residence at lunchtime for an informal scientific and technology discussion on climate change and the Arctic. Ambassador Lucas would be delighted if such an eminent figure could find a few minutes to share his ideas.'

Lucas handed Carrie headphones with an inbuilt microphone. He pointed to a segment of the left-hand screen. 'Keep an eye on the voice recognition. Green indicates he is calm; red that he's nervous; shades in between.' He tapped keys. Fingers poised above the keyboard, he fixed his gaze on Carrie, waiting for her to indicate she was ready. She didn't reveal the cascade of questions splashing through her thoughts. How would it work? Why can't someone else make the call? Why Harry Lucas, in her apartment in the middle of the night? Why not a secure government bunker with backup plans and trained people with ID passes and salaries? An ambulance siren flared on Virginia Avenue below. Lucas got up, closed the window, and pulled down the blind.

'We're a go,' he said.

Carrie's heartbeat rose. She breathed in slow and long. A ringtone sounded through the headset. Then a click and voice. 'Yes?'

'Vice-Admiral Semenov,' Carrie said in Russian. 'I am calling from the British Embassy in Moscow.'

Not an immediate answer. A guarded man who understood security.

'This is Semenov,' he said.

'Ambassador Lucas would be delighted if, on the off chance, you might be in Moscow and able to attend a lunch discussion on Thursday on climate change and the Arctic.'

'A very interesting global issue.' A cautiously confident tone reflected in the pale green of the voice software.

'And share with us your thoughts on changes in sea-traffic technology due to melting ice.'

'I am honored that you ask.'

'Ambassador Lucas would be most grateful. The seminar runs from two o'clock, but come at one, if you have time, for a light lunch.'

'Could it be for just an hour? My late afternoon schedule is full.'

'Of course. It is at the Ambassador's residence on Sofiyskaya Embankment, 14, between Kammenyy and Moskvoretskiy bridges.'

'I know it.' A change of tone. 'This is the British not the Americans?'

The reading showed hesitation. When Semenov had asked Carrie to tell 'them' he would have assumed she would go to her own government.

Carrie improvised, 'Yes. That's right, Vice-Admiral. These lunchtime seminars rotate. I believe next month the US is hosting, or it might be India.'

'I am in Moscow again next month,' said Semenov. 'Perhaps it would be better to wait for the next one.'

The final cadence at the end of Semenov's sentence indicated fear and uncertainty. Undulating lines traversed from pale green to maroon.

'Give him wriggle room,' said Lucas through her earpiece. 'Someone could have come into the room.'

'That's fine. These seminars are very informal,' said Carrie. 'Please come if you are free.'

'Tell your ambassador I will try.'

Semenov cut the call. Carrie took off the headset. 'What does that mean? He wants us to handle it, not the British.'

'Let's go through it.' Lucas pushed back in his chair. 'You fudged by telling him the US was doing something a month from now, and he went for that, but treading water for a month doesn't match the urgency of the burner phones and his call to you.'

'Is it that he doesn't trust the British?'

'It has to be more than that. He could have asked if the Swiss or the Norwegians were holding these seminars.'

'He only wants the US?'

Lucas replayed the conversation. Semenov's cadence remained stable at the beginning, a dark side of green, but measured, the usual contours of a businesslike phone conversation. The algorithm detected change after Carrie's directions to the Ambassador's residence and Semenov's words *I know it.*

'Did he realize that we knew where he was?' Carrie asked.

'He should have assumed. He didn't mind the British Embassy,' said Lucas. 'He got cold feet over the Ambassador's residence, or more precisely the route to the residence.' Lucas stood up. 'But who in the hell knows, Carrie? Betraying your homeland is never a straight path. You can be burying regrets into your grave.'

Carrie stayed quiet. This was Lucas' territory. She couldn't second-guess him. Then, to their surprise, Semenov rang back. Lucas sat down again. Carrie put the headphones on. There was a clear incoming call signal. Lucas opened the line.

'Carrie. You must help me.'

'I'm here, Uncle Art. What is the problem? Is it the British?'

'Why did they change it, Carrie?'

She told him straight. 'Ambassador Lucas is a personal friend. That is why I contacted her.'

'But why not the Americans?'

'You called me, Uncle Art. You need to trust me.'

'It has to be them.'

'I'm a doctor. I am not them. I contacted the one person I trust more than any other.'

Semenov's tone flattened. 'Will it work?'

'It will.'

'I don't know, Carrie. Why don't you come with your mother?' The voice recognition showed a bright red.

'I can ask her.'

'Don't tell her why. Just suggest a visit to Moscow.'

'How long will you be there?'

'Three days. Then I go back to Severomorsk where it is difficult.'

'I'll see if Mom can come.'

'Thank you. See you soon, Carrie.' Semenov ended the call. The voice color of his last two sentences flitted between light and dark orange, more indecisiveness than fear.

Carrie took off the headphones, stood up and reopened the window to a blast of cold air and the rumble of a truck passing underneath.

'You can't involve your mother,' said Lucas.

'I'll go,' she said.

Lucas' expression transformed from worry to surprise. 'No way. Moscow knows exactly who you are.'

Carrie leaned on the table, both hands flat on the surface. 'I go as someone else.'

'Not that simple. Fingerprinting at the airport. All sorts of shit.'

'The hospital will be happy to see the back of me for a few days.'

Lucas looped his hands behind his head. He was working it through. Carrie had planted an idea. 'You're not kidding, are you?'

'My uncle needs a familiar face.'

'You're not trained.'

'More than my mother, I am.'

Lucas unplugged his equipment. Carrie rinsed coffee cups in the kitchen. Neither spoke until Lucas had locked the two brief-cases. 'I'll get you a passport. You go via Europe and take a feeder flight.'

'I meet him and take him to wherever you need him to go,' said Carrie. 'It's not brain surgery.'

Lucas picked up his coat and smiled: 'You're right. It's not.'

Within Harry Lucas' trade, what Carrie had suggested was higher risk than the consequences of failed brain surgery. Far more than one life was stake. Carrie needed to go to Moscow with a safe passport. That meant no British, American, and most Europeans. Carrie's fair skin and blonde hair ruled out much of the world, which is why just before dawn Harry took a cab three miles north along Connecticut Avenue toward International drive, the neighborhood of many embassies, including that of Israel where a young Mossad agent whom he had never met handed him an Israeli passport and wished him well. An hour earlier, the friend in Tel Aviv who had arranged the passport fixed a hack into the Russian immigration database done in a single undetectable nanosecond. Carrie's fingerprints and other data were matched to Dr Sarah Mayer, aged thirty-six, consultant physician from Haifa. As a tourist, she could travel visa-free for ninety days, plenty of time to handle her nervous uncle.

FIFTEEN

Severomorsk, Murmansk Oblast, Russia

Vice-Admiral Artyom Semenov removed the headset he had used for the call with Carrie Walker. Ruslan Yumatov gave him distance and time to think. He kept his back to the room and studied Semenov through a reflection in the high windows of the apartment that had a view befitting a senior naval officer with an unblemished record of loyalty to his government. Over his decades of service, Semenov had broken boundary after boundary in submarine stealth technology such that the Americans now openly accepted that they had fallen behind. His large living room overlooked the dark, sullen figure of a fifteen-meter-high sailor holding an automatic rifle, standing on the sculptured conning tower of a submarine. The statue symbolized the city of Severomorsk's pledge to defend the Arctic from all enemies. Beyond it lay the wintry Barents Sea and along the coastline were docked Russian warships and submarines.

Even though Semenov was at the end of his career he retained an engaging curiosity about how things worked and how they could be made better. In the months that Yumatov had befriended him, Semenov tested ideas about Russian naval operations in Syria, a more efficient defense in the Atlantic, and how military departments could be organized with less rivalry. He was a likeable old man with a welcoming face, a full head of gray hair, and thick-lensed glasses. He had none of the pomp and arrogance carried by so many less capable senior officers. He wore his uniform with pride but scruffily. Semenov was not a parade-ground officer. He preferred books, science, and conversation, and he cherished his role in safeguarding Russia and restoring its lost greatness. His specialty was to give Russia the quietest and most disguised submarines.

His work had consumed him, costing him his marriage and weakening him enough for Yumatov to act. He had no children, and his wife of more than forty years had moved to Moscow.

Semenov placed the head set on a Scandinavian-style wooden table next to photographs of himself in bed with a beautiful young dark-haired woman whose affections for him had been as false as her name. Under instructions from Yumatov, Amy Vitsin had moved convincingly to fill the vacuum in Semenov's life for the purpose of blackmail. Should his wife ever see these photographs, Semenov would have no chance of rescuing his marriage and, without that, he had had no idea how he might keep going. He would be seventy next year, not a good age, he had thought then, to be alone or to try to start over again.

'What now, Colonel?' There was no anger or defeatism in his tone. Semenov understood his mistake, assessed, and had made his decision to comply.

'You wait to hear if your niece is coming. We fly to Moscow. You meet her. She takes you to the embassy and you hand over the data.'

'Was it necessary to bring in my family?'

Yumatov laid a conspiratorial hand on his shoulder. 'It is far more natural for a vice-admiral to enter a NATO embassy socially, with your niece, than to walk in unannounced.'

'At least show me what I will be delivering.'

Yumatov plugged a small flash drive into a laptop on the table. Semenov adjusted his spectacles. The first image showed an engineering diagram for air-independent propulsion that made a submarine quieter. Yumatov moved away, leaving Semenov to scroll down, seconds only on each image, faster and faster until he looked up, perplexed. 'I don't understand,' he said. 'There is nothing here that the Americans don't know.'

'You are correct. The importance to NATO will not be the quality of data, but that it is you who delivers it and that Russia is offering.'

Semenov took off his spectacles and placed them on the table 'But why threaten me? If your plan is to reach out to NATO, stop this dreadful talk of war, why not just ask me?'

Yumatov let out a short disparaging laugh. 'You could have called the Kremlin and that would have been the end of it?'

'You say Foreign Minister Sergey Grizlov is behind this, and I believe you.'

'He is. You know as I do that Russia is split. One foot in

Europe, the other heading toward China. Grizlov and I need to prevent that, which is why we are reaching out to the West.'

'A scientist is a bad navigator of human need.' Semenov rubbed his eyes. 'You are promising that if I do this, I can continue my work, and this blackmail will go away.' He picked up one of the photographs of the woman he thought had cared about him.

'You have my word. It was only ever an insurance. I knew your views about Russia's future were aligned with mine, which is why I chose you.'

'We are Europeans. We are not Asians.' Semenov shrugged. 'So, yes, I am with you. We fly to Moscow and I will see my niece.'

From the small balcony of his apartment, Artyom Semenov watched Yumatov leave the building and turn right toward the Barents Sea. He let the freezing air clear his mind and, only when he was certain of his next move did he go back inside, lock the French window, walk across his spacious living room to his study, which looked inland over the dreary architecture of Severomorsk.

It was here that Semenov kept computer hard drives containing his most secret work. Technically, it was illegal, but he did not know any military scientist of his stature who allowed decades of work to be kept only by the government. The only other copy was in his workshop less than a mile away. None was stored on any cloud, however secure and encrypted, and none was known to any intelligence agency from the United States or NATO.

This was far more valuable than the information that Ruslan Yumatov wanted him to hand over, and far more dangerous.

By blackmailing him, Yumatov had also opened a window. His high-class hooker had shown Semenov a glimpse of a life awaiting him, should he choose. She might have been a fraud, but there were other beautiful young women, honest and loving, happy to enjoy the company of an older man and his pension while he traveled the world speaking at seminars, feted for his brilliant career.

As Semenov activated the electronic code to open the safe, he hummed an American tune from the Sixties about never walking alone. He should stop being afraid. What was the point of pleading with Marissa to try again at their marriage only to return to their same unhappiness? She was building her own new life in Moscow and, within a few days, he could be celebrating in New York with his sister and his two lovely nieces. Carrie and Angela could become the daughters Marissa had failed to give him.

He would walk into the British Embassy with Carrie, hand over Yumatov's anodyne drive and, at the same time, offer more valuable technology on condition that he fly back with Carrie to New York. He would have preferred to go straight to the Americans, but they and the British were as thick as thieves and if Carrie had chosen the British so be it.

The Americans would play hardball. They would mock Yumatov's naive offering as not even an olive branch. Some of the material was open-sourced, discussed at security conferences, not enough to convince the United States that Russia wanted to end hostilities and do a deal. If Semenov were to escape with a New York apartment and a well-paid professor's post at an Ivy League university, the Americans would need to see his game-changing submarine technology. Semenov had decided to give it to them.

Working on a laptop, Semenov structured the data into compact files that, taking up no more than eight hundred giga-bytes, could fit onto a small one terabyte flash drive. He copied them, zipped the drive into his jacket pocket, and locked the safe. While waiting for Yumatov to take him to the airport, he surfed the Internet looking for apartments in Brooklyn.

Fifteen minutes after leaving the vice-admiral, Yumatov pressed the identity code to a low-rise office building two blocks from Semenov's apartment. There was no logo on the gray wooden door badly in need of a coat of paint. In this closed military city, most work was conducted out of the eye of civilians and of rival agencies. The building was owned by Russia's foreign intelligence service, the SVR, the equivalent to America's CIA. Yumatov took the stairs to the top floor, which was occupied by a unit within the SVR known as the Seventh Department for the Center of Self Security. Attached to that was Yumatov's highly classified military unit, Zaslon, which translated as Screen.

Zaslon's official task was to keep safe Russian diplomats, embassies, and their secrets. Its members had proven themselves in Ukraine, Syria, and other less famous theaters. Zaslon troops reported not to the Russian armed forces, but to the civilian SVR controlled by the Foreign Ministry that was now led by presidential hopeful Sergey Grizlov. Yumatov had engineered his recruitment to Zaslon while in Syria and identified it as the best-placed unit with which to achieve his goal.

He punched a code into a black keypad next to a steel door. Inside was a wall of windows that carried a similar view as from Semenov's apartment across the ice floes of the Barents Sea except from a lower angle. The floor covered an open space with computers in one corner, a sink and a kitchen area, weapons in another space, and a gym machine and a brown leather punchbag.

'What the hell went wrong, Joe?' Yumatov stepped in and pushed shut the door.

Josip Milotic was the driver who had worked with Yumatov on the successful Gerald Cooper operation. He had also been tasked with the failed operation the following day to capture Rake Ozenna and Yumatov wanted to know why.

'The navy, sir.' Sweat dripped off Milotic's forehead and lined his neck above his black tank-top T-shirt. He held out his boxing gloves. Yumatov pulled off the right glove and laid it on a steel table. 'They sent in a Ka-27—'

'I know about the helicopter, but who and why and whose idea was the fucking armored vehicle?'

Unphased by Yumatov's tone, Milotic pulled off his left glove. 'The navy thought having Ozenna in custody would complicate plans to get NATO to wind down the Dynamic Freedom exercise.'

'You know that or you're guessing that?'

'I know it.' At the level he operated, Milotic's contacts were excellent and not only in Russia. He was a product of the 1990s, born in Russia, raised in Birmingham, England, trained by the British army with combat in the Middle East. He moved on to private security contracting and, in Syria, was spotted by Yumatov, who identified his torn loyalties. Yumatov became an understanding ear, explaining that the days of shared values and flung-open borders were over. People were retreating back into tribes. Milotic was a Russian Slav, as was Yumatov. They must never forget who they were.

Yumatov snapped the top of a bottle of water and took a sip. 'How did the navy know?'

'GRU told them,' said Milotic. 'If we had our own resources, we could have handled it.'

'We don't, and we need to keep it small.' Yumatov handed the bottle to Milotic, who drank heavily. 'I need you in Moscow.'

Milotic finished the water, crushed the plastic bottle between his fingers, and dropped it into a trash can under the table. 'Permission to speak openly, sir.'

'Go ahead.'

'How much do we need Ozenna?'

Yumatov crossed to the punchbag and landed a fist hard in the middle of the rough leather. He steadied the slow swing and punched a second strike with the left fist. His knuckles tingled. A black and white pattern had been sewn into the top of the punchbag of an eight-spoked wheel known as the Kolovrat, an ancient symbol representing the spiritual and material strength of the Slavic people. The Slavs were Europe's biggest ethnic community, stretching right across Russia to Asia. At the end of each rigid spoke, a blade ran at right angles like an ice pick. The Kolovrat had many meanings and over the centuries had been hijacked by Hindus in India and Nazis in Germany, who had turned it into the Swastika. Its origins were about infinity, the repeating cycles of life, and the power of the sun. Today, for Yumatov, it combined political power with ethnic identity, which is why his unit had sewn it into the punchbag which helped them build strength and hone fighting skills. It was this symbol that he had cut into Gerald Cooper's severed ear.

Yumatov took another drink of water while weighing up Milotic's question about Ozenna. 'In the Diomedes two years ago, Ozenna murdered our young men,' he said. 'If we capture or kill Ozenna now at this juncture of our history we show Russian people a new hope. It would be a great moment for the nation. Leadership is about messages, delivering certainty and a vision that people want to follow. For that we need to show our people two paths, the certainty of hope and the certainty of revenge. So, yes, Joe, for our mission, we do need Ozenna.'

SIXTEEN

Rake's phone lit with a second message from Carrie. *Heading out. Next time.* His concentration shifted. The panel moderator, wrapping up the question and answer session, shot him a disapproving glance. A slim man, exceptionally tall, with a tight, drawn face was on his feet. He identified himself as a reporter and said, 'This is for Major Rake Ozenna.'

From the edginess of his tone, the rigidity of his body language, Rake braced himself for a hostile question. Whyte gave him a pointed look, tapping papers in front of him. Stick to the talking points.

Rake and Whyte sat at one end of the podium table. Whyte wore the same uniform as last night. Rake was in the full-dress uniform of the Alaska National Guard that had been sent to his hotel room, the medals, a blue emblem with eight small yellow stars that placed him with the Alaska State Defense Force whose origins lay with the Eskimo Scouts, giving him a brush of pride. Two years ago, Rake barely knew places like the Center for Political and Global Studies existed. Now, because of his race, the Diomede crisis, his West Point lectures, the army wanted him on panels as a poster boy with blood under his fingernails. Rake had warned he could be a liability. The army hadn't listened.

In the middle of the podium was the moderator, on the other side was a trim, middle-aged woman with neat, short blonde hair who ran a peace-keeping operation in Asia. At the far end sat a Harvard professor, an expert on Latin America who had come up with a catchphrase, *The Guevara Trap*, about making heroes out of terrorists that had caught on among academics.

The audience occupied circular tables with water jugs and cups of coffee. Each wall carried a screen. It was 10:27, three minutes before the break for coffee.

Rake typed into his phone: *Where you going? Boccaccio?* The name of the Kabul restaurant where he and Carrie first had dinner. A joke. Apart from one time, Carrie had pretty much shut down on him since they had parted on Little Diomede.

A television lamp snapped on, projecting harsh light straight into Rake's face. 'Are you with us, Major Ozenna? Or should we all wait until you have finished your private business?' the reporter challenged.

From his accent, Rake guessed he was Russian, early middle age, long, thin face, light, straggly hair, swept back over the forehead. He wore a dark pin-stripe suit, once a soldier; maybe still was.

'Apologies,' replied Rake with a smile, except his smile never moved much beyond his lips, no shine in the eyes, no crease of skin of the around the cheekbones.

'Major Ozenna, will you now confirm that you are the American who murdered nine young Russian men in cold blood on the island of Little Diomede; that you carried out these murders without orders at a time when Russia and the United States were in friendly negotiations; and that your irresponsible actions made war between our two nations more likely?'

Rake sifted through answers and couldn't find any that were good. His eyes stayed on the reporter. He didn't react to the lamp's brightness. Sun on Arctic snow was far worse. Since childhood, he had narrowed and hooded his eyes against glare, making his expression difficult to read. The army uniform helped tidy him up, dilute a wild, cold, weather-rawness that was etched into his features.

'And could you, Major Ozenna, the cold-blooded killer, now apologize to the families of the young men you murdered?'

The wall screen, with a live wide shot of himself, the reporter, and the audience streamed across the world. His answer would be picked up by Russian social media, a key weapon in low-intensity conflict. Rake had warned. The army hadn't listened. He scanned the room for allies and couldn't be sure, except for Mikki, who was at a table near the reporter.

Mikki loosened up, shifting in his chair. This was not a venue for a Russian to accuse an American serviceman of murder. Faces in the audience became tense and surprised; lobbyists and congressional staffers in suits and ties calculating political fallout;

casually-dressed academics and reporters, curious, observant, antennae out for a good story; mid-career uniformed military officers, gauging allegiances. A wrong word in this room could be a promotion maker or breaker. 'It is a yes or no question, Major Ozenna,' challenged the reporter. 'Will you apologize, and will the United States apologize to the Russian people and hand Major Ozenna over to be tried for the war crimes he has committed?'

Rake had to say something. To stay silent would indicate wrongdoing. He reached for the microphone. Whyte muttered, 'No, Major. Do not.'

Rake leaned in.

'Thank you for that question, sir,' said Rake. 'It's a good one and a tough one to answer and fortunately for me, I am a foot-soldier, a few days back from Afghanistan and the very important issues you raise are way above my pay grade.'

Relief flooded across the moderator's face. She cut in, apologizing for being out of time, thanking the panel, thanking the audience, pointing to coffee urns and cookies outside. The screens returned to the conference logo.

Whyte reprimanded, 'Ozenna, you disobeyed a direct order.'

The reporter clocked security officers walking toward him. Like a greyhound off the block, he leapt forward, knocking over a chair and jumping onto the podium, a trained military man. With the television crew, there could be at least three in the room.

Mikki reached inside his jacket. Whyte got to his feet to block the reporter, who hit him four times, very fast, a fist to the kidneys, a kick to the testicles, a blow to the left temple on the upper skull and the heel of the same hand under the chin, which propelled Whyte toward the floor, gashing his head on the sharp edge of the table as he went down, leaving barely two feet between himself and Rake. The reporter held a double-bladed knife, high-carbon stainless steel, sharp on one edge, serrated on the other, designed for quiet battlefield killing, its blade long enough to enter the body and destroy vital organs.

He was six inches taller than Rake, giving him a lethal reach. Rake's mind raced. Was he acting on orders? Was his television crew a military unit, here with a 'don't mess with Russia' message, taking advantage of the live-streaming to show how

Russia's enemies will be hunted down, even to the heart of Washington? The cost to Moscow would be minimal. Three Russians arrested in DC and three Americans would be picked up in Russia. A year or so on there would be a swap.

Or was it personal, a man driven by revenge, a grieving father who had lost a son on the Diomedes? Nightmare by nightmare, he would have imagined this final moment of closure and that meant he would make mistakes because he needed to be a soldier, focused, not a father grieving. Like oil and water, military training and personal feelings didn't mix.

Rake whispered in Russian: 'Screw your pathetic little family. I'll kill them all.'

Fury creased through his enemy. His arm swung back. Rake shifted to his left. The attacker stepped the other way, knife clasped, not a throw, a curling strike that would end up as an upward thrust to the throat to avoid body armor. His wrist muscles tightened. His eyes were tormented and diluted. Rake guessed right. This was about family, revenge and human frailty. Rake judged speed and direction. Too early, he would be floored. Too late, the blade would cut him. Rake leaned back to avoid it and raised his forearm to block it.

The attacker's knife arm moved above the hip up to the sternum where he lined it up to strike Rake's carotid, the artery that pumps directly into the brain. Rake chose to intercept between the sternum and the neck, when the Russian's sense of revenge was at its height. He struck the elbow, then the wrist. He gripped the attacker's wrist, turned the arm on its own momentum and guided the knife onto a ninety-degree trajectory into his right eye, the softest path for the serrated blade to plunge through into the brain. The Russian fell with a trickle of blood at exactly the moment that a high-powered bullet smashed into the Harvard academic's face, shattering his skull like a watermelon.

Why the professor? Was it a shot meant for Rake? The man who had shone the lamp in Rake's eyes held a microphone rod like a rifle. Black, long, metal, round, his finger on a hidden trigger.

Whyte pulled down the moderator and the UN official, covering them with his body. Rake jumped off the podium toward the gunman. A second shot smashed into the wall behind him. A third hit the ceiling. Mikki had thrown his knife. The gunman was down. Dark arterial blood jetted from his neck, splashing in an arc of red onto a white table. He grasped against air. Mikki pulled the bloodied knife from the dying man's neck and turned, poised to strike again. Rake's focus shifted to the third man. There were three in the crew, one left alive. The television camera was on his shoulder, but he was no fighter. Rake punched him in the belly, drove his fist upwards into the jaw. The camera fell to the floor. Rake pushed him down.

'Clear,' he shouted, spreading the cameraman face down.

Whyte's polished black shoe pressed onto the prisoner's back. 'One hell of a knife throw, Detective.' He tilted his head toward Mikki. 'We need to get you both the hell out of here.'

SEVENTEEN

Moscow

Ruslan Yumatov heard a little boy's cry for his daddy and shut down the news feed from Washington, DC. He had seen all he needed. The killing of Rake Ozenna had failed, but then he had never expected the team to get as far as it had, and the point had been made: if you fuck with Russia, you will never be safe.

'Andrei, excuse me, for a moment. I have to see to Max.' With him was Andrei Kurchin, commander of one of Russia's quietest submarines, the Yasen-class *Kasatka* docked in Severomorsk and imminently scheduled to head out to sea.

Yumatov had asked Kurchin over to his Moscow apartment to watch the feed from the Center for Political and Global Studies. Kurchin had become engrossed in the stealth-technology data on hard drives that were found in Semenov's apartment. As soon as the vice-admiral had become airborne toward Moscow, a Zaslon technical team had searched Semenov's home. The team broke open the safe, took the hidden hard drives, cracked the encryption, and saw that Semenov had transferred just under one terabyte of data onto a smaller, portable drive that, presumably, he now had with him. Kurchin was studying it while keeping an eye on mayhem from the conference in Washington.

'Will this throw us off course?' Kurchin asked amiably, although his expression made no secret of his concern.

'I allowed for it,' answered Yumatov. 'It was a long shot. Russia sent a message and the fallout is self-contained. Our fingerprints are nowhere.'

'I admire your balls, Ruslan, I really do.'

Yumatov walked out of his study, closing the door and scooped his son, Max, up in his arms. 'So, what's all the fuss, young man.' He kissed his forehead. Max had thick, deep blond hair and the clear blue eyes of a future leader. Tonight, though, they were brimming with tears.

'Why, Daddy. Why do we have to go?'

His wife, Anna, sat by the front door on a wooden upright chair decorated with folk art drawings that had belonged to his mother. She was elegantly dressed for the journey, her dark hair pinned back under a gray mink fur hat, and a dark-blue woolen overcoat. Natasha, dressed in a miniature manner to Anna, sat next to her, drawing in a coloring book.

'The car's here,' said Anna with no emotion in her voice.

Yumatov lowered Max to the carpeted floor. 'When you're grown up, Max, remember tonight, how you looked after your mother and little sister and helped Russia in her time of need.'

'I don't understand.' Max wiped his eyes. 'I have no friends in England.'

Yumatov rustled his hair. 'You'll have so many friends in England so quickly that you'll never want to leave.' He picked up two envelopes from the dark wood hall table and squatted so that he was eye level with his children.

'Hold out your hand, Natasha.'

His daughter rested her crayon in the seam of the book. Yumatov upended an envelope and tipped into her hands a silver-plated brooch shaped like a shield with a woman's face and a hammer and sickle in the middle. 'This belonged to my mother, your grandmother,' he said. 'It now belongs to you.'

'Thank you, Daddy,' said Natasha turning it around in her hands. Anna opened her daughter's overcoat and pinned it inside on her jacket.

Yumatov turned to Max, whose hands were out waiting. He took a watch from the envelope and placed it in his son's hands. It was large with bold white markings on a black face. 'You can wear this when you get bigger and older,' he said. 'It belonged to my father, your grandfather, and was given to him by the factory where he was the foreman for many years.'

Max hurriedly tried to fit it onto his wrist. It was too big and slipped over his hand onto the floor. The family laughed together. Yumatov picked it up. 'Remember, Max, this watch means you are a man and you have to make sure your family is safe.'

'Yes, sir.' Max looked at his father for a beat, then lowered his gaze to the floor.

There was a rap on the door. Anna opened it and pointed to a row of suitcases. Two men picked them up.

Yumatov rested his hands on Anna's shoulders. 'Will you be OK?' he asked.

Anna gave a short laugh. 'And if we're not, will you stop everything you've planned for so long?' She gave him a deep kiss. 'We'll be fine, my husband. Now, you do what you need to do and make our country strong again.'

Yumatov embraced the children. Anna took their hands and left. Yumatov slowly closed the door, catching the last glimpse of her fur hat vanishing around the stairwell. He gave himself a moment to regain his composure before going back into his study.

'All good?' asked Kurchin. The television ran footage of the attack in Washington.

'Anything new?'

'The FBI have issued a statement, saying two Russians are dead and one surrendered.'

Yumatov opened a cupboard. 'Whisky?'

Kurchin shook his head. 'I won't, if I'm heading out tomorrow.'

Yumatov poured himself a Scottish single malt and drank it straight down. The strong peat aroma warmed his mouth and calmed him. The sight of Anna and the children disappearing down the stairwell moved him more than he had expected.

'What's your conclusion about Semenov's material?' Yumatov sat on the sofa next to his friend.

'Can you stop him?'

'Why?'

'It is the encryption antidote to our latest cloaking technology.'

'Explain.'

'I have rigged up the *Kasatka* so that she transmits a false sonar signature. When we're out there, NATO will think we are a friendly vessel. Semenov has with him codes to break through that disguise. If the Americans get this technology, they will know exactly who we are, and our mission will fail.'

EIGHTEEN

Moscow

'Enjoy your stay in Russia, Dr Mayer.' The immigration officer stamped Carrie's passport. She walked briskly through customs wheeling a dark-blue hand-carry case. She spotted her driver, holding up an iPad with the name Dr Sarah Mayer underneath the logo of the Intercontinental Hotel on Tverskaya Street chosen by Harry Lucas, a big enough hotel chain to offer some protection, cheap enough not to notice a young doctor on holiday.

They walked through the cold to the parking lot, where he held open the door of a black Mercedes sedan. Inside were leather seats, bottled water, a copy of the English language *Moscow Times*, and tourist leaflets. A familiar landscape of expressway, modern buildings, and snow-covered pine trees unfolded. Carrie had been to Moscow a lot, and Russia was in her blood. Each time, she noticed something new, a bridge, a hotel, a road, but they did little to draw Russia away from its enveloping mood of gloom, anger, despair, arrogance too, too often released with drink, music, and poetry.

The Intercontinental lay two miles north of Red Square, which Lucas had designated as her fallback should anything go wrong. She was to go to the Beluga Caviar Bar inside the GUM shopping mall, a sprawling site that was once the massive State Department Store of the Soviet Union, now lit with global brands and filled with enough tourists to give Carrie a solid protective layer. Once there, British agents would bring her to safety.

The British Embassy, where she would be taking Artyom Semenov, was three miles south-west of the Intercontinental. Carrie was to walk it, about an hour, to ensure she wasn't being followed. Lucas' watchers would keep track. She would meet Semenov just over halfway outside the museum of the tragic poet Marina Tsvetaeva, who had lived through revolution, famine, exile, and the loss of her child. The location was Carrie's choice. Her mother adored Tsvetaeva and kept her photograph framed above her dressing table. Semenov had accepted the rendezvous without objection.

If Lucas thought it were not safe, Semenov would not be there. Carrie was to go into the museum for thirty minutes, then catch a cab to Red Square and follow the fallback plan. What if no one was at the Beluga Bar, she had asked? Call me, Lucas replied, handing her a phone; but only as a last resort. 'And if you don't answer, Harry?' pressed Carrie. Lucas didn't waver. Head for the airport. Get out of Russia.

At the Intercontinental, Carrie was given a large room with a huge bed, great for a lovers' weekend. She hoisted her case onto it, drew out a red sweater, leather gloves, red scarf, and black woolen hat to pull over her ears. It was just past three in the afternoon. Dusk would come in half an hour. The outside temperature was minus ten Celsius. She and Semenov were to arrive at the embassy late afternoon, after dark. She didn't shower or change. She kept on her black thermal waterproof jacket, thick cotton pants with side pockets down each leg, and brown leather boots for rain and snow. Everything was new, even the small laptop inside the case. Everything was Sarah Mayer. Nothing led back to Carrie Walker. She splashed water over her face, cleaned her teeth, applied lip balm for cold chapping, locked the case, and put it in the wardrobe. She pulled on her hat and tied her scarf around her neck and mouth so barely any of her face was exposed. She unlocked the door, hooked the *Do Not Disturb* sign on the handle, and walked out to meet her uncle.

Carrie headed toward Tverskaya metro station, two blocks south. Tverskaya, a wide, dominating, store-filled boulevard, was Moscow's main shopping street, now shrouded in snowfall, vehicle exhaust clouds, pedestrians wrapped in coats, scarves and caps moving through each other like the flows of competing rivers. Streetlamps were snapping on, beams blurred by weather. A vehicle's warning beep broke her thoughts. A small dirty yellow bulldozer mounted the sidewalk, causing people to jump out of the way, and drove toward a side-street junction. Sirens followed. Two police cars drew up to block the side street.

Carrie joined a small crowd watching the bulldozer. Unlike

the main road, slush and uncleared snow covered the side street, some fresh, some frozen and piled high on the sidewalk. Etched into it like graffiti on a wall were two rows of large green lettering, in Russian Cyrillic apart from the first word, which in capital Roman script read *FUCK*.

Police handcuffed two men in jeans and black leather jackets and marched one to each vehicle. The bulldozer destroyed the snow wall, crushing a can of spray paint under its treads. The police shouted that no photographs were allowed. People must move on. Carrie did. There was no time to get caught up in a small local protest.

She walked fast with added urgency. The first line read *FUCK Lagutov*, the ageing technocrat president, kept in office because Russia hadn't yet decided the type of leader it wanted. The second read *Grizlov for President*, a reference to the polished and debonair Sergey Grizlov, the newly appointed Foreign Minister who had achieved a rock-star, champion-of-the-people status while dressing in expensive tailor-made suits, speaking English and French like a native, and being on first-name terms with American and European leaders who were slated as Russia's enemies.

She had half an hour of daylight left, which would give her time to get to the museum. They would do the final mile to the embassy with streetlights, easier to vanish if needs be. She weaved through throngs, took stairs into the metro, leaving crisp city winter air for a brightly lit underpass lined with stalls of souvenirs and cheap clothes. She walked back up into the cold on the south side of Tverskaya, watching for ice-patches, in awe of how stylish women, even in heels, navigated frozen sidewalks. She stuck to the route agreed with Lucas, not the shortest, but the best lit, south-west along Tverskoy Boulevard, cutting in from the main sidewalk to a foot path inside a narrow tree-lined park. Traffic noise dropped to a low hum.

Lucas had told her the footpath would make it easier for his watchers to verify that she wasn't being followed. At the end, she crossed busy main roads, cutting through west to get onto Malyy Rzhevskiy Pereulok, which led to the Marina Tsvetaeva museum. She was making good time.

The museum was a nineteenth-century yellow building, well maintained with a canopied entrance outside. Carrie stayed on the opposite side of the road, walking quickly, keeping the building at the edge of her vision, as if it were not her destination. A couple came out of the main door and lit cigarettes. Pedestrians passed, a scattering, not like the crowds in Tverskaya, brisk, end of work, end of school, heading somewhere. Nothing alarmed her. There was no one hanging about and no Artyom Semenov either. The museum faced a junction. Carrie stopped as two cars drew up, then pulled out into the main road. She would walk for one minute, then loop back on the museum side of the road. If Semenov were not there then, she would buy a ticket, go in and stay until closing time.

She was crossing the road when, as if from nowhere, Semenov fell into step beside her. He wore a dark overcoat and traditional fur hat with flaps down over his ears. Large crow claws spread from his eyes, which smiled at her, not the eyes of a man about to betray his family. Or his country. He wanted to see her. She was his niece.

'Little Carrie.' Semenov laid his hand on her arm. 'You've grown into such a wonderful young person.' He wore no gloves. Two fingers were slightly curled, some form of arthritis. Small liver spots peppered the back of his hand. He wore no rings.

'Are you OK, Uncle Art?' said Carrie.

'Now that I am with you.' His expression danced around like a child. 'I am excited.'

'It's good to see you.' She meant it. She squeezed his hand and took a step to start them walking south. 'You must tell me everything. How are you? Where do you live?' She spoke as if they had met normally, distant relatives, after a long time.

'You, too, Carrie. Your lovely mother, my sister, is she happy? Is your father treating her well? My, didn't they fight so much? And your little sister. Angela? She was a baby.'

'Angie is a doctor.'

'Like you.'

'Yes, but she is married. Two lovely children.'

They walked side by side. One moment Semenov gushed with enthusiasm, the next his eyes darted around, anxious. When they reached the much wider New Arbat Avenue, Semenov insisted they switch sides. 'These crazy Moscow motorists.' He put Carrie on the inside and him closer to vehicles speeding by.

'You haven't married, Carrie?'

'Not yet.'

'But how can a woman fall in love if she is always in dangerous places?'

'And you, Uncle Art?' said Carrie.

'I am divorced. Marissa is lovely. We are like old gloves. She did not like my work. We had no children. She hated Severomorsk. It is a military place with many restrictions. I bought her a place in Moscow. I hope it makes her happy.'

Semenov adjusted his hat and looked away as if embarrassed, sad, eyes like dark unsettled moons, his buoyant mood suddenly punctured. It was a face Carrie had seen often in bad places where people craved escape. Motive was not a question. Semenov wanted out of whatever nightmare he was in, work, divorce, age, Russia.

Only small talk, she had agreed with Lucas. Nothing about why. No detail about Semenov's work. Keep moving. Cover the mile to the embassy fast without running. Give him no chance to change his mind. Fifteen minutes and they would be there. End of job. Carrie would see Stephanie Lucas, maybe dinner. If Steph was busy, Carrie would cab it back to the hotel, then her tour itinerary, early morning, high-speed train to St Petersburg, there by lunchtime, a river city trip and a short evening flight to Helsinki.

How Semenov escaped Russia, if he wanted to leave, was outside her remit. She imagined a reunion in Brooklyn, her mother cooking up a storm, Angie curious about the whys and where-fores, her doctor husband perfect with the two kids, and her father chipping in against Russia, the Soviets, and how everything was better in Estonia.

The traffic roar at the massive intersection of New Arbat and Novinsky was too loud for conversation. Semenov took the lead, guiding Carrie into the underpass with lines of little shopping stalls, more shabby, less jammed together than in Tverskaya. He became nervous. 'Are you sure it will be all right, Carrie?' he asked, stopping under a florescent lamp.

'I'm sure.' Carrie tapped his elbow. 'Only a few minutes now.'

Semenov obeyed. They walked purposefully along Novinsky, turning right past a bright cafe into Protochnyy where volume levels dropped, traffic thinned, and snow-laden trees gave off a freshness which seemed to relax him. 'So, it is the British,' he said. 'Not the Americans?'

'Yes. British. It is better. The Ambassador is a friend.' Carrie took his arm. 'Trust me. The coffee will be better.'

'You are so nice, Carrie.' Semenov smiled. 'My niece is a clever, funny woman.'

Carrie pointed to the river as it came into view at the end of the road. Semenov stopped again. 'But, Carrie, they will be watching. We can't wait in the street. They will see me. We must be let straight in.'

She coaxed him along with another affectionate tap on his arm 'It'll be fine. The British know we are coming.'

Semenov took a step. 'OK, Carrie. I know you are brave. I trust you completely. I wanted to say—'

He paused mid-sentence. A man stepped out from a side street just ahead. He wore a black jacket with the British flag and embassy logo on the left side. He waved enthusiastically.

NINETEEN

'Dr Walker, Admiral Semenov, I am Alan Scott, embassy security.' He spoke in a regional English accent with a reassuring smile. 'Come with me down here and we'll go in the back door.'

He gave Carrie a wink, turned on his heel, and headed back into the street marked as a dead end with uncleared piles of snow. It was dark, barely a light, a few sedans parked on each side. On their left was a bank and a vandalized cash machine, on the right, a children's playground covered in snow, icicles hanging off the swing bars.

Scott seemed to read Semenov's worry. 'Only a hundred yards down here,' he said chirpily. 'An alley to the left that leads us into the compound.'

'That is diplomatic property,' replied Semenov, half question, half statement.

'It is, Admiral. You will be a hundred percent secure.' Scott strode ahead reaching a thin red and white striped car barrier on the left. He pointed. 'Just through here.'

Beyond was a small parking lot, then a fence and hedge. Semenov shifted his hat a fraction, his hand shaking.

'Admiral, you first,' said Scott. 'Dr Walker, you stay back to give a clear run for the facial recognition.'

Semenov didn't move. 'Carrie, no.' He turned to her, his eyes bleak.

'Come on, Uncle Art,' she cajoled. 'We're home free.'

'No,' Semenov repeated, this time with grit, a naval officer, no longer an uncle. A bullet slammed into his chest. Carrie saw the flash from the chamber before she saw the weapon in Scott's hand. A burning coldness enveloped her. She fought to keep her mind. In front of her was total horror. Semenov swayed. Another round hit him, close to the first. He stumbled forward, his face creased tight, his eyes filled with despair as if his worst prediction had come true. He reached out to her as if for comfort. The fingers of his right hand curled into a fist. She had led him to his death.

'Nooooo!' she cried out.

Scott fired a third round into his back. Carrie caught his fall. She had to tear herself from overwhelming panic. Her uncle was dying, his vital signs racing away. He was heavy. She was somewhere else, Iraq, Liberia, Libya, gunfire, shelling, urgency, wounded, life draining away. She managed to hold him, keep his head from smashing into the road. Saliva bubbled from his mouth. He clawed at her jacket before losing all strength. She sank down with him into the snow.

'Move away.' Scott spoke softly in Russian, like she would in a trauma room, something that had to be done. He knew Carrie understood. How?

Blood thumped through her temples. She held her uncle's head in both hands, knuckles in the wet snow, not daring to look up, not knowing how she would react. She knew about people with guns, but nothing like this. It froze her thinking.

She laid his skull on the snow, kept her gaze down. Her hands were sticky with blood. She had to keep thinking.

'I said move away,' Scott repeated.

Why hadn't he shot her? A flash of relief spread through her and fear. He could kill her any time. He smiled so warmly when he greeted them. She couldn't look at him, didn't want to show her terror. She began to push herself up. Her muscles locked in self-protection. She had to force herself through it. Either she stood up or he would pull her up.

What was happening? Her uncle was dead. Carrie was alive. Meaning she wasn't on his kill list? What then? She stood up, stepped back from the body. Scott kept his eyes on Carrie, weapon ready. He ran his hands through Semenov's jacket, bringing out wallet, cards, money, keys.

'Did he give you anything?' Scott asked.

Carrie shook her head.

'Over here.' Scott indicated with the gun. He wanted Carrie to move out of sight of the intersection to a patch of unlit street. She stayed silent. She didn't move.

'American doctor being bitch.' He stood up, leaving some of Semenov's things on his body, some on the snow coloring with blood. His weapon was down. Relaxed. He carried the blankness of a man who often killed to order.

'Turn out your pockets,' he said.

Her skin tingled with revulsion. *Why don't you fucking shoot me, then search me?* She tried to shout defiance, but her mouth hung open, her throat parched.

Scott took a step toward her. Carrie braced. She could run, and he might not shoot because he had orders not to. Could she get to the main road before he caught up with her? Should she—

Scott's head vanished in front of her, evaporated into a brown, maroon, and orange exploding ball. Carrie's legs gave way. Flesh, skull bone, blood, and brain sprayed into the air. Some fell on her. She stumbled, found her balance again. Scott died silently, an explosive bullet to his skull. Carrie heard no shot. She looked for the weapon, expecting her world to go dark, too. She fought bile rising in her throat, the body's reaction to total terror. She was alone with two fresh bodies and lightly falling snow, watched, not shot. Raw, red muscles and arteries spilled from Scott's headless neck.

Carrie ran.

She fled the street, drawing ice air deep into her lungs, causing her to cough. She kept going, careful with her feet on the ice. She reached the sidewalk of the main road with traffic roar and splays of light from yellow streetlamps. A police car passed her. No siren. Two guys chatting. No alert about a double murder in a side street by the British Embassy.

She carried Semenov's phone in her right hand, fingers curled right around it. She looked behind her. Nothing. She reached the Novinsky intersection and slowed to a walk. She repressed rising nausea, spat out the greenish-yellow fluid. She knew that if she slowed, she would weaken. She needed to process shock by focusing on a small detail of logic, something that would make her safer. She talked to herself. *I am in Russia to take my uncle to the British Embassy. But he has been shot dead . . .* She kept walking and told the story to herself, straightforward, unemotional like a medical report.

She needed to get help and for that she needed a new phone. There would be a phone stall in the underpass. She would call Harry Lucas and take it from there. Except. Fuck! She reached the

top of the steps and made a three-hundred-and-sixty-degree turn.
Where the hell were Lucas' watchers, the guys who were meant
to have tracked her to the embassy, made sure she met up with
Semenov, who should have had her back?

Where in God's name are you?

Her phone vibrated, the one Lucas had given her for emergen-
cies. Incoming call. Unknown. Russian script. Carrie pressed
accept, held it to her ear, said nothing. Familiar voice.

'It's Steph, Carrie. Disappear. Don't use us—'

'Steph, what the—'

The line cut. She felt lost, empty. For a split moment a chance
of safety. Gone. She walked on, not into the underpass. She
needed to stay in the open where she could run. She could stick
to her plan. St Petersburg. Helsinki. Really? Back to the
Intercontinental? No way? What about Harry Lucas' fallback
plan, Red Square, the GUM shopping mall, Beluga Caviar Bar
from where the Brits would whisk her to safety? Except. Stephanie
said: Just hide. Disappear. Fallback blown? Unsafe.

She put Semenov's phone in her side pocket, then realized
that she could be tracked. She took off her gloves, sticky with
her uncle's blood. She sprang out the SIM card, dropped the
phone in the bin. She doubled back into the underpass where
she had seen a stall that advertised MTS, Beeline, and Megafon,
the main network carriers that any tourist can get onto at the
airport. Face covered with her scarf, hat unrolled over her ears,
speaking in English, she used the passport of Dr Sarah Mayer
to get a new phone, not the cheapest because she needed it smart
and dual SIM. Not one phone, but two, just in case, with different
carriers.

She headed east along New Arbat, working a route that would
take her to Leningrad Station, train to St Petersburg, where she
could hide away for a day and get the plane to Helsinki, not the
one booked. Another. Last minute. Except, if that rendezvous
was blown, so would St Petersburg be blown. Why had Lucas
pulled his guys? No way St Petersburg until she could trust Lucas
again.

Stop, Carrie. Stop. You are making yourself crazy. Her mind
had nowhere to go. She walked against the traffic, looking through
windscreens at impatient drivers, bored passengers, animated

conversations, belches of black smoke from old engines, battered cars, lopsided trucks, dark-windowed limousines. Evening rush hour. What in hell's name to do?

Carrie tightened her scarf, hunched her shoulders and slid her hands into her pockets. She wanted to fold herself up, head tucked away like a porcupine. Down in her right pocket, underneath a handkerchief and loose change, she felt something small, hard and square. She bought it out, tight in her fingers. A flash drive with a USB connection. Tiny. Her dying uncle had clawed her jacket. What presence of mind! Was this it? Was this what people were dying for?

Carrie passed two Internet cafes before choosing one which was busy, casual, and ran on a cash-operated system. She picked a workstation with no one on either side and slid Semenov's drive into the USB port. The computer's immediate recognition was a good sign. The drive could carry one terabyte. It was eighty-five per cent full, which was a lot of data. Files unfolded on the screen. Their titles were long numbers, like serial codes. Carrie opened one. Password protected. Another from a different folder. Encrypted. She tested more, randomly. None opened. Either encrypted, password-protected, or code appeared which to Carrie was meaningless. She took phone screenshots and left. She had been there for less than five minutes, came out and kept walking east. She imagined dangers that vanished. She ran across a red-light intersection because she saw two men in black jackets with a logo she mistook for the British flag.

She took a sidewalk table at a large cafe, gas warmers, blankets, instant Wi-Fi. No log on needed. She needed to eat and ordered borscht soup, carrots, onions, beetroot, stewed beef cubes, potatoes, comfort food, calories, strength injection. Black coffee. She scanned the street. Her hand shook as she lifted the coffee cup. Her nerves were going wild.

She ate the soup, chewed the beef slowly, allowing space to calm. She needed to do something, but what? How fast you died if you got it wrong.

She swabbed gravy with a last piece of bread, pushed the plate aside, drew her coffee close and warmed her hands around the cup. There was one person. Rake whom she had let down big time, who shouldn't give her a second thought. But they had been messaging and, on this, she would trust him completely. He was in DC. He wanted to see her. She told him she had to cancel because she was heading out but didn't say where. He had messaged back: *Where you going? Boccaccio?* An Italian restaurant in Kabul. Their first date. Rake throwing intimacy into a four-word text. She transferred his email address to the local number, attached two screenshots of the serial numbers and code from Semenov's flash drive, keyed: *In danger. Please.*

She sent it, paid the bill, and wrapped herself warm again. She walked, no idea where she was going. Two men left the cafe, similar military gait to Scott. Or was she imagining it? Carrie kept on. An embassy? Swiss. Norwegian? Canadian? Yes. Canadian. That's what she would do. Easy. Why didn't she think of it before? Or Israel? The nationality of her fake passport. No. Lucas had set her up with it. Not safe.

She stopped outside a brightly lit store window, mannequins draped in elegant evening dress, blacks and dark blues. The phone map showed the Canadian Embassy back the way she had come south of New Arbat close to the British Embassy. Like hell would she go back down there! Anyway, it closed in five minutes. They all would.

Her phone beeped. Rake. Straight back to her.

TWENTY

Rake looked at the two images from Carrie that had just appeared on his phone. He was in a crowded basement room in the Pentagon watching a live feed of a stalled FBI interrogation of the surviving member of the Russian television crew. Apart from claiming innocence, he had stayed silent.

Carrie's images were grainy and static, one a scroll of files identified by sixteen-digit numbers, the other yellow folders, similar to those seen on any Microsoft folder file and with shorter names. Rake had no idea what they were. They were shots taken on a phone of a computer screen. Carrie had been going out of town. Now she was in danger. But where? What danger? He sent a message back: *On it. Where you?* He needed to be careful. There was a reason that Carrie had only contacted Rake, a reason, too, that a Russian hit team had broken through all intelligence networks to get to him, a reason a human ear had been sewn into the carcass of a dead reindeer.

Within minutes of the shooting, Rake and Mikki had been taken out of the building and put into an SUV that sped across the Potomac River to the Pentagon. Rake was unfamiliar with Washington. Windows blackened, he couldn't see a thing anyway. They had slowed to go down a steep curving slope into the massive Pentagon complex, stopped in an underground parking lot with stripped overhead lighting, into an elevator, down three floors, through fingerprint, voice, and facial recognition, and to an area where there had been statements, briefings, interviews, even a polygraph, and a cell-like room to sleep. Now, a day after the shooting, Rake, Mikki, and Whyte were in a crowded communications room, not big enough for a board meeting, but not too small, government paint, functional, four chairs, only two used, two walls decked with screens and computer equipment.

Whyte held rank but seemed to be as much in the dark as

Rake and Mikki. The only person in charge appeared to be a technician, holding the fort, running through the footage of the attack, keeping tabs on the FBI interrogation, waiting for some kind of authority.

Others were men and women from an array of agencies, unafraid to conceal suspicion of each other. Careers would ride on this crisis. Rake was army and Whyte was navy, which was why the Pentagon had prevailed over the FBI, which tried to claim jurisdiction for a federal crime committed on US soil and failed. The CIA wanted to muscle in, insisting it was a foreign intelligence issue, and might have succeeded had its intelligence stopped the gunmen before they arrived. Other agencies and units within agencies were there. For a case like this, everyone wanted to be in the room.

Concentration focused on the FBI interrogation. The surviving team member had given his name as Dmitry Petrov, aged fifty-nine, a freelance camera operator for Moscow television stations. Petrov had checked out. He was well known in his trade, competent, workmanlike, divorced, relatively sober, and had gone to Washington because it was a high-paying foreign job. He had not worked with his two dead colleagues before. A surface investigation showed he had no links to organized crime except the usual protection and pay-offs that drew in most Russians. In his mandatory two years' military service, he had seen no combat. He had offered his name, address, and profession like a soldier with rank and serial number. He had asked for a lawyer who turned out to be a consular official from the Russian Embassy. Since then, he had not uttered another word.

Rake showed Carrie's images to the technician running the computer console. He was late middle age, quiet, fast at his job, working a shift, and Rake judged he would have no skin in the career game. The technician looked at both, made a call, and put Rake on the line. 'Thank you, Major.' No identity for the voice. 'We're telling everyone to hold fire. Someone will be along in a couple of minutes to take over. You need to wait outside the room.'

The outside corridor had low ceilings, dim light, gray walls, and a smooth concrete floor. To the left, it ended with an emergency exit door. To the right, it curved round like a river.

Round the curve came two military cops, broad, no-nonsense men, flanking someone. Rake couldn't work out if the MPs had him under arrest or were protecting him. Seeing Rake, he moved ahead of the cops. 'Major Ozenna. Harry Lucas. We met briefly at Bagram.'

The MPs took up positions either side of the door. Lucas was casually dressed in jeans, a red checked denim shirt and trainers, quiet on the concrete. He carried a look of controlled impatience, a man with a puzzle where the rules kept changing.

Lucas held out his hand. Rake grasped it. Strong fingers curled around Rake's. 'Those images you just received, are they from Carrie Walker?'

Rake covered his surprise that Carrie was locked into something that reached deep into the bowels of the Pentagon. He handed his phone to Lucas, who looked at the two shots, switching them back and forth. He led Rake toward the emergency exit door out of earshot of the MPs. 'I'm running Carrie's operation. She was helping us with a defector, which is why she is in trouble.'

'Where is she?' Rake's expression stayed unchanged, crow claws splaying out from the edges of his eyes that looked half-closed but were concentrating on Lucas.

'Moscow.' Lucas handed back Rake's phone.

'Why?' A brief fury swelled that Carrie was in danger doing work she wasn't trained for. But anger wouldn't help. Governments did what governments did.

'I will give you more details further along if necessary,' said Lucas. 'As far as we know, Carrie is unhurt and she's free because she sent those screenshots.'

'Why to me?' Rake was placing Lucas, former Chair of the House Intelligence Committee, a Republican, special-forces war veteran, a bad marriage to a British diplomat and rumors of drinking, although Lucas came over as composed and knowledgeable.

'My guess is she chose you because she knows you're capable and she trusts you. The operation went wrong. Have you got back to her?'

Rake showed him the message: *On it. Where you?* There had been no reply.

'Leave it like that for a few minutes while we track the phone.' Lucas jerked his thumb toward the door of the room. 'There may be a connection between what went down in Moscow and the attempt on your life. I'm going to ask you questions about what happened in Norway which you are authorized to answer.' Lucas handed Rake a note on the letterhead of the brigadier-general of the Alaska National Guard, instructing him to work with Congressman Lucas and brief him on the Norway operation. Whyte had failed to produce a similar note.

'You and Detective Wekstatt have flown in from Kirkenes in Norway. Is that correct?' said Lucas.

'It is.'

'Did you cross into Russia with the Norwegian police to retrieve a reindeer carcass?'

'Correct.'

'And you were with police inspector Nilla Carsten?'

'Correct.'

'The same day you were summoned to Washington for the panel?'

'Correct.'

'How long had your visit to Kirkenes been scheduled?'

'Not long. I was redeploying from Afghanistan. You never know exactly when you're going to get out.'

'With Detective Wekstatt?'

'Correct. He was already there on secondment to the Norwegian Police Service.'

'Were you on a mission?'

'It was vague. Someone was due to be coming across the border. We were to be involved only if called upon. That was it.'

'When you were in Russia, was any attempt made on your life in any way?'

Lines deepened between Lucas' brows, as if he knew and Rake's confirmation would clarify the mess. Rake didn't read Lucas as a manipulative man. In the Bagram canteen, Lucas had been alone, no entourage, no pomp. Rake told Lucas about the border trip from the crossing to the intervention by the navy helicopter.

'What's your take, Major?'

'A rogue op, sir, which the navy put a stop to. The reindeer had been dumped there.' He opened his phone again. 'Then, once the carcass was across the border, we found this.'

Lucas examined the pictures of the severed ear with the unidentified insignia cut inside. 'Who have you showed this to?'

'Norwegian intelligence was at the border. Nilla handed over to them. They saw it.'

'Keep it like that.'

'Who is the victim?'

'I don't know, but someone on our side does. When we step into that room, my authority will be questioned. Everyone will have their own view on the attack here, but they know nothing about Carrie in Moscow or Norway. I need you to have my back.' He signaled to the military police that they were ready.

'Then you need to tell me what happened,' said Rake firmly.

Lucas drew in his lips, lowered his gaze toward the floor, and stayed quiet. The military police saw and didn't move. Rake helped him out. 'Not everything, sir, but what we are dealing with.'

'Carrie is in Moscow because her uncle offered us something,' said Lucas. 'He was losing his nerve. She went to help him deliver it. He was shot dead. Carrie is on the run. From what she sent you, it seems she has whatever her uncle was offering. We need to get it. If there is a connection between the attempt on your life here and what happened on the Norway border and in Moscow, we are up against a powerful and dangerous enemy. It might be rogue, might be the Russian state. And that, Major, is why, when we step inside that inter-agency fight-pit of a zoo in there, I need to know you're with me. You're the hero of the day. Your voice will carry weight. Even if you have no idea what I am doing, ride with me.'

Moscow

Ruslan Yumatov opened the message on his tablet, and a picture appeared of Josip Milotic's disfigured body sprawled in snow, streaked with dirt and blood. The fragmented skull was unrecognizable. The message came with an attachment containing the contents of the drive recovered from Semenov's body. There was only one file, the harmless one that the Americans already knew.

He messaged: 'How many drives?'

'One,' came the reply.

'On Josip?'

'Only on the vice-admiral. None on Josip.'

Semenov must have given the drive to Carrie Walker before he died. She would have run.

'Where is the woman?'

'We're searching.'

'Find her,' snapped Yumatov. 'Find her now.'

TWENTY-ONE

Carrie edged through throngs outside St Basil's Cathedral at the south-east end of Red Square. Tourists stretched in front of her, camera flashes leaping from their phones, capturing sleet, darkness, shapes of Russia's symbolic buildings, some lit, some shadowed. She maneuvered around tour groups, overhearing snatches of history, yelling or recited through a megaphone, tour guide like politicians on a soap box.

'If you think the name Red Square comes from Red Communism, you would be wrong,' shouted a woman, hat off, short gray hair, a Canadian flag held as if a baton. 'The word is *krasnyi*, meaning both beautiful and red. It refers to St Basil's Cathedral here with its nine colorful cupolas.' She pointed skywards. The dozen heads in her charge followed. 'See, small bright domes at the top. It is from these and not Lenin's tomb that we have the name in English of Red Square.'

Carrie broke her step to listen. It was safe. A few minutes. Even if she was being followed, they wouldn't snatch her here.

'Excuse me—' A hand on her elbow. 'Do you speak English?' Adrenalin shot through her like a tidal wave. A guy, twenties, straggly brown hair under a woolen hat. American accent. Dark-blue down jacket.

Carrie stopped. *Yes, I speak English along with a thousand other people around. Why me?*

'This is Red Square, right?' He had a map, one in every hotel foyer. He took a step toward her. 'Is Lenin's Mausoleum around here anywhere?' He unfolded more of the map, spreading it in the air as if Carrie should hold a corner.

She didn't. She thumbed behind her. 'Lenin is down on the left, straight across from that big shopping arcade. It'll be on your map.'

'I'm dyslexic. I have trouble with maps.' He smiled, cheeky, immature, on the road, strange place, fired up, hitting on her a bit. Alan Scott was friendly, relaxed, murderous, killed her uncle

a few hours ago. She pointed toward a huddle of German tourists. 'Find one of these groups with English. Tag along and you'll
hear all about Lenin and his tomb.'

As if on cue, an Irish-sounding guide strode past with a group.
'Immerse yourself in the wonders of Russia's vibrant Red
Square—'

'There you go,' said Carrie. 'Enjoy,' she shouted, loud enough
to turn heads, eyes on him for her protection. She walked quickly
away, her stomach rippling, her tongue dried with fear, weaving
through. She glanced back to check he wasn't following. She
couldn't see him, couldn't see anyone dangerous. But how would
she know?

She spotted familiar dark green canopies at the northern end
of a McDonald's store and headed there, realizing how much she
craved familiarity. A PTSD therapist once told Carrie she had a
fear of things collapsing because of what happened to the Soviet
Union when she was child. That was why she was drawn to
unstable places, but within that she sought out familiarity, like
right now, a McDonald's.

She bought a coffee and took an inside gray plastic seat far
from the door. She wanted to be warm, to see who was coming
in, and she needed Wi-Fi. Her best cover, until she thought of
something better, would be her people, doctors, nurses, medics.
Overhearing trauma talk would give her a sense of safety and,
if she found the right place, there might be someone she knew,
whom she had worked with in a shithole, who could help her
get out of Russia.

The Sklifosovsky Clinical and Research Institute for Emergency
Medicine was the best in Russia. It was a couple of miles north
and she could walk. Carrie sipped her coffee, clicking through the
forums and social media pages until she found the cafe where
trauma staff hung out after shifts, a penthouse roof top, flaming
torches, long bar, young clientele, her kind of people.

She stood up and glanced up at a television screen showing
flashing ambulance lights and gurneys from a shooting in
Washington, DC. She hadn't looked at the news since she arrived.
A group of Americans began to speak loudly about gun control.
She hooked her bag over her shoulder, took a step away from
her seat, then turned back as if she had left something behind to

check that no one had got up to leave with her. All seemed normal. She moved aside at the door for a gaggle of Chinese tourists, stepped out, and let the door close.

She walked quickly, breathing deep and focusing. She was a fucking doctor. She needed to stay calm. She reached the Bolshoi Theater, grand columns lit up yellow and white, like a palace, limousines pulling up, exhausts clouding the air.

She kept up the fast pace. Afternoon shift at the Sklifosovsky Institute ended at six thirty. Time to change and head out would be half an hour, maybe less. She would get there around seven. She checked her phone. Nothing more from Rake. Who else to call? Her mother would flip. Her father would blame Russia. Her sister would try to help, but by the book, which could be lethal. Angie's street wisdom wasn't great. She spotted the bar with the flashing yellow sign Врачи-кафе, Doctors' Cafe, in a shabby, paint-peeled building a block from the hospital on Prospekt Mira. A red and green laser logo danced on the frozen sidewalk. Two torch flames flanked the doorway. A hat-check girl offered to take her coat. Carrie kept it, refused the lift, climbed five flights of chipped concrete stairs to the roof where arcs of warmth from gas heaters mixed with icy night air.

Just inside a door alcove, she eyed trauma bags in the corner, left like briefcases in a cloakroom, heavy duty kit, that would contain blood-clotters, intravenous drips, tourniquets with buckles, and powerful drugs. She had called it right, a place for serious medics. There was a bar, glasses and bottles reflected in its polished stainless steel, with stools and small tables. She saw no barman. White muslin curtains hung from the ceiling to separate the bar area from a dining room. No one there, either. Another space by a white brick fireplace with comfortable white chairs, chess and backgammon tables. Empty, too. Further in there was low lounge jazz music and conversation buzz, more commentary and argument, far from the relaxed unwinding bar-room medic conversation she had expected. About forty people, some in paramedic tunics, mostly jeans and leather or denim jackets, clustered around a television screen on the wall.

'We need to nail him,' said a woman at the back, pausing from drawing a cocktail through a straw. 'Whatever it takes.'

'Yeah, but not like this,' answered a young guy next to her.

'Crazy,' came a remark from somewhere in the middle.

'Mad fucking world.'

Carrie edged in far enough to see a news network with slowed footage, images enlarged, music and commentary embedded. Then what she came face to face with made her breath tighten. Muscles clenched around her jaw. She made sure she was seeing it right as she watched a close-up shot of Rake Ozenna kill a man by plunging a knife into his eye. The network played and replayed the same footage. It moved to widescreen. A few seconds earlier, Rake's victim jumping onto a stage in what looked like a conference hall. An elderly man, spectacles perched on his nose, gray hair wisped across his head, sitting at a long table collapsed. The footage slowed to show a gunshot wound to his head. It ringed someone in the audience with a cane or a rifle.

'What do you think?' A barman wiped the surface with a cloth. Strength draining, Carrie perched on a stool.

'I've just walked in. What's happened?'

'That shootout in Washington. They say it was a Russian TV crew. Some conference. But the American soldier on the stage, he's the one who murdered our people on the Alaskan border. Remember?'

'Kind of. Do you have a Coke?' She needed to keep her sugar levels up.

He took a bottle from the cooler, snapped off its top, and poured into a glass for Carrie. 'Three dead. Two from the TV crew and a professor.'

Carrie bought out money. He waved his hand; on the house, bad day for everyone. The screen now showed footage of Diomede. A still shot of Rake, eyes almost invisible under folded lids making him look cruel. Then. Fuck! One of her. The fiancée. Turning as she climbed into a helicopter. Another in a business suit on a panel in Moscow. Dr Carrie Walker. Father and mother Soviet citizens. She lifted her scarf to cover more of her face. Relax, Carrie. She wouldn't be recognized. There were young blondes everywhere in Russia. What now? The day her uncle gets murdered, someone takes aim at Rake. In medicine, coincidences were present in everything that could go wrong. The news show switched to a live a shot on a Moscow street, the suave figure of the Foreign Minister, Sergey Grizlov.

'Many senior figures are calling for us to act on Major Ozenna,' said the anchor. 'Your view, Foreign Minister.'

'Terrible, terrible situation. My thoughts are with all the families of those who lost their lives.' Grizlov flattened the lapels of his overcoat, stern-faced for a stern occasion, a big man in Russia. Some wanted him dead, some wanted him President, like the two graffiti guys with the green spray paint outside the Intercontinental. 'I must be clear, however, that nothing justifies an attack like this.'

'Ozenna murdered our people with impunity. How can Russia allow him to be free? If we had acted earlier, they would have been no reason to—'

'Russia operates under the rule of law—'

'Screw you, Grizlov,' said the barman. He held two glasses, dripping with water, a dishcloth over his wrist, eyes burning onto the screen. There was real anger in the room, the type that led to no good place.

A woman in a paramedic jacket pushed back from the group towards the bar. 'The Americans kill people all the time. If we had dealt with him back then, this would never have happened.'

'But Grizlov's right. You can't just send a hit squad to—'

'Why not?' snapped the barman.

A bar stool next to Carrie scraped back and a gloved hand fell on her shoulder.

TWENTY-TWO

Carrie didn't move. The glove was new. Carrie smelt leather. It stayed on her shoulder. She had no idea what to do. You thought you were hardened. You keep your heart rate steady and your nerves in line. Others sweat and tremble. But you are the doctor. You have seen it all, the unexpected, the violent, the hopeless. In the past hours Carrie had become like a nut in a clamp, sides moving in on her until the shell held no more and it cracked.

She steadied herself. At the edge of her line of sight lay medics arguing around the television screen. On the other side was the doorway, but too far, too much time to get there. In front of her was the barman, alert, seeing a new customer. Carrie raised her hand to bring him over faster.

The scarf came down, hazel-green eyes, a curl of short dark hair, a thin looped silver earing, squat nose, a sharp, jutting chin, all of which she might have not recognized without the down-to-earth confidence that enveloped all of that. 'Steph?'

'It's me.'

'What—' She signaled the barman to hold back. 'I mean how—'

'I've a car downstairs.'

A binary decision. Go with Stephanie Lucas who had a lethal leak in her network or stay in a place where half the room seemed to want to kill her ex-fiancé and her own face was being paraded on news networks.

A black Mercedes SUV was parked outside, engine on, driver waiting. A bodyguard opened the back door for them. Carrie got in behind Stephanie. 'I need your phone, ma'am.' He had dark closely shorn hair, a square narrow head. Carrie shot Stephanie a glance.

'Carrie, meet Craig Slaughden, my principal protection officer,' said Stephanie. 'Do what he says.'

Carrie's hand was deep in her coat pocket, fingers curled

around the phone which carried the screenshots she had sent to Rake. She shook her head. 'No, Steph. You have a problem with security—'

'Don't be an idiot.' Stephanie took off her gloves. Her tone was low and cool. Slaughden remained on the sidewalk, door open, left hand on the top rim, right hand ready to take the phone, eyes watching around him.

'Once we're safe.' She sounded defensive.

Stephanie replied softly, confident of her control. 'The thing about burner phones is that you use them and dump them. You used a Russian burner phone to send an email to Rake Ozenna, but you didn't dump it and that is how we found you and that is how your enemies will find you.'

Carrie knew her argument had been weak, and Stephanie's was strong and right. She handed the phone to Slaughden, who stripped it, flipped out the battery, dropped it on the sidewalk, stamped on it with the heel of his boot, and kicked it into the gutter. He got in and closed the door.

'Sorry,' said Carrie. 'I was stupid.'

Stephanie pulled down an armrest for them to share. 'Being stupid might have saved your life. It's the only way we found you.'

Carrie buckled the seat belt. They were separated from the front by a transparent screen, like in a New York taxi. There was a click as the doors locked internally. Carrie held back saying anything. She didn't like being locked into a car. They pulled out. Headlights from a vehicle behind swept across the back window. A second chase car followed.

'We're going to the residence. It'll take about half an hour.' Stephanie wore a world's gone to shit look. She pulled off her hat, shook loose her hair, and ran her hand back through it. She patted the fur hat on her lap and shrugged. 'I can tell you what I know. Except I'm not sure what I know.'

'Try me,' said Carrie. 'Who was Alan Scott? Where are Harry's watchers who were meant to be looking out for me?'

'We think they're dead.' Stephanie's cadence wavered. 'Harry had four people on you. One is missing. Three bodies have been found.'

'Bodies. Where?' Carrie tried to absorb. The watchers were meant to be protecting her, and they were murdered.

'Still clarifying.' Stephanie checked her watch. 'It came through about an hour ago, after your escape.'

Carrie looked out at blurring lights, the wide, busy road, exhaust mist. 'But how come you didn't know until then? Weren't they meant to report back?'

'Not blow-by-blow. Harry didn't want to risk intercepts. They clocked your airport arrival and your leaving the hotel. They were to call in after Semenov got to the embassy, then again when you were back at the hotel. Between your leaving the hotel and your uncle's murder, they were taken.'

'Who shot the guy who killed my uncle?'

'One of us. We had your back and we still have it.'

'Then why didn't you bring me in? Why leave me swinging in the fucking wind?'

'It wasn't safe. They have infiltrated the embassy. They took Alan, got his uniform, and did all that—'

'Why didn't they kill me?'

'Your uncle must have been the target. Not you.'

The more Stephanie tried the explain, the more Carrie struggled. 'But how come it went to shit, Steph? Harry had a plan. I did exactly what he told me to do. Meet my uncle and bring him in, so how come you weren't there, how come—'

'I was. We all were. What we didn't know was that Alan was missing, and Harry didn't know he had been compromised.' Stephanie let out a long sigh. 'We thought this was about a Russian naval officer defecting. It's much more. Harry's convinced it's connected to the shooting in Washington.'

'Me here. Rake there. People getting killed.'

'Never overestimate a coincidence. That's what my father told me, and he was a conman and used-car salesman who would have handled this mess a lot better. My take, for what it's worth, is that the Washington shooting and your uncle's murder are separate symptoms of a deteriorating relationship with Moscow. That's the connection. Nothing more. This thing against Rake seems to be a crazy revenge attack. Your uncle was a naval engineer with information to sell and that involved intelligence and governments.'

Stephanie's phone lit, Cyrillic script on the message screen. She took the call, listened, and said in Russian, 'I could make seven thirty, eight.' She heard the reply, shook her head. 'What's so urgent?' She listened again. 'It's difficult . . . OK . . . No. Not the Foreign Ministry . . . Not the Duma . . . Your suite at the Four Seasons.'

She ended the call and opened the dividing screen. 'Craig, we need to divert to the Four Seasons, the one next to the State Duma.'

Slaughden shifted round to face Stephanie. 'Ma'am, we need to get you to the residence. This isn't—'

'It's Foreign Minister Grizlov. It's the Four Seasons. It's safe. Drop me, get Dr Walker to the residence, then come back for me.'

'I'll get a second team in.'

'Now, Craig,' snapped Stephanie. 'Have the chase car wait for me. You head back with Dr Walker.' She sank back into her seat. They were heading south down the massive Garden Ring which encircled central Moscow. The driver turned off taking them south-west back toward Red Square. 'Grizlov wants to see me now,' explained Stephanie.

'The Foreign Minister? About this?' said Carrie.

'He wouldn't say. Said it couldn't wait.' Her face was taut. 'I tried to put it off an hour. He was adamant and that it had to be in person. Sergey's a friend.'

'I know. You told me, since you were in your twenties.'

'The only guy in Moscow I begin to trust, even then only a fraction. If he knows what's behind this cluster fuck, I need to see him.'

Carrie had no idea the forces Stephanie was juggling. The pit of her stomach churned. Just as she was picked up, Stephanie got the call. Just as she was outside the British Embassy, her uncle was murdered. If Stephanie could track her movements, so could the Russian government. She did not want to be in an SUV with two military-style guys in the middle of Moscow. She would prefer to have stayed in the bar, where she had a measure of control.

'I don't like it, Steph. Maybe, I'm overreacting—'

'I don't like it either.' Stephanie's voice hardened. 'We've lost five people, Carrie. I have obligations to their families, to find out what is going on and put a stop to it. If Grizlov can help in that—'

'Two minutes out,' said Slaughden.

'You called me, Steph,' said Carrie. 'You yelled at me to disappear and hide.'

'They're not after you. If it were about you, you would be dead by now. It's about something else.' Stephanie opened the armrest cover between them to reveal a revolver. 'My weapon of last resort.' She gave Carrie a quick smile. 'The button underneath the lid automatically releases the safety. If someone's coming in to get me, I'm meant to pick it up and shoot them. Never had to. Love that it's here.'

She snapped the cover closed. Carrie slipped her fingers under the lid, which sprang up. She shut it back down. Stephanie checked her face in a compact mirror. She pushed back her hair and put on the hat, pulling down the earflaps. The SUV swept into the hotel forecourt, the chase car behind. Slaughden got out and opened Stephanie's door. Sergey Grizlov appeared, raised hand, a confident wave. He came forward, flamboyantly opening his arms to greet her. A concierge opened the main hotel door. Craig got back in the vehicle. The SUV pulled off into the Moscow traffic. With his hand resting on her back, Grizlov guided Stephanie inside.

Ruslan Yumatov had gone straight to the Four Seasons after intercepting Grizlov's call and hearing that two British diplomatic vehicles had been located through automatic number-plate recognition on Prospekt Mira near the Sklifosovsky clinic, parked outside a bar frequented by medics, a natural sanctuary for a terrified Dr Carrie Walker. Facial imaging recorded her in the bar watching news footage of the violence in Washington. It failed to detect the person with whom Carrie had walked out until, on the sidewalk, gait recognition suggested this was Stephanie Lucas, the British Ambassador to Moscow.

Surprisingly, at the Four Seasons, the British protection unit separated. The Ambassador's vehicle with Carrie Walker continued its journey to the British residence. Stephanie Lucas, without protection, went into the hotel with Grizlov.

The Pentagon, Arlington County, Virginia

'We've found her,' Harry Lucas told Rake quietly. He shifted his chair so Rake could move in to get a closer look at a center screen showing a live feed from a hotel forecourt. 'She's with the British Embassy. This is the Four Seasons in Moscow. The British Ambassador has gone in for a meeting with Foreign Minister Grizlov.' He pointed to a black suburban pulling out of the driveway. 'Carrie is in this vehicle. She has armed protection. Within half an hour, she'll be at the ambassador's residence.'

A wave of relief flooded through Rake. He had watched with admiration as Lucas had taken control of the room. First, the technician had deferred to him. Then came dissent and turf pitching. Calls were made to head offices asking who was in charge. Messages came back to stand aside and let Lucas handle this side of the investigation. Stephanie had notified Lucas about the meeting and he activated cyber-cracking software to break into the hotel's surveillance.

'Can you play it back?' Rake asked Lucas, who glanced up curiously.

'Keep the live feed,' explained Rake. 'Play back the Ambassador's arrival.

Lucas complied. Mikki leaned against a wall in a place from which he could see everyone. Rake studied the feed, the driveway ramp, the columns, the porter's desk, the wide hotel doors to the lobby, the flow of vehicles and people. His eyes squinted to cut out peripheral vision, improve depth of field, ensuring his retinas would only receive what he needed to see. Rake read the screen like he would something lit by sun reflected off ice.

A green circle settled on the British Embassy vehicle as it drove into the Four Seasons' forecourt. The occupants were identified as Stephanie Lucas, Ambassador, Dr Carrie Walker, passenger, Craig Slaughden, principal protection officer, and Peter Eklid, driver. Rake examined eye directions of people around the front of the hotel. Heads turned to look at Foreign Minister Grizlov greet Ambassador Lucas outside the front door. People craned to see.

Far from being sidelined by the Kremlin as before, the Foreign Ministry's profile had been lifted by Grizlov's appointment. He was a political superstar, in the frame to succeed the lackluster Lagutov as President. But why was he seeing the British Ambassador? Britain was of indeterminate quantity. Germany and France were the powers in Europe. So why today of all days does Russia's Foreign Minister entertain the British Ambassador in the luxury of Moscow's Four Seasons Hotel?

'Carrie's still on the road in Moscow,' said Rake. 'She's not yet safe.'

TWENTY-THREE

The Four Seasons Hotel, Moscow

'What the hell are you guys doing with this insane military exercise?' Grizlov smiled broadly as he steered Stephanie through. Bodyguards spread around the lavish lobby area, inelegant men among softly decorated pastel beige and white.

'Two hundred aircraft, seventy ships, fifteen thousand military vehicles.' Impeccably dressed and mannered, Grizlov walked with the assured air of a man who understood the contradictions of power and how to deploy its nuances. Not only had he survived every Russian regime since Gorbachev, he had grown with them, collecting favors, sharing influence, promoting, protecting, mentoring, showing the way, apparently clean, but impossible in today's Russia, to get to where he had without dirty hands.

Stephanie smiled back. 'Routine exercise, Sergey. Proportionate and transparent.'

Gas flames roared around a replica log fire underneath a high marble mantelpiece. A camera flashed, which might be exactly why Grizlov had asked her, to be photographed objecting to a military exercise inside Russia's backyard. NATO called it Russia's Bastion of Defense, an area that led off its coastal waters and stretched down to a line that ran diagonally across the North Atlantic from Greenland, Iceland, and the United Kingdom. Operation Dynamic Freedom was designed to make sure things worked. Russia didn't like it.

Grizlov directed her toward the elevator bank. 'The West is being deliberately provocative. You need to understand how dangerous this is.'

Stephanie did. But the United States led the charge and picked off governments one by one. One day China. The next Iran. A swipe at Europe and this month, Russia. She and Grizlov had discussed it many times. 'Nothing unusual, Sergey, and you didn't bring me here with such urgency to protest against NATO military exercises.'

Two of Grizlov's people stood at either side of the end elevator, door open. They rode up in silence. Grizlov led the way into the suite. His men stayed outside.

'They've swept it,' said Grizlov. 'It's clean.'

Clean for him, perhaps. Not for her. The suite carried a similar decor to the lobby, low tertiary colors, light shades, comfortable but unobtrusive furniture. From a narrow balcony, there was a view across Red Square, the GUM shopping arcade lined with lights like Harrods in London and St Basil's Cathedral, a spangle of contradictory colors. Stephanie rested her handbag on the arm of a sofa and pulled loose her scarf.

'You're looking good, Steph,' said Grizlov.

'That caps one hell of day,' Stephanie replied grimly. 'How are you bearing up?'

'If you had agreed to marry me when I asked, we might not be where we are now.'

That bought a smile. 'I recall you dumped me and headed off to a mining deal in Siberia and if we had married, I would be tearing out walls as the wife of a Russian oligarch or you would be a bored billionaire in London running soccer clubs, getting burned by your mistresses and sanctioned by my government.'

She let her answer run because she needed time to gauge what was going on. Grizlov was tense. Usually, when alone, catching up, he would flop into a comfortable chair, curious as to what she had been doing, telling her his latest theory of Russia's plight, where it was heading, why it would be a disaster. Today, he stood arms folded, conversation light, body language rigid.

Three years older, Grizlov was fifty-six. They had known each other since she had gone to Moscow to practice her business skills in Russia's 1990s' chaos. She taught him Western business tricks. He guided her through post-Communist anarchy, keeping her and her money safe. Nothing had prompted them to become lovers or to end their affair. They were young, attractive, ambitious, on the move, no acrimony, no fidelity questions, no discussions of a future. When Grizlov made her a partner in a tech venture, he said he would take out ten times more than her because he needed that to fund his survival. Stephanie believed him. She made her first million because of him and, as he maneuvered through the mood swings of Russian politics, she made sure they stayed friends. Stephanie grew her businesses, entered British politics, and, mistakenly, married Harry Lucas, a counterpart politician in America, although for a reason she had never yet worked out, she still kept his name.

However high Grizlov rose or rich he became, he kept in touch, often with a joke. He made chairman of the State Duma, was now Russian Foreign Minister and poised in the minds of many to be the next President, the West-facing candidate with comparisons to the eighteenth-century's Peter the Great, who made Russia a European power and embraced Western culture and science. In today's environment, Grizlov was a cheerleader for those fed up with the embrace of China and enmity toward America. As he became more popular, his dress sense had become snappier, more expensive. Unlike in Britain, Russians respected style more than they begrudged wealth.

Stephanie circled the suite, pushing open doors to the two bedrooms and two bathrooms, making sure, as much as she could, it was just the two of them. The place was freshly cleaned, the bed made, flowers on coffee tables, gels and soap in the showers.

'You summoned me at a moment's notice, and I came,' said Stephanie. 'Whatever it is, NATO, those shootings in Washington, anything else, just spit it out.'

Grizlov's eyes bore into Stephanie in way she had learnt to read over the years, half reprimand, half warning. From his suit pocket, he drew a dark-blue British passport and handed it to her. She opened it. A British driver's license dropped out together with a British Airways gold club card. They fell on the floor. Grizlov picked them up. Stephanie looked at the passport.

'Do you know him?' asked Grizlov.

A white male with blotched red cheeks stared out from the passport. The picture was laminated with symbols, birds, a compass, shapes, half circles, stars, signs that told immigration officers more about a person than eyes, nose, lips, and hair. As a diplomat, Stephanie knew some of the tells, but only from a half-day course some years back and she had no idea if there was anything obviously wrong. It was passport type 'P,' which everyone carried; code GBR which meant Great Britain; a nine

digit passport number; surname Cooper; given names, Gerald
Malcolm; nationality British citizen; date of birth, Cooper would
turn thirty-four in the New Year, sex, male; place of birth,
Middlesbrough, North Yorkshire, an expiry date nine years on.
Stephanie flipped through the pages and saw only the Russian
visa and stamp, a new passport, unused apart from this single
entry.

'I don't know him,' said Stephanie.

'He's dead,' said Grizlov. 'Murdered.'

'In Moscow?'

'His body was found in a place called Kola, a southern suburb
of Murmansk, hit badly as if run over by a truck. Was he one of
yours?'

'Not one that I know and what do you mean "as if run over?"'

Grizlov stepped across to the dining table. He pulled open a
drawer, brought out a transparent plastic folder, tipped out photographs, and spread them out. Cooper's killers had left him a
mess. His head lolled in a way that meant his neck must have
been broken. His right leg was bent double, his foot on his torso,
looking as if it had been wrenched from its hip socket. He wore
a black down jacket which bore the imprint of a vehicle tire. His
pants were torn at the top revealing exposed skin, turned black.

'The vehicle didn't kill him.' Grizlov separated off two pictures.
The first was a close-up of Cooper's head and neck: a line of
frozen blood where a knife had cut his throat curved around the
neck.

'My God!' Stephanie gasped.

Grizlov moved the photograph away and slid in the other one.
The corpse lay on a gurney, head arranged to the left. Light and
focus were bad. Stephanie couldn't work out what she was seeing.
Grizlov picked up the print, held it between them, and pointed
to the side of skull. She looked down again at the photograph.
Cooper's killer had cut off his ear. She leant on the table, both
hands, arms supporting her. 'Why?' she whispered.

'I don't know,' replied Grizlov.

Stephanie ran her gaze over the photographs, about a dozen.
She separated them so they were not overlapping. She turned
each over. There were two types, those at the scene where she
could see a sidewalk, lights of a gas station, buildings. They bore

what looked like a regular local police stamp. The second were Cooper on the gurney, closer shots in a controlled setting, showing the ear and the neck. They were stamped with the logo of a gold-handled sword and gray-lined shield that carried a yellow and red double-eagle motif in its center, the symbol of the Federal Security Service of the Russian Federation, the successor agency to the Communist KGB.

'FSB's involved.' Stephanie tapped her finger against the logo.

'The FSB control the border. Cooper was a British citizen. I'm only guessing. I got this stuff less than an hour ago.'

Stephanie perched on the arm of a sofa, the passport open on her lap. 'Let's work through normal consular procedures. British citizen is murdered in Russia. We inform the family. We identify the body—'

'That's the problem,' Grizlov interrupted. He held up one of the photographs like a shield. 'That's why I asked if he's one of yours—'

'He's not.'

Grizlov continued, 'Gerald Cooper had been a major in the 16 Air Assault Brigade, 3rd battalion of the Parachute Regiment. He served in Iraq, Afghanistan, and was a founding officer in Britain's new Joint Expeditionary Force, aimed at rapid reaction against Russia in northern Europe. He resigned his commission a year ago even though he was on a fast trajectory path to the top. So, my question is: why would an officer with such potential leave the army unless his government asked him to take another job serving his country?'

Stephanie stayed quiet. She saw where this going and wanted Grizlov to get there himself.

'The talented young officer turns up murdered in Russia near the city closest to the border he had been trained to protect,' concluded Grizlov.

Stephanie stepped directly in front of Grizlov. 'Read my lips, Sergey, Gerald Cooper was not one of ours.'

A condition of her taking the ambassador's job had been that she would be kept informed of any intelligence operation that could compromise the embassy. She held a weekly meeting with the Secret Intelligence Service station chief, who appeared grateful for her insider perspective of Russia. If Cooper were on the payroll and had been tasked for something up in Murmansk, Stephanie would expect to know about it.

'Why don't we return to official channels?' she said. 'We'll notify the family, do the paperwork, send someone up to identify the body, and get it back for a funeral.'

'Cooper's body was cremated this afternoon.' Grizlov moved to the table, stacked the photographs into a pile, and slid them back into the envelope. 'A British Embassy official was there. He identified the body, agreed to waive a post-mortem, and signed off on the cremation.' He brought documents from his inside jacket pocket. 'Here's the paperwork.'

Stephanie stiffened her wrist muscles to keep her hand steady. There were stamps, signatures, boxes and ticks, a photograph of the body in an open cheap wood coffin, another of it sliding into a crematorium furnace. There was the seal of Murmansk Oblast, the administrative area and the logo, in blue and yellow, a ship, a fish, and a spiky aurora which was meant to represent the Arctic Circle. Everything was in Russian Cyrillic apart from a box on the second sheet reserved for the witness signature. Inside, there was a signature and a printed name, Alan Scott.

Shock and fear hit Stephanie, not head on as in physical threat, but a creeping, untouchable, and slippery anxiety where you think you see danger, convince yourself it is imaginary, then like a monster rearing up from a lake, it is there, lethal and unstoppable. Alan Scott was missing and probably murdered presumably by the same people who killed Gerald Cooper.

'Who the hell is feeding you this?' said Stephanie. 'Alan Scott is a security guard at the embassy. He is neither consular nor chancery. He would not be authorized to sign this off.'

The hotel phone rang. Grizlov picked it up. 'Tell him to wait in the lobby.'

He picked up her coat. 'Sorry, Steph. Another crisis. On something like this, we have to work together. Russia is not one government, but I will get to the bottom of it.'

'We both have to.'

'I'll see you—'

He was interrupted by a commotion outside the door. They heard a raised male voice: 'If the Ambassador is in there, I need to get in.' English over the Russian. The handle turned. The door shook. Grizlov strode across and opened it. Behind his body-guards, Stephanie saw Craig Slaughden, forehead cut, fresh blood, shoulder of his jacket torn, holster empty, composure rippled.

'My security,' said Stephanie.

'Let him in,' instructed Grizlov.

The bodyguards melted back. Slaughden pushed through.

'What is it, Craig?' asked Stephanie quietly, trying to bring calm.

'The vehicle, ma'am.' He ran his hand through his hair, patted his empty holster, arranging his thoughts. 'We were attacked.'

TWENTY-FOUR

Black balaclavas covered the heads and faces of the two captors riding with Carrie. The interior of the van smelt of polished leather and gasoline, the roof high enough for her to stand. There were sliding doors on both sides and a steel, sealed panel between the driving section and where she was. The windows were tinted. Carrie made out roads, traffic, and street-lamps. No landmarks. Drab suburbs. No idea where. The van moved smoothly, routine weaving for Moscow traffic, no sudden jerks and turns, no flashing headlights. No horn.

One of her captors sat beside her with a pistol on his lap, the other on a jump seat across from her, weapon in a shoulder holster. They looked in shape, not fanatical body builders, but fit and not giving off male militia smells, sweat, tobacco, bad breath. They didn't talk to her or each other. There were two more men in the van's front seat, making four in all.

She had been so near. Why had they taken her so close to Stephanie's house? Why had her driver crossed the river on the Moskvoretsky Bridge instead of the closer Kammeny Bridge where they could have looped straight into the forecourt and British diplomatic territory? How did her captors know to put the snowplow across Bolotnaya Ploshchad which ran around the back of the property? Too many swirling questions.

Slaughden had been chatting, reassuring, half friendly, half military. He loved New York, had walked the Brooklyn Bridge. Windy. Great views. That sort of thing. There had been a burst of radio traffic. They were five minutes out, he had said. They went over the Moscow River and a right turn into Bolotnaya Ulitsa, less than a minute with an empty road and another right into Faleyevskiy Pereulok, then the fated right, curving round a parking lot. Their headlights picked up the unexpected shape of the snowplow, its yellow streaked with rain dirt, a cigarette's glow in the cab. A Kia truck, headlights off, boxed them in, a big operation with one driver in the snowplow, two in the truck, two motorcycles on each side of the road and four in the van with her. Nine in all.

Slaughden reassured her: 'You're safe inside the vehicle. They can't touch you.' He snapped shut the divide with the driving section. Doors clicked locked. The vehicle was armored. Carrie's captors appeared outside. They had some kind of drill for locked and armored vehicles. One guy, head down, focused on the door like a locksmith. *Rat. Tat. Whir. Rat. Tat. Whir. Rat. Tat. Whir.* Another behind, face out protecting him. A third, a few paces away, keeping a wider watch.

Slaughden flung open his door, right fist around his weapon, and barely touched his feet to the ground when the third guy pistol-whipped him across his forehead, followed by a gloved fist hard against his right cheekbone, followed by a snow-covered boot up and fast into his groin. Another kick sent him down, snapping the wing mirror on the way. Slaughden was military, these men were in another class. Slaughden was down. He was brave, but he achieved nothing.

The driver moved both hands from the wheel and placed them on his head. He stared straight ahead, rigid, not moving, not even shifting his glance when Slaughden was being beaten. His job was to protect the vehicle, Slaughden's to protect Carrie.

Carrie had released the clip on the central armrest and put her hand on the pistol that Stephanie showed her. Once the lid opened, the safety would be off, weapon ready to fire. The locksmith kept drilling until her door burst open. She was hit by a blade of freezing air. The guy keeping watch came forward. She could have shot him, two of them. Maybe all three. Then what? Soldiers were like mosquitoes, down one and another one's there straight away. Besides, doctors don't shoot people. Not generally. Not Carrie.

Her captor reached in and took the gun. She read him as much as she could through the balaclava. A slit in the wool. Two brown eyes, calm, no anger, threat, or fear.

He grasped her wrist, like a mountain climber helping a friend. She went with him. She saw Slaughden, fallen on his side, face cut from shards of the wing mirror, impossible to tell through thick clothing if he were breathing.

Carrie pulled to get a closer look, which was the only time

her captor spoke. 'He'll live,' he said in Russian in a way that she believed him. He walked her round the Kia truck to a Mercedes Sprinter whose side door was open. The seats were black leather, wide and comfortable like a luxury minibus shuttling guests into town from a private airfield. They didn't cover her face with a sack. No tape across the mouth. No blindfold. They kept themselves disguised instead. They didn't speak. The Sarah Mayer passport, credit cards, travel itinerary, Semenov's flash drive sat in her pockets untouched.

Her wrists were lightly bound with plastic wire. They clipped in her seat belt, leaning across her, no sense of treat, no touching. They were very professional. But they removed her boots and thermal socks. She was barefoot, warm on the floor carpet of the van. Outside she would barely last a step. Then they searched her and found the flash drive her dying uncle had put in her pocket.

Sergey Grizlov offered his car to take Craig Slaughden to a hospital. Stephanie knew enough first aid to conclude that Slaughden could fix himself up when they got back.

'Anything more you need, call.' Grizlov tapped his phone as he walked them to the lift. Stephanie nodded. Polite. Diplomatic. Grizlov stayed in the corridor. The elevator doors closed. Small lamps played across the top. Grizlov counted it down to the lobby and waited. The lights indicated the doors opening at the bottom, pausing, closing. It started its journey back up again. The elevator pinged. Grizlov took a step back as the door opened. His new guest wore the khaki uniform of a colonel in the Russian army with a custom-made dark green tunic, thin red threaded lines around the lapels, a jungle green shirt, and black tie. Grizlov ushered Ruslan Yumatov into the suite.

TWENTY-FIVE

The Pentagon, Arlington County, Virginia

Rake examined a live feed coming from the forecourt of Moscow's Four Seasons Hotel. Using facial and gait recognition, most of those in the lobby had full profiles pulled up within seconds. They were a mix of well-heeled tourists and Moscow oligarchs and politicians. Some bodyguards and staffers came up blank. Most were identified.

Rake studied the digital footage much as he would a hunting scene in the Alaskan wilds, narrowing his gaze, taking in a panoramic sweep, identifying specific elements, cutting out the wider arc and focusing on detail. He said to Lucas, 'Go back to when the Ambassador entered the hotel.'

All heads on the forecourt turned towards Grizlov and Stephanie Lucas, except for five. Three of Grizlov's bodyguards kept scanning. A porter stepped out to stop a taxi coming up while the Foreign Minister was vulnerable, and the gaze of a bodyguard or staffer by the porter's desk moved directly across the forecourt, nowhere near Grizlov.

'Put this figure left of screen,' said Rake. 'Enlarge around, brighten and whiten it.'

He worked better in contrast and less color. Dark sky, sea ice, and islands were mostly hues of gray. Even moonlight reflecting on snow did not do much color.

'What exactly is it you need, Major Ozenna?' intervened an agent, mid-forties, close-cropped blond hair.

'Monochrome.'

'We have software that does this work faster and cleaner,' persisted the agent.

'A moment, Jeff,' said Harry Lucas.

'Keep enlarging,' said Rake. 'Ignore pixelation.'

The image ballooned out. Shapes became blobs of dark and light, indecipherable, except to an experienced eye. What Rake was looking for appeared as a distorted light-gray circle, which he judged to be halfway down the driveway heading east. Within that circle lay a pinprick of light.

'Bring it back.' Rake unfolded his arms, put both forefingers to his lips, waiting for the image to return.

'Here.' He tapped the screen. 'Separate off that section. Check facial recognition. He's using his phone for something.'

The shadow shape Rake identified was blown up with colored lines that followed identifiable human contours. Within seconds, it had a match. The hotel forecourt once again became full screen. The footage spooled, stopped, and a red circle appeared around the half-turned head of the figure. An hour after Grizlov met Stephanie Lucas the same person walked purposefully into the hotel lobby a step or two ahead of his bodyguards. CCTV picked him up inside, meeting with two of Grizlov's men who escorted him to the elevator bank. He was dressed in full military uniform.

A nervous edge fell on the room as details of the man's identity appeared. Colonel Ruslan Yumatov, attached to the 14th Separate Special Purpose Brigade at Ussuriysk in the Eastern Military District, a spetsnaz veteran of the Syrian, Venezuelan, and Diomede campaigns, aged forty-three, married to Anna, with two children, Natasha, five, and Maximilian, seven, who lived in Moscow.

'That's him,' said Rake. 'He was expecting the British Ambassador. He was signaled by the guy at the porter's desk that the British Embassy car was leaving.'

'How did he know who was in that vehicle and where it was heading?'

'They knew the route?' interjected Jeff, the CIA agent, running his hand across his short hair. 'The Brits let them hack into their GPS.'

'Or the kidnappers fabricated traffic and road closures prompting them to take the back route?' said Lucas.

'And who are you?' said Rake quietly. He didn't work well with people in suits in cramped spaces, the smell of ambition and trampling.

'Agent Jeff Auden, CIA. I report to Director Ciszewski.'

Quizzical expressions crossed the dozen or so faces, including Lucas. This was not a room where it was good to show or pull rank.

'We have the British Ambassador,' said Lucas.

The hotel forecourt picture vanished, and a video link appeared, not of Stephanie Lucas, but her bodyguard, former Parachute Regiment captain, Craig Slaughden. He was clean shaven, wearing a dark jacket and casual shirt with no tie. A fresh dressing covered a gash on his forehead. He looked straight into the camera, a soldier on debrief.

Harry Lucas had Slaughden's statement on a tablet in front of him. 'They knew you were coming?' he began.

'They did, sir.'

'Were you using satellite navigation?'

'Not on the vehicle. We use encrypted navigation on our phones. We take the back route often, particularly at that time of day, when traffic's busy.'

'Anything abnormal?'

'Nothing, sir.'

Lucas nodded as if the answers satisfied him. 'From what you know about the assault in Washington, and I appreciate it would be what you have seen on television, could it be the same people?'

'What I saw in Washington were two armed men in a surprise shooting who were easily neutralized,' said Slaughden. 'There was a much higher caliber of organization and skills here in Moscow.'

The door opened with yet another new face. The name tag on the white naval uniform read Matthew Allen, a captain from the Office of Naval Intelligence. He saluted Rake. Tilted his head in respect to Mikki.

'What you got, Captain?' asked Lucas.

'The long single-file numbers are the craft identification numbers and hull identification numbers of US naval vessels,' said Allen. 'The shorter numbers attached to the yellow files are the NATO pennant numbers applicable to Canadian and European naval vessels. Basically, this is the same information but with different methods of registration. There are thirty-three vessels on the screenshots, seventeen in the US group, sixteen in the NATO one. Each is taking part in the upcoming Dynamic Freedom exercise. Most also took part in the last Trident Juncture exercise, which would not be unusual. Therefore, this could be an old compilation. Most would be in the North Atlantic theater now.

Their current positions are classified. These registration numbers are open-source information.'

'You're saying this stuff any teenage kid in his bedroom could put together?' Harry Lucas pushed back his chair and stood up.

'Yes, sir.'

'Then, what exactly is it that's worth killing for?'

'My guess is that whatever else is inside that flash drive is gold dust on submarine warfare.'

TWENTY-SIX

Moscow

Sergey Grizlov had his back to Yumatov. 'Who is responsible?' he asked, looking out from the hotel windows over weather sweeping across Red Square, through lights on onion domes, crenelated high walls, and spires. 'Even if you don't know, tell me what you suspect.'

Yumatov took his time, gauging how much to tell. Carrie Walker was in his custody. The stolen data was secure. His men had found her carrying Semenov's one terabyte flash drive. It was time to deepen his deception against the Russian Foreign Minister and move on to the next stage.

It was just over a year since Yumatov had been granted a five-minute meeting in President Viktor Lagutov's everyday office in the Kremlin's Senate Building. Lagutov, an introverted academic, had appeared irritated, bored with his role as a stand-in president, keeping the office warm until Russia could find a vigorous leader to hold the country together. He had aged, thinning gray hair, spectacles too big for his colorless face, no energy in the eyes.

The President had agreed to see Yumatov because of the Diomede operation, which had given the young colonel the temporary superstar status of a Russian folk hero. Television loved his looks, his elegant wife and adorable children, his ruggedness, his composure in crisis, his ease in dealing with people, his turn of phrase, not least because Yumatov described convincingly how the Diomede had been a victory against American aggression.

'So, Colonel, what plan does the Russian military now have for the future of our country?' Lagutov began, staying behind his desk in the dark wood-paneled room and not offering Yumatov a seat.

'NATO's Trident Juncture exercise has humiliated Russia, sir,' answered Yumatov, referring to the recent large North Atlantic military exercise. 'We have no way to balance it.'

'You have not come to tell me what we cannot do.' Lagutov waved his hand with impatience.

'Reverse tactics, sir. For the next exercise, instead of whipping up hostile rhetoric, you initiate a peace summit with the American President. Let us see how the world reacts should he refuse.'

Lagutov tapped a folder on his desk. 'The file says your father was a good party loyalist, the foreman at a steel factory in Magnitokorsk which collapsed when it was privatized.'

'Yes, sir.' Yumatov had not expected the President to have called for his file.

'You went on to join the military and did well.' Lagutov spun the folder round and beckoned Yumatov to his desk. 'Is this correct? When you were recruited by Admiral Vitruk for the Diomede operation you were asked about your motivation. This is what you replied. Read it to me.'

The interview with the commander of the Alaska incursion had been more an afternoon conversation on a long, uncomfortable plane journey when both men had spoken of their backgrounds and experiences. Yumatov stepped forward to the President's desk, glanced quickly at two short paragraphs. 'It is correct, sir.'

'I asked you to read it.' Lagutov's tired expression was unexpectedly taking color.

Yumatov picked up the single sheet of paper. 'Admiral Vitruk asked Major Yumatov how his personal life influenced his vision of Russia's future. Yumatov replied: "We were honest working people until the catastrophe of the 1990s. My father was a respected factory manager. My grandfather, too. When the factory was privatized my father was promised that every worker would be given shares by the new owners with guaranteed pensions, housing, and medical. That was a lie."

'Admiral Vitruk asked: "What exactly was the lie?" Yumatov replied: "First, we were told it would take time for the privatization to come through and we would have to live without wages. Then, a flashy young prick came along and offered to buy our shares. We needed the cash so we could eat. My father trusted him and sold the idea to his men. He stole our factory. Families became destitute, while this prick bought himself yachts, fancy suits, and fast cars."' Yumatov felt his mouth dry as he read it. He placed the sheet of paper back on the President's desk.

'Was it wise to speak so honestly?' asked Lagutov.

'Had I lied, he would have seen through me.'

'And this "flashy young prick," who was he?'

Yumatov ran his tongue around the inside of his mouth. He needed moisture to make sure his voice didn't sound parched. The President knew the answer, or he wouldn't have asked. There was only one answer to give. 'The flashy young prick, sir, was State Duma Chairman, Sergey Grizlov.'

'Indeed.' Lagutov's expression remained unchanged. He took back the file, slid it to one side of his desk, and rested his chin in steepled fingers. 'Russia is filled with such stories and their contradictions.' He took a pen from a cradle and wrote a note on white Kremlin letterhead note paper. Without folding it or using an envelope, he gave it to Yumatov. It read: 'Sergey, please work with Colonel Yumatov.' There was a single line scrawl of a signature.

'I will soon ask Grizlov to be my Foreign Minister,' Lagutov said. 'Take it to him. If Russia is to be modern and at ease with herself, it will take the charms of the man who ruined your family.'

Yumatov suppressed a smile at the successful outcome. He could not have hoped for better and had misjudged Russia's President as a lame duck. He was also convinced that Lagutov was far too clever to be allowed to live.

'Thank you, sir. I will.' Yumatov turned to leave,

'And when is the next military exercise?' Lagutov asked as he was reaching the door.

'December 15th to 23rd next year.'

'Then I have plenty of time to think about your suggestion.'

Yumatov was unsure how much Grizlov knew about him. The Foreign Minister turned in from the window. 'If you're not certain, Colonel, let me recap for both of us,' Grizlov said. 'The purpose of this initiative is to usher in a new era of trust between Russia and the West. A major obstacle has been a routine NATO military exercise on our borders that reeks of war. Our plan is for Russia to initiate a face-to-face meeting between Presidents Lagutov and

Merrow during Dynamic Freedom. The Norwegians have agreed to host the summit, but nothing is to be shared with the Americans until the Kremlin issues an official invitation.'

Yumatov said nothing. Grizlov stepped further into the room. 'As a sweetener, we offered naval intelligence to the Americans, a gesture of cooperation and goodwill, in security terms, relatively harmless. You arranged for the material to be delivered to the US Defense Intelligence Agency via the Norwegian Intelligence Service. It was not sent electronically because the size of the file could have alerted our intelligence services. The Americans chose the route across the border and hired the courier, a British freelance, Gerald Cooper. He was murdered outside of Murmansk. We don't know by whom. You then tried to deliver the same data direct to the British Embassy using Vice-Admiral Artyom Semenov. He, too, was murdered. My question, again, Colonel: who are we up against? Our own government? Your colleagues in the military? The Americans who don't want peace with Russia?'

'I believe this is the work of a crime syndicate from the Far East based out of Vladivostok,' said Yumatov.

Grizlov raised his eyebrows. 'Vladivostok is a long way from Murmansk.'

'The syndicate represents the interests of China, Japan, and North and South Korea with the aim of spreading influence through Asia to Europe. Any alliance we make with the West will threaten its plans.'

'And how did this syndicate know what we were doing?'

'Through the Americans.'

'The Americans? How?'

'The syndicate uses the name Extreme Path or Gokudo, which is the old translation for the Japanese Yakuza. American gangsters are patriotic and cannot be seen to be supporting Chinese-led crime, because American crime goes deep into their defense and political establishment. Japan is an ally, so a US–Japanese crime alliance, in their minds, is acceptable. That is how Gokudo knew how to intercept both Cooper and Semenov.'

Grizlov whistled through his teeth. 'Can you fix it?'

'I believe so, sir. It might be messy.'

'Damned if I've worked this hard only to see my country

become an Asian gangster state. Fix it, Colonel, and we'll clean up the mess afterwards.'

An hour later, Yumatov trod slowly through the Gorky Park snow, hands deep in pockets, head raised to feel the weather on his face. He walked toward the river, shrouded with blurring lights from the Kymsky Bridge. Slow-moving barges pushed through ice floes on the water.

His account to Grizlov had been convincing and most of it accurate. Black-market Asian money was pouring into Russia but Yumatov had not revealed his own role in bringing in the Japanese Gokudo as his partners. Nor would he. Sergey Grizlov and others needed to be punished. They had lined their pockets by sucking up to the West and ruining the lives of hard-working Russians. Revenge would taste very sweet indeed. Grizlov's people would know they could never fuck with the Russian people again. With upheaval inevitable there would be a run on the ruble and Yumatov needed Asian money to prop it up because the money around Moscow and St Petersburg was too entangled with Europe.

On leaving Grizlov, Yumatov had called an urgent meeting with the Gokudo, who had suggested Gorky Park where, in this weather, it would be deathly cold, and they could talk unseen and undisturbed.

Yumatov spotted his contact pacing up and down by two empty benches. He had expected a familiar face, but this was a slight, bespectacled kid with Asiatic features. Yumatov raised his hand in a wave. The young man took off a glove and held out his hand. 'I am Ivan,' he said. 'Welcome.'

Yumatov shook his hand and saw that the tip of the left-hand little finger was missing, a traditional punishment and act of loyalty toward a Gokudo member's superior. Ivan's face showed a nervousness as if the mission were out of his league.

'The shooting outside the British Embassy does not jeopardize our operation,' said Yumatov.

'We know about the shooting and that Vice-Admiral Semenov was carrying technical data that would destroy your plan.'

'The data is secure.'

'We also know you have Dr Walker.'

Yumatov had called the meeting but his business partners were steps ahead of him. Ivan spoke precisely as if he were wired and his words scripted. 'I am instructed to tell you that unless we see Semenov's data, funds will be withdrawn, and our partnership will be shut down.'

Yumatov bundled his black woolen scarf tighter around his neck and buttoned the collar of his military greatcoat. 'I understand your concern.'

'I am instructed to ask on what grounds you trusted Vice-Admiral Semenov,' Ivan said. 'Because of that mistake, we have these problems now.'

'In any operation, a setback is rarely caused by one single mishap,' answered Yumatov.

Ivan took off his spectacles and wiped them clean, only to find wind driving new snow onto them, melting and smearing with the warmth of the lens. 'My task is to return with any response you might have.'

Yumatov stepped so close that their breath clouds mixed. 'I will deal with this issue. Our enemies will never see Semenov's file. Nor will you until the operation is complete.'

'That is not the answer we were hoping for.' Ivan had given up with the spectacles, which he held tensely in his gloved hand.

'Then, report back and we'll meet again soon.' Yumatov held out his hand. As Ivan's arm came forward, Yumatov grabbed it. With lightning speed, he held the little finger, snapped it back inside the glove at the point it joined the hand, twisted it, and moved it back and forth. Ivan's face creased. He sucked his lower lip and bit down with his upper teeth to counter the excruciating agony. 'We have an agreement, and those who break their word and threaten Russia pay the price.' Yumatov let the hand go. 'Make sure your people have the funds your promised.'

Yumatov walked away toward the grand colonnade entrance of the Gorky Park Museum. Four of his Zaslon men fell into step back and front of him, big, black-clad figures, openly carrying weapons for the Gokudo to see. Giving them Semenov's data would be handing it to the Japanese, who would go straight to the Pentagon and NATO. But, then, if Gokudo knew about Semenov's death and Carrie's kidnap, they would know where she was now, which meant Semenov's material was far from secure.

TWENTY-SEVEN

Carrie's captors had let her keep her watch. She checked the time. 21:08. They had given her water, sparkling, a bottle of Narzan, a glass. She could have smashed it and used its jagged edges as a weapon. Except not with her two captors, identities hidden under black balaclavas. They were cool and self-assured. They gave her food, a packet of Lay's white mushroom and sour cream crisps. When she finished, she lifted up both bound hands and wiped grease off her lips. She picked crumbs off her lap and flipped them onto the floor. She smoothed and folded the empty green crisps bag, making it smaller and smaller into a tiny square while her captors watched without reacting. Three times she asked for the bathroom. Three times she got no response.

The van was parked up somewhere. Lights streaked through its blackened windows. Horns blared. Sirens. Occasionally, voices, a group walking close by. They were in a parking lot or a side street. Four times the side door had slid open. Snow swept in with freezing air. Carrie dug her bare feet into the van's floor carpet. Stuff was handed in, food, a tablet, an envelope. Not a word was spoken.

At 21:14, the door opened smoothly like a low-frequency drum roll, steel casters on a well-greased mechanism. A vehicle head-light glared, causing Carrie to squint. Two boxes were delivered. The door closed. The captor opposite drew a small knife from his belt and opened the first box. There was a phone inside with original packing, a Chinese Huawei Android. He did the same with the second, an Apple iPhone also in original packing. He turned them on and worked the keyboards to test them. He took out earphones, charger, and cables. He pulled two slim weather-proof zip bags from his pocket, put a phone with its accessories in each. He offered them to Carrie like a plate of food. She put them on her lap. The other captor, the one sitting next to her, sent a message from his phone.

The van moved off. The captor opposite cut her wrist cuffs with his knife. His colleague reached over to the back and gave her her boots and socks, scarf and hat. She put them on, balancing in her seat, as the van turned and turned again.

'So, is that it, guys?' she said, drawing on reserves of confidence. 'Is it party time?'

There was no answer. The iPhone buzzed. A message in Russian. 'Check into the hotel. Room paid for.'

What hotel? What room? The van stopped in a side street with streaks of lamps and headlights through the tinted glass. The captor opposite opened the door. He whipped off his balaclava, stood up, and got out.

She glanced at the other one. He nodded. *Go.* She checked her leg strength and balance, got out carefully and stiffened with the cold. The captor offered his hand to her elbow. She studied him, mid-twenties, short blond-brown hair, life in his eyes, a guy at the end of a shift about to go home.

'Thank you,' she said.

'Good luck,' he replied in English. He handed her her uncle's flash drive in a Ziploc transparent bag together with a small brown envelope. He got back into the van, pulled on his balaclava, and closed the door. The van drove off. The number plate was smeared with dirt and ice and unreadable. She faced a budget hotel, part of a chain all around Europe that she had used a few times.

She was in central Moscow, with two new phones which would track her wherever she was. She opened the envelope. A new dark-green American passport. The owner, Dr Carrie Walker, with her photograph, her accurate date of birth, and a Russian visa and entry stamp with her arrival date today. The passport photo was not her current one, but it was her. Nor was it her passport number. But overall this was a good job. Taped to the back was her MasterCard, gray and plain, but the same sixteen-digit number, same three-digit CCV security code on the back.

The hotel lobby was brightly lit. A Chinese couple sat on an orange bench sofa, looking at a map. A young European guy with a dirty red backpack stood at the reception counter. To the right of the main entrance was a restaurant.

She walked through the revolving doors enveloped with

warmth. The receptionist, young, long black hair, Asian-looking, smiled, and welcomed Carrie in English. Carrie reeled off the booking reference which came up straightaway. The receptionist hooked her hair behind her right ear, looked across the lobby, half lifted her hand to beckon a porter, and broke into a frown seeing no one there.

She tore off a numbered luggage tag attached to Carrie's booking document. 'There's stuff for you to pick up.' She apologized to a couple who had arrived behind Carrie, then walked along the counter to a door that opened into a luggage room, shelves of backpacks and suitcases, tags hanging off handles and zippers. Carrie followed. The receptionist lifted out Carrie's hand-carry case, the one she flew in with and had left at the Intercontinental on Tverskaya Street.

'Someone dropped this off for you before I came on shift,' said the receptionist.

'Oh yeah. Thanks.' Carrie answered as if she were expecting it. She stared at the case, last neatly placed in the small hotel room wardrobe, now here. The receptionist said Carrie was in room 416, turn left at the top of the lift, to the end, a quiet room with a queen bed as requested on the booking. Carrie took the small cardboard envelope with two electronic keys, the room number hand-written at the bottom. Carrie moved toward the elevator. One of the phones rang. The iPhone.

'Get out, Carrie. It's dangerous. You're not safe.' An instruction and an explanation.

'Who are you?'

'Go, Carrie. Go now.' English. East coast American. Traces of a foreign accent. Carrie was in the middle of the lobby halfway to the elevator bank. She scanned the outside. No black vans. No smeared number plates.

'Tell me who you are, or I cut this call, throw both these phones away, and walk straight into the American embassy.'

'You won't make it, Carrie. You'll end up like your uncle.'

A jolt of panic. 'Who are you?' A low, tight barely audible whisper.

'You do not recognize my voice?'

She didn't. *Don't plead. Don't show fear.* 'Stop dicking around and—'

'I am Colonel Ruslan Yumatov.'

Carrie brought her hand up to her face in a jerk of a movement that prompted the receptionist to look across. She tried to remember the smarmy Russian officer from the Diomede, oblong head like a bad sculptor, blond hair neatly styled, tall cheekbones, narrow mouth, and smooth skin, like a model. She pulled her case to the edge of the counter. She tried to sound in control: 'Is it you handing out phones, changing my hotel room, cooping me up in a van all these hours?'

'Get out of that hotel, Carrie.'

'And go where?'

'Out of Russia.'

'How?' Her question pleaded a straight answer.

'St Petersburg. Once there, a ferry ticket to Helsinki. I will arrange it and call you. The credit card I gave you is clean. Keep the phones.'

Yes, now she remembered Ruslan Yumatov, smooth, merciless, showing her dead body after dead body on Little Diomedes.

'I tried to help you before, Carrie. I couldn't. Now I can. If either of us are to survive this, you need to trust me.'

The line cut. The lobby bustled. People came in stamping feet, blowing on hands. The receptionist slid key packs across the counter. There was laughter and foreign languages.

Carrie sat on the sofa next to a Chinese couple, huddled over a tourist map. A wet gust of sleet cut across the street outside. If Yumatov was setting her up, would she be safer here? If she walked out, would it be into another black van with smeared plates? Would she be greeted by a smiling, welcoming man who would shoot her dead like her uncle.

She remembered Yumatov's line from the Diomede that they were two small people caught in a screwed-up world running out of control. Therefore, she should work with him. She watched the pace of the hotel. Check-ins. Check-outs. The flow to and from the restaurant; to and from the washrooms; to and from the elevator banks.

Carrie formed an idea. She stayed where she was and waited. The Chinese couple left. An elderly German couple, walking poles dripping with melting ice, took their place on the sofa. There were two women checking in at reception, mid-thirties, a calm brunette and an impatient blonde. They spoke Quebec French and English with Canadian accents, arguing with the receptionist about not being allowed to take their luggage into the restaurant.

'I am sorry.' A roll of the eyes from the receptionist. 'I did not design the hotel. Please, take your bags to the storeroom.' She tore off luggage tags for each case, one black, one yellow. They were hand-carry style with wheels. The brunette held open the luggage-room door. Carrie could see in. The blonde lifted the two bags onto a middle shelf. They left. Midway to the steps that led to the restaurant, the brunette remonstrated and pointed back. The blonde said. 'It'll be fine. No one will touch it.'

A tour bus pulled up right outside, windshield wipers on full. South Koreans came in, led by a guide with a national flag above his head.

The receptionist's attention moved onto new guests. Carrie slipped into the luggage room and closed the door. The brunette's yellow case sat at eye level, wheels out. Carrie turned it round. The main case was locked, but not the outer zipper pockets. Carrie opened one. There were a pack of tissues, gum, Halls lozenges. She unzipped the top pocket. There was a plastic transparent folder with flight schedules, hotels. The black case was to the left, wheels in, no need to turn it round. Carrie zipped open the bigger top pocket, slipped her hand inside, and felt a linen pouch, a money belt. It was empty. A thrum of irritation ripped through her. A walking pole was strapped to another case. She slid it out and levered the weak lock until it broke. Inside, there was a transparent plastic bag with a passport, credit cards, driving license, the works. She tried a bulging side pocket and her run of luck continued. There was a phone and charge cable, but no adaptor. Enough. No need to press her luck. She undid her own case, put toiletries and underwear in a small grab bag, and closed it. She opened the door an inch and froze.

Ruslan Yumatov had warned her, and they were here. Military-style men fanned out through the lobby. Or were they his men, looking for her?

Carrie counted four, working in pairs. They were plainclothed and their side arms holstered. They moved as if they owned the place. The receptionist ignored them, working through a pile of

South Korean passports. The tour group clustered to the right of the door. Two of the men spoke to a back-packing couple. The woman, late twenties, long dark hair, showed her passport to them. They didn't ask to see the man's passport. Once they had covered the lobby, they would move onto the washrooms, the luggage rooms, the restaurant.

Carrie pulled her black woolen hat over her head and ears. She wrapped her red scarf around her, right up over her nose. She opened the door of the luggage room, walked out, and turned left toward the washroom. She didn't look back. She pushed open the washroom door, went into an empty end cubicle. The women's washroom was not the place for a showdown with male Russian thugs. It was a place to prepare and gather resolve. For reasons unknown, her captors had given her back her uncle's flash drive. She needed to honor him by getting it out of Russia. That would be at risk if she kept it in her jacket pocket. She unwrapped a tampon, worked it loose, closed it round the drive, and lubricated it generously.

She left the washroom, holding the door so it closed quietly without a rush of air. The lobby was packed, the guests nervous and edgy about the intrusion. People were gathered outside. The South Korean tour bus was still there, engine on, baggage doors open. The driver had his hand over his eyes looking toward the end of the street. Carrie walked swiftly, wheeling her case, pushing through, passed the reception desk, passed steps to the restaurant, passed the orange sofa, through a cluster of South Koreans blocking the revolving door. She pushed the cold, wet edge of the revolving door with her free hand.

Two of the military men stepped in front of her. They had stubble. One had a bent nose, broken long ago and set badly. His eyes were red, and his breath reeked of tobacco. These were not the same caliber as in the van. 'Passport,' he demanded, holding out his hand.

'Excusez-moi,' said Carrie.

'Passport.' French. Russian. English. Passport sounded pretty much the same anywhere.

Carrie drew the dark-blue Canadian passport from her outer pocket and handed it to him. The photo wasn't unlike her. The name was Gagnon, Sofia Alice. His colleague said: 'Hat. Off.'

Carrie peeled back the hat, held it in her right hand. Her blonde hair fell. In the passport, the hair was brown. The colleague tapped the open page. Carrie spoke in Russian, a few words, as if she was learning it on a podcast. 'Brown. Now blonde. I dyed it.'

The one holding the passport, lowered his head, conferring with his colleague. 'No,' he said. 'Mayer. Walker. Not Gagnon.' The colleague nodded. Carrie took back her passport. She began putting her hat back on.

'Stop,' said the one behind. Carrie held the hat midway to her head, stared at him, using every strength to rein back her *who the hell are you* look. 'Where you go now? It's late.'

'Convenience store. Water. Some food.' She looked down at her bag. 'To carry back.' All in bad Russian mixed with bad English. They had lost interest. Their eyes were on other blondes arriving in the thirties age range. Their task was to find a woman with a passport that read Sarah Mayer or Carrie Walker. They were not Yumatov's people. But he knew who they were, that they were coming, that they were dangerous.

Outside, wind and sleet hit her hard. She pushed through people around the bus whose engine and headlights pointed toward the end of the street.

'Be careful.' A male voice in English; may have been speaking to her; may have been to someone else. Carrie cleared the crowd. There were less people on the sidewalk, mostly Russians, familiar with how their city worked. She asked what was going on. Police were at the end of the street, best to cross the road and keep outside the cordon.

Two police cars were parked at angles across the road, their blue and red lights static. Cops signaled pedestrians to stick to the sidewalk and keep moving. Beyond the cordon, as she got closer, she made out dark shapes, smudges within shadows, a meat wagon for corpses, two ambulances, security and police vehicles. A black minivan was skewed across the road. A cop shone in a flashlight. Carrie drew a sharp intake of breath, cold on her tongue and back of her throat. She stopped without thinking. A cop told her to keep going. Carrie obeyed, bumping her case along ridges of ice. She kept her gaze on the vehicle, her black van, the Mercedes Sprinter, its windscreen shattered. A man's body collapsed over the steering wheel. Dead. Lines of bullet holes along the side, clear, jagged holes through which she could see lights from the other side.

Two bodies lay on the snow, faces covered, torsos bloodied. Police made way for a senior officer, wearing a black ankle-length greatcoat. Two cops crouched down, lifted the dead men's heads and pulled off their black balaclavas.

Carrie stayed with the flow, walking quickly, looking back like everyone else. She recognized her captor, the one who wished her luck, the guy with no emotion who had given her the phones, whom she clocked as looking forward to the end of his shift. She slowed again, couldn't help it, until a cop told her to go. Her phone vibrated. It was Yumatov calling from the same number as before. She ignored it. Instead, she used the Canadian phone to message Rake.

TWENTY-EIGHT

The Pentagon, Arlington County, Virginia

'We need the room.' Rake slid his phone across to show Lucas the latest message from Carrie. *$750 in rubles, Western Union, Moscow Leningradsky. $750 St Petersburg tomorrow by 10.00. Sofia Alice Gagnon.*

'With respect, Major,' objected the CIA agent Jeff Auden, 'you do not have the authority to clear this room.'

There was a murmur of agreement from different agencies, one moment at each other's throats, the next fighting for a common cause.

'Congressman Lucas, General Whyte, Detective Wekstatt, and myself,' said Rake. 'The rest need to leave now.'

Rake included Whyte because the marine general was the highest-ranking military figure, and this was a Pentagon room. He needed Mikki to watch his back, and Lucas because he held sway in a way that Rake had yet to work out. Auden whispered to others. Heads shook. Phones lit as messages were punched in. Rake said, 'General Whyte, could you give the order, please.'

'It's not up to you, General,' interjected Auden. 'If you want this room cleared, you will need authorization from ODNI, Director of National Intelligence.'

Dozens of rooms throughout Washington would be filled like this one, similar distrust, same topic. What made this special was that Rake, Wekstatt, and Whyte were here, the men at the heart of the action. Anyone who voluntarily left this room would be ceding ground to rivals.

'Then we'll do this somewhere else,' said Rake. Mikki headed toward the door.

'Hold it right there, Detective,' said Jeff Auden. 'On whose authority—'

'Alaska State Police,' said Rake. 'If you want to stop him

walking out that door, you need to call the Alaska Department of Public Safety.'

Lucas' chair scraped back. He glanced at Rake as if to say *trust me*. He stood in front of Auden, touched his elbow, gave time for his gaze to travel the room so he had everyone's attention. 'You need to loosen up, Jeff. We've lost people in the field. There is a leak. We don't know who or where, but it's lethal. We have an American citizen on the ground in Moscow who needs help. We're against the clock. For us to deliver that safely, you have to leave.'

'I'll need more than that.' Auden held Lucas' gaze.

Others shuffled, heads lowered, weighing career choices: Side with Auden? Side with Lucas?

Whyte stepped in: 'In the interests of national security, you all need to get the hell out.'

'You get the signature of the ODNI, I'll comply,' said Auden. 'If not, I represent Director Ciszewski, and I stay.'

Rake took Auden's left wrist and bent his arm behind his back, just below the point it would break. Mikki gripped his right arm and held open the door. Rake pushed him through into the corridor. Auden didn't resist and the way Rake read his face, anger in his eyes, how an animal communicates threat, Auden's enemy was not Rake, Wekstatt, or Whyte. It was Lucas. Maybe they had history.

Like tidal waters, people followed. The FBI led. Rake didn't keep track of the other twenty or so who filed out. The door closed.

'Do we know it's her?' said Whyte as he read Carrie's message.

Lucas pulled up a satellite map of Moscow. 'The phone is registered to a number in Montreal, Canada under the name Sofia Alice Gagnon. Gagnon is a pediatric nurse at Montreal Children's Hospital. She entered Russia through St Petersburg three days ago. She took the train to Moscow today. Gagnon checked into this hotel, here just over two hours ago, a three-star, frequented by tour groups and budget travelers. Her phone is currently, here, half a mile north, by the Peter and Paul Church. The phone keeps moving north, logical destination would be Moscow's Lenigradsky Railway Station where she's asked to pick up money and more in St Petersburg. It's now eight past midnight in Moscow. The next train to St Petersburg is at 01.15, which gives us just over an hour.'

'I'll be damned,' said Whyte. 'She stole the phone and passport.'

'How long's she got?' asked Rake.

'The theft hasn't been reported yet,' said Lucas. 'At least until the train leaves. At a stretch until morning.'

Carrie had requested clever amounts, fifty dollars below what would have needed a higher level of authorization, a passport number and an ID reference. Less than $800 and Carrie could collect with a picture ID at the Western Union rail station sub-offices, which were dotted around Moscow. She would need to answer two confidential questions and she could walk away with some 50,000 rubles, enough to pay cash for a first-class ticket to St Petersburg and a flight or ferry to Helsinki. The 'send' instruction would go with a Homeland Security tag at the US end, meaning that Western Union, an American company, would clear its path and fast-track the money. It should be ready for Carrie within minutes.

'Security questions?' asked Lucas.

'Favorite Italian restaurant. Answer: Boccaccio. Favorite color: yellow.'

'These are subjective, not factual,' said Lucas.

'They'll be fine.' Rake and Carrie had discussed Boccaccio's menu and the pros and cons of yellow as a favorite color enough times to lock them in concrete. If she didn't know them, this wasn't Carrie. If she was, she would know Rake was the sender. Lucas punched keys to transfer the money.

Rake said, 'We need to get a new passport for her to St Petersburg. The theft of the one she's using will be discovered by then.'

'We have a consulate there,' said Whyte.

'Possibly.' Lucas sounded unconvinced. He was concentrating on numbers across the screen as the money went through. Rake read his skepticism. They had yet to identify the breach that had left so many dead.

'The consulate is safer than leaving her exposed on the street,' answered Whyte.

'We need a guaranteed option,' said Rake. 'Not the best of bad choices.'

'Done,' said Lucas. 'Seven hundred fifty dollars to Leningradsky

Station. Seven hundred fifty to St Petersburg station. Pick-up anytime.' He swiveled round to look at Rake. 'I've set up an account with another Montreal-registered phone. From that we will message back "done." More letters than that, there would be a chance of it being detected. She'll have to trust it's from you.'

'Then it needs to be more personal,' said Rake.

'Like what?'

Rake pulled up his sleeve where his O-negative blood group was tattooed on his right forearm. Carrie had told Rake that if he wanted to marry her and stay a soldier, he would have to get his blood group tattooed onto his body. She didn't want to have her husband die because of something as dumb as not getting the right blood transfusion. They ended up having it done together. Carrie carried her A+ on her inside right wrist.

'O-neg,' said Rake.

'Good,' said Lucas, pressing a key.

'That money won't make Carrie safe.'

'I know,' said Lucas.

Attention went to the live shot of Dmitry Petrov, the Russian cameraman in the FBI interrogation room. A left column appeared of the identities of his two dead Russian colleagues, headshots, passport details, brief biography, brief family history, whatever was in the intelligence community files.

The one Mikki Wekstatt had killed was Valentyn Golov, aged sixty-three, former spetsnaz sniper, attached to 14th Separate Special Purpose Brigade based out of Ussuriysk about seventy miles north of Vladivostok, where he now lived. The tall one whom Rake had killed was Adrik Syanko, a serving sergeant in the 83rd Airborne Brigade, also based in Ussuriysk, aged forty-one.

'Yumatov's unit,' said Rake

'You know them?' asked Lucas.

'Those units were deployed to the Diomedes and would have been under Yumatov's command.' Rake recognized names, first Golov, then Syanko, on Russian casualty lists from the Diomedes. But these were not the Russian soldiers he had killed. 'We need to match their facial recognition with Yumatov,' he said.

'On it,' said Lucas.

While the computers did their work, Rake ran a plan through

his mind. What they were doing now wasn't good enough. Russia
was ten steps ahead of them, even more, because in Washington,
they weren't even off the starting block yet. They didn't even
know there was a starting block.

Within minutes, facial-recognition matches began coming in.

'This is worse than we thought,' said Lucas.

'We need to get there,' said Rake. Lucas agreed.

Harry Lucas rode in front with the driver. Rake and Mikki were
in the back, the same vehicle that had brought them into the
Pentagon. Whyte, on the jump seat, faced them. They headed
south past Ronald Reagan National Airport, through Potomac
Yard into Alexandria and were running parallel to the
Potomac River. There was a black night sky, stars and thin
moonlight reflected on the river water.

Dozens of matches had come in from facial recognition of the
two dead Russians, Valentyn Golov and Adrik Syanko, with Ruslan
Yumatov. One photograph and two phone videos stood out.

The images showed a memorial ceremony, bleak light, harsh
rain, dark, cloud-scudded skies by the river outside Khabarovsk,
headquarters city of Russia's Eastern Military District. Golov and
Syanko, identified by red circles around their faces, were gathered
in a group of fifty-three people, wives, children, a military family
affair with national flags and regimental emblems. At a podium
stood Russian President Viktor Lagutov, a man of no great
charisma. At his side was Sergey Grizlov, then Speaker of the
State Duma, skilled at manipulating Russian political sentiment.
Next to him stood the Chief of the General Staff of the Armed
Forces, Makar Za, and a line of dignitaries. At the edge was
Ruslan Yumatov, neither with the families nor with the dignitaries,
vigilant as if it were his show, in full-length military coat, war
medals, and a Soviet old-style gray sheepskin hat, embedded red
star in the front. Golov and Syanko were fathers grieving for sons
killed in action and honored with this ceremony.

There were phone videos of Yumatov escorting Lagutov from
the podium and initiating a discussion with Lagutov, Grizlov,
and Za in a conspiratorial huddle. Yumatov held a large red
umbrella over them all, collars up against an oncoming downpour.
Finally, another of Yumatov opening the back door of a Mercedes

limousine for Grizlov, then walking round and getting in the back seat to ride with him.

Lucas had arranged a plane and passports for them and Carrie, ten hours to Helsinki and from there a commercial flight to St Petersburg by noon. Carrie's train, if on time, arrived around 11.00. She would have a vulnerable hour on the streets, but by then they could guide her.

'Why can't she go to the consulate?' Whyte asked again.

'She wouldn't trust it,' said Rake.

'We let her down,' corroborated Lucas. 'The Brits let her down. If I were her, I would feel safer outside of our protection.'

'Why Ozenna?' insisted Whyte as if Rake wasn't there.

Rake let Lucas continue. 'Dr Walker knows him. She sent Ozenna the message. No one else. Once she gets a visual sighting of Ozenna, she will trust his lead.'

Lucas had secured a plane to leave from Andrews Air Force Base within the hour. It would take Rake and Mikki to Helsinki, then drop Whyte at the Bodø Air Station, Norway's joint armed forces command center, eight hundred miles north of Oslo, also command center for the Dynamic Freedom exercise. Lucas had argued that Whyte should go because he had become involved randomly, by being on Rake's panel, no previous skin in the game. Whyte hadn't needed persuading. With all that was going down, Dynamic Freedom would be good for anyone's CV. Lucas would stay in Washington, DC.

A Gulfstream G550 was fueled up, waiting, blue and white, a US Air Force plane, too big for the three of them, but one that was available, pilots in the cockpit checking flight plans, plenty of range, seven thousand miles, meaning they could turn back to Andrews at any time. An air force sergeant, rugged up in a black windbreaker, met them and gave Lucas three passports with matching driver's licenses. He flipped through and handed them to Rake. They were high quality, even had Finnish entry stamps for him and Mikki. Rake was John William Gray; Mikki, Vincent Douglas Joseph; Carrie, Hilary Elizabeth Lawrence with her real photo and year of birth. Hers had a Russian entry stamp and a visa that ran for another two weeks. They were all US citizens.

Mikki and Whyte climbed the steps to board. Lucas ushered

Rake under the aircraft's wing out of the windchill. 'You asked why Carrie is in Moscow.' Lucas' face was creased and not against the weather. 'Semenov called her. Carrie called Ambassador Lucas, who brought me in. Carrie spoke to Semenov three times. We didn't know what he had, how many lives it might save, whether it was gold dust or bullshit. Semenov wanted his sister, Carrie's mother, to be with him. That was when Carrie insisted that she go.'

'But you made it happen.' Rake brushed rain off his face, trying to work out how straight Lucas was being with him.

'She had the bit between her teeth. She knows Moscow. She speaks Russian. She has good track in dealing with difficult situations. I had no idea it would be so dangerous.'

'When did you know?' Rake lifted his arm against a ferocious gust of wind. His sleeve slid back, ice drizzle on his skin.

'First, when you found the human ear. It turns out the Defense Intelligence Agency was running the operation that brought you to northern Norway. It was expecting classified Russian naval information. Instead it got the severed ear of the man tasked to get it across the border. His body has been found near Murmansk. He is British and the Russians cremated him without formalities. DIA didn't loop in any other agency. From facial recognition, we know more things are piecing together. The attack on you has a direct connection to Yumatov and the Diomede crisis. Carrie's uncle must be connected to the DIA border operation. The timing, too, is significant, right before Dynamic Freedom.'

Rake pushed the toe of his boot through a rivulet running across a kink in the tarmac. He understood more, but not enough. He looked across to Lucas, taking a squall of rain on his face. 'Who's authorizing you?'

Lucas met Rake's drizzle-swept gaze. 'When Ambassador Lucas called, I reached out into government at a high level and was warned that this could not go higher. President Merrow is deaf to hearing anything bad about Russia. He is obsessed with using it to contain China. Even so, the intelligence community needs to know what Semenov had. I was authorized to set up a standalone operation, and that's what this is.'

Rake didn't like the shape it was taking, nor that Carrie was the target. Lucas was running something outside government because when it turned to shit it would be deniable. A steward with an umbrella stood at the top of the airplane steps. Lucas raised his voice against another gust of wind.

'We won't know exactly what the stakes are until we retrieve the flash drive, which is what you need to get. You have a personal relationship with Carrie Walker, and she trusts you. But listen hard, Ozenna. Your task is to retrieve that drive whatever the cost.'

Rake understood, and anger rose within him. He loved Carrie; could never shake that off even though they had become strangers to each other. A howl of wind tore round the fuselage, trembling the end of the wing. 'Off the books!' he shouted. 'With an air force plane, access to every intelligence database. Off the books. Bullshit.'

'Off the books from the White House,' Lucas conceded. 'That's how things are nowadays.'

Rake didn't give a damn about government squabbles. He cared about Carrie. 'While we're in the air you need to do some-thing.' Rake delivered it as a condition. A flashlight shone down from the aircraft steps. It was time to go. Lucas kept his attention on Rake, both faces lashed with rain. 'By the time I'm in Helsinki, we need to know how in the hell Yumatov is involved in this,' said Rake. 'You want a link. He's the link. We want to beat this, he's the one to beat. The head of the snake.'

Lucas' expression didn't change. He ignored the rain, ignored the flashlight beam. He didn't show if he agreed with Rake, if he thought Rake was overreacting. 'If I had known, I would never have let Carrie go to Moscow,' he said. 'But we are where we are, Ozenna, and I need to trust you on this. I am truly sorry it is Carrie.'

TWENTY-NINE

Moscow

The Western Union office for Moscow's Leningradsky rail station doubled up as an electronics store, selling phones and local cards, a clothes stall with hats, scarves, gloves, and T-shirts, and a souvenir shop with Russian dolls and Moscow ornaments. It was flanked by competing stores on the edge of the station in Komsomolskaya Square, a vast area, where three rail stations served different areas of Russia, busy even at this time of night, bursting with Christmas lights. Kazansky station dealt with the east and southeast; Yaroslavsky station handled the Trans-Siberian; and Leningradsky, where Carrie was heading, sent trains west to St Petersburg and Europe.

Carrie walked past the Western Union store twice, wheeling her hand-carry, watching for threats within a regular hum of life, the elegant, grand curves, the spires, columns, clock towers, colors, taxi lines, the flow of people, a direct opposite to Moscow and the corpses and shot-up van she had passed just over a mile away near her hotel.

On her phone were scrolls of messages from Sofia Gagnon's friends and families, asking her to be safe, telling her they envied her travels, missing her, recommending the Café Pushkin in Tverskor Boulevard, 'not as posh as it looks,' and was she going to Peredelkino, the village outside Moscow where Boris Pasternak had lived. Amid them was Rake's message, short, coded in a way that she knew it was him – *O-neg*.

She allowed herself an inner smile. It was intimate and clever. The message had been routed through a Montreal server, which meant he had resources to do that kind of technical thing and that gave her confidence.

Carrie waited in line at the Western Union counter. Two customers ahead of her moved quickly along. She showed the

Canadian passport, kept hold of it, and said in broken English with a French accent. 'I have money to collect.'

The wire-thin young man behind the counter in a black woolen hat and black leather jacket with a crucifix earing hanging from his right ear was fast and alert. He punched in the name, looked back at the exchange rates listed on a screen, and said. 'Two questions, Miss Sofia Gagnon. Favorite Italian restaurant and favorite color?'

Rake again, bringing them together, making sure she knew it was him.

'Boccaccio,' she said, 'and yellow.'

He looked down, punched more buttons, shook his head. 'No, sorry, Sofia. That's not correct. No money.' He worked on the keyboard beneath the counter.

Carrie broke into Russian, not fluent, traveling podcast level. 'Say the questions again.'

'This is not a guessing game, Sofia. Please, respect the regulations of Western Union.' His expression was stern. Carrie ran through options. She could risk the credit card and get picked up immediately. She could—

'Only kidding, Sofia.' Laughter pealed from behind the counter. 'You see, because your favorite Italian restaurant should be Grabli, do you know it, in Arbat Street. My uncle owns it. I can take you there.' He waved at the line behind. 'One moment. One moment.' He pushed an envelope of rubles across to her. 'You can count, but it is right. I have never got it wrong. 48,933 rubles. I give you 48,000 and with the 933, you can take a beautiful new hat and scarf and a souvenir for your loved one.'

Carrie fingered through the nine orange-brown 5,000 ruble notes and four blue 2,000 notes. 'Can you break one of these down into thousands,' she said.

He slid over five crisp new notes. Carrie picked a red floral hat, matching scarf, two plain blue T-shirts, two burner phones and SIM cards, and two tiny flash drives almost identical to the one she carried in her pocket from her Uncle Artyom. As she glanced back, he reached across with a bag. 'That much, Sofia?' His lips pursed in a quizzical frown.

'How much do I owe you?'

'Give me a thousand.' He gave a grand gesture of his right

hand, then said: 'Forget it. You are beautiful. On the house, Sofia, on condition you have dinner with me at your favorite Italian restaurant when you come back.'

'A deal,' Carrie laughed. A real laugh.

'Happy travels, Sofia. See you soon.'

Carrie walked off, wishing she didn't have to, wishing she could have dinner with the ear-ringed currency whiz-kid at his uncle's Italian restaurant. To buy two tickets, Carrie used the gray and red ticket machines; Moscow to Murmansk leaving at 00.41 third-class open sleeper 7,500 rubles, using the Sofia Gagnon passport number. She fed in notes. On the other, same train, same open carriage lower-bunk sleeper, except only to St Petersburg, costing 3,000 rubles.

She had forty minutes before that train left from platform five. The concourse was designed like a mall with three blue-green levels of shopping and brand names. She found a pharmacy where she bought the most expensive emergency medical kit for 7,000 rubles and over-the-counter medicines like antiseptic cream, pain-killers, lubricant, cough syrup, vitamins, even a stethoscope. Many Russian pharmacists kept antibiotics and other prescription drugs for sale to anyone who claimed to be a doctor. This was one of those pharmacies.

She bought a canvas *I Love Russia* bag for her medical purchases and felt much better with it. As she walked back to the concourse, she used the Huawei Android phone to call Ruslan Yumatov, who was pivotal to her next move. He had given her a warning that may have saved her life. He picked up on the second ring.

'Where are you, Carrie?'

'You know where I am.'

'Yes. At Three Stations Square.'

'That's right.'

Carrie's mother and locals called Komsomolskaya Square, Three Stations Square, pronouncing it just like Yumatov. Her mother argued with her father about how elegant and grand it was, the architecture of Stalin and the Tsar blended into one. Her father denigrated anything in Russia as a Soviet disaster. Three Stations Square was one of those lightning rods for all that was wrong with her parents' marriage.

Yumatov's tracking was out by several hundred yards. Carrie wasn't in Three Stations Square. She was inside Leningradsky Station.

'You are booked on the 1-28 Allegro to Helsinki,' said Yumatov. 'Take your passport to the ticket office. They will issue you the ticket. You have a first-class sleeper.'

'Thank you.'

'Promise you do that, Carrie. I can get you through. The FSB will handle the Helsinki route. The other routes are domestic, controlled by the police, even the GRU, and you will be compromised. Once in Helsinki you will be safe.'

She kept walking to see if Yumatov noticed her moving. 'The men who held me in the van, are they dead?'

'Yes.'

'Did you kill them?'

'No. What happened was terrible.'

'Did you order them to kidnap me?'

'Yes. For your safety.'

'I was going to the British Embassy. That would have been safe.'

'You're not meant to be in Russia, Carrie. This isn't your fight.'

'What do you want from me?'

'I want you safely out of Russia.'

'Then get me through an airport. UA to Washington.'

Yumatov's voice hardened. 'Don't be stupid and stubborn. Do what I say and tomorrow morning you'll be in Europe and safe. Don't and you'll end up shot like those in that van. I am telling you how things are about to go down. It's much bigger than either you or me, Carrie, and you don't want to be here for it.'

'You have my promise.' Carrie kept her tone flat.

'1.28 Allegro to Helsinki. Ticket booked under Sarah Mayer. Use that passport. Your new Carrie Walker is still good as back up. Travel well, Carrie. I hope we can meet in Washington one day and share a coffee.'

Carrie took the Israeli passport from her pocket. She wheeled her hand-carry into the uncrowded ticket office and straight to an empty booth where she showed the passport. A few seconds later she had her ticket, just as Yumatov had described. All she had to do now was board the train and wake up in the morning in Finland. If the rest of the day was any marker, her chances of that happening were not good.

The train was sleek and elegant, pastel gray, with emblems of red. A steward, a young good-looking blond man, showed her in her cabin, one up from the restaurant car, and how the bunk went up and down. When he left, Carrie shut the door. She lifted her bag onto the bed and sorted through clothes. She changed. She slid her bag onto the luggage rack with the Android Huawei phone inside. She left a scarf and a green woolen jersey on the bunk with the iPhone underneath. Both were switched on for clarity of signal.

She put extra clothes, washroom stuff, and what she had bought from the Western Union store into a canvas carrier bag. She inserted SIM cards into her new burner phones, left one off and activated the other. She had 30,000 rubles, about $450 left, and another $750 to pick up in St Petersburg. She had three passports, two false, one authentic, various credit cards, enough of a change of clothes, three phones, none tracked by Yumatov, her uncle's flash drive secured, and two empty drives that would be found in a search.

Sitting on the bunk, she sent the same message to Rake twice, one from the Canadian phone and one from her new burner phone. *A+Tks.* Her blood group and gratitude.

She opened the cabin door, hooked the carrier bag over one shoulder, the first-aid kit over the other, left the Moscow–Helsinki train and joined a flow of passengers onto platform five. The concourse was busier. Carrie looked different. She wore jeans, a white undervest, a blue denim shirt, and the same down jacket, but draped with a large red scarf, more of a shawl. She looked more Russian. The phone signals would locate her on the train and in the sleeper compartment. Two tracks along, at platform five, a burst of steam jetted up from the bright red snout of the 00.41 to St Petersburg and all stations from there to Murmansk.

Carrie had her ticket scanned and there was a cursory passport check. She was traveling Plakstart, third-class, the cheapest and safest way. She would be in a fifty-four-bunk carriage, busy, protected in numbers, many of whom would have been screwed by the system, people wary of authority, loathing of uniforms, suspicious of each other, better to be with them than locked in a luxury cabin waiting for the knock on the door. She found her bunk in an open compartment of four bright blue berths with a carpeted corridor for through traffic. There was no privacy. Three of the bunks were already taken.

Opposite Carrie's bunk lay an emaciated man, thin white hair, watery eyes, gray skin slack around his jaw and cheeks, gripping a walking stick so hard it made his knuckles white. He examined Carrie. She said good evening in native Russian, no podcast accent, this time. She didn't smile. These were poor people living on the edge. Friendliness was a preserve of the rich.

With his free hand shaking, he pointed upwards. One across to the empty bunk. On the top bunk was a man, about forty, with a long scar down the right of his face, sat legs dangling, failing to quieten a restless boy, around nine. He tried to put a brown corduroy jacket on the struggling boy, whose cheeks were blotted and nose running. The task was made more difficult because the man only had one arm. His right arm was amputated above the elbow. Carrie could tell by his awkward movements that he was right-handed.

The man acknowledged her in an embarrassed way. He wasn't doing well. The way his shoulder twitched, the way he turned, Carrie thought he must be imagining he still had the missing arm, only to keep being reminded it wasn't there. His brain had yet to implement the neurological transfer to give his left hand better control. He was failing to work the jacket buttons.

The boy sulked. 'Papa, it's hot. I don't need a jacket.'

'If you sleep, you'll get cold and sicker. That's what your mama would tell you.'

'Mama is not here. What Mama says doesn't count.'

The old man said to Carrie: 'His mama is my daughter. We are going to her wedding.'

Carrie climbed up and sat on the empty bunk opposite them both. 'Are you his dad?' she asked the man.

'His uncle. He calls me Papa because his father has gone.' His face carried scarred dead skin of a burns wound. His left eye was lame. His right held Carrie's gaze steady as if to say he was no one's servant, no one's victim. 'I am Hektor Tolstoye. Like the famous writer but not.'

'I am Sofia.' Carrie looked at the boy. 'What's your name?' The boy had an eye infection as well as snot around his nose and blotched circles on his cheeks, signs of diarrhea and fever.

'His name is Rufus,' said Hektor Tolstoye.

Carrie held out her arms. 'Come, Rufus. Jump across here and we'll get your jacket on.'

Rufus curled up on himself.

'His mother is getting married,' said Tolstoye. 'He is afraid. His father used to beat him and then left. He doesn't want a new father.'

'That stump must be driving you crazy,' said Carrie. 'I am a doctor. Let me take a look.' She climbed down to collect her bag. The old man touched the sleeve of her coat. 'I am Oleg Tolstoye. He is my son, wounded in Syria.' He pulled up his blue shirt to show a massive red scar across his torso. 'For me, Afghanistan. All stupid wars.'

The train jolted, pulling out of the station. Applause broke out around the carriage. Carrie hoisted herself up and examined Hektor's stump. 'How long since the amputation?

'A year.'

Carrie pulled on blue disposable medical gloves and touched the raw skin. Hektor flinched. It was bruised and infected and needed dressing. She opened her bag and pulled out a pack of Ampicillin, not perfect, but the best she had. She tipped two 250mg white tablets into her hand and held it open for him. 'Antibiotics. Take two three times a day for a week.'

Hektor swallowed them dry. Rufus watched, entranced at Carrie and all she was doing. She cleaned the stump. Hektor winced against stabs of pain. For the amputation and the burns on his face he may have had half a dozen operations. She covered the stump with antiseptic cream, tore open a pack of sterilized bandages, sealed the dressing with tape. It would hold for two or three days. Once done, Rufus held out his hand, his bloodshot eyes filled with longing.

'Are you going to put on your jacket?' Carrie asked.

Hektor held up the jacket with his left hand. Rufus slipped his arms through the sleeves. The jacket was too big on Rufus' torso and too short on the sleeves. Carrie rifled deep into her bag and brought out a chocolate nutrition bar. Rufus lunged forward to grab it. Carrie whipped it back. 'Let me examine you first, like I did your uncle.'

Sitting on the bunk, with the train swaying, beams of different lights slicing through from outside and vanishing, Carrie gave Rufus as full a medical as she felt she could. Tongue. Throat, Chest. Neurological reactions. He was healthy but run-down. He had a low fever, mild conjunctivitis in the left eye, and a sore throat. She gave him lozenges, vitamins, and mixed up a strawberry rehydrate from bottled water.

Rufus reached into his small yellow rucksack and pulled out a torn, faded, dog-eared children's book of Russian fables. He opened it to a precise place and handed it to Carrie. She read aloud a story called *Father Frost* about a daughter banished by her evil mother and rescued by the good Father Frost. Hektor brought soup and bread from the restaurant car. Carrie ate. A guard came. Tickets were shown and scanned.

'Does Father Frost also help little boys?' Rufus was drifting off to sleep. Hektor watched, relief on his face.

'Of course.' Carrie kissed his forehead. 'He watches over all children.' She climbed down to her bunk and lay, hands linked behind her head.

Unexpectedly, the rocking of the train enveloped her. She had not slept since getting off the plane in Moscow, since Harry Lucas had buzzed up to her apartment in the middle of the night. She woke with Hektor tapping her shoulder, crouching at the side of her bunk. The stump dressing looked good. That wasn't why he was there. Worry etched into his face. The boy. Snot-nosed. Rufus; was he all right? Not that either.

'Sofia, are you really Israeli?' Hektor said. 'Is your real name Sarah Mayer?'

THIRTY

Ruslan Yumatov's black Mercedes limousine drove south along the deep maroon fifteenth-century western wall of the Kremlin. A message came through that Carrie Walker had been found. Thanks to the determined fury of a French-Canadian nurse over her stolen passport, police discovered that a Sofia Gagnon had booked a third-class ticket on a night train to St Petersburg. He messaged his unit that Sofia Gagnon was Israeli doctor Sarah Mayer, who should be watched until the train reached St Petersburg, but not intercepted.

Locating Carrie Walker was a piece of good news that might signal his run of bad luck was over. He had been summoned to see the President, who had even sent a car. The vehicle turned through the Borovitsky Gate on the Kremlin's south-west corner. Once inside, they headed toward the ornate pastel-yellow Senate Building. Yumatov was always awed at how the Kremlin's grandeur had endured through so many upheavals. Just as an Italian architect was brought in to design the walls and towers of the Kremlin in the late fifteenth century so in the late twenty-first century his own great-grandchildren might see Oriental designs from Asia make their mark across Russia's seat of power.

To his surprise, when they pulled up President Lagutov himself was standing outside the main entrance of the Senate Building as if to greet him. Yumatov was about to leave his car, when the President signaled that he should stay, breaking away from a cluster of officials and getting into the back seat beside him.

'Too damn cold out there for an old man to think.' Lagutov took off his fur hat. Fragments of ice dropped onto the floor. 'Now, Colonel, I spoke to President Merrow and he's agreed. I wanted to thank you for suggesting it.'

'It was a privilege. Thank you, sir.'

'The Norwegians are helping out. We'll meet on their royal yacht.'

A convoy of seven presidential vehicles wound in and stopped in line at the entrance to the Senate Building. 'I'm opening an engineering faculty at Moscow University. I enjoy so much talking to the students. They are always full of ideas. We must never crush ideas like the Soviets did.'

'I agree, sir. Very much.' The confined space and the way the light played through the tinted windows of the limousine made it difficult for Yumatov to read the President. Lagutov had unusual enthusiasm in his tone, like a man with a new project, pulling out of a mood dip.

'Foreign Minister Grizlov speaks highly of your capabilities and I want you to oversee another event that will follow the summit.'

'Of course, sir.'

'On December 30th 1922 we created the Union of the Soviet Socialist Republics, the Soviet Union, and we delivered paved roads, sanitation, and electricity from here to Asia. How did the West succeed in making us ashamed of our achievements? Tell me that, Colonel.'

'It was wrong, yes, sir.'

'But no more. I have ordered a ceremony to mark December 30th and we will hold it in Severomorsk because from there Russia will protect its sea lanes of the future and its path to Asia.' A huge smile spread across Lagutov's face. 'The Presidential Regiment is already heading there, and I want you to run this for me, Colonel. Make it a celebration for all of Russia to remember.'

'Of course, sir. I am honored to be asked.

Lagutov opened the door an inch, letting in a rush of cold air. 'Make it a celebration to show the world that Russia is strong, and no one should fuck with her again.'

Barvikha Village, outside of Moscow

Stephanie Lucas didn't expect her early morning visit to Sergey Grizlov to be an easy one. She had insisted on seeing him after Harry Lucas sent photographs of the memorial service, and the Washington gunmen with Lagutov and Grizlov. 'It's on you,

Steph,' Harry had said. 'We need to know Grizlov's link to Yumatov and who Yumatov's working for.'

Grizlov had tried to stop her. It wasn't convenient, he argued; too far to come. He was tied up with other stuff. Stephanie countered: 'Give me one line on why you, Ruslan Yumatov, Viktor Lagutov, and the two Washington gunmen were on the Amur River outside Khabarovsk.'

'Who needs to know?' said Grizlov.

'I do, and I want to keep it like that.'

Grizlov had agreed.

They had left the British Embassy in lockdown with a fresh security team flown in to establish the level of infiltration and the fate of Alan Scott, the missing security guard. Streets around the embassy were cordoned off. Moscow morning traffic had yet to fill the roads. Sleeting rain eased and strong south-westerly winds shifted clouds and pollution to bring a clear, dark winter sky. Her black diplomatic SUV with chase cars front and back headed due west along Kutozovsky Avenue. Stephanie sat belted up and dressed in a sharp black pin-stripe trouser suit with a white blouse, starched collar, and deceptively stylish shoes, black leather, with small white buckles and sand-rubber soles so she could move fast if need be.

They turned right into the Ryblevkoye and headed north-west. A British Union flag flew on the hood to get through checkpoints quickly.

She looked out at dirty high-rise blocks of drab Moscow suburbs and found herself yearning for a London traffic jam, a bacon sandwich at a Soho cafe, a call center row over the telephone bill, things manageable.

They slowed at the first checkpoint. Keating, her new security guard, showed the email of Grizlov's invitation. The three vehicles were waved through. Barvikha Village began life as a Communist-era retreat with a hotel, spa, sanatorium, and dachas for political leaders. In recent decades, mansions had sprung up, mock-Tudor, open-space Scandinavian, a spectrum of designs, all huge, all with security posts at the driveway entrance, all with large satellite dishes, interspersed with car dealerships and luxury stores, Gucci, Armani, Lamborghini, a retreat for oligarchs and political elite. Sergey Grizlov was both.

All Russia's modern leaders, Lenin, Stalin, Khrushchev, Gorbachev, Putin, Medvedev, Lagutov, had had places in this dazzling swamp of power and money. Stephanie was rich but she couldn't have afforded a bathroom in one of these properties. Grizlov's mansion stretched across at least two plots. A snow-covered lawn between the carriage driveway where ice was melted with under-surface heating. The main house had three big doors with steps leading up. Its design lay somewhere between Baroque and Gothic with arched windows, brick chimneys, and green crenelated roof surrounds. Grizlov had never invited her and now she knew why. For a twice-divorced single man apparently living alone, it was way over the top. It might have been very Russian elite, but it didn't match the funny, self-deprecating Sergey Grizlov she had once thought she loved.

Headlamps from the British Embassy vehicles arced around the driveway and lit up the biggest set of steps at the front of the house. The vehicles stopped.

'Wait, ma'am,' said Keating. He got out of the vehicle, walked round, allowed time to scan the environment. He opened Stephanie's door. As she got out, two jeeps, four men in each, came around from the back of the house and boxed in the vehicles. The double doors at the top of the steps opened. A figure appeared in a black suit, no tie, and a large round head, creased like a football. He came down the steps, speaking in Russian. 'I am Yolkin, head of security for Foreign Minister Grizlov. They need to search the vehicles to ensure the Minister's safety.'

'That's not going to happen,' Stephanie said. 'This is British diplomatic property.'

Yolkin held a phone to his ear, spoke into a microphone hanging from an earpiece. He beckoned Stephanie to follow him up the steps, went inside, and left the door open. Stephanie walked into a badly lit entrance hall that looked like a shoddily curated museum. There were three gold-framed mirrors and a chandelier, heavy sets of furniture, a brown leather sofa with two armchairs, another with embroidered yellow covers, dark wood tables, and two television screens, one tuned to CNN, the other to Russia One, running on the story of the Washington shootings and still demonizing Rake Ozenna. The area was wide and at the end was an arch where Yolkin waited. Beyond were dark wood double doors. Yolkin pressed down the gold-plated handle and pushed it open for Stephanie to go in. Keating began to lead. Yolkin waited until he was close, then stopped him, hand directly on Keating's chest. 'Only the Ambassador,' he said.

Keating didn't resist, didn't move away. He waited instructions, stationary like a pillar. 'It's OK,' said Stephanie. 'Stay here.'

Stephanie passed Yolkin, who stood hands cupped in front of him like a concierge, huge head dipped, bald on the crown. Inside, there was a different room, stylish, homely. She recognized Grizlov's stuff, student posters, once taped up, now framed. *Suppose They Gave a War and Nobody Came* looped with rainbow psychedelic colors; a Munch poster, not *The Scream*, one called *The Dance of Life*, that they had bought together at the Norwegian National Gallery on a weekend visit to Oslo, two monochromes of a Rolling Stones tour, of whom Grizlov was a fan.

Yolkin closed the door. Stephanie couldn't see anybody. Like the entrance hall, the room was dimly lit, a desk light and a couple of standing lamps. It was hot and airless. The furniture was undemanding, colored bean bags, low white coffee tables, a desk to one side, and bookcases, as if Grizlov had ordered in from IKEA. No feminine touch. A bachelor apartment. Not a home.

A door to the left opened. Light flooded in, like driving from shade into the sun. Stephanie stayed back where she was, letting her eyes become accustomed.

'Stephanie. How good of you to come!' Grizlov's voice had less power than usual, and she could barely see his face. There may have been a stoop. It looked like he was wearing the same clothes as in the Four Seasons. His lips were poised tightly as if he planned to say more but decided not to. A second person stepped into the shaft of light and a cold electricity crawled through her body.

THIRTY-ONE

R uslan Yumatov was as tall as she had seen on television and as polished. He wore full dark-green military uniform. The tunic and trousers had lost some of their shine, stretched creases, crumples around the sleeves. Like Grizlov, tiredness etched his face as if, overnight, youthful arrogance had crashed into reality. From Grizlov's rigid body language, Stephanie sensed tension cloying the air between the two.

Stephanie's father told her many times that she had a natural talent for selling, a turn of phrase, knowing how and when to bend truth, not a skill that could be taught. You either had it or not, how a person presented themselves, how their mind worked because they had to believe the story they were telling, how they purveyed trust. Her father held his only child on a pedestal because she had inherited his talent for performing the perfect con, well suited to inherit his trade, maybe even better than him. Once she had reached her late teens, he changed his story. Sure, his little daughter had all those skills. She could rig, lie, and forge just like a man. But she was way too good for a used-car lot in South London.

Stephanie examined the confident expression held by Yumatov against the out-of-character self-doubt that enveloped Grizlov, his blue and yellow silk tie undone, his collar open, his face exhausted.

Yumatov was thirteen years younger, his eyes strained but still blue and sharp and devoid of any texture except determination. As silence hung, arteries pulsed in her neck. Grizlov came forward, held both her hands, and kissed her on the cheeks.

Stephanie said, 'Good of you to ask me, Sergey.' First name. Informal visit. Ignore Yumatov. Treat him like a valet.

Yumatov saluted. 'I am Colonel Ruslan Yumatov, Madam Ambassador. May I reiterate the Minister's gratitude for your coming here at such an unearthly hour.'

'Colonel,' said Stephanie with a nod. 'If you've a moment, Sergey, it won't take long.'

'Sure, but Colonel Yumatov has something that will be useful to us. He can brief you on that, then you and I can have a chat.' Grizlov looked across the room toward a dark area Stephanie hadn't noticed before where a wiry, small man stood by a table, like a butler. 'Some coffee over here,' instructed Grizlov. 'Steph, you're black, no sugar, right.'

'Right.'

'Anything to eat. Pastry? Croissant?'

'Coffee's good.'

Grizlov stepped across to a table under the Munch poster. 'Put your bag here, Steph. Perfectly safe. I assume you have stuff you want to ask about the Khabarovsk ceremony.'

'Embassy stuff.' She gave a quick smile and pointed to a single armchair with a coffee table by its side. 'Best keep it with me.'

A steaming coffee, strong, thick, and dark arrived. Yumatov took the chair next to her, Grizlov the sofa opposite, leaning forward, elbows on knees. She and Grizlov had worked on many negotiations together. She could read part of Grizlov, but not all. She realized she might be outflanked. The skill of how to tell a con was as crucial as how to con, and Yumatov was cold and strong-minded. She couldn't read him, which meant she couldn't read the room.

Yumatov took a tablet from his tunic pocket and put it on the coffee table. The photograph showed the gathering of Yumatov, Grizlov, Lagutov, other powerful men at the memorial for the casualties of the Diomede operation. The faces of the two gunmen were not ringed as in Harry's photographs. But Stephanie recognized them.

Grizlov said, 'I've asked Colonel Yumatov to explain why we are all here.'

Yumatov's intense eyes shifted in a disciplined way between his tablet and Stephanie like watchtower searchlights. 'Valentyn Golov is here in the second row, Adrik Syanko here in the front. These men are responsible for the shootings in Washington. Their motive was revenge. They are trained military men and went further than most grieving fathers in getting themselves to Washington to avenge the death of their sons.'

'We want to think of it as a crazy mass-shooting incident,' said Grizlov. 'The US is familiar with the motives and mental-health problems of such perpetrators.'

'America is far ahead of Russia with mass shootings,' added Yumatov. 'It is part of their culture, not part of ours or yours.'

'These men lost loved ones. They couldn't deal with it,' continued Grizlov. 'They bought their weapons in Purcellville, Virginia, an hour's drive from the venue in Washington, DC. The rifle was a .260 Remington. They knew exactly the weapon they wanted. They removed the stock and bought a hollowed-out microphone pole for the concealed fit. They drove to Rhode Island Avenue, parked their hire car, walked in, and tried to kill the man who killed their sons. They failed and died. They probably expected it. We don't know what was going through their minds. They had never processed their grief.' He looked at her with a glint in his eyes. *Trust me. Stay with it.* 'That's what happened, Steph. Not nice. Not big either. The surviving member of their team was an off-the-rack hired cameraman. He had no idea what he was getting into. We're giving him consular help, of course. Russia is not making an issue of it. We don't want the Americans to.' Grizlov shadowed his hand over the tablet. 'And this memorial was exactly what it was. Think of the President, the Secretary of State, a commanding officer at Arlington Cemetery honoring the dead from one of America's wars.'

'You might not be making an issue,' said Stephanie, 'but you're allowing the networks do the job for you.'

'The news cycle will naturally fade,' said Grizlov.

'We have no control over the networks,' said Yumatov.

Stephanie ignored the blatant untruth. She reached into her bag and pulled out the sheaf of printouts, shuffling through, discarding those from the memorial and keeping three, the blurry figure in the Four Seasons' forecourt, facial recognition of Yumatov, and electronic intelligence confirming he had used his cellphone to initiate Carrie Walker's kidnap. She laid them out, facing Yumatov. She sipped her coffee, cutting and harsh, tingling her lips, keeping her thinking clear.

Yumatov looked without curiosity. 'You're about to ask me why I was waiting in the forecourt of the Four Seasons Hotel when you were meeting Minister Grizlov.' He reached forward and turned them around, so they faced Stephanie. 'And why I triggered the abduction of Sarah Mayer from your vehicle.' He took a transparent plastic bag from his pocket and held it up to the light. 'Because of this, Madam Ambassador.'

Stephanie recognized a flash drive. She had to assume the meeting was being filmed and what unfolded next could be released to the world. Grizlov and Yumatov had been ahead of her ever since she had stepped into the over-heated room.

They were prepared for the Khabarovsk memorial, for the Four Seasons imagery, for Stephanie piecing together strands that led to Yumatov and Grizlov. The only flaw so far was Yumatov referring to Carrie as Sarah Mayer, and that might be deliberate.

'This was found on Vice-Admiral Artyom Semenov after he was shot dead at the back of your embassy.' Yumatov laid the bag on the table. 'It contains the same information that Gerald Cooper was to have sent across to Norway.'

Stephanie glanced at Grizlov. Until now Cooper had not been mentioned. 'We want you to understand,' said Grizlov. 'Cooper and Semenov were going to hand over an olive branch from modern Russia to NATO, technical maritime weapons data to show that we want to work with you and not against you. Now, we're giving it to you, Steph, in the hope that you can deliver it to its new home.'

Yumatov swiped his finger across the tablet to bring up the file.

A technical diagram appeared. There was no headline or title page. Stephanie read from the Cyrillic script that this was air-independent propulsion technology that quietened a submarine, making it more difficult to detect and therefore more dangerous. Yumatov switched to a profile of a submarine showing tanks and pipes in different colors. Then the back of a submarine, propeller and colored boxes, diesel engine, generator, motor batteries. He only gave each one a few seconds, letting Stephanie glimpse, but no time to take it in.

He stayed a few seconds longer on a slide headlined in Russian *Underwater Drone* with a diagram resembling a torpedo, only to move quickly to another entitled *Project 09852 (NATO)*. There was more, sketches, three-dimensional diagrams, photographs of naval vessels and shipyards. Some carried stamps, *особое значение, Of Special Importance*, the highest form of Russian intelligence classification.

Yumatov worked in silence, which became a weapon itself, stretching into a suffocating unease between them. Stephanie didn't plan to break it. Grizlov watched in a way that looked as if he might not have seen the file before. Yumatov worked with the impatience of a man too busy to be here, the corner of his mouth curled, his eyes hard and indifferent. He had seen these images too many times.

Yumatov finished. Stephanie counted fifty-two separate images. She had not noticed sloppiness or mistakes deliberately planted. She felt as if Grizlov and Yumatov were trying to draw her into a vortex of technology and facts that were impossible to verify. She placed her coffee mug on the table, sat back, and steepled her hands across her stomach, relaxed as if she had all the time in the world. Their play.

Grizlov leaned forward, elbows on knees, eyes on Stephanie. 'We're showing you this because we need someone who understands Russia, who can prevent the situation running out of control.'

Stephanie stayed quiet. She let her curiosity show through a crease of the brow.

Yumatov said, 'The Foreign Minister and I are convinced that Russia's future lies in an alliance with West and that Vladimir Putin was wrong to cause hostility with the aim of recreating some greatness of the past.' Yumatov's gaze drilled into her, unwavering. 'This file is our gift to the West. Twice we have tried to deliver it. Once on the border through Gerald Cooper. Then with Vice-Admiral Semenov to your embassy. Those trying to stop us work out of Vladivostok, a network run by Russian, Chinese, and Japanese criminals. They do not want a Russian–NATO alliance. They want a weak Russia, a weak West, and a strong Asia. The motive is financial. The weaker the governments, the richer they can become.'

Grizlov said, 'If I succeed Lagutov to the Kremlin, I will reach out to NATO and we could put a stop to these Asian ambitions. But first, I have to win the presidency and that won't happen if NATO's Dynamic Freedom exercise encroaches so far into our backyard. The result will be increased nationalism. Either NATO accepts or it will feel the wrath of Russia that will last for another generation.'

'And what exactly is it you are revealing with these diagrams?' Stephanie pointed to Yumatov's tablet.

'The most lethal weapon of modern warfare is the quiet submarine,' said Yumatov. 'If you're noisier than us, you will die first. Russia has submarine acoustic superiority over NATO forces. These files reveal selected technology. Air-independent propulsion allows us to operate without access to outside air. We can use laser instead of sonar detection. And so on. NATO technicians will understand immediately what we have.'

'Take me back to the beginning, Colonel,' said Stephanie.

Yumatov flipped back to the slide on air-independent propulsion. She saw immediately what she needed to know. 'I'll deliver it.' She stood up to leave. 'I'll relay your case.'

'It's all on here.' Yumatov held up a flash drive and handed it to Stephanie.

'I'm giving you full protection back to the embassy,' said Grizlov.

Stephanie smiled, an ambassador's smile. Yumatov fetched Stephanie's jacket. She slipped her arms through the sleeves, pulled on her gloves, knotted her scarf and zipped the flash drive into her side pocket.

'Thank you, and for the coffee,' she said.

'Look after yourself, Steph. Catch up soon,' said Grizlov as if they had just finished an evening cocktail. He kissed her lightly on each cheek.

'Who would have ever thought it?' she said. 'You and I doing this.'

In the vehicle driving back, escorted by FSB vehicles with flashing lights, Stephanie sifted through the discrepancies in Yumatov's presentation. Two stood out. The first, he had referred to Carrie as Sarah Mayer. Either he didn't know, or he was testing her. And the second, none of the images matched those Carrie had sent to Rake Ozenna. Stephanie felt the small drive inside her jacket pocket. Files are files. Copy them and they come out the same. That was how digital technology worked. She plugged the drive into her tablet and checked its size, 65.3

megabytes. Tiny. A vice-admiral with Semenov's access could have found a way to send this level of data electronically. What then was on the file Carrie now had that was so lethally different to the one retrieved from Semenov's body?

THIRTY-TWO

Train to St Petersburg

'I overheard the guards talking as I was getting hot water.' Hektor Tolstoye's voice was so low that Carrie could hardly hear him. Lying on her bunk, woken by a soldier who had lost an arm in Syria, Carrie stayed quiet and gauged risks around her, the bunks, the corridor where people moved back and forth, the old man, the uncle and boy, all staring at her. Streaks of hazy light wormed across the windows, snow, trees, emptiness, darkness, the rock and tumble of the train. Stale air was laced with smells of beef and sweat. The boy dropped down from his upper bunk and stood next to his grandfather, who held his hand. She remembered his name was Rufus. He had a slight fever and was traveling to his mother's wedding. His uncle, Hektor Tolstoye, had woken her with the question: 'Are you really Israeli? Is your real name Sarah Mayer?'

Hektor studied Carrie as if he were trying to find a way out for both of them. 'They have been instructed to check the train for an Israeli doctor, Sarah Mayer, and watch her until St Petersburg. They were arguing. The older one who scanned our tickets said it was wrong, like Soviet times. The younger one said it was their duty to protect Russia against foreign spies.'

'You must listen to Hektor.' Oleg's frail hand reached across toward Carrie, hovering midair to ensure he had her attention.

'People saw how you dressed my stump,' said Hektor. 'How you examined Rufus. They talked. The guards heard. They say you will get off at St Petersburg and catch a train to Helsinki. Do not do that. Stay on this train. We have found you somewhere safe. We got this in Moscow.'

Hektor handed her a plastic light-green wallet with a transparent front and a strap to hang round a neck. Inside was a Russian identity card, mandatory for all adult citizens. The face of a young woman stared out from the left. She had full round cheeks, tied-back brown hair, a friendly smile. She was thirty-six years old. Her name was Katerina Tolstoye.

'My daughter,' growled Oleg. 'The boy's mother.'

'If you are stopped. Use it. You get off at Olenegorsk. It is the stop one hundred kilometers south of Murmansk.' Hektor punched a message into his phone. 'I am asking a friend to drive you from Olenegorsk to Nikel. It is close to the border with Norway. It will take half a day. He will find someone to help you across.

'If this were Soviet times, they would stop the train now, check everyone's papers,' said Oleg. 'Today, they can't do that.'

'It is just as bad when they find you,' added Hektor.

'Worse,' said Oleg. 'The Soviet Union was founded on humanity. Now we have shit.'

Hektor nodded at Rufus, who slid into the corridor and ran toward the end of the carriage. To protect themselves, the family needed her away from them. But they would not turn Carrie in. Hektor and Oleg bore the wounds of a rotten system. They couldn't fight it. Nor would they join it. She had helped them. They would help her, up to a point.

She had been right not to follow Yumatov's instructions and get the Helsinki train. But that hadn't made it safe anywhere else. Carrie's brief but deep sleep had given her enough confidence to decide her next step. Uncle Artyom Semenov was family, her blood. Carrie hadn't asked for it, but there was no way she would allow his death to be in vain.

Hektor explained Carrie's false identity. Katerina Tolstoye. Occupation secretary, traveling to Kola, just south of Murmansk. She had been in Moscow to get divorce papers so she could remarry. He gave her a dark red patterned scarf to cover her head. He handed her a brown envelope containing the stamped documents, canceled marriage certificate. Hektor asked for Carrie's phone. She drew one from her jacket pocket, not the one she had used to message Rake. Hektor told her to keep it flat in her palm. Skillfully, holding his phone in his good left hand, he air-dropped phone history and contacts into it, giving texture to her cover.

'You've done this before,' said Carrie.

'In Syria,' he said. 'A different kind of fighting.'

Rufus returned, out of breath, excited.

Oleg said, 'Goodbye, Sofia, or whoever you are.'

Rufus went ahead, tuning left, backwards down the train away from the restaurant car. It was just past seven thirty in the morning, an hour before they reached St Petersburg. Hektor stepped out. Carrie followed with her bag and medical kit.

'Do you have a hundred dollars?' said Hektor.

Carrie turned sideways to let through a young couple, holding hands, smelling of tobacco. 'I have rubles.'

'Better. Give me six thousand.' Hektor took the money from Carrie. 'We are going to a part of the train controlled by the army. You should be safe there.' They went through another restaurant car, the second-class sleeper, the first class, then another third-class carriage. They passed guards who barely noticed them. Hektor explained that the search for Sarah Mayer was running from the other end of the train. That was what Rufus had gone to check. She kept glimpsing Rufus, waiting for them, making eye contact, then heading off to keep vigil for the next carriage.

It wasn't yet light. Countryside sped by, snow, lamps by the track, occasional car headlights. The wheels rhythmically clunked metal on metal through the early morning. Shapes from the darkness splattered the windows like an abstract painting. They reached the end of the train. Hektor pushed down a handle with his elbow. A rush of freezing air came through. Snow hit Carrie in the face. Fresh crystals melted on her lips. She tasted polluted rain. The two railcars were hooked up but with no cover. A soldier in green camouflage fatigues and a matching hat with ear flaps came out of a door, shut it firmly behind him, and stood on the narrow ledge, holding a rail. Hektor stepped across, gave him Carrie's money. He counted it. Hektor beckoned her to cross, too. There was open space. The train rocked. The two railcars moved against each other. Carried judged it and jumped. The soldier took her elbow while she got her balance.

She pressed a ten-thousand-ruble note into Hektor's hand. He looked embarrassed and grateful. He wanted to refuse it. He needed it. He stepped back to the main train. Rufus gave her a hesitant little wave. The soldier opened the door. A stench caught the back of Carrie's throat, so harsh and unforgiving that she coughed, then doubled over to suppress rising vomit.

The soldier pushed Carrie inside, shut the door, and pulled across two bolts, one high and one up from the floor. She could see very little, except for a shoulder-high wall straight in front of her. The only light came from narrow slits of frosted glass on either side of the carriage shaking with the movement of the train. She heard a sharp, cracking thud from halfway down the carriage. The soldier didn't react. Carrie fumbled in her pocket for a flashlight. The air tasted toxic and heavy, like something rotting in the tropics. She coughed. The soldier turned to the left and she saw that the wall was part of a container, several containers. She counted eight huge open boxes. She followed him, keeping her balance with her hands on the shuddering carriage wall, cold, damp grimy. Her eyes began to water. Another crack, this time against the container closest to her. A rumbling snort. A second smashing against the reinforced steel of the container. An exhalation of breath. A high-pitched bray. This was a carriage transporting horses, and Carrie knew enough about horses to know that kicking its hoof against the container meant an animal in distress. Hektor said the army controlled the railcar, which meant military horses and the sickening stench made sense. Some would be frightened, and fear made horses ill. Diarrhea was one of the symptoms. Carrie was breathing air filled with bacteria from decomposing horses' urine and feces. Chemicals, too. The soldier would be disinfecting with ammonia. But he couldn't clear away the shit. With the railcar exterior iced over, there was nowhere for it to go and horses shit a lot. Fifty pounds a day. Eight horses at least. Through the dark, she saw jumpy, pinpoint eyes of caged animals feeling insecure.

'How long have they been here?' she asked the soldier. He hadn't said a word. He didn't answer now. He pointed to a wooden three-legged stool for her to sit on. It was loose, not attached to anything in the carriage. On one side were bound bales of fresh hay stacked to the roof giving off a rich countryside smell, the horses' food. From the other side, piled high inside dirty orange plastic netting, came the stink that had caused Carrie to retch, damp, soiled straw, spilling out onto the floor.

Above the stool, a certificate was taped to the wall, carrying stamps and signatures. Carrie's eyes had adjusted enough to read that it was an authorization to transport eight ceremonial military horses from Moscow to Severomorsk, the city where her uncle had lived. The horses would have been on the train for at least twelve hours. The soldier sat on a stool on the other side of the hay bales. He brought out his phone, messaging or playing a game. He was around forty, a hard, narrow face, not a cruel one. He didn't want anything to do with her. He needed the money. His protection of Carrie was as thin as a paper screen. It was an hour to St Petersburg, then another twenty-four hours to Olenegorsk.

Using her hat as a backrest, she leant against the grimy carriage wall. She absorbed the pace of the railcar, snorts, neighs, and occasional thuds of kicking hoofs, the lumbering rhythm of the track, the sway, her throat and lungs accustomed to the bad air, light flickering from the soldier's phone.

She pulled out her phone. She should have checked earlier. Rake had messaged, short to avoid detection. *ETA 11:05*. That would be his flight into St Petersburg. Of all those involved in this mess, only Hektor and Rake had delivered. She had asked for money. He got it to her. Now he was coming to get her out. Except Rake couldn't go to St Petersburg because his face had been all over Russian television. Surely, he would know this. Then, like peeling skin from a bad fruit, a black thought hit her. They had tried to kill Rake in Washington and failed. They now wanted him in Russia, and Carrie was the bait. If Rake tried to meet her in St Petersburg, that is how it would play out. They would take him, display him, and string him up. It was a swirling thought, and the more she played it the more she was sure she was right. If Yumatov could get her a near-perfect passport, he could have got her on a plane out. But he insisted on the train.

She realized how often she had been asking herself, almost without thinking, how Rake would handle things. Carrie wasn't a hunter like Rake. She did fevers and wounds. She needed his take on what was happening now. She messaged. *Unsafe. Call.* Carrie needed a discussion, not a ten-character message.

THIRTY-THREE

Helsinki International Airport, Finland

All had been on plan until Rake saw Carrie's message to call her and warning him not to go. Human figures, gloved and hooded, wrapped in oranges and yellows, worked around the airport apron in Helsinki. Snow stretched away like a white sheet and de-icing spray bounced off aircraft wings. Colored lights glowed through the morning darkness to demarcate runways. From Helsinki, Rake and Mikki were less than two hundred miles away from St Petersburg and Carrie's train would be getting close.

Carrie liked to talk things through, sit down face to face, if not that then voice to voice, phone, Skype, or something. A couple of minutes. Stuff got missed with short digital messages.

The boarding announcement came for their St Petersburg flight. Mikki hoisted his bag onto his shoulder. Rake messaged Carrie: *U LED? Are you in St Petersburg?*

She sent straight back. *No. Do not come*

Where?

Call FFS For fuck's sake.

Rake called Harry Lucas who said: 'Keep it to less than three minutes.' The boarding lounge lit like a theater as headlamps from snowplows swept through the huge window. Rake dialed. Carrie picked up straightaway.

'Is it you?' Her voice was raised against background noise of the train, no name, no recognition risk, no courtesy, no time. To hear Carrie's voice was good.

'O negative. Yellow. Boccaccio.'

'They're expecting you. They'll arrest you. I have help. I have a safe place on the train. I get off at Olenegorsk, before Murmansk, another twenty-four hours. I have a lift to Nikel, close to the Norwegian border. Can you get me across?' She spoke firmly, in short bursts, like while traveling back to a hospital with a critically ill patient.

'I can,' said Rake.

'I have a flash drive. I sent you screenshots from it.'

'Good.'

'Hektor T-o-l-s-t-o-y-e,' she spelled out the name, 'and his sister Katerina Tolstoye. I need to know if they are real people.'

'On it.'

He heard the shaking of the train, an intake of Carrie's breath. He imagined her hand cupped around the mouthpiece to cover her voice. Maybe squeezed between passengers, protected by this Hektor and Katerina Tolstoye. The glare in the airport lounge faded as headlamp beams turned away to join a line of yellow snowplows, like a military convoy, heading far off into the airport. Rake wanted to ask Carrie if she were all right. Stupid. No one on a train in Russia with people wanting to kill them was all right.

'There's a security breach,' she said.

'Yes.'

'The second in command on the Diomedes. It's him. Unfinished business.'

'Copy that.' *So, Carrie knew.*

The call ended. Mikki stood at the back of the boarding line. Rake held up his hand to indicate he would be another couple of minutes. He called back Harry Lucas and kept the line open while Lucas sourced Hektor Tolstoye.

'Captain in Russia's 96th Separate Reconnaissance Brigade,' said Lucas. 'He lost his right arm and suffered third-degree burns during an ambush in Homs, Syria, April 20th 2017. Divorced. No children. The family comes from St Petersburg. Father, Oleg, fought in Afghanistan. Has a sister Katerina and a nephew, Rufus, aged nine.'

'Any connection to Yumatov?'

'Not that comes up here. Based out of Moscow, not Eastern District.'

Rake rang off, walked across to Mikki, and said, 'We're not going.'

Expression unchanged, Mikki unhitched his bag set it on the floor. 'Where to, then?'

'Kirkenes,' said Rake. 'I'll call Nilla.'

*　　*　　*

Leaning back on her stool, Carrie read Rake's message. *Ts check out.* She had an urge to hug him, wished she could sort him out in her mind.

She had last seen Rake a year ago. She was working at a trauma unit in Boston. He called her out of the blue asking if she might have time for coffee. Her first thought was no. What did he want? It was over. He explained he was designing a defense course at the Belfer Center at Harvard University, which stopped her dead.

'What the hell are you at Harvard for, Rake?'

'Army's show-ponying me,' he said off-handedly.

'You're kidding!' she laughed. Rake, a Harvard academic? She suggested a safe place, daytime, people. She wore a formal dark-blue work suit, her blonde hair twisted into a topknot, a kind of, I like you but keep your distance message, except Rake had never cared what she wore.

He slid into the seat facing her. Carrie felt a twitch in her abdomen. That creased, weathered face, the eyes gone sad: all that real-life experience. Other guys would spend an evening crowing about how great they were because they were teaching at Harvard. Rake couldn't wait to get away. He was heading out of town at the weekend, visiting friends at a farm. Would she like to join him? By agreeing, she would be stepping back into a danger zone. She told herself, what the hell, she was thirty-five, in her prime, didn't know people in Boston apart from doctors with families and partners. And it was a long time since she had had good sex.

'Sure,' she shrugged, hands protectively around her large warm cup of coffee.

'I'll pick you up.'

'No,' she quickly countered. 'Give me the GPS, in case I get called.'

Ninety minutes out of Boston, when Carrie turned off the I-291 into an undulating, snow-covered landscape lit by brilliant winter sun, she spotted Rake by the roadside, rugged up in animal skins, warming himself by a fire. She could have been in Alaska.

'You hungry?' he asked.

'I thought we were with friends on a farm.'

'Over there,' Rake pointed behind him. He led them up around a mound toward a copse of trees where, out of sight from the road, eight dogs lay resting in the sun. They were harnessed to a wooden sled draped in caribou skins. Carrie put her hand to her mouth, couldn't help smiling, couldn't help thinking she should turn back. The dogs' heads lifted. Two barked, setting off a chorus until Rake let out a high-pitched whistle and they quietened. They were all sizes. Some looked like mutts, shades of fur, brown, black, greys, whites; a random spread of strong winter coats. Rake had talked about huskies and sledding, but she had never seen him with dogs. He explained that these dogs were veterans of the great cross-country Alaskan sled rally called the Iditarod and he was settling them into a new home.

'Why here? Why not in Alaska?' she asked.

'Kids come with them from the Diomedes, Wales, Teller, and places, gets them way out into the world. They learn sledding, tour guiding, hospitality, and they get Indian Health Service so medical is covered.' He introduced her to each dog, giving the name and a character trait, cuffing his fingers under the throat, checking the harness wasn't too tight or loose. 'Meet Pepper. He's a little crazy. And Kani. She's strong, really solid in the long haul, I'm using her as the lead, and Jake, he's more timid, a follower, really good as team dog, and matching him with Carly, who's more happy-go-lucky.'

They went back to the roadside fire. Rake laid a caribou skin on the snow for them to sit on. He hadn't touched her, she realized. He cooked them salmon and steak. He had brought strong paper plates and knives and forks. He asked if she wanted to go for a ride. The dogs yelped, strained at their harnesses, which lifted from the ground and tightened. The sled jolted forward, swaying as Rake coaxed the dogs into a pattern, then settled onto a trail through woods and snow. Carrie sat, legs up, hands steadying her over the bumps with the sun on her face. Some way along, Rake insisted Carrie drive. He showed her the slow and hard foot brakes and how to shift weight like in a sailboat for the curves of the trail. She was a skier, not a sailor. She was clumsy. The sled tipped, spilling them into deep snow. Rake took over, and they ended up outside a large log cabin with kennels and outbuildings, snow covering the roofs and drifting up against the walls.

'An offshoot to the farmhouse,' said Rake. 'It's a couple of miles across there. We can hang out here or we can keep going.' There was no electricity. Water came from a well, heating from chopped logs loaded steadily into the stove. Light came through small square windows, growing dimmer as Carrie, dry and warm, watched the changing light of the vanishing sun. Rake lit candles. As she stood, surprised and marveling, he touched her shoulder and turned her toward him. 'Thanks for coming,' he said. They slept under thick goose down, warming each other, then naturally, their bodies seeking the familiar pleasure points, holding each other hard. She knew him well. Rake knew who he was. He knew what he wanted. It was her. The cold, the animals, the skins, the smell of fire and the quiet; she could hardly believe the memory. She hadn't met anyone like him, hadn't moved on because she hadn't stopped measuring other men against him. She had forgotten how much a person needed someone they could trust to keep going.

Hektor and Rufus came in with a bowl of steaming borsch soup and a chunk of bread. Hektor explained what she should do once she got to Olenegorsk. His cousin Mikhail would meet her. He was driving a green Skoda sedan. Carrie should keep her head covered with the dark red scarf he gave her and use the Katerina Tolstoye identity if she were asked.

The train slowed, and the soldier, playing with his phone, looked up, alert and tense. He slipped his phone into his jacket pocket and pulled across the zipper to seal it in.

'St Petersburg,' said Carrie.

He ignored her. With the change of rhythm, a horse became skittish, setting off others, a chorus of restless whinnying, hooves thumping on the floor. The train crawled forward, jolted, and stopped. The soldier peered through the narrow glass window. He unholstered his weapon, checked the chamber, slid it back in, leaving the flap unclipped. He spoke to the horses, calming them, feeding sugar cubes from his pockets, stroking their manes, necks, and heads. He glanced at Carrie. He put his finger to his lip. Stay quiet. Don't speak.

From the platform came raised voices, orders being shouted. The soldier watched. He showed no aggression, no apprehension, a soldier doing his job. There was a thump on the side of the carriage. There would be people out there waiting for her. Carrie sat rigidly on the stool, muscles clenched, thankful for the hot food, her mind alert. She hated having no control. Doors opened and slammed shut. Other carriages. Not Carrie's. She concentrated on her watch, tracked the rotation of the long, thin second hand. This wasn't one of the high-speed trains. St Petersburg was a stop, not a destination. The wait would be minutes. Not long. Five. Maybe ten. Not more.

The railcar lurched forward and stopped. A hoof smashed against steel. There was another jolt. The train moved ahead again. A whistle shrilled, merging back into the rhythm of the train regaining pace. The soldier pitchforked hay into the containers, poured himself hot tea from his flask, sat back down, and brought out his phone.

The silent soldier had not betrayed her. She pulled fresh hay from a bale. She arranged it as a mattress on the juddering floor. Warmed by the soup, she lay down. This time tomorrow, she should be in Norway.

THIRTY-FOUR

Washington, DC

Harry Lucas' surveillance alerted him that the CIA Director's vehicle was looping around Logan Circle and heading along Church Street to his apartment block. An hour earlier, Frank Ciszewski had called, saying he was being summoned to the White House. Ciszewski needed to drop by Harry's place after. It couldn't be done on the phone. Harry's automatic plate recognition flagged up that Ciszewski was riding in his official Cadillac XT5 Crossover with two escort vehicles. Harry Lucas and Frank Ciszewski had agreed to keep the Carrie Walker operation off the books. So why was Ciszewski now advertising his own involvement?

Harry put on a playlist from Ciszewski's generation, music from Queen, the Rolling Stones, the Doors, and bands that straddled his Yale college years and joining the CIA. He opened the door just as one of Ciszewski's security detail was about to press the buzzer.

'I'll take it from here,' Ciszewski told his men. 'It's Harry Lucas. I'll be fine. Place is like Fort fucking Knox.' Harry held open the door, Ciszewski walked in, loosening his white silk scarf, unbuttoning his black cashmere overcoat. 'You got one hell of a bachelor pad here, Harry. Gives me a view of a freedom I've never had.'

'Grass is always greener, Frank.' Harry hung the coat on a stand near the door and pointed to the coffee machine. Ciszewski shook his head. His cheeks were red from the cold. He sat heavily on one of Harry's black-leather easy chairs, resting his thick hands on his stomach. His brogue shoes shone with melted snow.

'I'm sorry about your guys, Harry. Dreadful stuff,' said Ciszewski. 'Sorry about Semenov, too. That's a mess that will be dissected for decades to come.' He pulled out a handkerchief, freshly laundered and ironed, and ran it over his bald, moonlike head, then down his face. 'You go first, then I'll tell you about Merrow.'

Harry perched on the arm of the sofa. 'Semenov carried two drives. One we were meant to see and one we were not. He was killed for the latter, which we hope Carrie Walker has. She should be in St Petersburg around now. We're meeting her there and getting her out.'

'Do you know what's on them?'

'Carrie managed to send us two screenshots from the one we were not meant to see. They showed the registration numbers of NATO naval vessels.'

'That's it?' Ciszewski looked at Harry curiously.

'That's it. Open-source material. But there's got to be more.'

'The other one?'

'Nothing new. Foreign Minister Grizlov gave the file to Ambassador Lucas. It mainly contained material about air-independent propulsion and submersible drones. According to Grizlov, it is a goodwill gesture, the beginning of a partnership, a plea for us to back off on the Dynamic Freedom exercise and help stem the rise of nationalism in Russia.'

Ciszewski folded the handkerchief and returned it to his pocket. 'How are you getting Walker out?'

'I'm using Rake Ozenna.'

'Jesus, Harry.' Ciszewski raised his eyebrows. 'The Russians just tried to kill him.'

'My network has a security breach. It might be wider, Frank, and I've no idea who or what it is. Carrie doesn't trust us. She trusts Ozenna.'

Ciszewski looked at Harry as if to say he didn't like it, but he understood. 'This is the Doors you're playing. Coppola used them in *Apocalypse Now*. Great film about another mess we created. Can't let our generation slip into the same abyss, Harry. That's what Merrow just told me. Went on and on about Vietnam and Iraq. Learning from mistakes.' He pushed himself to his feet, stepped to the window, which had a clear view to the street but was frosted on the outside so people could not see in. 'You got a map? North Atlantic. Something we can lay on the coffee table and touch without it lighting up and speaking to us.'

Harry brought down an Arctic and North Atlantic map from an upper shelf and unfurled it on the large, low coffee table. Ciszewski drew out a pen. 'Can I write on it?'

'Go ahead. It's stolen government property.'

Ciszewski drew a line down from the southern coast of Greenland, through Iceland to northern Scotland, the GIUK gap, which marked the outer boundary of Russia's Bastion of Defense. He drew a curve that sealed off the eastern area of the map, closer to Russia, the Bastion's inner sanctum, which Moscow insisted was its area of control. He tapped the pen inside that arc. 'Russia's inner Bastion of Defense takes in the northern Norwegian coast and Dynamic Freedom is going right in there, not just with subs but overtly, with aircraft and surface ships, a show of force like we have never done before. We can't allow Russia to control that area and Russia can't allow us to control it. President Lagutov has been on the phone to Merrow, who's called in the Chairman of the Joint Chiefs, who's asking the NATO Secretary-General. Everyone's flinging around slogans like "Peace through Strength," "America First," "Russia First," "New World Order," "Motherland," "Neo-colonialism," all that crap. And no one knows what the fuck they're talking about because the Russians have outsmarted us and Merrow's taken the bait.'

'You mean we're rowing back Dynamic Freedom?'

'Worse. Lagutov wants a summit with Merrow in theater during Dynamic Freedom to show the US–Russian friendship. I knocked it back. The Secret Service knocked it back. The Joint Chiefs. Madness. We suggested Vice-President Bennett, Secretary of State Diamond, which the Secret Service thought they could handle. Merrow was adamant. It had to be him and Lagutov. Russians are our natural allies and all that, rebalancing world power for the greater good.'

'Where?'

'Worse still and a damn unfunny joke. The Norwegians are bringing their royal yacht out of winter mothballs.' Ciszewski leaned over the map. 'Docking it in Kirkenes, a tiny one-horse town, but marked to become a big new port for the northern sea routes and melting ice and turns out, historically, that it's the sister city of Severomorsk, the Russian North Atlantic naval base.'

Ciszewski sat back and folded his arms. 'Merrow asked if there were any ongoing ops that could bite him in the butt. The wheels are moving fast, Harry. You need to bring Carrie Walker in before we pass the point of no return.'

When Ciszewski left, Harry tried to call Ozenna. As the line rang, a map came up that was meant to highlight Ozenna's location. It didn't. Harry went close on St Petersburg and Helsinki. There was nothing. He checked Finnair Flight 107 that Ozenna and Wekstatt were booked on. It had landed in St Petersburg. They did not board. He tried Wekstatt's phone. It rang through to a factory settings voicemail.

The Kasatka submarine, Barents Sea

Five submariners sat at the weapons panel in the control room of the Yasen-class Russian submarine, their faces colored by the red, blue, and green lights glowing off their screens. The commander, Andrei Kurchin, studied charts on the plotting table and examined the array of enemy ships stretched through the Barents Sea as the Dynamic Freedom exercise prepared to get underway. A green bulb lit on his communications panel and he switched on his headset. 'Merrow has agreed to the summit,' said Yumatov.

'We're ready to go.' After his evening with Yumatov in Moscow, Kurchin had had a good feeling about the mission. Yumatov was solid. Their friendship stretched back more than twenty years. They had become so close that Yumatov had made him godfather to his first-born. When Yumatov approached him, he laid out his plan in such meticulous detail and advocated the simultaneous assassination of two presidents as merely one stage in reaching an end goal. The sacrifice of two lives with inevitable collateral casualties could save the lives of millions. While the West has spread its influence around the world through slavery, murder, and nuclear weapons, China had spread its with barely a shot being fired in anger. It was time for Russia to learn from Asia.

'The venue is the Norwegian royal yacht, which is docking at Kirkenes now,' said Yumatov.

Kurchin and Yumatov had discussed variables of the summit venue and put in place fallbacks in case the two Presidents refused to meet. The current scenario was the best possible outcome. 'When are they boarding?'

'Within twenty-four hours.'

'We'll use VLF.' Communicating with submerged submarines was difficult because radio waves did not travel well underwater.

The most secure method was through sonic equipment laid on the seabed, of which there was a network around Severomorsk and along the north Russian coast. But, with security stepped up for the summit, the Americans would be intercepting. Kremlin security, too, would be all over it. Very low frequency radio waves could get through water in distances up to about sixty feet. The summit itself would have a narrow window, probably less than an hour. Kurchin would keep the *Kasatka* just below the surface for Yumatov to send a burst of VLF which would be his green light to attack, or to withdraw.

'I will signal once the targets are on board,' said Yumatov.

'You have Semenov's cloaking data?'

'Carrie Walker is on a train between St Petersburg and Murmansk. Consider the threat neutralized.'

The *Kasatka*'s mission could be finished swiftly with minimal risk. The sea around was crowded with naval hardware and attention would be split between the military exercises and the presidential summit. Norway would provide an immediate cordon of defense around the yacht. American, Canadian, British, and European warships, together with Russians, would form an outer ring to protect the two Presidents.

Presidential protection produced complex layers of security. Military exercises carried a realism of live conflict, but also an unrealism of pushing agendas, piling on decisions, and creating scenarios with pressure that would be unlikely in a real war. Both would fabricate a fog of war which Andrei Kurchin would exploit.

He gave orders to dive. On his screen, the captain watched blocks of sea ice scatter as the massive gray whale-like hull dipped below the surface. He placed his hands on the cool metal of the periscope shaft, half in prayer, half to feel the tremors of the submarine descending into dark, freezing water. The weather was due to break. The two Presidents would soon be on the Norwegian royal yacht. The timing was perfect.

Kirkenes, Finnmark, Norway

Rake had told no one where they were. He needed to get back to Kirkenes to get Carrie across the border and there was no time for discussion. He messaged her reassurance. *Close by. On plan.*

From Helsinki, Rake and Mikki flew to Oslo and took a connecting flight far north to Kirkenes. The temperature in the small airport parking lot measured minus seventeen Celsius. They walked across from the terminal. Mikki opened the white SUV they had hired using the passports and driver's licenses that Lucas had given them, John Gray and Vincent Joseph. Tire chains were fitted. They cleared windows of ice. Mikki climbed in behind the wheel and fired up the engine.

Rake would soon have to contact Lucas. First, he needed to get his plan straight.

At an intersection from the airport, Mikki swung the vehicle south. The gritted road looked like a winding piece of dark thread lying on white-speckled desolation. Headlamps swung through mist. 'Do we take Nilla?' he asked.

'Yes. She's good. She's independent. She's—'

'You slept with her. She wants more of you and you're asking her to help save the woman you love.'

'Nilla's bigger than that.'

'Jesus, Rake.' Mikki laughed out loud. 'You only knew her for a day.'

'As a team, we've been across there before. Nilla knows the border. She knows snow. And she's not the one who betrayed. Her security clearance is too low. She knows shit.'

'See. You're biased.' Mikki turned on wipers. The road sloped down between two jagged slopes. A wall of hail splattered onto the windscreen. The road rose out of the dip. The hailstorm ended as suddenly as it started. A dull light hung low casting a gray-orange glow over the white. Mikki held his hand loosely on the wheel, understanding how cold worked on a metaled road, letting the tires move naturally over the camber and stray ice patches, trusting the vehicle to right itself. He slowed on the outskirts of Kirkenes. Drifted snow piled against walls of dull apartment blocks. A few people were out, heads down to avoid windchill, faces covered against frostbite.

Rake called Nilla. It went to voicemail, said she was on leave, which only made sense if she were being investigated for what had gone down across the border. Mikki pulled up outside Nilla's building. The path had not been cleared of snow. Ice covered the windows. Rake trod through the snow to the front door. A frozen sheet of paper was pinned to it: *Gått til min gård.* Rake used his phone to get a translation: *Gone to my farm.*

It was an hour's drive south. Mikki drove fast on good gritted roads while Rake called Harry Lucas, whose tone was edged with irritation.

He briefed Lucas on the dangers of St Petersburg and Carrie's plan to get to Nikel and out of Russia.

'What do you need?

'To go through the border and back with a vehicle,' Rake said. 'FSB border guards on side and weapons in case it goes bad.'

'Who's going with you?'

'Mikki and Nilla Carsten.'

'Could you and Wekstatt do it alone?'

'Nilla Carsten has the language and local knowledge. She knows the FSB.'

'Point taken, Major. I need you back in Norway with Carrie and the drive by ten hundred, day after tomorrow. Merrow and Lagutov are holding a summit at the start of Dynamic Freedom. The venue is Kirkenes. She needs to be in Norway before the President's plane touches down.'

Rake's expression furrowed. Mikki glanced across, sensing that something had changed.

'Who called it?' asked Rake.

'Lagutov.' Lucas softened his tone. 'Yeah, I know. The Russians are way ahead of us.'

Mikki slowed at a small rotary where snow was heaped up against the walls of a shopping center. He swung left. The road ran alongside a gray iced lake edged by leafless trees. Wind came straight at them, buffeting the vehicle.

'Get me what I need,' said Rake, 'and we'll be wrapped well before the summit.'

THIRTY-FIVE

Train to Olenegorsk. Murmansk Oblast, Russia

C arrie was an hour out of Olenegorsk. She had become used to the rhythm, bad air, and animal sounds of the railcar. She had slept only to be woken by damp straw falling from high up onto her face. The soldier had still not spoken a word, except to the horses. He was good with them, calming, talking softly. They got jittery every time the train pulled out of a station. One had kicked hard enough to dent the steel of the container. A mare whinnied for a long, excruciating hour or more while the soldier pampered, coaxed, and soothed her to quiet. Every so often he went into a container to clean out soiled straw and splash around ammonia. Carrie offered to help. He put both hands up as if to say, 'Stay away from me and my work.'

The soldier was inside a container with one of the horses when they both heard a single rap on the door. It was followed by fast, sharp knocking. The lock shook. Voices, loud above the noise of the train, demanded the door be opened. Color evaporated from the soldier's face, not fear, not surprise. He took on a completely new demeanor, like a soccer player waiting on the benches and now called onto the pitch. He snapped a lid back on a can of ammonia, stepped out, and bolted the container door. He looked at Carrie, pointed to the door at the other far end, and spoke for the first time. 'Through there. Now.' Carrie picked up her gear, brushing away straw clinging to her coat. The solder spoke on his phone. He unclipped a trapdoor under his stool and lifted out a machine gun, a pistol, and other weaponry, prepared for trouble long before Carrie arrived. From outside, there was harsher, impatient thudding, forceful voices, threatening to shoot out the locks. The noise set off a stream of high-pitched neighs and whinnies from the horses. Pistol in hand, machine gun slung around his shoulder, the soldier led Carrie to the other door. As he crouched to lift the bolt, a single rap came from the other side, a rifle butt on metal and a command: 'Federal Security Bureau. Open this door.'

Both doors at either end of the railcar were blocked. They were boxed in. 'Not FSB,' whispered the soldier.

'Open this door now!'

The soldier replied in a firm, steady tone. 'This railcar is under the jurisdiction of the armed forces. I need to seek authority from the Security Council before I comply.'

'Two minutes.'

Another prompt from the door behind them. 'We have authorization to break in.'

'I advise you to wait for the Security Council decision,' insisted the soldier. Compared to the heated urgency from outside, he was calm and authoritative. The soldier's eyes searched every filthy crevice and dark space in the railcar. He pointed to the pile of soiled straw, loosely held within the orange rope netting that hung from the ceiling way above her head. Wet, filthy clumps bulged through, pushing out at the edges. Inside bacterial feces and urine rotted. Carrie suppressed an urge to retch. 'They're not after me. I can—'

'They are after Carrie Walker and that is you,' he said.

Her resolve crumbled. She slowed her breathing. The railcar tang that had become familiar seeped down her throat and churned her stomach. Nausea enveloped her. The soldier was right. The fetid mound of horseshit was the only place. He slid his pistol into his belt, unbuttoned a couple of squares of the netting, and used a pitchfork to hold the straw back from tumbling down, uncovering a stench sharper than anything in the air. The rapping on the doors became louder. The soldier's free hand reached for his pistol, Carrie thought to take them on, but he leveled it at her face. He wouldn't hesitate to shoot her. His expression had a hardness of determination. If she continued to risk his safety and of his horses, he would kill her. 'Take your bags,' he instructed. She put on her black woolen hat and leather gloves and picked up the bags. 'There is a trapdoor on the floor, bolts at each end,' he said. 'The train will stop either on a red signal or at the next station. Be ready. Open it, drop out, and run.' Using both hands, Carrie clawed open a space, pulling out clumps of straw and dropping them on the carriage floor. She climbed in, tearing out more, until she was in with her bags, her face pressed up against sickly excrement and scratchy edges of straw. The smell overpowered her. The soldier replaced the hay, pushing it up against her like closing a full suitcase. He sealed her in with the plastic netting. Dark, damp, airless, Carrie became disorientated like she was drunk. She took short breaths to prevent vomiting. Bile rose in her throat causing her to cough. Strands of straw caught in her mouth. She tasted horseshit, spat it away. She waited for the dizziness to pass. She eased the straw apart, just a fraction. She needed to keep her bearings. She heard bolts drawing across, the grind of the hinges, male voices, argumentative, loud enough to catch phrases. 'Where is she? . . . Who? . . . The American doctor . . .' A sway of the train. Rustle of straw. Lost next words. They were closer. She could see their heads and upper torsos. Carrie's soldier said, 'I am alone with the horses. No one is here, and this railcar is under the jurisdiction of the Presidential Regiment of the Russian Armed Forces.'

'Fuck the President.' There were two men, stocky, around six feet, one in a suit, tie, scarf, and dark overcoat, the other in a dark-blue down jacket. She couldn't see their hands. Their faces were jumpy, not in control like the soldier, who said: 'I care for the horses. I work alone. We are going to the December thirtieth ceremony at Severomorsk.'

'There won't be a ceremony if you don't hand her over,' said the one in the overcoat. The other in the down jacket stepped out of Carrie's arc of vision. She heard a crashing thud against the side of a container. A horse whinnied, the mare that the soldier had spent time calming. She screeched, hooves smashing against steel. 'She is pregnant,' explained the soldier. 'She is nervous.'

'Where is the woman, or I shoot your horse.'

'If you do, I will kill you.'

The soldier took a step toward the container. There was a jolt of the train. The man in the overcoat stumbled, reached out for balance, and found the rope netting, pulling on it, loosening the straw, freeing up Carrie's view. The other had his back to the container, elbows hooked over the side, like he was leaning against a bar. He wore a sneer on his face. He carried a machine pistol and another weapon in a shoulder holster underneath his jacket.

A batch of straw fell to the floor. Carrie pressed herself back to stop being seen. The train slowed, then jerked again. The wooden stool Carrie had been using fell over. To her horror, she saw a glimpse of red material. She had left the scarf there. The man in the overcoat saw it and shouted, 'They were right. She is here.'

THIRTY-SIX

The man in the down jacket unbolted the door at the back of the carriage and two more men stepped in. Each had a similar build and wore black jackets. They put their hands over their mouths against the stench. One coughed with a tubercular sound from deep within damaged lungs. Outnumbered, Carrie's soldier moved to protect the pregnant mare. A jolt of the train knocked the pitchfork, clattering to the floor. The man in the overcoat picked it up and seemed to look straight at her, but gave no reaction meaning she must still be hidden. Then, he said: 'Let's try inside this pile of shit.' He drew back his arm and plunged in the pitchfork, missing Carrie's head by an inch. The man with the cough said, 'Stand back. I'll give it a few rounds.'

He couldn't have been more than eighteen, a child soldier, a kid with a gun. His face was pale and thin, his expression cold, detached, also anxious, a weedy guy, sick, desperate to prove himself. He couldn't see her, but she could see every contour of his intent. He was about to kill her. Her jawline tightened as she tried to control her reflexes. She had never experienced such undiluted fear. She had seen how bullets tore flesh and organs apart. Half her mind went to Brooklyn, her bickering mother and father, Angie and her nephew and niece, life flashing by you stuff. The stronger half of her mind calculated bad options. If she screamed out and surrendered, there was no guarantee she would survive and a good chance the kid would open fire in panic. If Carrie was found, the soldier would defend himself and his horses over her.

'Go ahead,' the man in the overcoat told the kid. He leant the pitchfork against the railcar wall and folded his arms. The other two men held their weapons ready, but relaxed, watching. Bring on the fun. Let the boy make a fool of himself. The American doctor had forgotten her scarf. It lay bundled on the wooden stool. They had won. They were right. The one who had come in with the boy tipped a cigarette out of a pack. The soldier said: 'No smoking. Horses don't like it.' His tone was soft and assured and had no urgency that Carrie was about to be shot. He had his back to the container with the mare who was restless, stamping hooves.

'Screw you.' A lighter flared. In the next few seconds, several things happened. The boy fired into the mound of straw, high and blind. The rounds crunched through above Carrie. She heard their hissing. Smacking into the metal wall. One of the men said, 'Fire lower, kid.' Two crashing explosions of gunfire echoed around the carriage. The soldier killed the man with the cigarette. As he fell, the boy's face changed to terror, then bravado. He aimed right at Carrie. 'Stop!' she screamed. The boy's expression turned to surprise. Carrie stumbled out, tearing at the straw, wet, scratching her skin. Gunfire from the soldier smashed into the boy. His warm arterial blood splattered onto Carrie. From deep on the other side of the railcar came a single shot that hit the soldier. He flinched, stayed on his feet, and responded with four rounds, shattering his attacker's legs and ripping away half his face. The man in the overcoat, close to Carrie, fired three rounds toward the soldier, who fell heavily against the container. Carrie couldn't see exactly because the boy had toppled forward, his head caught through the rope netting, like in a noose. His corpse blocked her view, staring straight at her with wide-open empty eyes.

There was quiet apart from skittering horses. The man in the overcoat kept his weapon on Carrie while he freed the boy's head and let the body thud to the floor. Only he and Carrie were left. The mare reared up and unleashed her hoof against the container wall. Other horses did the same, creating an overpowering sound of frightened animals. Fresh cold air streamed in from the two open doors. The stink of horseshit mixed with the smell of gunfire. Carrie clung onto the rope netting. She spat a strand of straw from her mouth. Given they had used the manure heap for target practice, the surviving gunman would have no orders to take her alive. He could kill her and display her body and his would be a job well done. They examined each other. The overcoat hung well on him; drawn in at the waist with a matching belt. He looked out of place. He could have been a commuter heading to the office. He was broad-shouldered and slim. His face was long, his look shrewd. He lowered his weapon. Three confirmed dead. Two probably dead. Two survivors. 'Are you Dr Walker?' he said.

Carrie nodded. She took off her glove and wiped her face with the back of her hand.

'A lot of men have died because of you,' he accused. Nothing to say. Carrie stayed quiet.

'Passport.' He held out his hand like a guard at a checkpoint. Carrie unzipped an inside pocket from her jacket and brought out the false passport that Yumatov had delivered to her. Her captor didn't have a scanner so he couldn't verify it. He read the name, leafed through to the Russian visa, and, to her surprise, gave it back to her. 'Sit.' He pointed to the wooden stool, which had tipped over, the red scarf tangled in one of its three legs.

She moved toward the straw, stepped across the boy's body, picked it up, folded the scarf, made sure the legs were firm on the floor, and sat. He took a flashlight from his coat and shone it high along the wall. It stopped on a smudged and dirty red plastic handle just above head-height behind the stack of soiled straw, the alarm that would bring the train to a screeching halt. He turned the flashlight off. Carrie saw her soldier move his leg. A speck of hope rippled through her. He had only been protecting his horses. Her captor saw it, too, and shot the soldier with two rounds, one in the torso, one in the head. Carrie recoiled and looked away. Then she spun back, torn with anger. 'Fuck you, whoever you are!' she yelled. 'No one has died because of me. They have died because of pricks like you.'

He typed into his phone. Outside dawn had broken. The rising sun managed to stream light into the carriage. For a fleeting beat a shadow fell across the open doorway, enough for him to notice and turn, but not tense, not expecting trouble until a new crescendo of gunfire filled the carriage. He stood still, mid-turn, like a marionette, battered in one place, then the other, so ferociously that he couldn't even fall. Some shots went wide. None hit with accuracy. When they stopped, he fell onto Carrie's stool and slid to the floor. His phone tipped out of his hand, message unsent.

The door was closed and bolted. Hektor Tolstoye, limb hanging loose, came forward. He had shot with his left hand. He looked around, saw the soldier he had bribed, took in the other corpses. The horses quietened as if they understood that something terrible had happened. He tilted his head down to a green canvas bag hanging from his shoulder. 'Help me, please. I need a fresh magazine.'

The bag was coarse, heavy canvas material, weighed down by ammunition. Carrie counted three long magazines, a shorter one, and a pistol. The metal was ice cold, sticky on the skin. Hektor Tolstoye unclipped the spent magazine with his thumb. It clattered to the floor. He held the weapon steady while Carrie clipped in the fresh one. 'Check for wounded,' he said.

Carrie obeyed as if they were working together in the field. She began asking herself where Hektor Tolstoye got his weapons, which would be a big risk to have on a train. But this was Russia, a violent place. He had them. He had shot her enemy. He had his reasons for helping her. She went through the process of checking the dead, laying her fingers against the neck of each one, skin warm, cooling fast, nervous systems settling, muscles twitching, first the boy and she worked her way around. The soldier who loved horses lay curled up against the container, protecting his pregnant mare. Dead.

Hektor picked up the scarf and handed it to her. It was warm, weighty, full of colors. He lifted the trapdoor near the stool. Clumsily, with just his good hand, he removed metal bars on which the soldier had hidden his weapons. 'Before Olenegorsk, the train will stop on a red signal,' he said. 'You go down through here and come out on this side.' He pointed to the right of the railcar. 'There is a bank with bushes which will give you cover. Stay hidden until the train has gone. Go up the bank and you will come to the road. If there are people, stay hidden, and wait. If it is empty, walk north a hundred meters to a bigger road. Mikhail will be there in the green Skoda. Wear the red scarf, so he can recognize you clearly.'

Beneath her feet, through the trapdoor, the ground rushed by, rail track, sleepers, caked ice.

'What about all this?' She swept her hand around the carnage.

'I will arrange. You leave. I close the doors. They find it in Murmansk.' He reached into the bag and bought out the pistol and a spare magazine. 'For you.'

'No.' Carrie had often been offered a weapon and always refused.

'Give it to Mikhail. He needs it. For me. A favor.' It wasn't a favor. He wanted her to be able to protect herself. But this was not a time to argue. She opened her bag, let him drop it in.

'There are people who want to destroy Russia,' said Hektor. 'But why so much over you?'

'I don't know.' Carrie tensed her muscles protectively around the flash drive.

'Rufus asked if you could be his mother.' Hektor attempted a brief smile, clawing at a lighter future.

'Tell him sure. We can be pen pals first.'

'Pen pals?'

'We email each other. Keep in touch.' Carrie clasped her hands together, looked at the blood on them. The train slowed. Hektor checked his watch. First came a jerk of the engine cutting speed, brakes gently applied. Carrie arranged her bags with the medical pack at her front like a parachute and the other slung around her back. 'Too dangerous.' Hektor lifted it off her. 'I will give you.' The train slowed more. Hektor tottered and reached out for balance with the right hand he didn't have. He leaned against the wall. The moving ground came into focus through the trapdoor. There was clarity in the dawn light, the red signal reflected off the snow, a final judder, and the train came to a stop.

Carrie swung down her legs and lowered herself to the ice. Her right foot slipped. She held the edges of the trapdoor until she felt secure and took the bag from Hektor. His eyes remained steady on her until her closed the trapdoor. Carrie was bent double in a glare of morning sun on ice. Wind whipped between the track and the carriage. She shivered and drew in freezing fresh air which caught in her throat. The railcar shook. A huge wheel clicked forward. Carrie scrambled out as the railcar lurched. She ran until she reached undergrowth, branches scratching her face, brittle, spiky, and cold. Above lay the bank that would lead to the road. She waited for the train to pass. Railcar after railcar, four or five like the one with the horses, others open with guns, tanks, and military equipment. She watched the train disappear into the distance where there was mist and the contours of Olenegorsk.

THIRTY-SEVEN

Carrie grasped branches and found footholds in the ice. The bank was steep and slippery. There were plastic bags blown onto bushes and frozen hard. She pulled herself up to a vast white landscape. She looked for a green Skoda, saw only a narrow, rutted road flanked by thin, dark trees. The phone signal was good. She messaged Rake: *Off train. Olenegorsk.* It helped her feel normal. *I'm here. Running late. Where are you?* What a luxury! Rake was her go-to guy. Yes, she thought, let's sort out today's shit and make it work. Two words came back from Rake. *On plan.* She tried to think of something useless, funny, affectionate. Normal times, she would take a photo and send it. Normal wasn't infected with electronic tracking surveillance and burner phones.

The sky looked restless with jagged, black snow clouds, wisped with white ones which twisted and curved into a river-like line of deep blue. On one side of the road stood spiky, barren trees, on the other slanted, wind-battered telegraph poles, snow clinging to their frozen wood bases, icicles hanging like a modern-art installation, cables drooping, but holding up. She saw vehicle movement by the intersection ahead, this the smaller farm road crossing the bigger one that led to the town. There were two vehicles. She swiped away her breath cloud like smoke obstructing her view. One vehicle stopped, taller than the other, maybe an SUV. The other kept coming slowly, weaving around potholes and ice packs. It was green and had to be the Skoda as Hektor had described. She lowered herself back down the bank, out of sight to stay under cover until she could see the make of the car.

The vehicle sloped down on the driver's side. Its green bodywork was peppered with rust spots. The bonnet was silver, the passenger front door a dirty faded blue. A front-wheel hubcap was missing, and a crack streaked right across the middle of the windscreen. In the middle of the upper radiator cage, almost unblemished, was the winged arrow of the Skoda logo.

Carrie draped the red scarf over her hat and let it fall onto her shoulders. She scrambled back up the bank. The Skoda drew up beside her, fogged with cigarette smoke until the driver lowered the window.

'Mikhail?'

He pushed open the passenger door. The leather seat was torn. Rust had eaten through the floor. Carrie climbed in, kept her medical bag on her lap, the other at her feet. Mikhail tossed his cigarette out the window. He wore black woolen gloves with finger holes, missing the right-hand middle finger. A scar ran down the left side of his face which was gaunt, cheeks drawn in, covered in a couple of days' growth. He was extraordinarily thin, veins protruding from his wrist and neck, which was disproportionately big. He was not a well man, might be an overactive thyroid. Carrie drew the pistol from her bag. 'This is from Hektor.'

'Keep it,' he said.

'But—'

'Keep it,' he repeated. He moved the stick into gear, made a single turn in the road, and began back toward the intersection.

'Who's that?' Carrie pointed ahead to the second vehicle.

'Friends. Better car to take you to Nikel.'

They rode in silence. Carrie messaged Rake. *In car.* There was no heating. Windows were down. Wind cut through, unforgiving, tearing through the trees and telegraph poles, sending icy pellets against Carrie's face. She drew the scarf tighter and dabbed lip balm onto her cracked lips. The second vehicle was a black SUV stretch, which would be sturdy and warm with good suspension and solid heating. A driver sat behind the wheel. A second man leaned on the hood, seemingly oblivious to the cold. Mikhail stopped some yards away. He leaned across her to open her door.

'What—' Carrie felt a churn in her stomach. It wasn't right, although everything made sense, the new vehicle, the friends, keeping the gun she had anticipated. Mikhail's surly, monosyllabic conversation. *Stay calm.* She checked her phone. Nothing from Rake.

'They will take you.'

They, not him, Hektor's cousin. Mikhail kept his gaze straight ahead. He pulled out another cigarette, unfiltered and crushed, from his top jacket pocket. He hung it between his lips and pushed in the Skoda's lighter. Carrie got out, gripped the top of the door to stay steady on the ice. Between her and the SUV what looked like a farm sack lay in the middle of the road. She leaned down to check back with Mikhail. He plucked out the lighter and lit his cigarette, inhaling deeply, not looking at her.

The man waiting outside the SUV pushed himself off the hood, arm outstretched in beckoning wave. She hoisted her bag more securely onto her shoulder. Treading carefully, she walked to meet him.

He shouted something, lost in a howl of wind. Carrie's eyes watered. She pulled the scarf right around her face, protecting everything except her eyes. His face was covered, too, small goggles over the eyes, quality cold-weather clothing. He walked fast on the other side of the road, pointed to the Skoda, held up his right hand, five fingers splayed as if to say: *Got to talk to Mikhail. Give me a few minutes.*

There was someone else in the SUV. Carrie spotted movement in the back. Its engine ran, exhaust white, vanishing in swirl. She stepped left to skirt around the farm sack. Except, closer, when she saw what it actually was, her strength drained. She had to stop herself buckling. She cried out from deep in her belly but had no voice. She squatted down to see more. She put her arm out to check and pulled it back because it was pointless. The amputated arm was enough. The red, scarred face lay on the ice, the neck twisted. She recognized the brown jacket. Less than an hour earlier Hektor Tolstoye had saved her life. Now, he was dead, his body here as a warning. She looked back toward the Skoda. Through the cracked, filthy windscreen, she saw Mikhail, just as she had left him, hands on the wheel, cigarette in mouth, eyes straight ahead, Hektor Tolstoye's cousin. Or so she had been told.

The man from the SUV leaned on the roof of the Skoda, head at the window, as if casually chatting to Mikhail. In his right hand was a pistol. He killed Mikhail. The wind carried the two cracks of pistol shot. Blood splattered the windscreen. The killer stepped back, holstered the pistol, and moved quickly toward Carrie. He pulled up his goggles and lowered his scarf. A broad smile stretched across his face. 'Ruslan Yumatov. Remember? I helped you in Moscow.'

He touched her elbow, informal, friendly, and moved on ahead to the vehicle to open the back door for her. Rufus sat inside, upright in the middle of the bench seat, the safety belt around him, clutching his battered book of fairy tales. He saw Carrie. His eyes glimmered with recognition and surprise. Carrie mustered every strand of broken energy to show him a face of certainty, to portray falsely that he would be all right.

'Hello, Rufus.' Carrie's voice cracked.

He looked at her expectantly. He would have seen his uncle murdered, which would have been Yumatov's point. Rufus' lips opened to speak. He said nothing and looked back down at his book.

'Great kid. Fantastic future.' Yumatov laid his arm on her again and switched to English. 'Do what I ask, Carrie, and he'll be fine.'

She didn't shake him away because she didn't want to give him the pleasure of her discomfort. She got into the back of the SUV and gave Rufus a tight, consoling hug. Yumatov shut her door and got in the front. The driver pulled away. Carrie looked back at the battered green sedan, the body lying in the middle of the farm track, misty snow. Rufus trembled, hands shaking, as he pretended to read Russian fairy tales.

Yumatov turned, arm slung over the back of his seat. 'You got your uncle's flash drive?'

Carrie didn't look at him, didn't answer. She ran her fingers through Rufus's hair.

'Work with me, Carrie, and we'll all be fine. It's four to five hours to Nikel and Rake's expecting you. The FSB are letting him through at the border. Message him that you're safe and on your way.'

THIRTY-EIGHT

Svanvik, Finnmark, Norway

In car. Safe. Carrie's message came as Mikki swung into Nilla's farm near Svanvik, a sprawl of dark wooden buildings, smoke curling from chimneys, sleds lined up, and dog and boot prints on the snow.

'She's on her way,' Rake said. 'We have seven hours max.' He opened the vehicle door and heard barking. A young woman, using ski poles to stop herself sliding, came toward them.

'Nilla Carsten?' asked Rake.

She pointed down a short slope toward a wooden fence, an open gate, and a compound of kennels. Near the entrance, Nilla was giving a lesson on how to harness a dog. Kennels were dotted around behind her. A noticeboard allocated a dog to each kennel. Color-coding told their temperament and recommended which dog was suited to which. Rake couldn't help noting the combination; Skye, a lead dog, Jake and Ranta, an excellent pair of point dogs who came after the lead. Skye and Jake had the strongest sense of smell. Nilla held a wriggling brown and gray husky called Finn. Half a dozen students gathered round. 'You hold Finn between your legs like this,' she instructed in English. 'Bring your heels together like this.' She took her hands off the dog, held them in the air. 'That gives you control over her. See? No hands. She might twist around. She might try to get free. But you have her secured.' Nilla held up the yellow and red harness, which is when she saw Rake, took a beat, twisted the halter in shape, and kept teaching. 'Bring the harness into a loop, big enough to fit.' She slipped the halter over the dog's head, opened it out, secured it over the neck and through the two front legs. She beckoned over the young woman with the ski poles. 'I'll be back in a moment, Izzy. Get them to practice.'

She said to Rake: 'Hello, trouble. You caused hell in Washington, now you're on my farm so what's up?'

'Come to get you back to work,' said Rake.

'I've been suspended pending an investigation.'

'It's been lifted. Check your phone.'

Nilla drew her phone out of a jacket pocket and saw several messages. 'Why?' she asked with cool suspicion in her eyes.

'We need you to lead us back across the border.'

She pointed across the road where a sign said *Office*. Rake and Mikki followed her. Inside, cold-weather gear hung from wall hooks. Boots lined shelves. Fur gloves were piled up on tables. There were chairs, benches, maps, brochures, and a smell of coffee. A bearded man in his thirties worked a laptop behind the one desk. 'My brother, Stefan,' said Nilla. 'We own the farm. He runs it.' Stefan nodded, kept working, disinterested, people coming in and out all the time. Nilla pulled off her gloves and hat and let her hair fall.

She held Rake's head between her hands and kissed him full on the lips. 'You're dangerous and I forgive you.' She stood by the window, her lips moving silently as she read messages. She spoke in Norwegian to her brother, short enough and in a firm enough tone for Rake to get the gist. She needed the room. Stefan left. She kept reading. Mikki examined the cold-weather gear like he was in a shop, flipping through seal and reindeer skins, silk undervests, face masks, and fur gloves. 'Take your pick,' said Nilla, her eyes on her phone. 'We'll need it.' She scrolled her phone messages and looked intensely at Rake, a thin smile on her pursed lips. 'I am no longer suspended. My security clearance is restored. I am to work with Major Raymond Ozenna until further notice, blah blah, blah, so why doesn't Major Ozenna tell me what the fuck is going on.'

'We need to bring out an American citizen who's in danger.'

Nilla's jawline tightened. 'Is this to do with the shit last time?'

'Yes.'

'Who is this American citizen?'

'She got entrapped over there. A doctor.' Rake decided to tell her. Small teams in hostile environments don't work well with secrets. 'Her name is Carrie Walker.'

'Your ex-fiancée.' Not a muscle moved in Nilla's face.

'That's correct.' Rake kept his expression as flat and business-like as hers.

Nilla hissed, 'You come here, you fuck me, you ask me to risk my life rescuing your squeeze.'

'Sounds about right,' said Mikki, looking out from the storeroom.

Nilla spun round to look at Mikki. 'Why Rake?'

'Carrie trusts him, as do I,' said Mikki.

'I mean: why us? They have governments.'

'She's in trouble because there's been a leak,' said Rake.

'It's Finnmark and Russia, what do they expect.'

From the tightness of her face and the edge of her voice, Rake saw he needed to do more. He took her hand and brought her toward him. She didn't resist. He cupped the back of her head and kissed her slowly, confidently. He was not gentle, nor was he rushed. Her mouth tasted of mint gum. She kissed him back. Her hand ran down his back, pulled out his shirt to feel his skin. He did the same, feeling her warmth underneath her layers and silk vests. She shuddered, pressed herself against him, then pushed herself back, suppressing a smile, clearing her hair from her face. 'We go get Carrie Walker,' she said. 'Send her on her way, then we go to my place and fuck. Tell me it's a deal or I don't go.'

'It's a deal.' Rake gave her a light hug. A message came in from Harry Lucas. He checked it and moved to the map on the wall. 'Come out from lusting over those skins, Mikki,' he said. 'I need you here.' The map showed the border area with looping sled trails. Nilla and Mikki stood either side of him. Nilla brushed her hand against his leg.

Rake said: 'We head back north. It's been arranged for Einar Olsen to meet us with a police vehicle at Hessing outside of Kirkenes where the road heads east to the border. He has weapons. The FSB border guards have the green light to let us through.' He traced his finger along the route. From Nilla's farm to Nikel as the crow flew was about twenty miles. By road it was close to sixty miles, due north, across the border, then due south. Rake circled Nikel. 'Carrie will be somewhere here. We'll get confirmation. We pick her up, pay the guy who's helped her, bring her back.'

'Does she have a passport to get through?' asked Nilla.

'She does,' said Rake.

Nilla cupped her hands around her cheeks and studied the map.

'If we get opposition like last time, they could close the border. We'll need an alternative route out through the fence.' She ran her finger south from the border post toward Nikel, examining the line between Norway and Russia. 'Don't meet her at Nikel. Meet her here, just south of Salmiyarvi, across the bridge where the road goes down to water level. That's on the lake, less than two miles to the border, and it's smoother and faster than the sea ice you're used to. The fence is broken along here. If there's no trouble, we go back in the vehicle to the border crossing. If there is, we get across this way. We bring skis, snowshoes, and that's how we do it.'

Nilla pulled open the door and shouted for her brother to return.

Stefan appeared, stamping his boots to shake off the snow. Nilla spoke to him in Norwegian.

'Stefan was with FSK, that's our special forces,' said Nilla.

'I will be here,' said Stefan pulling a file from his laptop that showed the border fence and terrain. 'Nilla and I, we will make sure your girlfriend will be safe and back in Norway.'

THIRTY-NINE

Murmansk Oblast, Russia

C arrie's hands rested on Rufus' head as it lay on her lap. The child slept, breathing evenly in the air-conditioned warmth of Yumatov's vehicle. They bumped fast along the unrepaired road. Desolation cloaked the landscape, settlements of huts and houses, dirty snow, trees sagging, bleak and endless. The dashboard showed the outside temperature as minus fourteen Celsius. A flash drive she had handed to Yumatov protruded from a USB port next to the satellite navigation screen filled with a logo, *SanDiskSecureAccess*. Yumatov flipped back and forth. There were instructions on how to use it, links to download, offers to sign up.

Yumatov's face clouded. There was cold quietness in his voice: 'What's this, Carrie? You take me for a fool?'

'Get your tech guys onto it.' She matched him with tense calm. When he had asked her to hand him her uncle's flash drive, she gave him one she had bought in Moscow. 'Maybe it's encrypted or something.'

'You have something else?'

'The guy was dying. I didn't know it was there until I was running. Search me if you want. But, yes. That's it.'

Yumatov sent messages on his phone. He told the driver to speed up. He made calls, asking questions, giving monosyllabic instructions. Rufus slept. The driver chewed gum and kept his eyes on the road.

'Even if you do have it, Carrie, you're not going anywhere, so nor is that drive.' Yumatov settled back in his seat. They traveled in silence until they turned west off the main Murmansk road. Carrie asked where they were going. Yumatov did not answer. Rufus shifted on her lap. His fairy-tale book fell to the floor. She picked it up and laid it at the end of the seat. She gave time for tension to drain and tried a gentler approach, 'Why not tell me what's going on, Ruslan. Where we're going, what's happening? Maybe I can help you.'

Yumatov turned in his seat to look at her, his face smooth like marble, his body fit, worked out, attractive even. 'How old are you, Carrie?'

Carrie answered straight. 'Thirty-seven, turning thirty-eight.'

'What is your sister's name?'

'Angela.' She told herself to ride with it.

'Is she older or younger?'

'Younger.'

'Married.'

'Yes.'

'Children.'

'A boy and a girl.'

'That's nice, Carrie. Family is good. Children bring stability, don't you think?' His tone matched hers, kind, conversational. He showed her a photograph on his phone, two children, heads together, big smiles, in a park somewhere. 'Natasha. See that cheeky grin? She's five. And Max. He's seven.' Yumatov flipped to another photograph, himself and an elegant woman, around forty, in a dark blue evening dress standing outside the Bolshoi Theater in Moscow. 'Their mother. Anna. She is a professor. I am so lucky to have found her. So, so lucky.'

The vehicle jolted. His finger accidentally swiped the picture away. 'I don't know what I would do if anything happened to her. That's what confuses me. I am forty-three. You are thirty-eight. We are children of the same generation. We understand about our broken Russia. I look at you and I hope to see an American with the blood of Russia who understands why we do what we do.'

The vehicle swerved. Carrie steadied herself against the back of Yumatov's seat. Outside, a reindeer carcass lay on the road. Two black crows pecked at the frozen hide.

Yumatov tapped his head. 'You're crazy, Carrie. Look at you. Stinking of horseshit when you could have been showered, smelling fresh, and on a plane to New York.'

'Right now, Ruslan, I would love to be in New York.'

'Funny, Carrie. Very funny. You're desperate to get away from the safe Brooklyn life your parents built for themselves. You are suffocated by the thought of being like your sister and her perfect family. You're ambitious. I like that. That new job at Washington General Hospital.'

A chill ran through Carrie that he was playing her with so much personal information. She felt the rhythm of Rufus's breathing. She touched his forehead to check his temperature, which was fine. Rufus opened his eyes and gripped Carrie's hand. 'I need the toilet,' he whispered.

Carrie said in English, like they were a couple out for a weekend, 'We need to stop. Rufus needs to pee.'

Yumatov caught her eyes in the mirror and nodded to the driver, who pulled up at the side of the empty road. Carrie secured Rufus' jacket, tightened his scarf, wound her red scarf around his neck as extra warmth, and pulled his woolen hat over his ears.

'I'll go with him,' said Yumatov.

Rufus looked at her, terrified. Yumatov was out of the vehicle, banging his hands together, clouding his face with condensation, looking around at the emptiness. Rufus scrambled out stood with his back to Yumatov.

'Where are we going?' Carrie asked the driver.

No answer.

'How long until we get there?'

The driver chewed gum and stared ahead. Yumatov took Ruslan's hand and led him back to the vehicle. Yumatov stayed outside, talking on the phone. He ended the call, got in, turned back in his seat, and ruffled Rufus' hair. 'Feeling better?' he asked.

'Thank you, sir,' muttered Rufus, staring at the floor.

'Good news, Carrie.' An expansive smile spread across Yumatov's face. 'We can relax. Your President has agreed to meet my President before the start of Dynamic Freedom. Thank God, everyone finally sees sense.'

FORTY

Moscow

Stephanie Lucas watched Sergey Grizlov's motorcade pull up under the stucco balcony of her ambassadorial residence and ended her conversation with the British Prime Minister. Kevin Slater had called about the suddenly announced US–Russian presidential summit on Norway's royal yacht in a small town in the Arctic Circle. Slater was a life-long left-wing activist who started in office a couple of years earlier raw and over-keen. It took all efforts to stop him dismantling Britain's nuclear deterrent and demobilizing half its armed forces. Slater became more measured and earned a reputation as a pragmatic elder statesman, a win-win with British voters who had had enough false dreams over Brexit.

Slater told Stephanie she was to stand in for the British Foreign Secretary at the summit. 'Ambassador is the right level, Steph, not Foreign Secretary,' Slater said. 'We can't be too close to America. Can't be appeasing Russia, and I want your expert eyes and ears on it.'

Stephanie didn't conceal her enthusiasm to be a fly on the wall of history. She thanked Slater as Grizlov stepped out of his limousine in the elegant nineteenth-century forecourt. Grizlov held his brown wolf-fur hat in his left hand and smoothed down his overcoat lapels with his right. He had called her less than an hour earlier asking if he could drop by. She rigged up a sound feed for Harry to listen in.

'Sergey, what a pleasant surprise.' Stephanie led him to the dining room with its huge mirrors, black marble mantelpiece, and corniced ceiling, all decorated with deep yellow gold leaf. She pulled out two red velvet hard-backed chairs, creating an informal atmosphere in a grand setting. Grizlov stayed on his feet. He hadn't even given her a cursory kiss.

'Ruslan Yumatov has gone rogue,' he said. 'There's been a

mass killing on a train to Murmansk. Five bodies were found in a railcar. All male, all shot to death.'

Stephanie couldn't blame Grizlov for being so wound up. Yumatov was his man. She kept a smooth control of her voice. 'You're sure Yumatov's responsible?'

'Carrie Walker was on that train, trying to escape Russia.'

Stephanie sat down heavily, realizing now why Grizlov had come straight to her. 'Is she all right?'

'She befriended a family in third class. When Yumatov's men came looking for her, they hid her in this railcar.'

'But is she all right, Sergey?'

'Her body wasn't found in the railcar, which was under the control of the Presidential Regiment transporting horses for a ceremony in Severomorsk that is to take place after the summit. Carrie is missing, somewhere around the city of Olenegorsk south of Murmansk.'

Stephanie let out a long, grateful sigh that, at least, Carrie hadn't been killed or captured. Harry would have that information and would need to find a way to get her across the border. 'What ceremony?' she asked.

'Lagutov wants to cap the summit with a parade in Severomorsk on December 30th. That was one of the trains transporting armaments and equipment there.'

'December 30th is the anniversary of the creation of the Soviet Union in 1922, the Union of Soviet Socialist Republics. The old empire.'

'Exactly.'

'What's Lagutov playing at?'

'I hope I'm wrong, Steph, but let me show you this.' Grizlov put his tablet on the table and brought up a picture of a male corpse in a mortuary, most of the skull blown away. The body lay on its front, the back exposed showing an intricate circular tattoo. 'Do you recognize this?'

Stephanie did. It was a Slavic pagan symbol that had bedeviled Europe. Hitler had even stolen its design to create the swastika. 'The Slavic Kolovrat.'

'Correct, and this body belongs to a Josip Milotic, the man who stole the identity of your security guard and murdered Artyom Semenov. Someone from your embassy took him out.'

Grizlov gave her an appreciative look to which Stephanie did not react. He moved to another image of two male bodies on a night-time street and a black van filled with bullet holes. He gave Stephanie a few seconds to absorb and changed to a close-up of the bodies in a morgue. 'See the tattoos.'

'The Kolovrat,' whispered Stephanie.

The next picture showed Gerald Cooper's severed ear that had been embedded in the reindeer carcass. Stephanie examined the curve of the cut and saw how it could be interpreted as a rough attempt to show the eight-sided spoked wheel. Grizlov moved to a picture of a study or office, books about Europe and Slavic history, the legends of the Kolovrat and more recent events like Russia taking Crimea and the West taking Kosovo.

'We raided Yumatov's Moscow apartment,' said Grizlov. 'These photographs are barely an hour old. His wife and children have left for London. She has a visiting professorship at the London School of Economics. They were given visas three months ago.'

'It was planned?' said Stephanie, wanting to say something more sensible, but not knowing what.

'Yumatov went to the President in August last year and sold him the same line that he sold me, about Russia's need to ally itself to the West. Lagutov gave him a hand-written note asking me to work with him.'

'And his real aim was the exact opposite?'

'Yes.'

'But why kill Cooper, why the severed ear, why such an elaborate show of brutality?'

'A message of power. Just because he is intelligent and well-read doesn't mean that violence is not Yumatov's natural home. He is clever to use Slavic nationalism because it goes wider than Russia. It includes Central and Eastern Europe, the old arc of Soviet power, Poland, Serbia, Slovakia, a lot of countries that are turning authoritarian. We know from military flight records that Yumatov traveled from Moscow to Severomorsk on the afternoon that Cooper was killed. Milotic was stationed in Severomorsk. They both flew to Moscow the next day. They had worked together in Syria.'

Her strength back, shock subsiding, Stephanie stood up and swiped the tablet images back to the shot-out van and the two corpses. 'But these are Yumatov's men. Why would he kill them?'

'He didn't,' said Grizlov. 'Yumatov told me an Asian crime syndicate was out to wreck any détente we had with you guys. What he didn't say was that, here in Russia, he is leading it. We asked the CIA and your people what they might have and heard nothing. But the Japanese got back to us straight away. There is such an Asian organization with broad plans as Yumatov outlined.'

Afternoon winter sun fell onto the table. Stephanie played her fingers in and out of its dancing patches of light while sorting through what Grizlov was revealing. At the center stood Ruslan Yumatov, who planned to use Asian money and a revival of pan-Slavic nationalism to change the face of Europe. Even if Yumatov was just another man with a gun looking for relevance, it was a theory that should not be underestimated. The bloodshed in the Balkans and the origins of the First World War carried similar Slavic symbolism. Stephanie steadied a rising panic that Carrie wouldn't get out, that she would be murdered on some frozen steppe for an ancient pagan symbol and flash drive with a big swinging dick.

'Then it's not Yumatov who's gone rogue.' Stephanie took Grizlov's arm. 'He's working with the Kremlin. Soviet ideology might be dead, but Russian Slavic nationalism isn't. December 30th we'll see a ceremony with tanks, missiles, and horses and the symbol of the Kolovrat. Isn't that right, Sergey. Isn't that what all this about?'

Grizlov glanced down at her hand then at her. His skin was pale with a deep crease across his brow. But his eyes shone with energy. She had seen him like this, physically drained and mentally driven, back against the wall and excited about a way out. He took her hand off his arm, but kept hold of it, part affection, part in a formal handshake. He leaned forward to kiss her on the cheek. With his mouth close to her ear he whispered, 'Carrie has a six-hour window to cross into Norway. Until the end of the current FSB border guard shift.'

The Kasatka, Northern Fleet, Russian Navy, Barents Sea

Andrei Kurchin detected the small Gotland-class Swedish submarine *Halland* north of Vardø as she made her way to Kirkenes from the country's main naval base in Karlskrona in the south of the country. She was traveling at seventeen knots, without using her air-independent propulsion system and other stealth measures that would have slowed her speed and made her more difficult to find. The Gotland-class was one of the world's quietest and most nimble submarines, which is why Kurchin had chosen her for their target.

The *Halland*'s timing and location, thirty miles north of the Norwegian island of Vardø, was so precisely accurate that Kurchin yet again marveled at the reach and professionalism of Yumatov's network. Kurchin knew only a fraction, something about Yumatov that he admired and feared.

'Arm torpedo,' he ordered.

He was using the Shkval torpedo, whose rocket propulsion could send it to targets over long distances at up to 200 miles an hour. As it sped along, the Shkval vaporized water in front of it using a technology that engineers called supercavitating. For Kurchin, it was a better weapon, nothing more. He did not enjoy murdering fellow submariners. He brought his submarine to within three miles of the *Halland*, touched the black steel pendant of the Kolovrat that hung from a hook on the periscope, and gave the order to fire. The Shkval was noisy. But with its lethal speed, by the time the *Halland* crew understood what was happening, it would be too late to intervene, and they would be seconds from death.

Skorskog, Norway–Russia Border

Norwegian border police waved though Rake, Mikki, and Nilla in the late morning. They were traveling in an armored Land Cruiser. The temperature was minus thirteen Celsius with a chill factor created by strong wind. Pine trees flanked the road, making it feel as if they were gliding inside a cloud-filled canyon. Nilla slowed on approaching the Russian side, expecting an FSB Land Cruiser to pull out and drive with them. There was nothing.

Lights were on inside the timbered Russian buildings, but no one in sight, no traffic either. The Russian guards had melted away. Daytime moonlight casts a silver glow over the landscape. Cellphones switched to Russian networks. Rake fired up the encrypted satellite link and told Harry Lucas they were across.

'Future comms, your call sign is Sword Edge. Mine is Excalibur.'

'Sword Edge. Excalibur,' repeated Rake, words that would cut through noise from the worst blizzard.

'We're running drone surveillance along the border. Carrie is at a farmhouse three miles south of a place called Salmiyarvi, thirty minutes south from where you are now. She arrived ninety-eight minutes ago. We counted eleven people at the property, four vehicles. Carrie has a child with her. She walked him or her to the house. We are running advanced ID on the thermal image to confirm Yumatov is there. We have visuals on your vehicle, but not for long. The weather's coming down bad.'

'Bad weather can be our best friend,' said Rake.

FORTY-ONE

Salmiyarvi, Murmansk Oblast, Russia

Ruslan Yumatov opened the door onto the wrap-around wooden balcony of the old farmhouse south of the settlement of Salmiyarvi. A howling wind smashed into him. He steadied himself against the wall and kicked the door shut. Frozen clumps of mist swirled through the grounds. Before the blizzard knocked out satellite communications, Yumatov had made contact with technicians in Severomorsk and confirmed that the drive Carrie had given him was a fake. He had searched Carrie's bags. He had gotten the farmer's stupid wife to search Carrie herself. They had found nothing. As long as the real drive did not fall into the hands of NATO before the presidential summit, it could not pose a problem. The blizzard would ease. Rake Ozenna would be captured and the American murderer from the Diomede would be paraded in front of the Russian people. Any military planner worth his salt allowed for bad weather. The cellphone signal was still up, and Yumatov could see that the whiteout stretched north into the Barents Sea where the royal yacht HnoMY *Norge* had been hauled out of its winter dock to host the summit. News reports covered dignitaries arriving in Kirkenes and boarding the *Norge* with close-up shots of Foreign Minister Sergey Grizlov in a group with British Ambassador Lucas. Yumatov had identified the farmhouse the day after he murdered Gerald Cooper. The caretaker farmer was only too keen for the money and to accommodate such a famous Russian patriot. Although isolated, the house was close enough to the road and its land flat enough to take a helicopter. Encircling trees gave protection.

Yumatov took the stairs to the ground floor. Outside, under the cover of the balcony, six men sat on plastic chairs, hands cupped skillfully to keep their cigarettes alive against the weather. They stood up and saluted. Yumatov briefed the sergeant. He wanted two men on the field to guide in the helicopter when the weather quietened, two watching the road running north, and one in Salmiyarvi to alert Yumatov once Ozenna's vehicle had passed through.

The sergeant and the remaining man would stay in the house tasked with keeping the boy and Carrie safe. He needed Rufus Tolstoye to ensure Carrie stayed in line and he needed Carrie to lure in Rake Ozenna. Once the destruction of the Norwegian royal yacht and the two Presidents left the world reeling, Ozenna would be taken to Severomorsk for the ceremony and Carrie and the boy would die. The killing could be here, bodies burnt, ashes left in permafrost.

Carrie didn't look up when Yumatov walked in. He stood over her, arms folded. She concentrated on a yellow flame dancing around burning logs in a black iron stove that stood between two windows. 'I will explain how we worked in Syria,' he said. 'You decide what course to take.' He unbuttoned his greatcoat, took it off, folded it across the back of one of the chairs, and walked over to a scrubbed wooden table by the window. This was Yumatov's second visit to the room. It was a large, rambling building with rusting pipes and broken windows. Carrie had counted three black Land Cruisers outside. Yumatov had led her and Rufus into this spacious front room that was barely furnished. One part was warmed by the stove. The rest was ridden with drafts coming through windows on three sides. A red floral carpet covered most of the area. Three worn brown-leather armchairs circled the stove and, across the room, was the table with the wooden toys, where Yumatov now stood.

Earlier, he had brought in a kindly faced woman around sixty whom he introduced as Lydia. She carried a battered cardboard box which she placed on a table across the room and brought out colored wooden toys, cars with broken wheels and farmyard animals with missing legs, their paint chipped and faded. Rufus ran across to the table, picked up a toy cow with a leg snapped off. Yumatov said the toys would keep the boy occupied while Lydia body-searched Carrie outside. Lydia took her across the hall, where two of Yumatov's men stood by the door, into a freezing restroom with ice wrapped around ceiling pipes. Lydia explained she and her husband were caretakers for the house owned by a family now living outside of Russia. It was once lavish. Three decades of neglect had worn it down to what it was now. Lydia talked and apologized. She was cooking a stew for them. Her children had left home and were in Moscow. Money was so difficult now. Carrie said she understood what Lydia had to do, explaining she had given Yumatov everything she had. She asked if Lydia had any sanitary towels. Lydia shook her head. She was past menopause and they had no children here. Carrie told her not to worry. She would keep the tampon she already had. Lydia was embarrassed, ashamed, and she was not a nurse. The search was over in barely a minute. They had returned to the large room and Lydia had brought in steaming beef broth and chunks of bread. Yumatov had gone outside, issuing orders to his men. She calculated there were between six and twelve, although there could be battalions in the grounds.

Now he was back. He tipped all the wooden toys onto the table and flattened the cardboard from the box. He took Carrie's medical bag and placed rolls of bandages and antiseptic ointment at the end of the table. He unsheathed a knife from his waist and laid it next to them.

Rufus was running in circles in and out of the warmth, his hands stretched out pretending to be an airplane. His face was fixed like a statue of a child crying, no sound or tears. Yumatov called his name, asking him to come over to the table. Rufus's stopped, his arms dropped, like a shot bird. He ran to Carrie. Yumatov stepped across, pried Rufus' hands away from Carrie's shoulders, and carried him to the table. Lydia rested both her hands protectively on Rufus's shoulders. Carrie prayed for him to play up, yell out, slip away, give them hell. But she recognized his expression of helplessness, terror, paralysis.

'In Syria, we identified the strongest in the household.' Yumatov retained the same tone of courtesy and charm making his words even more chilling. 'Usually that was the husband and the father. We did not touch him. We cut up his wife and children while he watched. A human being can endure pain until death, but few can watch their loved ones suffer without talking. Tonight, Carrie, you are the head of the family and little Rufus is your loved one.' He walked back to Carrie, pulled round a chair with his foot, and sat down. He was wearing a shoulder holster with a pistol on his left side. He faced Carrie directly. His eyes were unsettled. They didn't match the certainty of his voice, something slight, like someone who had drunk too much coffee, suppressing jumpiness, like someone who tried to be the smartest in the room, but wasn't sure.

Carrie took advantage: 'How you doing, Ruslan? Max and Natasha good, are they? Cutting up Rufus is a sure way to win Anna's love and respect.'

Yumatov's face blackened. Lips pursed, muscles of his right arm tensed as if about to raise his hand. He stopped himself. 'I need to know what you have done with your uncle's data, Carrie. It is not on the drive you gave me. You are not carrying it. I will run through questions. If the answers are satisfactory, no one gets hurt. If you lie to me, Rufus will lose a finger. That will keep happening until you tell me the truth. One lie, one injury.'

Carrie leaned forward, elbows on knees, eyes unyielding, hard into Yumatov, upbeat tone the same: 'OK, Ruslan. I'll give it my best shot.'

Yumatov needed fear and control. Carrie responded with flippancy. He brushed his hand against his pistol as if to draw confidence. 'Vice-Admiral Semenov left you a military-grade drive containing classified information. Where is it?'

Carrie shrugged: 'I gave you what I found.'

'One lie, Carrie. I'll give you a pass and try again because I like you. When did you know Semenov had passed you the flash drive?'

'As I was running from his killing.'

'What did you do?'

'I was scared. I kept moving.'

'Where did you go?'

'A place called the Doctors' Cafe near the Sklifosovsky Clinic.'

'Yes, and did you give the drive to Stephanie Lucas when she found you there?'

That was unexpected. *How much did Yumatov know?* She couldn't help looking across to Rufus, the back of his head, a tuft of black hair needed combing, at Lydia the housekeeper, gray hair falling out beneath her head scarf, holding Rufus steady.

'I planned to give it to Ambassador Lucas once we reached

her residence. She was called to the Four Seasons to see the Foreign Minister and then you know what happened.'

Yumatov held up the tiny black drive. 'I ask you again, Carrie. Is this what Semenov left for you?'

'Yes.'

Yumatov swiped his tablet and handed it across to her. 'Then what is this?'

There was a video-surveillance picture of Carrie in the Moscow Internet cafe. It was a frighteningly high-quality image of Semenov's drive plugged into the side of the computer showing the long list of numbers she had sent to Rake. 'Internet cafes are a priority for our intelligence agencies,' he said. 'Especially those who only take cash and require no registration. By trying to be so clever, Carrie, you were very stupid.' He reached over her, smelling of sweet aftershave. 'What is this, Carrie? This is not on the drive you gave me.'

She shifted back on the chair. Yumatov swiped to a close-up of the flash drive in the cafe computer's USB port. He laid the drive Carrie had given him next to it. 'What did you do, Carrie? Paint it like those toys. This one that you gave me is black. It has a commercial logo in red. SanDisk. The one I am looking for is red with no logo because it is a military-standard drive.' His tone hardened. 'You have five seconds, or the boy loses a finger.'

Carrie folded in on herself, clawing at the depths of her reserves. She kept her voice low to prevent it from cracking. 'Wrong call, Ruslan. I'm a trauma surgeon, remember? I calculate priorities. Soon as you injure Rufus, you lose me. One finger, five fingers, no difference. I have what you want, but you need to be smarter. Why don't—'

Yumatov struck the back of his hand hard across her face. Carrie's head jerked back. The noise of the blow rang in her ears. Her eyes welled. She put her hands on each arm of the chair to steady her posture. Lydia held Rufus' shoulders, whispered in the boy's ear. A guard walked into the room and held down Rufus' wrist. Yumatov's voice was barely audible. 'Five, four, three, two . . . Carrie?'

Yumatov reached for the knife. Lydia shouted: 'No. Stop.' The guard struck her hard and she reeled back.

'Come, Carrie,' said Yumatov. 'Let's move the chairs closer so you can choose which finger you are causing this innocent little boy to lose.' He raised the knife. Rufus' cry cut through the room. It undulated loud, then soft, loud again, a whimper, a scream. Yumatov's hand stopped, the knife hovering just as automatic-weapons fire burst just outside the window. Carrie hurled herself forward bringing Rufus down onto the floor.

FORTY-TWO

Salmiyarvi, Murmansk Oblast, Russia

As they drove through Salmiyarvi, Rake made out a handful of low-rise buildings next to a frozen river, no lights, and the shapes of small, squat houses back from the road. There was no one in sight, as he expected. The weather had become ferocious, which for Rake was an advantage.

'Mikki and I can do this,' he said to Nilla. 'This isn't your fight.'

'You need me,' Nilla replied.

'Might get uncomfortable,' added Mikki. 'Rake and I are not trained in diplomacy,'

'I'm your ticket in. They won't fire on the Norwegian police.'

Rake didn't answer. It was decided. Lucas had supplied a floor plan posted by a real-estate agent twenty years earlier when the property must have been on the market. Three large rooms on the ground floor, a couple of smaller ones, a wide staircase, then bedrooms and on the top floor an open-plan space and a water tank. This was the location of Carrie's phone but that didn't mean she was there. Lucas had given them a description of the layout of the farmhouse and the geography, straight driveway from the road, grounds with a barn, two smaller buildings, a pond, an orchard of some kind, and beyond that woodland. Lucas had identified three guards at the front door of the property and two at a checkpoint at the entrance to the drive.

Rake and Mikki armed up. The weapons were standard Norwegian special-forces kit, high quality, modern synthetic oil to withstand the cold, which had fallen to minus thirty.

Rake and Mikki put on Kevlar jackets. Mikki chose a Heckler and Koch MP7 submachinegun and a .45 caliber pistol, making him more agile for knife work. He strapped an M72 light anti-tank weapon around his shoulders in case of an armored vehicle. Rake took a Heckler and Koch HK416 assault rifle and an attachable

40mm grenade launcher, together with a .45 caliber pistol. They put the rest in the rear compartment and locked it down. Yumatov's people would have to tear the vehicle apart to get to it.

They pulled on thin inner gloves, then mittens with flaps freeing their fingers to handle weapons. They wore sealskin jackets over thinner clothing, silk and wool with warm air trapped between layers. Finally, to keep in the heat, and give them less risk of exposure to thermal imaging, they wore balaclavas that covered head, face, neck, and shoulders. Ventilators over the face protected the lungs from frostbite and dissipated breath clouds from the mouth. They clipped on snowshoes to prevent them falling into unseen drifts.

Nilla stopped a quarter-mile from the driveway entrance. The blizzard whipped against them as they got out. They tested the wind, tested the snowshoes. Mikki took the left side, Rake the right. He slapped the side of the vehicle. Nilla moved ahead at walking pace. In between squalls, Rake could make out a straight road, trees on Mikki's side, white scrubland on his. Nilla's headlamps reflected crazily, crystals melting on the lamp glass, freezing fog rolling through, beams bouncing off snow on telegraph poles and trees.

'Checkpoint.' Nilla's voice in his earpiece.

A Land Cruiser, engine running, was parked at the entrance to a driveway to the left. Two hundred yards along were three more Cruisers and the house. The weather roared in cycles, raging, then dropping, then raging again. Rake timed a lull and sighted four men in a group under the balcony. He thought a dog was running behind the house, but it turned out to be three deer. Nilla kept going steady and slow. Rake dropped back, using the vehicle as cover. A flashlight came on from the passenger seat of the checkpoint Cruiser, shone right into the windscreen. Nilla stopped. Rake slipped away. A guard got out and walked to Nilla's window. She let it down, bringing weather noise into Rake's earpiece.

The guard shouted in Russian. 'No vehicles allowed!'

Nilla showed her identity card. 'I am Nilla Carsten, Norwegian Police Service, from Kirkenes. I am expected.'

The guard spoke into a radio. Nilla looked ahead, unruffled, gloves resting lightly on the wheel. Rake made out one lamp in the grounds, near what must have been the front door. There was light coming from a corner room at the front, curtains drawn across, which could be where Carrie was; another light from the top of the house. The middle floor with the balcony was dark. The guard walked along the side of Nilla's vehicle. He peered in, circling and coming back to her window.

'Where is the American soldier Ozenna?' he asked.

'My instructions are to come to this house.' Nilla drummed her fingers impatiently on the wheel.

The guard returned to his radio. 'She doesn't know about an American soldier.' The second guard opened his door to get out of the Land Cruiser. They both walked toward Nilla. In the next few seconds, Rake needed to decide if Nilla's cover would hold.

'Ready?' he asked Mikki through the radio comms.

'Copy,' answered Mikki.

The guard tried to open Nilla's door. It was locked. 'You need to come with us,' he said.

Nilla delivered him a dismissive glare. 'I stay with my vehicle.' The second guard standing just behind let off a burst of machine-gun fire at the front of the vehicle, spraying up ice. Rake stepped out of his cover, hands high above his head, and walked briskly toward him. 'I'm Ozenna, the American soldier,' he shouted. 'I am unarmed.'

The guard spun around, machine gun raised. Mikki was behind him and plunged his knife through the back of his neck and up into the brain stem, head twisted round to snap the vertebrae and cut the spinal cord. He dropped the body.

Before the second guard could react, Rake hurled the knife he was concealing in his raised hand. It flew blade first, no turns in the air, with a slight upward trajectory anticipating the target rising on the balls of his feet as he prepared to fire. The knife caught him on the side of the neck, not enough to kill, but enough to cause him to slip, falling hard on his back. Rake smashed his snowshoe onto the skull and kicked away the weapon. He tore off the man's radio, turned to check on Nilla and Mikki when he realized his target had a second weapon from an ankle holster now raised at Rake, who drew a second knife and stepped to his left just as the wounded guard fired and missed. Before he could pull the trigger again, Rake sliced the knife across his throat. Blood poured onto the ice. Rake moved away, took a moment, then spoke into the radio, the wind covering his voice, laidback, like a police officer handling a Saturday night drunk. 'Bringing in the American and Norwegian.'

'Go ahead,' came the reply in a similar casual tone, meaning they had not seen the deaths.

Rake was at Nilla's window. She looked alert like a fox. There was no fear or surprise. Her gaze was fast and everywhere, checking everything.

'Are they dead?' she asked.

'They are,' said Rake. 'Mikki and I will take their vehicle. Are you still coming in?'

'Of course.'

'Then, you follow.'

'No. I go ahead. I'm your body armor. They will not open fire on me. But if they know about this, they will fire on you.'

From their hostile tone against Nilla a few minutes back, Rake wasn't convinced. But Nilla had a will and there wasn't time for argument. 'OK. You go ahead.' Rake walked to the Cruiser. Mikki got into the passenger seat. The cruiser was new and stank of cigarettes and male sweat. Rake took the wheel. Mikki arranged weapons. He wiped his knife. Harry Lucas' drone fed through more information; four men at the front door, two in the grounds, and a significant level of heat coming from the corner room at the front of the house, to the right of the front door. There was sharper moonlight. Rake could see the house, dark and imposing like a church. There was an old gypsy caravan at the end of the driveway, a single wagon wheel sticking out of the snow, and a tractor outside a barn at the back.

The weather was forecast to close in again in just over five minutes. If they retained surprise, they could go in with lethal entry, killing anyone who got in the way, and bring Carrie out within a couple of minutes. A gust knocked ice off a telegraph pole. It smashed down onto the bloodied ground between the two corpses. A wall of sleet slewed across the windscreen. 'Go,' said Rake.

Nilla entered the driveway, same slow pace, tires crunching snow. They passed two tall gateposts, a sign on the right side showing the name of the property. The road surface improved. Nilla speeded up slightly, steered to her left, away from the middle of the road. As Rake followed her, he spotted a flicker of light from underneath the balcony, a muzzle flash of gunfire. He veered hard left. The front windshield exploded, showering them with tiny chunks of glass. Mikki opened his door and jumped out. Dozens of high-velocity rounds tore through the hood and into where Mikki had been. Rake spun the wheel, skidded the Cruiser round, hurled himself out. The vehicle smashed into a bank of snow. Bloodstains smeared Mikki's seat.

Rake lay flat. He couldn't see Mikki. Nilla stayed in her seat, protected within the armored vehicle. She had both hands on the wheel. Rake picked out two men by the front door. Two more on the empty ground between the house and the trees.

Harry Lucas' voice in his earpiece. 'Sword Edge?'

'Taking fire.'

'Casualties?'

'We're good. We're going in.'

Through the howl of wind, he heard the higher-pitch sound of a helicopter. Not possible, he thought, not in this weather. 'Aircraft approaching,' he told Lucas.

'Hold.'

The curtain in the corner room of the house pulled back. Light spilled onto the snow outside. Rake saw Carrie, shouting, hand raised, trailing a bandage stained with blood.

Lucas came back. 'The aircraft is hostile.'

FORTY-THREE

Carrie covered Rufus with her body as the gunfire continued. The helicopter shook the timbers of the house. Yumatov spoke angrily using two phones. He pulled back the curtain an inch. The spotlight from the helicopter snapped on and shone through. 'Get up!' He leveled his pistol at Carrie. She scrambled to her feet, brought Rufus with her, stood in front of him, protectively. 'Move away from him,' commanded Yumatov.

'Fuck you, no!' yelled Carrie. With a barely detectable turn, Yumatov fired two rounds into Lydia, who was crouching on the floor. She toppled, blood pouring from her head. Rufus' whimpering stopped. Yumatov hooked his free hand under Carrie's shoulder. She lashed out, then saw his eyeline shift to Rufus, pistol hand raising for the shot.

'Stop!' she screamed. 'Just stop.'

Yumatov hurled her to the floor. Carrie went down, breaking her fall with her right hand, hitting her left shoulder hard.

One of his men burst into the room. 'Now, sir?'

The guard lifted Carrie with her left arm. Her shoulder screamed with pain. The outside door opened. A column of Arctic air streamed through. The wind was down. Moonlight on snow cast clear light. A Norwegian police Land Cruiser, engine running, stood at the end of the circular driveway. A woman sat at the wheel as if she were waiting for traffic lights to change. A black Cruiser was rammed into a snowdrift, windshield smashed, doors open. Floodlights from an approaching helicopter glared on the empty whiteness, its noise immense, its downdraft scattering loose snow.

Yumatov led. The guard kept hold of Carrie. She glanced back, saw Rufus at the window. Good. In the helicopter, Yumatov would kill him; throw him out. If Rake were in the grounds, Rufus would be safer staying in the house. Her feet sank into fresh snow. To keep going, she lifted her legs high like on a treadmill.

The guard stumbled, pulling down on her arm. His grip weakened. He had been shot. He jerked backwards, letting go of her, his balance gone, falling, and releasing Carrie. She stopped and turned back to the house, air biting into her lungs, helicopter noise clattering through her head, vision skewed by crisscrossing beams of light. She picked out her old steps to run faster. Yumatov chased her. She sensed him behind her, expecting him to shoot. There was no shot. He was faster than her, better in snow. She felt him reach out, snatch the edge of her coat, like getting snarled by a fish hook. She tripped and fell backward.

Rake followed Carrie through the sights of his rifle, Carrie skidding, snow spraying around her like dust. He tracked Yumatov's pursuit, waiting for a clear shot. He clocked five men in his field of fire, two by the skids of the helicopter, there to get Carrie in; one behind the tail with the flashlight; and two in cover under the balcony of the house. There would be more. The rule of thumb was kill what you can.

Yumatov was too close to Carrie for a safe shot. He reached forward like a sprinter and grasped her loose clothing, skewing Carrie's balance, which is when he made a mistake. For a fraction of a second he made himself a visible, stationary target. At exactly that moment, a blanket of automatic-weapon fire from the house opened up against Rake. Earth, ice, and snow spewed up around him. He pulled the trigger against Yumatov, who went down. Muzzle flashes came from behind him, and the hostile gunfire went quiet. Mikki's work. Carrie edged away from Yumatov, keeping herself flat, snaking along, no attempt to get to her feet. Yumatov crawled after her. Rake fired again, but the wrong trajectory, and he missed. The men at the helicopter let off covering fire against Rake and ran toward Yumatov, who struggled to his feet. His men each took an arm, dragging him to the helicopter. A shot from Mikki hit one, but he was not down. He staggered and kept going. Yumatov found his legs and lurched forward. Carrie was away and safe for the moment. Rake needed Yumatov, the head of the snake; kill while he could.

Three Russians were at the aircraft door. A hand reached down to pull Yumatov in. Rake fired, missed. He fired again and hit one target, who fell under the skid. Yumatov was inside the aircraft.

The second man, already wounded, climbed halfway into the aircraft when Mikki killed him, a clean shot to the head. The pilot began the takeoff. Downdraft scattered snow across the grounds. Rake switched to the anti-tank weapon. He stayed prone, the worst position from which to fire. He would have preferred to be standing, kneeling at least, but they would hit him before he got his finger onto the trigger. The helicopter was a Kazan Ansat, new, small, agile, used by oligarchs, gangsters, and generals. Rake would only get one shot. He rested his elbows in the ice, steadied the weapon, targeted the helicopter's fuselage. It was six feet off the ground. He fired. There was no recoil, only a small cloud from the back and a deadly lethal streak as the small rocket opened its stabilizing fins and sped toward its target. The helicopter twisted, either Rake's bad luck or a skilled pilot spotting danger. The rocket struck the point where the fuselage met the tail, glanced off, and exploded in the air. The helicopter yawed but kept climbing. Rake couldn't judge the damage. It turned north. A jet of flame leapt from the tail. The pilot took it up, reached the trees, and more flame streaked out. The aircraft kept going, increased speed, no lights, fading into the dark blue sky and out of sight.

FORTY-FOUR

Rake listened for the crash of the aircraft. He heard quiet-ening engine noise and the growing sound of the wind. Two bodies lay in the snow near the imprints left by the skids. Two lay by the house.

'Carrie, stay down!' Rake shouted, switching back to the rifle. He kept his cover and scanned the grounds in Mikki's direction. He couldn't see him. If Rake were Yumatov he would have posted a marksman on the top floor of the house with a three-sixty panorama. Yet, when the stakes had been highest and Carrie needed to get to the helicopter, no covering fire had come from that area. Where were they and how many?

'Mikki. Check,' Rake said.

No answer.

'Nilla, check.'

'Check.' The emergency lamp of Nilla's police vehicle came on. Beams of blue streaked the landscape. Nilla's voice bounced out from the public-address speaker. 'I am Chief Inspector Nilla Carsten from the Norwegian Police Service. I am getting out of this vehicle to help the wounded. Do not open fire. I repeat. Do not open fire.'

'Nilla, stay,' urged Rake. 'They're—'

'I'm secure. We need to find Mikki.' Nilla opened the door and stepped out. She held her pistol casually. She snapped a powerful flashlight onto the house. The front door hung open. Plastic chairs outside were knocked over. She shone onto the faces of two bodies, one with blood pooled around the head, the other dead but with no sign of injury. She played the beam higher along the walls. There was nothing on the upper balcony floor, nothing around the window at the top. As she brought the beam down, she saw something and shifted the light to the front door. Through night vision, Rake had a clearer view. He checked the immediate area for threat, saw first a pair of eyes, tensed his trigger finger, then relaxed when he saw a boy, face etched with terror. Nilla's light hit him full face. The boy put up his hands to shield his eyes. She moved the beam away. Behind the boy was a tall figure, face obscured by a black balaclava helmet. He held a pistol to the boy's back and with his right hand, an automatic weapon leveled toward Nilla. He stayed in the doorway behind the boy.

'I will take your vehicle,' he said. 'I will leave the boy at the road. There need be no more killing.' His voice was loud, in control, authoritative. His friends' bodies lay around him.

'Are you the only one?' Nilla put the flashlight beam straight into his face. It was thin. He was around thirty. His eyes were confident, not cocky.

'I am. I need to leave.'

'What's your name?'

'Call me Lev.'

'OK, Lev.' Nilla leant against the hood. She kept her pistol down. 'Why not just walk? Keep your weapons. Get to the road, take the first vehicle you see.' She brought the flashlight away from his face, an act of conciliation. 'I need my vehicle to get home. If you think you have to kill the boy, go ahead. I don't give a shit.'

'How many of you?' he asked.

'I'm alone.'

'Bullshit.' His face tightened.

'Not bullshit.' Nilla didn't move. 'There's an American doctor out there. She may be dead. American soldiers came to rescue her. They may be listening. They may be dead. I have no idea. But I am from the Norwegian Police Service. Norwegians and Russians do not fight. You want to walk away and take the boy, that's fine, too. He's Russian. Russia looks after him. But the longer you keep us here doing nothing, if any of your people are alive, they'll be bleeding out or dying of hypothermia.'

'Guarantee my safety.'

Nilla reached inside the vehicle for the public-address microphone. 'Anyone out there, do not kill this man. He is leaving.' Her tone dripped with nonchalance, no sense of urgency, like a station master announcing a later train. If Rake were Lev, he would have laid down his weapons, walked out, and put himself under Nilla's protection. Lev was trained but not smart. If Nilla let him walk, why would he not be back to avenge the death of his friends? Nilla would be thinking these things. She played the bored cop wanting to get home. Rake sensed Lev knew the corner he had gotten himself into. Nilla could not guarantee his safety and she didn't care about his hostage. All Rake needed was the clear shot. He did not like the prospect of a cold-blood kill, but sometimes that was the way gun battles worked.

Rake least expected what happened next. From the trees came automatic fire, smashing into the hood of Nilla's armored police vehicle. She dropped to the ground and snapped off her flashlight. The boy tore himself away and ran toward Nilla. Lev stepped out of the doorway, weapon raised, changed his mind, and began to backpedal inside when Rake pulled the trigger in a shot that tore the back of his head away. The boy was halfway across to Nilla, running into the field of fire laid down from the woods. 'Rufus, stop,' yelled Carrie from her cover. 'Lie down. Now. Rufus.' Rufus did for a second, then quickly scrambled up again and sprinted off with his arms out like the wings of an airplane. He circled away from Nilla toward Carrie, running from the firm ice of the driveway onto mushy fresh snow of the grounds. He stumbled. Gunfire from the trees threw up snow in a line toward him. Rake saw Mikki on his knees, grenade launcher in hand. Rake sighted the flashes, emptied his magazine to give cover. Mikki fired. The explosion erupted in a blinding glare. Fire came back toward Mikki. Rake put a fresh rocket into his anti-tank weapon. A single flash from the left. Rake pressed his trigger. The rocket hit a target with flames licking up the trunk of a snow-covered tree. Armor-piercing shrapnel cut through the air. Rufus ran. Carrie got on her feet to hold him.

Rake shouted, 'Carrie, down!'

She ignored him. She grabbed Rufus and brought them both down into the snow and a sudden quiet. There was no more fire from the trees. Rake checked along the moonlit treeline. The core character of a good combat decision, wait, watch, and decide. Rake examined the crashed Cruiser in the driveway, the shape of Carrie and the boy in the snow, Lev's body fallen across the doorway, Nilla crouched by the wheel of her vehicle.

'Nilla, check!' he called over their comms.

'OK.'

'Carrie?' he shouted.

'We're OK.' Carrie's voice was clear and professional.

'Mikki.'

'I'm hit.'

Carrie was on her feet, bag slung off her shoulder. She held the boy's hand, bringing him with her. Nilla shone her flashlight to pick out Mikki. He had stayed well hidden by hewing out a small snowhole. Bloodstains and weapons lay around him. Carrie let go of the boy's hand. She broke into a run toward him.

'Excalibur?' Rake asked Lucas.

Nothing.

'This is Sword Edge to Excalibur.'

Silence.

'Excalibur, are you reading?'

White noise.

Rake's phone vibrated, a call with the Norway number. He opened the call: 'Swor—' The line fell into digital static.

FORTY-FIVE

Norwegian frigate Thor Heyerdahl, Kirkenes, Norway

'Sword Edge,' Harry Lucas tried again. 'Sword Edge, this is Excalibur. Sword Edge. Are you hearing?' He watched his voice pattern undulate in green across the screen and go flat in the absence of an answer. Harry had seen with dismay images of the firefight from a NATO Global Hawk flying in Norwegian airspace along the Russian border. Its thermal imaging had pinpointed Rake Ozenna and Carrie Walker. He had seen Yumatov's helicopter take off under fire. Then the feed went blank. He contacted Rake on the satellite line, which fell silent. He tried on the regular line. That, too, was cut.

'Is the drone down?' he asked the Norwegian naval technician assigned to him.

'Negative, sir.'

'Then what the hell's going on?'

'Russian electronic interference.'

Contrary to all presidential summit agreements, Russia was jamming GPS and communications.

Harry had been allocated a corner workstation on the bridge of a Norwegian frigate stationed alongside the royal yacht. He could see the *Norge*'s yellow funnel with two deck levels, colorful ensigns, and the red national flag with its black and white cross off the stern flying strong in a blistering wind. The yacht carried an air of rushed preparedness, technicians fixing light bulbs, cleaners polishing wood, decks being scrubbed. She had been taken out of her winter home with a quickly assembled naval crew, many unfamiliar with its workings. The American Secret Service and Russian Presidential Security Service were combing the decks and cabins, bickering over turf.

Harry called Frank Ciszewski. The CIA Director was in the Situation Room in the White House in direct contact with President Merrow, who was on the presidential plane just landed at Kirkenes airport. On his news feed, a presenter was making the point that this was not the traditional Air Force One Boeing 747, but the Boeing C-32A usually allocated to the Vice-President which, with maximum reverse thrust, could handle the short Kirkenes runway. The President would stay on board until he and Lagutov could drive together to the dock. Lagutov, too, was using a smaller version of the regular presidential Ilyushin-96 and was due in soon.

News reports switched to the Dynamic Freedom exercises with rare shots of troops at work in command centers, generals and admirals giving interviews, and dozens of NATO vessels gathered at sea, including American, Russian, and European submarines whose locations had been declared to safeguard the summit. Never before had a military exercise been conducted with such apparent transparency.

'Harry, we're up against it here. This had better be good,' said Ciszewski as he came across the line.

'Ozenna has reached Carrie Walker,' said Harry. 'It's a hostile situation. We need to delay the President until we get them back across the border.'

'Merrow wants to get this done now.' Ciszewski carried irritation in his tone.

'Carrie Walker has Semenov's drive,' said Harry. 'Its data could expose a danger about the summit.'

'Like what?'

'Vessel identification linked to Dynamic Freedom. The summit is insecure. An hour. That's all I'm asking. We can upload immediately Ozenna crosses the border.'

'I doubt Merrow will go for it.' Ciszewski let out a long, tired audible sign. 'But I'll try.'

Harry was certain Ciszewski would not push it. He called Stephanie, looking out toward the yacht in case he could spot her among the crush of dignitaries visible inside the yacht's stateroom. Stephanie answered. He saw her edging to a window, giving him a short wave.

'Ozenna has reached Carrie,' said Harry.

'Thank God! Is she OK?'

'As far as we know. They have a vehicle. They could be at the border within thirty minutes. Can Grizlov keep it open?'

'That's the agreement. Until the end of the current border guards' shift. Why would it close?'

'There've been casualties. Several dead.'

'Jesus, Harry! Who?'

'Yumatov's people. There were firefights. Yumatov escaped in a helicopter. Frank Ciszewski's asking Merrow to delay so we can see what Carrie has. Merrow probably won't agree. So, lean on Grizlov to keep his President back until we give the all-clear.'

'Delay much more and you won't have dignitaries left. They call this a stateroom, but it's no more than a private living room crammed with a hundred people. I'll pitch it, but I have to tell Sergey what's happened.'

'Tell him Yumatov's guys fired on the Norwegian police.' Harry closed the call, glanced inquiringly at the technician, who shook his head and kept working his keyboard. The drone feed was still down.

Harry's personal laptop emitted a buzz alerting him that his facial-recognition scan of Ruslan Yumatov had finished another level of penetration, constructing a pattern of Yumatov's travels and whom he had met. He accessed sites on the dark web and used Chinese and Russian software, technically illegal in the United States because of its power in penetrating facial-recognition identities. The scan scoured every accessible server for matches of Yumatov's face anywhere in the world.

Harry scrolled through. Over the past two years, Yumatov's work had taken him on a jet-set lifestyle, hotel suite to airport lounge to conferences, lectures, and military academies, mostly with his wife, occasionally with another woman. The software cross-referenced those Yumatov had been with, resulting in thousands of identifications which it prioritized and narrowed down. The speed of technological development continued to amaze Harry and injected a new danger that he least expected. Even though comms were down, he pressed the microphone button to try again. 'Sword Edge. Sword Edge. This is Excalibur. Come in, Sword Edge.'

Nothing.

Harry felt a rush of blood flow through his neck. He found his hands trembling as he called Frank Ciszewski for the second time in the space of a few minutes, this time through a video link.

'What now?' Ciszewski wiped his glistening brow with a white handkerchief.

'You need to see this.' Harry shared surveillance images of Yumatov in hotels around Europe, some grainy, some barely recognizable, some blotches and shapes identified only by computer-generated subtitles. He needed to stagger the information to ensure Ciszewski did not automatically dismiss it. 'These are Yumatov's confirmed locations. The dates match his travel itinerary.'

'A Russian military officer traveling around Europe is not unusual.' Ciszewski's tone was impatient.

'But this.' Harry moved to a new set of images. 'The same person with him in all those places. Going into a hotel room together. Getting out of a car in another. Meeting in a foyer?'

'So, he's having an affair. What's your point, Harry? Who is she?'

'Her name is Nilla Carsten. She is with the Norwegian police—'

'The Russians and the Norwegians meet at conferences all the time.'

'Nilla Carsten is with Ozenna right now in Russia. Frank, you have to alert Merrow. You have—'

'I don't have to do anything.' Ciszewski's large, hanging chin moved up and down as he answered. 'You want to be down there right now in the Situation Room, Harry? We've got threats coming in by the bucketload. You're getting too close to this. Step back. Think clearer. Handle it until this summit is done. Then we'll talk.'

'No, Frank. Now.' It was Harry's turn for impatience. 'Nilla Carsten has met Yumatov in four locations in Europe in the past two years and right now she is with Rake Ozenna, who is extricating Carrie Walker from Russia. I can't raise him because the Russian military is jamming our comms. That's not coincidence, Frank. This is Yumatov running rings around us.'

FORTY-SIX

Nikel, Murmansk Oblast, Russia

Ruslan Yumatov removed his flak jacket and examined two welts on the Kevlar that had saved his life. He was lucky. He should have anticipated Ozenna's ruthlessness. But Nilla Carsten would make sure they would not cross into Norway, and his priority was to contact Andrei Kurchin on the *Kasatka* in the Barents Sea. To even get a short message to a shallow depth underwater needed a powerful military-grade transmitter, and Yumatov had set up a direct line to the navy's very low frequency transmission site just outside of Severomorsk. The contact would be only one way. The submarine could not message back.

The Kasatka, Northern Fleet, Russian Navy, Barents Sea

Proceed. Andrei Kurchin read the one-word message and ordered the crew to begin cloaking procedures to disguise the signature of an underwater drone attached to the hull of the submarine.

Codenamed Bear-1, the small unmanned submarine, twenty-four meters long and one point six in diameter, was the result of more than twenty years of research, mistakes, and ambition. It could operate half a mile underwater at speeds of up to sixty miles an hour. With a range of six thousand miles, it was designed to hit an American city with a nuclear warhead. Today, it was not nuclear-armed and its mission was to travel a short distance to destroy the Norwegian royal yacht, kill two Presidents, and create the chaos needed to structure a world order in Russia's favor.

Bear-1 had never been to sea. NATO had no record of its unique signature. Uncloaked, it would stand out as dangerous and unidentified amid the range of vessels in the Barents Sea. Both Russia and its enemies had technology that could cloak a submarine in an acoustic shield with a disguise mechanism whereby it appeared to be another vessel. The Russian Bear-1 underwater drone was programmed to emit the signature sounds of HSwMS *Halland*, the diesel-powered Swedish Gotland-class submarine that Kurchin had sunk hours earlier. Sweden was not a member of NATO, therefore there was less sharing of military databases. But Sweden was taking part in Dynamic Freedom with its status as an Enhanced Opportunity Partner. The *Halland* provided Kurchin with the prefect false identity.

If the data drive reached Norway, Bear-1's real identity would be revealed within seconds. Kurchin trusted his friend to stop Rake Ozenna crossing the border, just as Yumatov trusted Kurchin to accomplish his mission of assassinating the two Presidents.

'Completed, sir,' said the chief engineer.

Kurchin now needed a second message to confirm that the two Presidents had boarded the Norwegian royal yacht.

Royal Yacht Norge, Kirkenes, Norway

Stephanie Lucas sensed the increasing impatience of the dignitaries crammed inside the homely stateroom of the Norwegian royal yacht. There was a high number of military uniforms. The latest to arrive was the NATO Secretary-General, who had visited the British aircraft carrier HMS *Queen Elizabeth*, where he was met by the First Sea Lord and the Chief of Naval Staff. They had taken a helicopter to the carrier USS *Harry S. Truman* to link up with the American Chief of Naval Operations. All made it on board just as a new blizzard confined the two Presidents to the terminal at Kirkenes airport. There were also several heads of governments, mostly from smaller European countries, vulnerable to Russia, circling Sergey Grizlov like moths, wishing him well in his quest for the Kremlin. Stephanie caught his eye, and he broke away for her.

'They're expected at the border in half an hour,' she said.

'Well done.' Grizlov had a skill of completely honing his attention on whoever he was with.

'If they're late, can you keep it open for them?'

'Will they be?' Grizlov sipped his drink, which looked like champagne but was alcohol-free sparkling elderflower.

'Yumatov's men went rogue, opened fire on a Norwegian police vehicle—'

'Fuck, Steph! You mean on Ozenna's team.'

'Traveling under the protection of the Norwegian police.'

Grizlov turned toward the huge window. Outside, people were braving the cold, waiting to witness the arrival of the joint presidential entourage. 'Who knows about this?'

'We had a drone. Not sure about your side.'

'Where?'

'Near a place called Salmiyarvi.'

Grizlov's eyes narrowed. 'We have three hundred troops stationed in barracks there.'

'Meaning?'

'It could be to our advantage. Where's Yumatov?'

'His helicopter landed at Nikel. We're trying to get Merrow and Lagutov to delay.'

'Lagutov won't.' Grizlov tapped his phone. 'As soon as I am officially notified of this beautiful mess, the border will have to close. Until then, I'll do my best to make sure Ozenna's team can get across.'

FORTY-SEVEN

Salmiyarvi, Murmansk Oblast, Russia

'You need to leave with this now, Rake,' commanded Carrie, pointing to the flash drive she had just pressed into his hand.

'No,' challenged Rake. 'We all go.'

'We can't all go, and I'll be damned if I'll let you fuck around worrying about Mikki and me.' Carrie spoke in the tone Rake had heard a hundred times before; no room for argument. This was what Dr Carrie Walker deemed would happen.

Mikki Wekstatt lay wounded but conscious on a mattress in the front corner room of the farmhouse. He had two injuries, one close to the femoral artery on his right leg. Another had torn the Achilles tendon on his left ankle. His Kevlar jacket had stopped rounds and shrapnel. Carrie had found a military first-aid kit, treated him with a tourniquet and clotting agent, and got Mikki to concentrate his mind by reading fairy stories to Rufus.

Carrie and Rake had had a reunion of sorts, but not like in the movies with rainbows and music. Rake yelled at her to stay down, ran across and flung himself in the snow next to her, his arm firmly across her back like a straitjacket strap. Their eyes met. For a fraction of a blink there was something between them. But the first words she said to him were: 'I've got it.' They reverted to skillsets, things they both understood. They lifted Mikki into the house. Carrie fixed Mikki up while Rake and Nilla checked the vehicles. The Russian Cruisers were shot up, tires blown, windows smashed, high-velocity rounds in the engine. Nilla's armored Cruiser had come through better. Carrie walked out to them, Nilla shone a flashlight in her face, moved closer to Rake, and rubbed her hand affectionately down his back.

'Mikki needs a hospital,' said Carrie.

The closest hospital was Nikel, but that would mean surrendering to the Russians. The best hospital was Kirkenes. That would mean getting Mikki across the border.

The weather kept chopping and changing. In a sudden lull, visibility cleared. If Yumatov's men were still around, they could get a clear night-vision shot. Rake led them inside. It was then, as soon as they were back in the house, that Carrie dropped the flash drive into Rake's hand and told him to leave her with Mikki and deliver it. But there was no way he would let them stay in this house with the Russian bodies freezing over in the grounds acting as lightning rods for revenge. When Rake objected, Carrie stepped close to him, her face up against his, eyes straight into his. 'Don't fuck around, Rake. You came for this, not for me. They're not going to kill us. Yumatov's finished. Mikki and I can wait it out.'

'We all drive to the border crossing.' Rake stamped ice off his boots.

'No way that will work,' dismissed Carrie. 'What, with a patient with gunshot wounds?'

'Carrie drives Mikki and the boy,' said Nilla, peeling off her hat and goggles that were hitched above her head like sunglasses. 'I take Rake across the lake and through the fence.'

'They'll still stop us,' said Carrie.

'I'm good at what I do.' Nilla pulled off her gloves and ran her finger down a map on her phone screen. 'The border itself is only two miles west of here. We can be in Norway within the hour. At the end of this road is the lake where we should get a Norwegian phone signal. I call through and alert them that you're coming.' She looked up at Rake with a smile. 'And I'll call my brother Stefan and he'll guide us to a safe gap in the fence.'

'And the road crossing?' asked Carrie.

'Twenty miles north. You could be there in half an hour. They might waive the police vehicle. More likely they will stop you. But by then, I should have got through to our people on the other side.'

Mikki shouted from the front room. 'We'll be fine, Rake. I can't walk, but I can shoot.'

Mikki lightened the mood, but no one spoke. Silence clawed the air. They waited for Rake's decision. Nilla made sense, high-risk, the only way through, an hour, possibly less, the same for

Carrie. The border could be difficult, but there would not be shooting. They laid Mikki on the back seat of the cruiser. He insisted on being propped up with weapons in case there was trouble. Carrie strapped Rufus into the front and took the wheel. Rake stood by her open window. He leaned in and wedged a pistol between the pack and her seat. Carrie took his head between her hands, drew him to her and kissed him, not like a brother but like she used to, slowly and softly on the lips.

'Thank you.' She squeezed both hands through his gloves. 'Sorry I yelled at you.' Without giving Rake time to respond, she reversed and headed out of the driveway.

Rake and Nilla dressed for the cold. They gathered weapons and ammunition from the dead. He tried contacting Lucas again, first through his phone which still showed no carrier and then by the satellite line which showed a strong signal. There was no response.

Rake secured both phones in his jacket and zipped the flash drive into an inner pocket. The weather was coming back, uneven wind, blackness in clouds, fresh snow swirling like leaves. He covered his face and pulled down his goggles. Nilla did the same. She handed him a pouch and a small canister of water. They clipped on snowshoes and set off down the driveway. He held back out of earshot away from the sound of Nilla's tread. He listened for aircraft or vehicle engines. Nothing. He looked for moving lights. None. He slipped off his goggles and examined the long black driveway flanked by snow-laden trees and weather-twisted telegraph poles. An icy tang of fresh snow fell on his face. He followed the tall, confident shape of Nilla up ahead. Wind gathered, then dropped, then strengthened again, so loud that he could only hear its howl. Then, in the quiet, he could hear only the crunch of his snowshoes and, if he allowed it, the pounding of his heart in his ears.

FORTY-EIGHT

Norwegian frigate Thor Heyerdahl, Kirkenes, Norway

'Visuals restored,' the technician told Harry. 'No audio.' He flipped the main screen to the feed from the drone patrolling the border. Two figures shimmered in the greens, yellows, and reds of thermal imaging. The software showed their location and pinpointed the farmhouse. It tracked the path of the moving human images along the short driveway onto a road heading west and then down to a path that led towards frozen water straddling the Norway–Russia border. They were identified as Nilla Carsten and Rake Ozenna.

The ice separating the two countries came through as a deep blue with a clear view of the fence on the Russian side. Nilla Carsten was forty feet ahead of Ozenna, walking quickly. Ozenna moved more cautiously, holding back, checking around, watching the sky. From the drone's arc, Harry saw they were alone, no threat from the air, none on the road. Apart from the fence, they had an unimpeded line across the lake into Norway. Harry could see Rake, but he could not warn him.

Royal Yacht HNoMY Norge, Kirkenes, Norway

'The royal yacht *Norge* measures eighty meters and was built in Britain in 1937 for the famous aircraft designer Thomas Sopwith,' Sergey Grizlov told the increasingly restless guests whom he had just told yet again about weather delaying the arrival of the two Presidents. Grizlov stood behind a long table set up for Peter Merrow and Viktor Lagutov against a backdrop of the Russian and American national flags. 'The Norwegian government bought the vessel in 1947 to mark the late King Haakon's seventy-fifth birthday and I am now at liberty to reveal that her first voyage of the summer will be to visit our beautiful Severomorsk, which many of you will know as a closed military city. What many of you might not know is that Severomorsk and Kirkenes are sister cities and the Russian and Norwegian people feel that a visit by the *Norge* is long overdue.'

The Kirkenes mayor gave a whoop of support followed by applause which Grizlov shortened with a louder clap saying, 'I have also just been informed that the presidential motorcade is minutes away from the jetty.'

Stephanie looked out of windows streaked with melting hailstones to see security agents take up positions. Merrow's armored Cadillac stopped just beyond the gang plank that led to the deck of the yacht. Lagutov's Russian-made Aurus Senat pulled up just before it. Both Presidents got out of their vehicles simultaneously, shook hands for the cameras, and walked on board.

Grizlov weaved through guests toward the door, beckoning to Stephanie who edged across to him. 'They've closed the border,' he said. 'Troops from Salmiyarvi have been deployed along the E-105.'

That's it, thought Stephanie. Best efforts and mission failure. Grizlov joined the Norwegian Foreign Minister and American Secretary of State in the greeting line. A naval helicopter took off from the Norwegian frigate behind them. Stephanie's phone vibrated. 'We've found Ozenna,' said Harry. 'I'm heading down there, now.'

Nikel, Murmansk Oblast, Russia

Ruslan Yumatov watched the news feed and sent a two-character message to Andrei Kurchin on board the *Kasatka* through the very low frequency transmitter outside of Severomorsk – *GO.*

Kurchin repeated the message to his chief weapons engineer. He watched the Bear-1 detach itself from his submarine. The screen blurred with a rush of white water as software within the unmanned drone adjusted the vessel, found its direction, settled, and set off on its programmed course. The two Presidents were due on board the *Norge* for just under an hour. By then, they would be dead.

Salmiyarvi, Murmansk Oblast, Russia

A blizzard arrived with slicing hail that smashed against Rake like a drum roll. Shrieking wind was strong enough to stop Nilla in her tracks. Rake kept on, lifting his snowshoes high, slowing his steps, leaning forward to keep balance. They were off the road on a narrow track sloping down to the lake, trees on both sides. Clumps of snow thrown off by raging weather drifted in the middle. Visibility cut, Rake felt his way through. He sensed more than he saw hazards on the path. He stepped around them. An inch too far and he would sink into a drift. In this weather, the Russians could never track them. All they had to do was keep moving. He lost sight of Nilla. He stayed on the path. He didn't want to go past her. He thought he saw her shape, reached out, and found it was light and ice playing tricks. She found him, her hand stretching, probing, like searching inside a dark cupboard. She grasped his arm and pulled him toward her, close enough to see each other. She pressed her gloved hands down on the air: *Stop until it passes.* Rake put his hands together as if in prayer and pointed ahead: *Keep moving.* She ran a finger under her throat: *Too dangerous.* Rake tapped his chest. *I will go.* Nilla could stay, build a snowhole, keep safe. Nilla waved her hand across her face: *Both go.* She shouted something, but he couldn't make out what. He clasped her wrist like a mountain climber.

Rake led. The downward path became steeper. A gust shook clumps from a tree, part snow, part ice. They landed on the path like a rockfall. Rake side-stepped; Nilla with him. She was good. The treeline ended. Fresh snow was blown away by the wind. The bank to the lake was made up of uneven ice, leading to an expanse of hazy, barren desolation. Rake fumbled with his night vision, got the lenses over his eyes, and saw they had almost walked right into a Russian fence in front of them. It ran along the banks of the fjord and would have sensors and alarms to override the weather if they were working. He judged it about twelve feet high with razor wire at the top. Nilla was by his side. She knew what to do. She led, hand clasped around his wrist, with each step snowshoes locked skillfully onto the ice, picking safe areas, guiding them along the fence, looking for a gap. She moved with confidence as if she knew where one was.

Without warning, the wind dropped. There was sudden quiet, clarity and extreme danger. They were right up against rows of razor wire, like a film coming into focus. At the bottom, wire was pulled out of the ground, splayed up onto the other side, probably the work of a brown bear. Nilla crouched down and used her gloves to wrench the wire out further. She lay on her front. Rake held the broken fence clear of her clothing. She crawled under. Once through she lifted the wire for Rake. He went crablike on his back, wanting to keep a line of sight around him.

Once through they needed to get onto the frozen fjord and keep going. The border was unmarked, and this was Nilla's land. It was why Rake had brought her along. Nilla showed Rake a path with her flashlight, prodding with her pole. Shore ice was the most dangerous, where land became water, where animal warmth and plant growth disrupted, where it was difficult to tell what was under a deep fall of snow. Nilla stopped thirty feet out, shone the flashlight back again to confirm her route. Rake followed. His phone buzzed. He looked down through the transparent sealed pocket in his jacket. They were in Norwegian signal area. He kept walking, trying to work his finger through the plastic to see who called. Lucas. He needed a secure place, but he didn't want to lose Nilla. He stepped where she had stepped, prodded his ski pole where she had prodded. He felt the crumbling of old snow beneath the fresh first layer. Lucas' call became a message. His snowshoes hit the smoothness of the lake's ice. Nilla's back was to him. She ran her flashlight toward the border, finding a passage of thin snow and flat ice to get them there quickly. Rake glanced at the phone again. Lucas again. *Nilla—* He couldn't see more. Wind smashed iced mist against his goggles.

The snow was more than two feet deep. He lifted his shoe high to be sure to clear it for the next step. He brushed the shattered ice from his jacket and tried to read more of the message. He couldn't see it. He lowered his foot, pole out, and secure in case the wind struck again. Something cut into his leg. It gripped both sides, sharp metal breaking through his protective clothing and throwing him off balance. The pole snapped out. His right knee buckled, and Rake fell. A cast-iron circle of steel weighed down his right leg, its teeth biting through his reinforced cold-weather pants. Rake knew bear traps. This was a powerful one, about forty pounds, designed to immobilize a big animal. The way the teeth bore into his leg, he knew the spring had been set for maximum tension. The trap would keep up pressure, cutting through material, into skin, muscle, and bone. Nilla had her back to him. She was on the phone, as if she hadn't seen him. He leaned forward to take hold of the trap. Its teeth penetrated his leg more, cold steel breaking through his skin. He felt for the springs either side of the plate, began pushing down on them, began feeling the pressure ease. Nilla turned, casting her flashlight over him.

FORTY-NINE

The way the snow swirled, Rake more sensed her than saw her. Nilla crouched next to him. His left hand worked the spring of the trap. His right patted down his jacket until he reached his pistol. In between the cycles of wind, he heard the high-pitched engine of a snowmobile. Nilla cupped her hand around Rake's ear and shouted, 'Give me the drive, I'll take it across.'

Nilla's suggestion didn't match anything that was happening. She could free him within seconds because she knew animal traps. 'Help me open it,' he yelled against the weather. He kept the pressure on the trap's spring, easing the pain. 'Here, where my hand is.'

She reached toward him, not for the trap, but for his jacket pocket, her hand ungloved, fingers feeling for the zip. Rake didn't think. There was no time to work out what was going on. It wasn't the first time for him that a friend turned enemy. He struck her with force across the face. She fell back into the snow. Rake brought out his pistol. The trap, embedded in the ice like a pole in concrete, confined him. The teeth cut into his leg. He couldn't see her. He could twist to the right and left, but that was it. Nilla wasn't there. Her boot landed hard between his shoulderblades, jerking him forward. She kicked the gun out of his hand. 'Stop, Rake, and listen,' she screamed into his ear. 'My job is to deliver you to Russia. It's not that fucking drive. If you need to get it across the border, I'll take it.'

She shifted round, facing him. She pulled up her goggles so he could see her. 'I know how much it means to you,' she said.

Nilla had played him from the moment he arrived in Norway. She had run her flashlight over the exact spot of the bear trap, guiding him into it. She had suggested just he and her cross the border on foot. As they drove to the farmhouse, she had swerved sharply to the right, giving Yumatov's men a clear shot toward himself and Mikki behind her. She had been as cool as a statue during the firefight, knowing she would never be a target. And before that, she had got permission for Rake to cross the border with her where the Russians tried to take him in. If Rake was her mission, she had carried it out pretty much to perfection. Except, until now, she had failed.

'No,' he said.

'Then you're stupid, Rake Ozenna.'

'What do you need?' shouted Rake. 'To help me out of here.'

'Nothing.' Nilla pointed north. Rake heard the whine of approaching engines and saw lamps of snowmobiles, flickering across the ice, blurred in fog.

'They'll take it when they get you, Rake. Trust me. You have my word, I'll deliver it.'

Rake's right hand eased the trap's spring back further. His left hand gripped the handle of his knife, ready to use against Nilla. She put back on her goggle and face mask, started making a phone call. She abruptly turned, picked up Rake's pistol, and dropped it onto his lap. Then, she was gone, engulfed by the weather, walking towards Norway.

The snowmobiles became more distinct. He could see the lamps of each one spread across the ice in a military cordon. There were not just snowmobiles because pairs of headlights emerged, higher off the ground, trucks driving across the fjord as if it were a field, not just one line, but a second layer, more trucks, with a snowmobile on each flank. Far away there was a more powerful spotlight sweeping the landscape behind and Rake heard the clatter of a helicopter. Was all this just for him? The noise of approaching engines became louder, competing with the roar of the wind. The headlamps glared, obscured, vanished, shone through again, depending on the mood of the snow fall and the fog. Rake put all his concentration on the trap. Both hands prized down the spring, easing the pressure on his leg until it was unlocked. He drew his leg out. The cold on the broken skin sent a jolt of extreme pain. He pushed himself up and tested his weight. It was not fine. It hurt like hell. But it would hold.

He judged the snowmobiles were three minutes out, more if the weather worsened. He unzipped his jacket, untucked his shirt, and cut a large strip off the bottom of his silk vest. He dabbed the material on blood from the cut skin on his leg, tied it around one arm of the bear trap, and secured the trap back in the snow. He zipped up his clothing, put on his gloves and facemask, picked up his ski pole, and followed Nilla's steps west for seventy-five yards within the effective range of his pistol. Nilla had kept to the path across the ice. On either side was deep snow. Rake sank himself into one and carved out a space that protected him from the wind and gave him a view back toward the trap.

Clearly defined now, he could see seven military snowmobiles, two of which he identified as the powerful Berkut 2 with a 1,000cc engine, carrying at least two men, and a 7.62mm machine gun on the back. Five were smaller, more versatile, with just a driver. The vehicles behind them were a distorted blur of lights. He heard pulses of the helicopter's engine, but couldn't see the aircraft. This level of force had not been deployed just to take in Rake. It was a show of strength that NATO was incapable of rescuing an American soldier in harm's way only a few hundred meters from its border.

He had a full Norwegian signal on his phone. The snowhole gave him protection from the noise of the wind. He called Harry Lucas, who picked up. 'Excalibur,' said Rake. 'This is Sword Edge.'

'What is your situation, Sword Edge?'

'Fifteen minutes out.'

'Do you have Carrie?'

'Negative.'

They should have been across by now, but if they were, Lucas would know. He didn't react.

'Nilla Carsten is hostile and she is coming across now.'

'We have her tracked. If you're where the locator says you are, you have Russian hostile forces approaching.'

'Correct,' said Rake calmly. 'Tell Stefan to prepare two sleds, eight dogs each, and, repeat, I will be with you in fifteen minutes.'

Rake slid deeper into the shallow snowhole. The wind was steady, the snow light. A lamp from the lead snowmobile washed across him. There was no reaction, meaning he was adequately hidden. The first snowmobile was smaller with just one driver. Then a larger Berkut 2 broke from the formation and cut across to join it, one man in its closed cab, another on the back with a machine gun. Others circled. The single snowmobile skirted around the bear trap and stopped. A soldier got off. He held a pistol ready and a Kalashnikov on a strap around his shoulder. The flashlight from his helmet cast an arc around the area. He signaled to the crew of the larger vehicle as if to say, 'nothing here'. As he turned back to his vehicle, Rake shot him in the face and a second round in his right leg made sure.

Rake leapt out of the snowhole. The second snowmobile caught him in its beam. Rake shot the machine-gunner, riding exposed on the back. He used the same double tap, head and leg. The door to the cabin flew open. There was only the driver inside. Rake fired and missed, but bought himself enough confusion to pick up the automatic weapon hooked to the body of the man he had just killed. He aimed half the magazine toward the cabin, fifteen rounds, in a line of fire that cut through the driver's torso. The driver fell out, wounded, arms flailing. Inside the snowmobile cab were four hand grenades, another Kalashnikov, and a bag of six thirty-round magazines. Rake carried them to the small snowmobile which would be faster and versatile. The engine was still running. The GPS on the control panel showed the Norwegian border 550 meters due west.

Five snowmobiles sped toward him, ignoring the unpredictable terrain of deep snow and unseen bumps that could quickly flip them. Ice on top of a lake was the most dangerous condition for a snowmobile. Nothing was guaranteed. Rake sensed rash orders from a commander with his back up against the wall, probably Yumatov in the helicopter, shouting instructions.

Rake let off the brake and eased out the accelerator. He cut the lamp and followed Nilla's foot track with his naked eye. She had kept a steady, unwavering pace. The powerful engine below him could go more than a hundred miles an hour. Rake stuck to below twenty, a choice of fine balance; the slower he was, the more chance the enemy had of closing in; the faster he was, the more chance of smashing into an obstacle or veering off into a snow drift. Twenty miles an hour covered nine meters a second. If he were able to keep straight and free of deep snow, it would be just over a minute before he reached Norway.

One Russian snowmobile was ahead of the rest, zigzagging toward him, its light jumping up and down. One second, he was in its beam, the next it was gone. Rake moved into a cloud of frozen ice, stinging his skin and cutting his visibility. He couldn't even see his hands on the controls. The wind whipped up. He slowed to walking pace.

Bullets smashed against the back of the snowmobile, wild firing from his left. They were guessing. They couldn't see him. Rake was unable to see Nilla's tracks. Without them, he could sink into a drift. If he turned on the lamp, he would be dead. Rake kept going, feeling the turning of the treads, the sliding of the skis. He was three hundred meters from the border. They had thermal imaging and infra-red that could cut through the weather and pick up the heat from his engine. The weather was worsening by the second. He could try on foot. He could wait it out. He could risk a high-speed run, across the line. None was a solution.

A grenade exploded in front of him. Its blast cut through the wind. Flames leapt up from the snow. Shrapnel cracked the wind-shield. A second grenade went off to his left. They were ranging in on him like with artillery, firing until they hit him. Rake made his choice. He hurled a grenade to his left and one to his right. In an arc in front of him, he laid down a field of fire, using a whole Kalashnikov magazine, threw the weapon onto the snow, picked up another, snapped on the lamp, and opened the throttle. The engine pitched. Shots ripped through the air around him so close he heard cracks of bullets breaking the sound barrier. He picked up speed. An explosion threw up flames and snow on the exact spot he had just been.

Rake could see ahead, not to his right or left. He spotted the flickering beams of lights beyond the border. There was no line, nor markers, no wall. A searchlight from behind bounced off the cracked windshield and onto his face. His snowmobile shook as it was rammed from the back, its front skewed round to the left, the skids about to sink into deep snow. Rake put his weight to the right to correct it. As it came back, another Russian snowmobile cut across his path, crashing into him. The driver gesticulated but didn't seem to know what to do next. He touched his earpiece as if waiting for instructions. Rake shot him. Bullets from behind smashed through his control panel. Rake turned but saw no target. He threw a grenade into the vehicle. As it exploded, he hurled himself out, into the snow and away. Rake crawled round to the front, passed the driver he had shot who had fallen into the snow, half in and half out of the vehicle, his legs caught on a strap on the seat, alive and a weapon in his hand. Rake put a round in the man's head. He pushed himself up and ran, pain pumping through his wounded leg.

The path was icy and hard. He could see figures up ahead in Norway. The helicopter search lamp lit his track, picking him out. Rake kept running, weaving, as rounds from a heavy machine gun cut up ice around him. A single erratically moving figure in bad weather was a near-impossible target. His concentration stayed on the border line and the threat overhead. A powerful spotlight lit the path from Norway. Then came Russian from a loudspeaker: 'Halt. Do not come any further. This is Norwegian sovereign territory.'

Rake gave himself an extra burst of energy. He felt friendly arms holding him up, moving him forward, picking him up and dragging him to safety.

FIFTY

Svanvik, Finnmark, Norway

'One hell of an entry, Major,' said Harry Lucas, letting go of his arm. At the edge of the ice in a bank of trees, Rake saw ambulances, police cars, a large white truck with antennas and satellite dishes, a mobile communications center. Rake pulled off his glove, unzipped his pocket, brought out the drive, and dropped it in Lucas' hand.

'Is Carrie through?'

'No word yet.' Lucas began leading Rake to the truck when he recognized one of the men helping him in was Stefan, Nilla's brother.

'Nilla?' Rake asked.

'Over there.' Lucas pointed toward an ambulance. 'She got shot.'

Nilla had saved him, betrayed him, then saved him again by leaving him a weapon. Rake had liked her. He needed to know what was inside her head. He turned toward the ambulance.

'Ozenna—' began Lucas.

'You've got the drive, use it. I'm doing this.'

'Go easy.' Stefan's hand was on his arm.

Rake reached the ambulance, his hand ready on the door. There wasn't time for anger. But he needed clarity.

'Nilla doesn't think the way most of us do,' said Stefan. 'She compartmentalizes emotions.'

'Why did she do it? asked Rake.

'Our parents left debt which we can't pay off. The banks were threatening to take over our farm. Yumatov paid the debt and made Nilla work for him. He was promising to open the border and make everyone rich.'

'And you let her?'

'I didn't know.'

Rake opened the ambulance door. A paramedic put up his hand to stop him. Stefan spoke in Norwegian, and he beckoned Rake inside. Nilla lay on her back with a drip and oxygen. Rake couldn't see the wound. Her face was pale with red blotches. Her eyes trembled, sharpened when they saw Rake, then seemed to retreat again. There were two paramedics, both communicating a sad, blunt expression familiar to Rake, who had used it so many times himself: Nilla was dying. He took her hand, which was cold. Nilla opened her eyes and managed to focus.

'Did I fuck up?'

'You did great,' Rake encouraged.

'Will I make it?'

'You'll be fine.' Rake lightly squeezed her hand.

Nilla managed a smile. Her face distorted in pain.

A phone vibrated from the ledge above the gurney. Rake noticed three there, together with Nilla's wallet, a set of keys, her pistol, and other stuff. Nilla's concentration faded. Rake recognized a Russian number and answered it.

'How is Nilla?' Yumatov's voice, speaking in English

'Your people shot her,' Rake said calmly.

'Not my people. Will she make it?'

'She's good. Just a flesh wound. Where's Carrie?'

'She's not through. I'm trying to fix it. But she's OK.'

The line cut. Was Yumatov trying to do a deal, Nilla for Carrie? Nilla was unconscious, her breathing slow but steady. Rake collected her phones from the shelf, stared down the paramedics' objection, and stepped out again. He showed the phones to Stefan. 'Yumatov called Nilla,' he said. 'I told her she was fine.'

Stefan's face furrowed with curiosity. Rake replied. 'I'm going back in to get him.'

Stefan didn't hesitate. 'I'm with you. Two sleds, treated birch, eight dogs each. Strong teams.' Stefan knew exactly what was needed. Rake read him as a man like himself. He didn't say much but knew what had to be done. Despite Nilla, Lucas and the Norwegians must have trusted him. So did Rake. His plan was to use his torn sweatshirt and the dogs' sense of smell to get to the bear trap where Nilla had left him and where the gunfights took place. Yumatov might be tracking Nilla's phone. If he were, it would be like a magnet. Once there, Rake would bring Yumatov to Norway to find out who he was working for and who he was running in the United States. Unlike snowmobiles with their heat and infra-red signatures, dogs could blend into the environment so as to be near invisible.

Stefan prepared the sleds. Rake joined Lucas in the communications truck, which was warm and quiet. Banks of screens lined both walls throwing off a soft pastel light and showing graphs, diagrams, surveillance, and a news feed from the summit that was about to begin on the royal yacht, barely thirty miles to the north. There was a smell of electronic equipment and strong roast coffee. Einar Olsen, the Norwegian Intelligence Service agent who took charge of the reindeer carcass, worked at one of the screens.

He and Lucas looked expectantly at Rake, who shook his head. 'Sorry,' he said softly. He laid Nilla's phones on a worktop next to Lucas. 'Yumatov called. He said Carrie's not through yet and he was trying to fix it.'

'Whatever that means,' said Lucas. 'We had a couple of technical hitches, but we're now good to go.' He plugged the drive into the control panel. First to appear was the list of vessel registration numbers. Then the images went haywire, lines of code, white noise, flashes on diagrams, black as software decrypted data.

Semenov had divided his stolen data into three sections. The first began with the images Carrie had sent from Moscow with signatures of NATO's ships and submarines including some taken from two top-secret acoustic measuring sites in Alaska and Norway. These were facilities where sonar signatures were recorded in near-laboratory conditions, picking out intricate elements that might otherwise be missed, highly classified information stored only on a hard drive. The data had been stolen by gaining entry and, until now, the security breach had gone undetected.

The second section showed the signatures that Russia had fabricated for many NATO vessels. Russia had reached the equivalent of America's sixth or seventh generation of undersea detection. The Pentagon was barely beyond the fourth. The third section explained exactly why so many had died over this flash drive.

Lucas looked across to the live chart for the current Dynamic Freedom exercise where NATO's naval hardware was arrayed in the Barents Sea. It showed security around the royal yacht and the whereabouts of Russian submarines whose location had been made public because of the summit.

Tension spread across his face. Lucas injected Semenov's

technology into the chart. The screen went black, then lit again with the location of vessels rippling as pixelation settled. Harry scrutinized the screen, checking each vessel as it now appeared with Semenov's software.

Only one changed identity, a small diesel-powered Swedish submarine, listed as *Halland*. A cold shiver ran through Harry. He drew a breath and tapped his finger on the screen image of what had been a Swedish submarine and was now showing as a Russian underwater drone.

'What is it?' he asked Olsen.

'Poseidon UUV,' answered Olsen cross-checking on a separate database.

'Which?'

'Not sure yet.'

The Poseidon was the name given to a family of Russian underwater drones designed to attack warships or cities.

'Direction?' Harry opened two phone lines, one to Ciszewski in Washington and one to Stephanie at the summit.

'South,' said Olsen, who opened his own line to the Dynamic Freedom command center in Bodø.

'Speed?'

'Thirteen knots.'

'Distance from the *Norge?*'

'Four miles.'

'Time.'

'Sixteen minutes. I'm through to Bodø.'

Frank Ciszewski came across Lucas' feed. 'What's happening now, Harry?'

'The Swedish diesel-electric Gotland sub, *Halland,* four miles out, with false signature. It is a Russian Poseidon UUV.'

'OK,' Ciszewski said impatiently. 'We've got a lot coming in. I'll put you to presidential security.'

Olsen said, 'Bodø insists the *Halland* is genuine.'

'It's Swedish,' objected Lucas. 'Not even NATO.'

'The Norwegians asked for it as part of the summit security cordon. The Gotland-class is more modern than anything Norway has.'

Frank Ciszewski came back. 'The information you have is incorrect. The identity of the *Halland* is confirmed as authentic.'

'By whom, Frank?'

'Like I said, step back. You got too close and you're wrong.'

'Who's telling you this, our side or the Russians?'

'POTUS is arriving. I'm closing this conversation.'

Lucas suppressed his bewilderment and spoke into his other phone. 'You there, Steph?'

Royal Yacht HNoMY Norge, Kirkenes, Norway

Stephanie listened to Harry's warning as the captain of the royal yacht *Norge* led the two Presidents to their seats behind a long antique table where they were to sign agreements. She managed to pass it on to Sergey Grizlov before he took his position directly behind Lagutov. Writing pads, documents, and pens were laid out on the table. A roll of hail smashed loudly on the roof and against the windows. Roaring wind rocked the vessel. 'The Devil works to stop good men making peace,' said Lagutov into the microphone, bringing applause from his guests. Merrow slapped his presidential counterpart on the shoulder and laughed. Grizlov spoke into Lagutov's ear. The Russian President summoned his head of security. Grizlov spoke to them both. Stephanie tried to interpret the conversation, the taut expressions, the rigid body language, the nodding and shaking of heads, the mounting concern on Grizlov's face, the shrug from the head of security, Lagutov's fingers toying around the base of his microphone. Grizlov stepped back. Lagutov spoke to Merrow, who gave a thumbs-up signal to his Secret Service agent: everything was good.

'They're not buying it,' Stephanie told Harry.

'How long is the ceremony?'

'Thirty, maybe forty-five minutes. The Norwegians, NATO Secretary-General, then the Presidents speak. Lagutov will go on. Then, the mingling.'

'You've got fifteen minutes, Steph. If that. You need to get off that yacht.'

The door was closed and locked. The weather thundered against the vessel. Stephanie was close to a window streaked with storm. She was in a line with ministers, admirals, generals, and air marshals.

'I can't, Harry.'

Svanvik, Finnmark, Norway

Rake was at Lucas' side. 'What's the source of Semenov's data?'

'This one is the acoustic range at Hergernnes near Bergen, run by Norway, Germany, and the Netherlands.' Harry flipped through to another image. 'This is SEAFAC—'

'Ketchikan, Alaska.'

'Correct.'

'There was a breach there. About a year ago. I was called in.'

'What sort of a breach?'

'They didn't tell me. They wanted my input in re-securing the site.'

'Fourteen minutes out,' said Olsen.

'It'll be less,' said Rake. 'The drone is programed to speed up on its final approach.'

He recognized the ringtone of Nilla's phone. Rake answered.

'I will tell you this once, Ozenna,' said Yumatov. 'This is how it will work. Are you listening?'

'I am.'

'We know you have activated the de-cloaking software. We are holding Carrie, Wekstatt, and the boy at the border. The moment you destroy the Poseidon, they will die.'

'I understand.'

Yumatov ended the call. Rake kept hold of the phone. Sweat covered the palm of his hand. He repeated what Yumatov had said to Lucas, his face darkening into a fury.

'He confirmed the Poseidon?' said Lucas.

'And he didn't need to. He also said his people didn't shoot Nilla. Something way outside our radar is going on.'

The door opened and Stefan came in. 'We're going back,' said Rake.

Lucas acknowledged with a tilt of the head. He wouldn't stand in Rake's way. Rake gave Stefan his silk sweatshirt stained with blood, the scent trail back to Yumatov. Stefan opened the door and held it steady as wind howled into the truck. Rake stepped into a barrage of swirling snow, far worse than when he came in barely fifteen minutes ago. He pulled up his mask against hail chips stinging his face.

FIFTY-ONE

A Tigr armored vehicle was parked across the E-105 at the Russian border with Norway. It was painted in a camouflage of white and pale green. Behind its narrow windshields, Carrie saw two men in the front and on the roof, two unmanned machine guns side by side. Despite brutal weather, Russian soldiers stood a few paces apart lining each side of the road, stretching several hundred yards behind them. Their commanding officer was inside an immigration cabin with Russian border guards. So far, they had been disciplined and professional. They had stopped Carrie as she drove toward the border crossing. A young officer explained they had been called from their camp at Salmiyarvi to check all vehicles at the border. He had peered in at Mikki and Rufus and asked for passports. Carrie had shown the one Yumatov had given her. Mikki flipped open his Norwegian police identity card. The officer gave the documents back. Carrie had nothing to show for Rufus. The officer didn't ask. They did not search the vehicle. They asked Carrie to turn off the engine and run the heater off the battery, which she did. They had handed her bottles of water and Russian energy bars.

Rufus hungrily devoured one while playing games on a phone Carrie had given him. He stayed in the front seat, strapped into a seat belt, his fairy-tale book on his lap. Mikki had been lying on the back seat. He pushed himself up for the border check.

'Must be another turf war,' said Mikki. 'These guys are to keep us waiting. They don't know why, maybe until Yumatov gets here.'

Carrie caught his expression in the rear-view mirror. Mikki was in pain. She leaned over and touched his forehead. There was no fever. The tourniquet was holding. She wondered if Rake had made it through.

'The army is working with the FSB border guards,' said Mikki. 'That Humvee-type vehicle is the wild card. It's under another command. They used it when they tried to take Rake and me before.'

Carrie checked to see how she could get around it without getting killed. The Tigr was parked with its rear end just up from a rest area on the left. A few meters beyond was Norway. In a clear run, she could veer left, sweep through the rest area, and be in Norway in less than thirty seconds. Their vehicle was armored, one gift Nilla had left for her.

'I can get through,' she said.

'Start the engine,' said Mikki.

Carrie looked back, hesitantly. She meant in an emergency, not when they were sitting protected. 'Then what?'

'Someone will come over.' Mikki eyes were fixed with determination. 'That monster vehicle will react in some way. I need to see how. If I say "go," go.'

Carrie fired the ignition. The headlamps dulled by battery power became brighter. Its beams showed whirls of snow skidding across the road and the Tigr's outline, a dirty lump of a vehicle on the white and green around it. A tree branch snapped and flew out of sight. The door of the immigration building opened. The same officer stepped out, walking quickly toward them, his hands out indicating that Carrie needed to cut the engine. Six men fanned out around the vehicle.

'Do not lower your window,' said Mikki. Carrie did what he said. She engaged the gear, keeping her foot on the brake. 'Kill your lights,' said Mikki as he brought down his window. The officer shone a flashlight in his face.

Carrie flipped off the headlamps. A soldier climbed up from inside the Tigr to the machine gun.

'Any news?' said Mikki to the Russian officer in English, narrowing his eyes against the light.

The soldier replied in Russian. Mikki shrugged, looking bemused. Rufus looked up at Carrie with panic. 'We have to leave the vehicle and go inside and take Rufus with us,' translated Carrie. 'He says these are direct order from the Kremlin.'

More like direct orders from Yumatov, she thought.

'Sure, we can do that,' said Mikki, looking straight at the soldier with a smile. 'I need to take a piss anyway.'

Carrie translated and Rufus piped up in Russian. 'Me too.'
The soldier stepped back with an expression of relief.

'Go,' Mikki said softly, taking her by surprise.

His lock clicked as he began to open his door, putting the soldiers more at ease. She met his gaze in the rear-view mirror to confirm his instruction. Carrie let off the brake and hit the gas. The front wheels spun and twisted on ice that had frozen over while they had been parked. She speeded up, letting the wheels adjust themselves. Mikki slammed his door shut. Glaring searchlights illuminated them from both sides of the road. A siren blared. Gunfire from behind hit the back of the vehicle. Mikki didn't fire back. His target was the Tigr, which was reversing to exactly the spot where Carrie had planned to break through. A soldier swung his machine gun toward her. If Carrie kept on course, she risked smashing into the Tigr. If she veered away, she could skid and flip the vehicle. Mikki said nothing. He trusted her decisions. Deafening gunfire erupted, as Mikki unleashed high-velocity rounds toward the machine-gunner. Sparks flew off its chassis. Rounds smashed into the steel cladding. Mikki's intensity of fire was designed to terrify and kill. The gunner slumped over the heavy machine gun, his arm and shoulder ripped away. Carrie knew he was dead. The Tigr entered the rest area. Another five seconds and it would be blocking Carrie's path. Small-arms fire rapped against her windshield, cracking but not breaking it, not from the Tigr, but regular troops from the Salmiyarvi barracks. Carrie could not stop, could not go back.

She swung the wheel to the right to get around the other side. The back of the vehicle began sliding to the left. She corrected, but not enough and it smashed into the side of the moving Tigr and bounced off without a grip on the ice. Carrie tried to correct again, but it kept sliding. Mikki laid down fire against the Tigr's front windshields. Their vehicle spun round until they were facing back toward the immigration post. Carrie slammed into reverse, gauged distance with wing mirrors, and headed backwards. Mikki kept up covering fire. They cleared the Tigr. The siren kept blaring. A surge of fire smacked against her vehicle. It dipped, the wheel crushing down to the right in a tire blowout. Carrie ignored it, keeping up momentum, praying she could avoid another slide, skewing left, then right. She headed toward a barrier with red and white stripes and braced herself to smash through it. But the barrier swung up. Lights went on. A voice from a loudspeaker said in Russian, 'Hold your fire. This is Norwegian sovereign territory.' Carrie coasted, letting the vehicle slow naturally. Yes, a blown-out rear tire. She had guessed right. Yes, she was safe. They were on the Norwegian side.

Face twisted with pain from his wound, Mikki leant forward, grabbed her hand, and gave it a big kiss. 'Did anyone tell you, Dr Walker, you're one hell of a human being?'

FIFTY-TWO

Svanvik, Finnmark, Norway

'Where is the real *Halland*?' asked Harry
'She was at Karlskrona,' answered Olsen, referring to Sweden's main submarine base in the south
of the country. 'She left dock five days ago to join Dynamic
Freedom.'

'Has she checked in yet?'

'No. But she's signature identified, submerged, and scheduled.'

'Have any others not checked in?'

Olsen was on the line to the command center in Bodø. 'They're
closing down on us, Harry. Too much else going on.'

'That's what Yumatov's banking on,' muttered Harry while
calling Jim Whyte at Bodø. 'We need confirmation on the
Halland, General, and now.'

'*Halland* has been verified,' said Whyte.

'At least order her to surface?'

'You need to step aside, Congressman. The summit is secure.'

'Eleven minutes out,' said Olsen.

Harry studied the cordon around the royal yacht and the position of the vessels attached to Dynamic Freedom. He placed the
Poseidon or *Halland* center screen on the live feed of the Dynamic
Freedom chart. The underwater drone was three times shorter in
length than the *Halland* yet Russian technology enabled it to
emit a detailed acoustic signature that was fooling NATO's most
sophisticated defenses. If this were not the *Halland*, where was
the real one?

'We need to put out a debris search—' Harry enlarged the
chart, working out the *Halland's* route over the past twenty-four
hours. 'Start between Kirkenes and Tromsø. Fishing boats,
freighters, cruise ships.'

'It's ten minutes out, Harry, there's no—'

'Just do it, for Christ's sake.'

He opened the line to Stephanie. 'What's happening?' she asked. 'This is going—'

'Steph,' he interrupted. 'Do exactly as I say. Contact your Prime Minister now. Tell him to set up a line with Joint Forces Command at Northwood. HMS *Anson*, Astute-class submarine, is two miles outside the royal yacht's protective cordon. She has a trailing-wire antenna, meaning you can have direct communications. Within the next five minutes, I need the *Anson* independently to confirm the identity of a Swedish Gotland-class submarine, *Halland*, now showing ten minutes out. Do not work through NATO or Dynamic Freedom. Tell the captain that the *Halland* is suspect.'

Royal Yacht HNoMY Norge, Kirkenes, Norway

Stephanie didn't query Harry. She dialed Prime Minister Kevin Slater, who was watching the summit on television. 'God, Merrow's droning on,' he said. 'If he mentions freedom and democracy one more time, I swear I'll declare Britain a dictatorship.'

Stephanie broke his humor by repeating Harry's precise instructions. Slater immediately understood. 'Onto it, Steph. Keep the line open.'

She steadied herself as the yacht jolted against a ferocious gust of wind. Merrow reacted by giving the room a sweeping smile. 'As my friend Viktor told us, no spot of rough weather can come between the friendship of the Russian and American people. Together we have fought . . .'

Stephanie caught Grizlov's eye. She tapped her phone to say she was working on finding out what was happening. He slightly raised his right hand and crossed his fingers. Slater came across the line. 'The *Anson* will get back to us in three minutes.'

Svanvik, Finnmark, Norway

'Seven minutes out,' said Olsen.

Harry sipped his coffee. It was lukewarm. This was one of those short stretches of time in a military operation when a man needed to fight every straining fiber and do nothing. If the British submarine commander corroborated the *Halland*'s identity, meaning that no action would be taken against it, Harry would simply yell down the phone for Stephanie to get off the yacht and pray she survived. After that, if proven right, he would track down every strand and thread of Yumatov's operation and go wherever it took him to what Rake Ozenna called the head of the snake.

'Putting you through to the *Anson* commander,' said Stephanie.

'Captain Winchester here, Mr Lucas. What exactly are you looking for?'

'A Russian Poseidon UUV.'

'I'm reading a Swedish Gotland-class but with possible irregularities. Give me fifteen minutes and we can—'

'We don't have fifteen minutes. What are the irregularities?'

'This acoustic reading gives us no confirmation of the air-independent propulsion installed on the *Gotland* class.'

Slater cut across. 'Conclusively?'

'No. It could be turned off to increase its speed, so not enough to verify this is a false signature, sir.'

'Six minutes out,' said Olsen.

The *Halland* was marked as being allocated to the presidential summit, not to Dynamic Freedom. She would not be under NATO command but— There wasn't time to think and guess, he had to know. 'Does *Halland* have a trailing antenna?'

'She does,' answered Winchester from the Anson.

'Under whose command?'

'I'm next to the Norwegian Defense Minister,' Stephanie broke in. She went quiet for a beat. 'The *Halland* is under US Secret Service command for the length of the summit.'

The Secret Service could have ordered the *Halland* to surface. It had chosen not to, even though Harry had people at the heart of the operation, Frank Ciszewski in the Situation Room and Jim Whyte in Bodø.

'Can you sight the target?' asked Harry.

'Affirmative,' replied Winchester.

'Are you ready to take it out?'

'Only on authenticated word from the Prime Minister,' said Winchester.

'Five minutes out,' said Olsen.

The screen marker over the *Halland* blurred. 'Target's increasing speed.' Harry's voice was raised with urgency. As

Rake Ozenna had warned, a Poseidon could be programmed to break cover in the final minutes to ensure maximum impact at a stage in the attack when it would have been too late to intervene. A few seconds from now the royal yacht itself would be in the arc of the explosion and the weapon would be too dangerous to destroy.

'Take it out,' said Harry. 'Now.'

'Prime Minister?' said Winchester.

Slater said nothing.

'Three minutes out.'

'Prime Minister,' repeated Harry. 'This won't stop at the assassination of two Presidents. If you don't give the order now—'

'I know the consequences,' snapped Slater.

Olsen's face creased with surprise. His hand went to his earpiece and he spun around toward Harry. 'Debris found. North of Vardø.'

'What debris?' asked Stephanie.

'Red life jacket, blue fabric with yellow cross, the Swedish national flag.'

'Prime Minister?' prompted Stephanie.

'Destroy her, Captain.'

Less than a mile from the royal yacht, the British torpedo destroyed the Russian drone and the sea heaved violently, lashing out in a violent pitch and roll. A white and gray wall of water rose up from the surface, hurling broken packs of ice in a mix of spray and froth. The gale caught it and spread it away and within seconds of the massive explosion, the sea returned to the raging turbulence of the storm.

Stephanie caught sight of the blast through the weather-lashed window. No one else seemed to. Pounding hail and applause for Merrow's speech drowned out any sound it might have given off. Then, all hell broke loose as the Russian and American security details moved in to get the two Presidents to safety.

'Thanks, Steph,' said Harry as she joined a crush of dignitaries being pushed toward the gangway.

'Anytime, Congressman,' she said lightly.

'Brief Grizlov.'

'As soon as we're clear of this crush.'

'The Poseidon came from a Russian sub, the *Kasatka*. The commander is a classmate of Yumatov's.'

'Have you got him?'

'We will.'

'Yumatov?'

'We'll know within the hour. Rake Ozenna is across there now.'

FIFTY-THREE

Murmansk Oblast, Russia

Sixteen Alaskan huskies ran fast, tracking the smell of Rake's blood and his torn silk vest across the ice. Stefan drove the lead sled, its tough birch runners bumping over thin snow on jagged frozen water. Rake was behind. Snow pelted against his goggles with such ferocity that he had no visibility of Stefan. Night vision and thermal imaging were so distorted that they only confused. Rake was better with his natural senses. The dogs knew, heads down, working hard, discerning between the hazardous and the safe with far better accuracy than he. From the sky, heat signatures would be too faint and unrecognizable to read in the storm, while Yumatov and his snowmobiles would stand out and be easy targets. Through his earpiece, using the Norwegian cellphone system, Rake had lines open to Harry Lucas and to Stefan.

'Poseidon destroyed.' Harry's voice came through clearly. 'Well done, Ozenna. You saved the President's life . . . Hold . . . Moscow cutting satellite comms again. Losing visuals.'

The sled tilted sharp to the left as the dogs swerved to avoid a low wall of ice. Rake leaned to the right to balance the weight. As it corrected, Rake saw the dogs were avoiding a wrecked snowmobile that had hit ice and flipped. Flames licked up from the engine, reminding him of the short time he had been in Norway and come back. The dogs' harnesses tightened and they bounded forward, getting up enough speed for the sled to jump over the crushed legs of the snowmobile's dead driver. Rake could see only blurs of different shades of darkness, but the energy of the dogs picking up the scent he had left on the bear trap told him they were close.

Something hard and metal smashed against his jaw, cutting his face mask and hurling him into the ice. Too late, driving the sled, his concentration lapsed, he saw a dark shape in front of him. Harsh cold numbed his skin. The dogs stopped. Rake began to pull himself up and a boot crashed against his shoulder, ripping down his neck protection. Wind cut though to his muscles. Rake kept focus against pain, his vision wrecked from the force of the blow. But he could still sense danger around him, and when the foot came for him again, he deflected it, caught hold of the other leg, and twisted his enemy to the ground. He jammed his fist into the neck, heard a choking sound, and was reaching for his knife when an arm caught him round the neck and hurled him backwards. The new attacker snapped on a helmet flashlight, putting the glare right onto Rake's blood-streaked face. A second helmet light came on. There were at least three.

One crouched next to him, pulled back his head as if to break his neck, and shouted through the noise of the storm, 'Where is he?'

The air exploded in a barrage of gunfire. The man who asked the question crashed forward onto Rake. More rounds pounded his body and bounced off his Kevlar. The dead man protected him. Through relentless snow, Rake gauged muzzle flashes. He judged distance and shot direction. He waited for the weapon to fall silent, its magazine exhausted. He heaved the body aside, rolled away, drew his knife, and hurled himself forward against the attacker, bringing him down. Rake caught the man's arm as it swung up toward his head, and stabbed his knife into the face, pulling back the blade, pushing it up into the skull and drawing it out. Blood blew away. Some froze on his skin.

Stefan had saved him. He pulled Rake to his feet. There had been three attackers. Stefan killed two, Rake one. There was a hum of engine sound from the south. Again, without warning, the weather quietened. The snow fall stopped. The wind dropped and a blue-gray haze unfolded over the landscape. Rake and Stefan stood back to back, assessing. Ragged strips from his torn vest hung from the arm of the bear trap he had tied it to. The dogs, trained and alert, had scented and tracked their quarry. They waited in their harnesses, some on their feet, some down in the snow, the sleds held fast by steel anchors Stefan had embedded in the ground. Three wrecked snowmobiles lay in an arc around them from the battle less than an hour earlier. The engine sound was louder, not so far away, three, possibly four military snowmobiles.

From the north, a flat-bed truck sped toward them. The head-lamps were on high beam. An orange light flashed on top of the cab. Its wheels threw out spray and ice, and a white sheet flapped from a window, which could be a white flag of peace in war conditions or could have come loose from a load. The truck swerved erratically as the driver avoided hazards. It was traveling too fast. The higher the speed, the greater the vibrations through the ice, creating a destructive surge of water underneath. The vehicle would be three tons, meaning the ice needed to be at least ten inches thick to take its weight and that was at a slow speed. Rake didn't know enough about Norwegian winters to calculate more.

The truck was a minute out. The snowmobiles were three minutes out. They would have to be stopped on the approach. Rake signaled that they should take cover behind one of the wrecked snowmobiles and checked the line with Harry Lucas. 'Sword Edge.'

'Excalibur, reading you.'

'Do you have visuals?'

'Negative.'

'We have truck approaching from the north and four snow-mobiles from the south.'

'Copy that.'

A wind gust slid a fragment of broken metal across the ice. Rake's torn vest on the bear trap flapped like a flag. A few minutes of respite and the weather was coming back, which was good. Rake set up a firing position south over the burnt-out seat of a snowmobile. He expected the approaching snowmobiles to slow just over a mile out while the crews gauged what lay ahead of them. He turned to see Stefan, standing, examining through night-vision binoculars.

He came across to Rake: 'It's Yumatov.'

Yumatov? Rake questioned incredulously, then remembering how one of the attackers asked, *Where is he?*

To the south, two snowmobiles stopped. Two others went ahead but slowed to a crawl. With horror, Rake watched as men from the stationary ones set up light portable mortars. After one or two test rounds, they could target Rake's position accurately. Worse, the shells could be designed with explosives to melt and break ice. Stefan pointed to his sled. He would head out to distract the mortars. Rake would handle the truck.

The dogs jumped up on Stefan's command. They pulled away. Stefan hopped onto the back runner and guided them in a loop. A skilled musher with well-trained dogs would be a near-impossible target at long range. The mortar crews were stationary and vulnerable.

A roar tore under Rake's feet. The ground trembled like in an earthquake. A cracking sound like breaking glass ripped through the atmosphere. Rake signaled wildly toward the truck, which braked hard, but too late. It skidded and skewed to the left. A chasm appeared, tearing between two massive plates of ice. The weight of the vehicle and its speed created a surge of water under the ice like a tsunami hunting a weak spot, which it found near the bear trap, the spot where Rake had wrecked a snowmobile with a hand grenade. The ground tilted like a theater stage. Water washed up and the truck slid toward a black pool of swirling water. Rake saw the face of Ruslan Yumatov. His gaze met Rake's eyes tight with concentration. He smashed through his window with a metal rod. The truck's front wheels were in the water. Yumatov had to get out before water spilled inside the cabin. If he didn't, he would be as good as dead.

Rake ran to the edge with a snow anchor and rope from the sled. He hurled the rope toward the cabin. There was an ear-splitting screech as another slab of ice broke away. A burnt-out snowmobile tipped into the water, somersaulting, creating a whirlpool that sucked the truck down faster. Yumatov's head was out, his right arm flailing. He was trapped. A leg was caught inside the door.

Rake had to go in because he needed Yumatov alive. He wasn't the head of the snake as Rake had first thought. There were others, many more, like the men with the mortars and those commanding and paying them.

Rake drew as much air as his lungs could take and leapt into the water ensuring that his head did not go under. He felt his organs react to the sudden cold, his heart pumping, blood needing oxygen, his mouth closed to avoid drawing water into his lungs. Rake knew about cold-water swimming. Nerve ends on the skin sent signals to the brain that responded by rapidly adjusting blood flow. Once through that, and if able to ignore the cold itself, a man could survive for long minutes before exhaustion and hypothermia.

Rake pushed away floating ice debris. Water streamed through the truck's windows. Yumatov lashed out, striking Rake in the face. Rake smashed his glove onto the side of his head, knocking him out completely. The sinking truck was pulling them both down. Rake secured his grip on Yumatov by hooking his arms under his shoulders like a lifesaver. He grasped onto the anchor rope to counter the weight of the body and the pull of the truck. Downward drag tore against his muscles. He clawed at the rope, but against the strain of the two-ton truck and the sucking vortex of water, the anchor's hold broke, propelling Rake under water, the cold against his skin paralyzing all sensation in his face. He saw Yumatov's shape and how he could be freed. With a knife, he cut through clothing snagged by metal on the door. Yumatov shifted, and Rake pushed him up. They surfaced, struggling against the drawing down of the truck, keeping up momentum to get him to the edge of the ice plate. Stefan was there. They hauled the Russian up and laid him on the ground. A rush of white water erupted as the truck vanished from sight.

Far away, flames streaked up from a rumbling thud as the first mortar shell landed. Then, another. Even a novice would have a better aim, thought Rake, until he realized that the tactic was to cut their route back to Norway. A third shell crashed down in the same area. Rake heard gunfire. He couldn't see him. Visibility was down and getting worse.

Rake knelt by Yumatov, mouth over his, pumping his breath into his lungs, then hand on his chest pounding to get his heart moving, to choke out whatever was in his lungs. Yumatov coughed and vomited.

FIFTY-FOUR

Rake retrieved the pistol he had flung onto the ice and pulled a waterproof flashlight from his pocket. A mortar shell exploded from a trajectory much closer to them in a burst of flame, vibrations from the blast trembling the ice. The mortar crews were homing in for the kill. Wind cut through Rake's wet clothing, chilling him with a ferocity he had never experienced before. They needed to keep moving or they would die from the cold or shrapnel flying invisibly through the dark, storm-lashed air. The dogs, on their feet, strained at the remaining snow anchor holding them in place. They lifted Yumatov into Rake's sled. Stefan went ahead. Rake loosened the anchor. The dogs leapt forward, straining on their harnesses, shifting the sled, first with a jerk, then gaining traction and speed.

They drove through a blizzard of biting hailstones and frozen mist. Rake sensed the sway of sled, counter-balancing, braking when he felt the harnesses slacken because the dogs had slowed. The wind was straight behind him. His voice carried to the dogs. He spoke to them as Nilla would have done by name, soothing, coaxing, urging. Inside the sled, Yumatov was stationary, in soaking wet clothes in sub-zero temperatures. Rake, too, was standing still, barely moving. Unless they got dry and warm, hypothermia would set in, muddling his thinking, weakening his movements, and both he and Yumatov would die.

A weapon fired nearby, barely a hundred feet away, close enough to see the flash and hear the cracks of multiple gunfire. Rake pushed his foot on the hard brake and the dogs halted. Stefan came into sight. He signaled, his finger under his throat, his right hand chopping through the air three times, that he had hit three of the attackers. He gave Rake's dogs a wide arc and pointed toward the border. He would lead. If they could keep up the pace, they would be there in less than five minutes. Stefan was able to go faster because of less weight. He set off, looking back, adjusting to Rake's slower pace.

Rake heard the whine of a mortar overhead. The one you can't hear is the most lethal. It exploded in front of them, throwing up a geyser of water, meaning it had broken ice. Stefan braked, leaning forward, taking his lead from the dogs. Rake spoke to his dogs softly, Jake this, Ranta and Skye that. It would be up to the dogs to get them out.

The border lay a few hundred yards ahead. They had no communications with Harry Lucas. Rake's earpiece was ruined by water. The phone signals were jammed. They would have no idea when they had crossed. Gales pushed away clouds for seconds of low-light clarity when Rake could see across to trees and land well into Norway. Then, the wind brought new clouds, putting them back into a roaring darkness. It carried the scent of pollution from the factories of Nikel.

Rake kept the sled a good distance behind Stefan. The dogs pulled hard, sensing home, the point dogs toward the back leaping in the air against the harness. Stefan's huskies turned sharply to the left to avoid another low ice wall that would have destroyed a snowmobile. They swung back to clear broken ice where a mortar had exploded, then smoothly curved into what they saw as their trail. With each burst of wind, cold tore through Rake. He had to stay rigid and still to control the sled. If he missed an unseen drift or the tilt of a turn, they would be finished.

The whine of snowmobiles carried through a lull in the wind. For a few minutes, they had gone quiet, but not anymore. Gunfire ripped into ground between the sleds. The dogs yelped. Ranta lay down and, for a second, was carried along by the others under Skye's lead. Stefan turned to check. Rake signaled for him to keep going. Then came a glaring flash and a crack of a mortar blast to their right. The ice shifted, startling the dogs. A second mortar exploded close by. Skye led her dogs hard to the right and swerved back again as water splashed up from the ice breach caused by the mortars. Stefan was now on the other side. They were separated by torn ice and angry water. Rake regained their pace, looping away from the broken ice. Stefan kept vigil from the other side of the water. A fourth mortar landed with an earsplitting blistering crash, this time to their left, and the dogs kept going, terrified, determined, as Rake drove through the smoke cloud, breathing the smell of burning metal.

Yumatov slumped, blood draining from his arm. A spotlight from new vehicles to the north snapped on. Momentarily, the dogs lost formation, yelping and barking, as the beam glared into their eyes. Light swept straight across Rake. A hundred yards away, he saw two snowmobiles. The air stream of a rocket-propelled grenade jetted over them and slammed into one enemy snowmobile with a fireball that lit the landscape. Seconds later, the other snowmobile was destroyed.

The beam from another light fell on Rake and a snowmobile drew up next to him. Mikki was perched on the back, a rocket-propelled grenade launcher hanging from his wrist. He flipped the flashlight back. Carrie drove. Excitement, gratitude, urgency, rushed through him. 'You OK?' shouted Mikki.

'We're OK,' replied Rake. 'Yumatov's hit.'

Carrie unhooked a medical bag and went to Yumatov, who was inert.

'Ruslan, it's Carrie,' she said. 'You're safe. Can you hear me?' As Carrie spoke, she traced the source of the blood, reached into the medical bag, and brought out a tourniquet, which she wrapped around the upper arm and tightened. She checked Yumatov's eyes and pulse. 'He's alive. We need to get him back.'

Carrie mounted the snowmobile. Mikki held up his forefinger and thumb in a circle as if to say everything was good. Carrie set off cautiously, careful not to alarm the dogs, giving them time to form up and follow. Stefan was waiting up ahead. After Rake passed, he fell in behind. There was faraway gunfire and fire burning in the mop-up operations. It must have been the Norwegians. Rake wasn't used to being rescued. If the shivering cold wasn't so brutal, he could even enjoy it.

FIFTY-FIVE

C arrie stopped the snowmobile under a blaze of lights. Police, military, and fire vehicles were everywhere. The white communications truck dominated with its aerials and satellite dishes on the roof. None was any good when the mortars were exploding, which is why she and Mikki had raided weapons from their vehicle, stolen a snowmobile, and gone across themselves. Mikki had used a ski pole as a crutch and assured her that his aim was as good sitting down with a bad leg as it was standing up with a good one.

Rake's sled stopped behind her. Harry Lucas stood outside the communication truck waiting for him. Paramedics ran across with blankets. Lucas fetched Rake a blanket and took him inside his vehicle. Carrie checked her patient. Yumatov had survived; unconscious, but his pulse was strong.

'We need an ambulance to Kirkenes,' she instructed the paramedics.

'Well done, my favorite girl.' Mikki hobbled toward her. He opened his free arm to give her a hug.

Carrie looked at his leg. 'You need a new dressing.'

'You do it, Carrie,' he said, his voice laced with a plea. 'Hospitals and me, no good together.'

'Once I'm done here.' Carrie crouched, patting the dogs, stroking under their chins, feeling the ice melting on their fur, enjoying respite in them excitedly jumping at her, tired but happy, a run well done. She realized a quiet and slowness, urgency evaporated, danger gone, hum of a generator, storm silent, the sound of scraping dogs' paws on snow. She wanted to know what happened, why things unfolded as they had, what Yumatov was doing here. She was doctor, not a detective or a spy. Like the huskies, her job was done and more than anything she wanted to be in bed with Rake, with his warmth, his roughness, his reliability. Whatever unfolded, however strong the urge, she must not let that happen, not now, not when she was tired and vulnerable and wanted him so much.

Rake stripped off in the communications van, dried himself down, put on fresh cold-weather clothes. 'Any idea what the fuck is going on?' he asked, accepting a black coffee from Harry Lucas, who thanked him again for saving his President's life and filled him in about the Poseidon drone and the cloaking-busting software that Carrie had delivered on Semenov's drive.

'I don't,' said Lucas. 'At least not to the level you and I need to know.'

'The Russians don't know we have Yumatov,' said Rake. 'His truck sank in the ice. We'll tell them he died in it.'

Stefan came in with Mikki. 'Carrie's checking him,' Mikki said, looking at Rake. 'Then give the lady some time.'

'If she gives me some,' muttered Rake.

'Thank you,' Harry said to Stefan. 'America owes you, but I don't know what to say. I'm so sorry about Nilla.'

'She was my sister.' Stefan shrugged. 'I loved her. She was crazy. She got fixated. Men and sex, probably on account of our dad being a drunk.'

Alone, Harry turned on a screen. Rake watched a compilation of surveillance images, networked through facial recognition. Each image was captioned with identity and location, Oslo, Berlin, Singapore, Stockholm. They centered on Marine General Jim Whyte, showing him with Ruslan Yumatov three times and twice with Nilla Carsten.

Harry said, 'In the past eighteen months, Whyte visited the Norwegian military acoustic range in Heggernes and the Acoustic Measurement Facility at Ketchikan. The marine signatures held there ended up on Semenov's drive.'

'I checked security at Ketchikan,' said Rake.

'I know. After Whyte's visit, they knew there had been a breach. They didn't know what.' Harry snapped off the screen. 'I need you to talk to Yumatov and find out what he knows about Whyte.'

Two armed police and a paramedic watched over Yumatov as Carrie treated him. She first thought shrapnel had severed his axillary artery under his right armpit. But the cold had slowed the blood flow and after taking off his shirt and vest, she was pretty sure the wound was only to the cephalic vein. There was no sign of the shrapnel. An X-ray would find it. Or it had gone through. She used plenty of bandage tight around the shoulder. It was basic first aid that could have been done by the paramedics. 'You'll be fine,' she said, sealing the dressing.

'Why are you helping me?' Yumatov lay on his back, eyes fixed on Carrie while she worked.

'Because I'm a doctor.'

'Bullshit.'

Carrie laid the back of her hand on his forehead. She tipped two Tylenol into her hand and reached for a glass of water. 'You've a slight fever. Take these.'

Yumatov pushed himself up to swallow the tablets. 'How's Nilla?'

Carrie was about to answer when Rake half opened the door.

'Carrie, a moment.' His tone was formal and hesitant, like he didn't know how to be with her. Carrie felt the same, didn't like it. Why did people have to be so complicated, including her? She stepped out into a dry cold, even with a moon which reflected across the trees and rooftops of the farm building. 'How is he?'

'Light flesh wound.'

'OK to talk?'

'Yes. He asked about Nilla.'

'Did you tell him?'

'No.'

'Good.'

Carrie marveled at Rake. After all that went down in their day, they were still doing their jobs, talking fast, professional, like overtime on a shift. Therefore, she pondered, why not for old times' sake, to find sanctuary, to relieve tension. Just one night. They had both earned it. *Stop, Carrie. Don't even think about it.*

Rake dismissed the police and paramedic and stood over Yumatov, who sat sideways on an ambulance jump seat, wearing a blue medical smock, arms folded, staring at the shelves of medical equipment in front of him. He had a white bandage down his right cheek with specks of blood seeping through. 'You are a fighter, Ozenna,' he said with genuine respect. 'I wish you had been on my team.'

'Except, I wasn't.'

'How is Nilla?'

'She didn't make it.'

'You said she was fine.'

'She wasn't.'

Yumatov grimaced and touched the dressing on his shoulder.

'What did you give her?' asked Rake.

'Money. Hope. Love. Why else do people do things?'

Rake perched on a gurney. 'Who are those people who want you dead?'

'Russia has men with guns everywhere.' Yumatov's expression was haggard, his voice weak.

'Who?' pressed Rake.

'I am an aide to Foreign Minister Grizlov.'

'Not a good time to fuck with me,' said Rake quietly. 'If your plan had worked Grizlov would have died on that yacht.'

'Then ask President Lagutov. He assigned me to Sergey Grizlov.'

Rake scrolled through his phone and worked the keyboard. He read nothing of note and sent no messages. It was to hold a silence between them. Then, he said: 'So, this is how it will work. Tell me now who these people are, what's going on, everything you know, and I'll see what slack we can cut you. We'll get in touch with Anna and the kids in London and work something out.'

Yumatov's face turned ashen. 'You've spoken to Anna?'

'We have and we know where she is. For a few hours, I've got some influence. After that, I'll be gone, and you'll end up in a rendition site, Thailand or Egypt probably. Once they've got what they need from you, they'll kill you. Officially, Colonel Ruslan Yumatov is dead because you went down with the truck. We'll deport Anna, Max, and Natasha to Russia. Anna will lose her job. The kids will grow up without money or a good education.'

'Then I present you a gift.' Yumatov pulled a piece of damp fabric from the pocket of his tunic and handed it to Rake. The cloth was smeared and filthy. Rake recognized the symbol he had seen carved into the severed ear.

'The sign of the Kolovrat of the Slavs of Europe,' said Yumatov. 'Our culture dates back twelve thousand years and symbolizes infinity in the fight between good and evil. It pays tribute to the sun that grants us the warmth of life. Over the centuries, the sign of the Kolovrat has been found across Europe and Asia—'

'Give me names,' interrupted Rake.

Yumatov ignored him, his gaze fired with determination. 'The sovereign state is dead. Power lies in knowing who we are, not who is our government. You know that, Rake Ozenna. You are no more American than I am Russian. You are an Eskimo. Carrie and I are Slavs. We have no borders. We have our people.'

Rake glanced down at the Kolovrat wheel that was imprinted from a photograph of a brown-gray stone carving. Two of the wheel spokes were broken.

'If I tell you who those men are, I die,' said Yumatov.

'If you don't, you die.' Rake folded the material and kept it in his hand. 'So, stay in charge and die doing something good for wife and children.'

Yumatov lowered his head into his hands, drawing his fingers down his cut-up face. 'Don't follow the money. Follow the Kolovrat.'

'Is that your answer?'

'It's the right one.'

Yumatov's eyes bore into him with an energy that belied his injury and exhaustion. Rake judged it was enough. The first move. He rapped on the door for the police to let him out.

'Tell Carrie, will you?' said Yumatov. 'Tell her to remember who she is.'

FIFTY-SIX

Brandywine Street, Washington, DC

Mikki stayed in the car in the affluent night-time suburban street in northern Washington, DC. Rake followed Harry Lucas along a short graveled path to a detached house where the porch light had just snapped on. Their visit had been announced barely a minute earlier by agents watching the house. Frank Ciszewski had reluctantly agreed. The rotund CIA Director opened the door wearing a black overcoat over what looked like dark-blue pajamas.

'Thanks, for seeing us, Frank,' said Harry.

'It had better be good and quick.' Ciszewski didn't ask them in. He closed the door and stepped onto the porch. 'What is it?'

'We're looking for the head of the snake,' said Rake.

'What's he talking about?' Ciszewski said to Harry. 'And what are you doing bringing Ozenna to my property?'

'Jim Whyte is in custody,' said Harry. 'He'll cut a deal.'

'Fuck Jim Whyte. Who doesn't have bad apples? I've heard the transcripts. You bypassed your own government to destroy an unarmed Russian underwater drone. Now, we're having to clean up the mess. You've screwed yourself, Harry, at least in this town for all millennia. I suggest you go back to screwing interns and America will be a safer place.'

'We've got Yumatov,' said Harry.

Ciszewski rested his hand on the wall. His voice faltered. 'Yumatov is dead.'

'He's alive.'

Ciszewski brought a handkerchief from his overcoat pocket. 'He died in the truck that went through the ice.'

'He's alive, Frank, and he's talking.'

'Then why doesn't the CIA know?'

'He gave me this.' Rake brought out Yumatov's patch of cloth and held it under the light. 'This is a stone carving of a Kolovrat, which is—'

'I know what a damn Kolovrat is.' Ciszewski wiped his forehead with his handkerchief. 'What the hell do you think we were doing with the Russians and the Serbs and all that Balkan crap all those years?'

'Yumatov gave me this sample for a reason.' Rake kept his tone measured.

'We've traced it to the Tarim Basin in north-west China,' said Harry. 'Yumatov told us first to follow the Kolovrat, then follow the money. We've done both.'

'Set up a meeting. We'll talk about it in my office.' Ciszewski opened his front door. 'I'm not interested in a night class in archaeology.'

Rake heard footsteps and spun round. Ciszewski's protection officers were behind him. Two stood further back. 'You gentlemen need to leave the property now.'

They walked back down the garden path. 'How'd that go?' said Mikki as they got back in the car.

'As expected,' said Harry.

Museum of Contemporary Art, Chicago

'The penis of a walrus is the largest of any land mammal,' announced the exhibition curator, his boyish, bespectacled face dead pan with only the hint of a smile. 'God chose to give the male walrus an advantage over us lesser mammals by endowing him with a baculum or a penis bone that measures up to twenty-five inches or sixty-three centimeters in length.' Low laughter rolled through the audience packed into the hall where Ronan, Rake's protégé and the young artist from Little Diomede, was exhibiting his walrus sculpture. Ronan had elaborately carved a long walrus tusk that was now lit by colored spotlights, mounted like the hull of a ship and framed by four elegantly curved walrus penis bones. Ronan stood shyly nearby with Rake, Mikki, and Henry and Joan Ahkvaluk, who were the adoptive parents to all three of them. Nearby was a troupe of Eskimo dancers in tribal costume carrying circular drums made of stretched walrus stomach. Mikki propped himself on a crutch with his right leg hooked back in a sling. 'I can't believe you got me doing this shit,' he muttered.

'Serves you right for getting shot,' whispered Rake.

'Did anyone tell you Carrie's coming?' Mikki grinned.

That took Rake by surprise. He'd felt bad about not seeing Carrie before Lucas flew him straight back to Washington on Air Force One. He had messaged her, but she had just sent back one-line replies that everything was fine. *Let's meet when our paths cross again* was her latest.

Mikki pointed to the doorway as Carrie walked in as if she owned the place, in a navy-blue business suit, blonde hair tied back, a red patterned scarf, and holding the hand of Rufus, the Russian kid, which startled Rake even more.

'Henry and Joan are taking Rufus while things are sorted out,' said Mikki.

'You fixed it?'

'A cripple like me needs to do something useful.'

Rake waved. She spotted him, waved back, and Rake couldn't stop a good feeling sweeping over him. Joan and Henry got to her first. Joan embraced her like a sister, then kissed Rufus, whose eyes were everywhere, taking in the sound and the color, clocking the other children. Henry kissed Carrie on both cheeks, held her by the shoulders, looking at her beaming. They hadn't seen each other since the Diomede crisis. Henry tilted his head to Rake. 'Look after him, Carrie.'

'That's what Mikki tells me, too,' she smiled.

Carrie let Rake hold her hard. Everything was always great between them as long as there was more urgent stuff going on around them. 'You staying?' he asked. There was so much in those two words.

She showed him a late evening boarding pass from her top jacket pocket. 'I yelled at a surgeon and have a disciplinary panel at the hospital.'

The curator began to wrap up. 'Our young artist Ronan Ahkvaluk has been inspired by artists through the centuries from all over the world. His specialism, however, is inspiration drawn from ancient erotic Indian carvings which display sensual touch between all living creatures.'

More laughter surged around the crowd.

'You will find more about the walrus and Ronan's carvings in your program notes,' he concluded. 'Suffice to say that the baculum is designed specifically to maintain stiffness and aid the pleasure of sexual intercourse and that evolution is gender-balanced. The baculum's female equivalent is known as a baubellum.' He raised his glass of white wine. 'So, let us toast this magic of erotic art and our discovery of a wonderful new American artist and declare this fantastic exhibition from the Little Diomede open.'

Drummers and singers broke into music with songs from the Eskimo islands of the Bering Strait. Rufus skipped away from Joan to join children who were jumping and dancing to the beat in front of Ronan's exhibit.

Rake's phone lit with a message. *Ciszewski's dead.* He brought up his news feed: 'CIA Director shoots himself on banks of Potomac.' They must have hit one hell of a nerve. But what did it mean? Ciszewski might have been a fang, no way was he head of the snake. Carrie glanced over, clocking the change of mood. His phone vibrated. Rake answered. 'When can you get here?' said Lucas. Rake plucked Carrie's boarding pass from her jacket and read out the flight number.

ACKNOWLEDGMENTS

Many thanks to all who have helped with *Man on Edge*. I am indebted to the Mayor of Kirkenes, Rune Rafaelsen; Finnmark Chief of Police, Ellen Katrine Hætta and her colleagues Silja Arvola and Torstein Petterson of the Norwegian Police Service; Lars George Fordal of the Norwegian Barents Secretariat; from the Norwegian Embassy in London, Mona Juul, John Olsen and Kaja Glomm; Trine Beddari at Birk Husky on the Russian-Norwegian border and her team, specifically Kit Hardy who taught me skills and pitfalls of dog sledding and how to grill a fresh salmon lunch on a fire in the snow. On wider Arctic security issues thanks to Tamnes Rolf and Øystein Tunsjø, the Norwegian Institute of Defence Studies; Arild Moe, Fridtjof Nansen Institute; Dag Harald Claes, University of Oslo; Niklas Granhalm, The Swedish Defence Research Agency; Heather Conley, Center for Strategic and International Studies in Washington DC. And on wider geopolitical defence issues to Nick Childs and Joseph Dempsey, the International Institute of Strategic Studies; Karin von Hippel, Chris Parry and Charles Parton, Royal United Services Institute; Shihoko Goto, The Wilson Center; Matthew Henderson and James Rodgers, the Henry Jackson Society; Karin Landgren, Security Council Report; John Hemmings, Asia-Pacific Center for Security Studies; Robin Marsh, Margaret Ali and Tom Walsh, United Peace Federation; Tom McDevitt, Washington Times; Harlan Ullman, Atlantic Council; Adam Thomson and Ian Kearns, European Leadership Network; Vladimir Petrovsky, Russian International Affairs Council; Alexander Yakovenko, Russian ambassador to London; Alexander Nekrassov, and others of many political shades who would prefer to remain anonymous. Thanks to the people of Little Diomede, the remote island home of Rake Ozenna; to Joshua Brown who guided me through the labyrinth of flash drives and data transfers; Carrie Roller who straightened out my descriptions of trauma diagnosis and surgery; and Nancy Langston whose stylishly decorated

Washington apartment I couldn't help borrowing as Carrie's temporary home.

Untold thanks to supportive fellow writers, too many to name. You each know the process, but particularly to the great thriller author and adventurer Odd Harald Hauge who understands the Arctic better than anyone. Much gratitude also to the International Thrillers Writers Association, Society of Authors and Crime Writers Association, those networking and advice institutions that help keep us on track. By the way, K.J. Howe, you and your ThrillerFest team know how to hold great parties.

It takes many hands to produce a book. The author is just one part. Much appreciation to Don Wiese who handled and advised on the first drafts, copy editor Nick Blake who lasered in on discrepancies and details, and John Plumer who created a map that made sense of a complex region.

A special thanks to my editor, Kate Lyall Grant who, from a few lines of plot and concept on email, guided *Man on Edge* to publication and earlier commissioned *Man on Ice*, the first in the Rake Ozenna series. Great working with you, Kate, and looking forward to our next one. The team at Severn House and Canongate has been fantastic, professional, fast and fun to work with. Thanks, too, to Holly Domney and the exciting new Black Thorn imprint which has beautifully brought *Man on Ice* and Rake Ozenna to a fresh paperback readership.

None of the above would have happened without David Grossman, my agent since I phoned him out the blue in 1992 when I was a BBC Correspondent in Asia. Thank you, David, for your wise counsel over the years.

9 781780 296661